Also By T

Serpentine

Majestic

Headhunter

Skeleton

MetroCafe

Mule

Letters From A Killer

The Ascendant

sands press
Brockville, Ontario

The Ascendant

Peter Parkin
&
Alison Darby

sands press

sands press

A Division of 10361976 Canada Inc.
300 Central Avenue West
Brockville, Ontario
K6V 5V2

Toll Free 1-800-563-0911 or 613-345-2687
http://www.sandspress.com

ISBN 978-1-988281-73-5

Website: www.peterparkin.com

Edited by Laurie Carter
Publisher: Sands Press
Author Agent: Sparks Literary Consultants

'The Snake,' music and lyrics by Oscar Brown, 1963.

Publisher's Note

This book is a work of fiction. References to real people, events, establishments, organizations, or locales, are intended only to provide as a sense of authenticity, and are used fictitiously. All other characters, and all incidents and dialogue, are drawn from the authors' imaginations and are not to be construed as real.

For information on bulk purchases of this book or any book published by Sands Press, please call 1-800-563-0911.

1st Printing October 2019

1

She gazed up at him with those big brown eyes that he loved so much. The eyes asked a question—a simple one that didn't need words. Sandy responded by carefully breaking off one more piece of pepperoni pizza, cradling it in his hand and passing it over to his six-year-old daughter.

Whitney was her name, and despite her young age, she adored the music of her deceased namesake, Whitney Houston. Of course, if her parents hadn't also been avid fans she'd have had no idea who the singer was.

Her mother reached over with a napkin and wiped the tomato sauce from her chin as the child eagerly shoved the latest slice of pizza into her mouth.

"Maybe she's had enough?"

Sandy laughed and shook his head. "Does it look like she's had enough? Those little teeth are chomping away as if this was her last meal on earth."

Sarah cocked her head and displayed her most serious motherly expression. "We don't want her to be sick. You know how nervous her stomach is."

"Yeah, yeah, but this is Memorial Day, hon. A day for all of America to gorge itself."

Ten-year-old Liam piped up, not one to miss an opportunity. "Mom's right, Dad. She's going to throw up."

Sandy made a face at his son. "Listen to you, all of a sudden worried about your sister. Could this have anything to do with the fact that you've finished all of your own pizza?"

Liam smirked in his charming, shy way. "Well, maybe a teeny bit..."

"I thought so. Okay, Whitney, can Liam have a slice of your pizza?"

Her mouth full, a fresh smear of tomato sauce dripping down her chin, the little girl nodded eagerly.

Liam's hand flew across the table and snatched a slice before she had a change of heart.

Sandy and Sarah laughed together, as their happy kids ate to their hearts' content.

Sarah reached over and squeezed Sandy's hand. "I love this time of year, don't you? The end of May, spring in full bloom, everyone in a good mood."

"Yeah, it's gotta be my favorite time, too. We long for summer, but then it just gets so darn hot that we long for winter again. Spring is just perfect—wish it could be spring all year long."

Sarah glanced over at a juggler who had set up camp not far from their table. Whitney suddenly shrieked and pointed at a clown who was dancing comically on the other side of the street—to the tune of a guitarist who was happily performing in the hope that someone might throw a quarter or two into his open guitar case.

Yes, this was Memorial Day, always celebrated on the last Monday of May.

And this was Boston, one of the most beautiful cities in the entire United States.

Sandford Beech and his little family were enjoying the buzz of the holiday weekend at Quincy Market. It is a massive food and entertainment complex, closed off to vehicle traffic. It consists of four historic buildings, which contain over 100 shops, stalls, and pushcarts right on Boston's famous Freedom Trail. Famous for—well—only one of the most famous events in American history. The Boston Tea Party began on this very site. The rebellion of 1773 that became the iconic symbol of the American Revolution.

Ironic that the severing of British rule was festered by the destruction of—tea.

Quincy Market is right across from Government Center and is world-renowned as one of the best food markets on the planet. It is an old brick marketplace, beautifully restored, and the massive indoor and outdoor site has served as a meeting place for merchants and shoppers for almost four centuries.

Despite how busy it was, particularly on a holiday weekend like this, Sandy found it relaxing. It was a happy place for families and singles alike, a gathering of Americans celebrating one of the greatest cities on earth.

A chance to get out of the house and soak up some atmosphere—and there was plenty of that—especially on Memorial Day weekend when the market transformed itself into the Street Performers Festival. At least 200 acts roamed up and down the market all weekend, which was great entertainment for the kids.

Visitors could choose to eat inside in the massive food court, or, if the weather was nice, outside at the dozens of tables equipped with umbrellas. That was where the Beeches were today—outside, with a front row view of all the action.

Caught up in daydreaming, Sandy gazed off in the direction of another iconic event—which was less than a mile from where they were sitting. The finish line for the Boston Marathon. He pondered how the words "finish line" had more than just symbolic meaning for the three who were killed and the almost 300 who were injured back on April 15, 2013.

The Boston Marathon terrorist bombings.

He shook his head, trying to clear away the memories of that day. He hadn't been there, but had seen the images on the news. Had seen the explosions, heard the screams, and watched the body parts flying outwards in every direction. He normally wasn't one to cry, but he had that day. It was horrific enough to watch a terrorist attack live just like on 9/11, but to see one happen in his own city was more than he was able to bear.

He felt a tiny hand shaking his forearm. "Daddy, look at that plane up there," said Whitney, pointing. "It's pulling a sign along with it. What does the sign say?"

Sandy looked up. "It says, 'Happy Memorial Day.' Isn't that nice?"

"Yes, it is. But, doesn't that sign slow the plane down?"

"No, honey. Here's how it works," he said, launching into an abbreviated explanation of propulsion and lift while he sipped from his bowl of famous Massachusetts clam "chowda."

Whitney smiled and nodded. "I understand, Daddy. You're so smart."

He ruffled her blonde hair. "No, not really. I'm just a lot older than you, that's all."

She shook her head defiantly. "You're the smartest person I know!"

Liam decided to do some of his own sucking up. "She's right, Dad, you are."

Sarah rubbed his shoulder. "Isn't that sweet. You do miss it, don't you? I can tell."

"Miss what?"

"Teaching."

Sandy smiled. "Maybe a little bit. But, I'm challenged by what I'm doing now."

"You were a professor at MIT, for God's sake! You loved it, I know you did."

"Yeah, but it was time to move on."

Sandy didn't tell her that he'd had no choice in the matter—he'd never told her that. And, she didn't even know what he really did at his current place of employment.

He stared at the funny clown. Just…stared.

And remembered.

Remembered back to his West Point days—when he'd been selected specifically for a future assignment along with many other talented young men. The United States Military Academy, otherwise known as West Point because of its specific location in New York State, was as prestigious as a school could get.

It was tough to get into, and shortly after he'd enrolled, Sandy had found out he was considered "special." He was transferred into a secret division along with several other gifted students. They were told their futures were being determined for them right then and there—and that they would enjoy incredible training other students in West Point would not receive.

But, for Sandy, it hadn't lasted. Something had happened.

He'd been blown out of the unit and transferred back to the regular student population, where he studied for four years to obtain his undergraduate degree in physics and nuclear engineering. At the same time he'd learned the mandatory advanced military techniques that all West Point graduates had to learn. He'd become a soldier, but no one ever intended for him to actually perform as a soldier.

Even though they'd blown him out of the special unit, they weren't finished with him. They made it easy for him—financially, and mentally.

When he left West Point as one of their privileged graduates, his brain was a finely-tuned machine. And his body was a lethal weapon—one of the benefits of attending the finest military academy on the planet.

After West Point Sandy attended the Massachusetts Institute of Technology, otherwise known as MIT. He obtained his PhD in experimental nuclear and particle physics and not long after that he became a full professor, teaching nuclear secrets to a bunch of snot-nosed twenty-somethings. Kids who fantasized about being involved in the next Manhattan Project.

Where had the years gone? How had he allowed himself to get caught up in this stuff?

MIT was founded in 1861 in direct response to the industrialization of the United States. Since then it had produced eighty-five Nobel laureates, forty-five Rhodes scholars, and thirty-four astronauts. It specialized in anything technical, anything with a technological or physics bent to it.

MIT's first foray into military research began in World War II and surged after the conflict was over. It was up to its neck in nuclear weapons, microwave radar, ballistic missile guidance systems, and high-altitude photography. It was one of the key players in the old Apollo space program, and now it was an innovator in drone technology.

In the 1960s, concerns were being raised about MIT becoming more of a military defence—and offense—school than anything else. War research was feared to be dominating its reason for existence. In response, the school set up a separate operation in 1969, called the MIT Lincoln Laboratory. All of the classified military research was spun off into this new operation.

This move accomplished two things: firstly, it satisfied all the crybabies that MIT would once again be "pure;" and, secondly, it allowed the U.S. Department of Defense access to the nation's best and brightest nuclear scientists and physicists in a facility disguised as a branch of MIT, when in reality, it was just another branch of the Pentagon.

Five years ago, Sandy had been told he had no choice but to give up his teaching job and move his ass over to the Lincoln Laboratory. As a consolation, they'd given him the honorary title of professor emeritus with MIT, which allowed him to still teach once in a while and get invited to all faculty meetings and summer picnics.

In other words, it was all bullshit.

His main job was with the Lincoln Lab, and he couldn't discuss the stuff he was involved in with anyone, not even his wife. At the time, Sandy had considered it a demotion, but it was actually a massive promotion with a salary higher than he could ever have dreamed.

But, despite all of this fascinating and lucrative history, his mind still wandered back to those early days at West Point when he'd been one of the "chosen ones" for a unit that no one ever talked about.

And, how, so quickly, he became one of "the unchosen."

Sandy felt a soft hand running through his light brown hair—actually more blonde, at times, which was the color it had been when he was younger.

He looked into Sarah's eyes. "Are you horny?"

She laughed. "Always! But, no, I was just wondering where your mind was. You were gazing off into the distance like you tend to do sometimes. What were you thinking about, dear one?"

"Oh, nothing important. Aside from how nice it would be to just curl up in bed with you right about now."

"I like the sound of that. Those blue eyes of yours remind me of the ocean. Hey, why don't we head down to the cabin next weekend—just the two of us? I can get my sister to babysit. What do you think?"

Sandy squeezed her shoulder. "I'd like nothing better. Let's do that."

"Great!" Sarah squealed. Then she grinned. "And, it's only fitting that we own a cabin on the beach in Cape Cod—what with your name being Sandy Beech!"

Sandy winced. "Okay, Sarah Beech, you've made that joke far too often. I hate my name, I don't know what my parents were thinking."

"I think they wanted you to remember them in a lasting way—either that, or you were the most miserable baby and they wanted to punish you into eternity."

Sandy chuckled. "It's bad enough to have the name Sandford, but it's just as bad when I shorten it to Sandy, considering my last name."

"I think it's cute. Makes you unique. And the name Sandford sounds very professorial, which of course is appropriate."

Sandy leaned over and whispered in her ear. "Your teasing turns me on. We're going to have some naughty sex in Cape Cod next weekend."

"Promises, promises!"

He laughed and turned his attention back to the clown, who was jumping up and down and making funny noises. All of the kids loved it.

Suddenly there was the ding-dong sound of bells. He turned his head and watched as three ice cream wagons came down through the middle of the promenade, pulled by beautiful palominos. Whitney and Liam jumped to their feet.

Whitney could barely get the words out. "Can we, Dad? Can we?"

"Of course." He pulled out his wallet and gave each of the kids a five-dollar bill. "Go treat yourselves."

They ran over to the first wagon along with a horde of at least two dozen other children.

Sarah smiled at him. "What a perfect day, huh?"

"It sure is."

And then it wasn't.

The sound of fireworks.

Thumps of bodies hitting the ground.

The clown lying on the cement, staring up at the sky with considerably more red goop smeared on his face than he'd had mere seconds before.

And Sarah's beautiful face gazing up at the umbrella, a mask of wide-eyed shock as her pink camp chair tilted backwards, an insanely perfect hole in her insanely perfect forehead.

2

TWO YEARS LATER...

It was a hot one, right in the middle of the dog days of summer. Downtown Boston was crowded as usual on a July afternoon.

But, today was different—people were there who wouldn't have normally thought to make the car or train trek downtown. This wasn't a workday; it was a Sunday—a church day, a picnic day, a cut the lawn day.

Anything but a downtown Boston day.

But this Sunday was different. It had been just over two years since the Quincy Market terrorist attack, and the memories were still raw, still seared into the consciousness of a gentle and peaceful city.

For one man in particular, the memories were especially painful.

Sandford Beech sat on the dais that had been set up in the middle of the promenade.

He gazed out at the crowd.

Several hundred people were sitting on the convention chairs brought in for the affair. And at least a couple hundred more stood at various spots around the mall, waiting for the proceedings to begin. He noticed numerous ladies waving their programs in front of their faces in a desperate attempt to stay cool. Men, on the other hand, just slid the sleeves of their shirts across their faces, leaving telltale signs of sweat on the material.

Sandy smiled as he watched several kids running around in circles chasing each other.

Then he wiped a tear from his eye.

The market looked very much like it had on the day it happened. You would find it hard to believe that such a horrific tragedy had occurred here—the hustle and bustle was just like it used to be; the buildings looked the same, the sidewalk and cobblestone road were no different than they had been back before the blood began to flow.

The sun was still shining, and the sky was still blue.

People were still laughing, crying, screaming and yelling. Merchants were still selling hot dogs and hamburgers—and, yes, there was even the pizza cart. The very same cart that Sandy had bought four small pepperoni pizzas from two years ago this past May.

But, he didn't notice any horse-drawn ice cream carriages.

This was the first time Sandy had been back since it happened. Despite living just outside the Boston city core in a suburban center named Lexington, he hadn't made the trip downtown in more than two years.

There was a good reason for that, of course. It simply gave him the shivers, even on hot days like this. In fact, he was shivering at that very moment as he gazed out over the happy crowd.

Why were they so happy?

He had forced himself to make the trip downtown today, back to the scene of the crime. Back to Quincy Market. He did it because he was asked to. He did it because he felt it was the patriotic thing to do, the right thing to do. An obligation.

At first, the event had been scheduled to be held in March, at Arlington, Virginia, where all of these award ceremonies took place. But, for some reason it became political, or perhaps intended to be sensational. Someone changed the agenda and went outside the bounds of tradition.

So, it was decided that it would instead take place right in Boston, right where the tragedy happened.

And not just in Boston. But, in Quincy Market itself.

Some government marketing genius must have convinced everyone that the optics would be perfect if the ceremony were held in this place, the actual site of the bloodbath. No one thought to ask Sandy how he felt about this, even though the ceremony was supposed to be honoring him.

All of the major news networks were there. Sandy noticed the CNN, FOX, ABC, and NBC logos on the predator vans, and recognized several prominent anchor faces hanging around with their video teams close by.

Yes, news loved tragedy, and everyone loved a hero. In fact, politicians and news networks worked hard to create heroes sometimes—sometimes when they didn't even exist.

Today Sandy was being presented with the highest honor that a citizen of the United States of America was allowed to receive for bravery—the Citizen Honors Medal, awarded by The Congressional Medal of Honor Society.

Up on the dais there were eight chairs. Sandy was sitting in the second one to the left of the podium. Next to him, on his right, was a four-star general whose name Sandy had already forgotten. The man had greeted him in military fashion, held his left hand over his heart while he shook Sandy's hand. Then he sat down and hadn't said a word since. He was holding a mahogany case, which Sandy presumed contained his medal.

The remaining chairs were occupied by a couple of senators and congressmen who Sandy recognized, as well as the mayor of Boston and a couple of other people who he assumed were aides. The mayor was the official master of ceremonies today, and the crowd was waiting for him to begin.

And, begin he did.

"Ladies and Gentlemen, welcome," said the mayor, pausing as he let his gaze scan across the crowd. "Just over two years ago, our great city suffered a tragedy that will never be forgotten. Two hundred innocent people lost their lives on that horrible day, a day that began with laughter and song and ended with tears and prayers. And, lest we forget, back in 2013 Boston suffered another terrible tragedy to the evil of terrorists, at the finish line of the Boston Marathon.

"This time they hit us on Memorial Day, a day that our country dedicates in honor of those who bravely served and gave their lives in military service.

"Islamic radical terrorists chose that day to hurt us; to once again try to turn freedom into fear, good into evil, happiness into sadness. Of those two hundred souls who were lost that day, more than half of them were children. Lives that were just beginning their quest for the full and happy futures offered by the greatest democracy in the world.

"We will never be defeated by the forces of evil, and that unassailable fact is borne out by the many examples of bravery that we witnessed that day.

"Today, we are honoring one of our citizens," the mayor said, turning to look directly at Sandy, "Dr. Sandford Beech, for acts of valor that went above and beyond the responsibility of a normal civilian. He is being presented with the Citizen Honors Award, the highest such award that any citizen of our country can achieve for acts of bravery. And he is fully deserving of our respect and love on this day of dedication for his selfless acts of courage."

The mayor paused for a few seconds as the crowd erupted in applause. He nodded and smiled at several people in the front row. Once things settled down, the mayor continued.

"As means of introduction, Dr. Beech is a Professor at MIT, and one of our chief researchers at the Lincoln Laboratory, a specialized division of MIT. He has a PhD in experimental nuclear and particle physics, and is also a graduate of West Point, the world's foremost military academy. That fact alone may explain his bravery on the field of battle two years ago.

"Before I introduce General John Huntsman to present the award, we have a special guest who will speak to you. Her name is Lynne Mansfield, a mother of three and a resident of Boston. Ms. Mansfield was one of many witnesses who came forward with descriptions of what happened that day. She told us her story, and has agreed to share it with all of you. Please welcome Lynne Mansfield to the podium."

A tall, long-haired brunette rose from her seat at the far end of the dais and strode confidently to the microphone. The crowd applauded, and Sandy even heard a few insensitive wolf whistles. Lynne Mansfield was a striking woman, no doubt, but classy in her demeanor and in the way she was dressed.

"Thank you for allowing me to speak today," she began, her hand shaking as she adjusted the microphone. "I'll be brief, because I'm a little bit nervous. But, I do need to share my story with all of you. It is painful to relive it, indeed, and I'm fortunate that I personally didn't lose any loved ones that day.

"I was sitting at the table next to Dr. Beech and his family," she said, turning as the mayor had done, to acknowledge Sandy, who sat stony-faced, staring at the crowd. "My children ran over to one of the ice cream carriages when they arrived. I was quite surprised to see horse-drawn carriages coming down the promenade—my immediate thought was that it was a dangerous thing to do with so many children around. But, the kids were so happy and the carriages were brightly painted in rainbow colors—it all seemed so harmless.

"Suddenly, the side doors of the three carriages swung open—I was stunned to see men standing in the open doorways holding machine guns. Then they just started firing, swinging their guns from side to side, and mowing down children and adults—anyone unlucky enough to be standing or sitting in the wrong spots on the promenade.

"I dove to the ground, screaming for my children. I noticed Doctor Beech turn his table over onto its side, throwing the umbrella out onto the ground. Then he ran towards one of the carriages, holding the heavy table in front of him like a shield. He didn't stop—he just kept running until he reached the first carriage. I could see bullets ricocheting off the table top, but that didn't stop him. He reached the carriage and rammed the table up against the opening, striking the shooter in the head. The gunman fell forward onto the ground and Dr. Beech pummelled him several times in the head with his fists, then lifted the table up high in the air and smashed it down onto the man's face. I think he was dead then.

"I was in awe as I watched Dr. Beech pick up the terrorist's machine gun and run over to the horse that had been pulling the carriage. It was lying on its side, on top of two children. Somehow, the horse had become disconnected from the harness of the carriage, and it appeared to be dead—possibly hit by bullets.

"While this was going on, the shooters in the other two carriages were still firing into the crowd. The street was littered with bodies, and thankfully my three children had already rejoined me on the ground underneath our table.

"But, I couldn't take my eyes off Dr. Beech. He slung the gun over his shoulder and dragged the two children out from underneath. He then carried them, one under each arm, over to the empty carriage and left them inside.

"He could have stayed there in the safety of the carriage with them, but he didn't. With the machine gun in his hand, he raced back to the dead horse. Diving to the ground, he shoved his body up against the back of the animal. From that vantage point, he began firing upon the men in the two other carriages. Within seconds there was silence. The terrorists didn't stand a chance, and it appeared as if they couldn't even see where the shots were coming from. That silence was only a brief respite, however, because the sounds of crying and screaming quickly replaced the noise of the gunfire.

"I was astonished—to this day, I'm still astonished. I've never seen such a heroic act in my entire life. He could have hid inside the carriage, but, he didn't. He sacrificed his own safety to bring an end to a massacre. I will always remember that day; the noise of the machine guns, the screams, the blood, the bodies. I'll always remember being afraid for myself and for my children. I've never been so afraid before, and I don't think anything will ever compare to that again. I believe that I'm a stronger person now than I was before that horror."

She paused and turned her head to look back at Sandy. It was a nice touch and a wonderful photo-op.

"But, what I'll remember most is that brave man, that hero, stopping a slaughter."

The audience erupted in applause. Lynne Mansfield smiled warmly at Sandy as she headed back to her seat. The applause continued as the Mayor started to introduce the general to the crowd. But, he quickly abandoned the idea, and waited a respectful few minutes before trying again. Somewhere in the din he managed to recite the credentials of the soldier and his war record, but no one was listening. They were still applauding the movie scene that had just been painted by the very visual Lynne Mansfield. Sandy thought that of all the witnesses who must have had stories about that day, Ms. Mansfield was carefully selected for some very specific reasons.

As General Huntsman began to speak, a swirl of emotions began to make their presence known in Sandy's stomach. He felt the burn, sensed that this was going to be one of those moments. Moments that had come upon him once in a while over the last two years, but usually just in the privacy of his own home. Today it would be public.

Somewhere in the recesses of his brain Sandy heard his name being called. He stood and walked to the podium amid thunderous applause. The loudest yet.

He stared into the cold, official, emotionless eyes of the four-star general and lowered his head slightly as the man draped the medal around his neck. Huntsman took his seat and left Sandy alone with the microphone.

The crowd fell silent as Sandy adjusted the height of the instrument. Then he glanced down and examined the medal. The sash was red, white and blue—naturally. And the medal itself was bronze colored, with the words Above and Beyond engraved in a separate little plaque just over the disc. On the face of the medal were three figures holding hands. Sandy had no idea who these people were supposed to be. And, he didn't care, either.

He shifted his feet forward, tilted the mic towards his mouth and began to speak.

"I've listened to all of the words that have been shared with you folks today. And I have to admit that I'm stunned by the glaring omissions. I'll be even briefer than Ms. Mansfield was, because I really just want to go home. And while this medal is nice, and is supposed to be one of the highest honors in the land, I don't want it."

There was a hush in the crowd as Sandy withdrew the medal from around his neck, turned around—and threw it at the general.

"Put that back in its box, General. And, give it to someone who cares about your propaganda stunts. I'm not your boy."

Sandy turned his attention back to the audience. The shocked murmurs from the crowd were reaching decibels that challenged applause.

"No one over the last two years has questioned why there were horse-drawn carriages on the promenade that day. This hasn't been investigated, and I want to know why. There's been nothing but silence. There were supposed to have been barricades, and security personnel restricting access to the pedestrian mall. Where were they?

"And, the comments pertaining to how the killers in those carriages were Islamic terrorists? That just isn't true. They were American citizens, home grown terrorists with names like John, George, and Bill. I don't recall that an Islamic terror connection was ever made.

"No one has questioned why individuals like these were allowed to possess AK-47 machine rifles. Why is there always such a focus on propaganda *after* tragedies happen, but no action on prevention beforehand?

"Why was this event today scheduled to be held in this place? At the scene of a slaughter? Why wasn't I asked?

"I've refused to talk to the media since that fateful day two years ago. I've heard words today recounting what happened, yet no officials on this stage bothered to vet their comments with me in advance, or show any interest in my own words. Why is that? Would my story perhaps be less hero-worthy? Was that what they were worried about?

"I'm being honored today purportedly for heroic acts to save others. I'm sorry, folks, but that wasn't what motivated me that day to use my skills. I wasn't trying to save the people of Boston. I was simply trying to save my own family.

"I'm astounded that no one on this venerable stage even mentioned that I lost my entire family that day. Instead, they have tried their utmost to paint me as a selfless citizen acting for everyone else with no fear for my own safety. How is it possible that amongst three speakers, not one of them paid homage to my family, my loss?

"My lovely wife, Sarah, was one of the very first victims—shot through the head right where she sat. But, I couldn't even spend the time to tend to her, to see if perhaps there was a chance to save her. Because I knew she would have wanted me to rescue our kids first. So, I didn't even check for a pulse, didn't even kiss her goodbye. Yet...I adored her.

"Those two children that you were told I pulled out from under the horse? They were my own children, not someone else's. Liam and

Whitney. I loved them with all my heart. I carried them to the carriage for safety, but they were probably already dead. Their chests were crushed and the backs of their soft little skulls were flattened. I didn't check for their pulses, nor did I have time to give them goodbye kisses. All I could hope for was that perhaps they were still alive and could be tended to later.

"Yes, I graduated from West Point, and one of the things they teach you at a school like that is to eliminate the threat before trying to save a life. So, that's what I did. I was on auto-pilot, and perhaps if I hadn't been I might have been able to tend to my family and save their lives. That has haunted me for two years, but, I've found consolation, oddly enough, by remembering how horrific their injuries were and how hopeless it probably was.

"Horror has brought me solace. Isn't that ironic?

"And isn't it ironic that in this spectacle you were invited to attend here today, no one thought to pay homage to the family of the selfless hero they chose to put on stage? I'm sure it wasn't deliberate; I'm sure they didn't mean to dishonor my loss. They just got caught up in the moment, the propaganda, and the example of yet one more hero to motivate the American people to support an agenda. To get them fired up, angry, patriotic.

"I, for one, don't want any part of it. Find another hero."

With that, Sandy turned and began to walk off the dais. Out of the corner of his eye he could see that all of the esteemed guests on stage were sitting as stiff as boards, shocked into paralysis.

He passed by all of them without a second glance and began to walk down the stairs onto the promenade. A promenade that had been covered in blood not so long ago.

That's when Sandy saw him. Walking directly towards him, confident head held erect, jaw clenched, a sneer on his mouth, and fire in his steel blue eyes.

It was a face he'd seen on television many times over the last few years, but not in person since West Point. A face that never failed to summon a myriad of emotions in Sandy. First in line was always the sickening sensation of overwhelming revulsion.

3

Sandy's stomach was doing flip-flops by the time he reached the bottom of the stairs. All he wanted to do was head home, but that simple desire was going to have to wait for a bit now. A face that he truly hated from deep in the depths of his soul was assaulting his space for the first time in about twenty years.

Sandy stopped and waited, studying the man as he approached. He hadn't really changed all that much—sure, he was a lot older now, but so was Sandy. His hair was still blonde, his eyes were the same sinister blue, and he still had that cleft chin that Sandy had punched more than once.

Strangely, they'd always kind of looked a bit alike—as if they were brothers. And for a while, back at West Point, they'd even behaved like brothers. Close, but also distant. Friendly, but also competitive. Protective, but also jealous.

Just like brothers.

Then, gradually, it all went to hell.

"Hello, Sandy," said the man, coming to a stop directly in Sandy's path. "I see you're making a name for yourself once again."

Sandy nodded. "Lincoln, you're looking well."

Lincoln chuckled, a cruelness curling around the edges of his mouth like it always had. "Oh, let's not be so formal. Call me Senator."

"No, I think I'll just stick with Lincoln. Or, do your friends and enemies still call you Linc?"

Lincoln sneered at him, then turned around for a second and motioned to three burly men standing a discrete distance behind him. He pointed at several members of the media that were headed quickly in their direction. The security detail responded quickly—whirling around and holding their arms out wide, effectively keeping the reporters at bay just by their menacing presence.

Lincoln turned his attention back to Sandy. "You still have a tough time showing respect, don't you? Just like the old days, and just like up there on stage today. I'm a U.S. senator now, as you well know, so people know me that way. I was even asked to sit up there today, but, out of respect for you, I passed on that honor. I figured it might upset you. And it's a good thing I refrained. I would have had to sit through watching you make a spectacle of yourself. Those photo-ops aren't the type I would want my face showing up in."

Sandy started walking. "It's been a pleasure, Linc. Let's hope we never bump into each other again."

"Hey, don't you walk away from me!" Sandy felt a heavy hand on his shoulder. And a memory shot through his brain...

He was running through the woods, branches scraping against his bare skin. Several members of the cadet platoon had already fallen off to the side. The heat of the day had taken its toll, and, as the famous school liked to extoll, only the strong survived.

The strongest were up front, way ahead of the stragglers.

The winner of the day's marathon would have privileges—extra time off, exemption from some military exercises—not much in the grand scheme of things, but for a student at one of the toughest academies in the world, those were like gifts from heaven.

There were only about five miles left in the grueling twenty-six-mile run, and Sandy was breathing hard. His T-shirt and shorts were soaked with sweat, and he could taste blood; the product of one particularly nasty branch. For the last hour, it had been dripping down his cheek and across his lips. He actually enjoyed the salty taste, and it somehow seemed to spur him on. Maybe it was just psychological, knowing he'd already sweated away a lot of salt since he'd begun the ordeal.

Sandy grimaced as he thought how West Point couldn't just schedule a normal marathon—along flat roads, fields and tracks. No, no, this one had to be through a dense forest—cadets had to not only be competitive and the best at whatever they attempted, they also had to be tortured once in a while. But, Sandy knew that it was also part of the character-building that the school was famous for. The tougher the better, and he embraced it. In fact, knowing that he would finish this marathon in his best time yet gave him a rush of adrenaline.

He knew that right now he was in second place. His best buddy, Lincoln Berwick, was up ahead somewhere. Because of the denseness of the forest he couldn't see him. He'd heard Linc for a while, crashing through the underbrush, but for the last couple of miles he'd gone silent. He glanced from side to side as he ran along, worried that his friend might have fallen into a ditch.

These races usually followed the same pattern. Sandy won, unless it was a day when he didn't feel at his best—like a flu bug or something. But, he normally won at everything and Linc seemed to take it okay. He was a competitive guy as well, and they always trash-talked each other no matter what sport they competed in. But, Sandy still generally won, and sometimes he felt bad about that. Linc tried so hard, but usually finished second. The two of them, famous for being the best athletes, were always the one-two punch. With Sandy in the number one slot.

Technically, he was losing to Linc so far in this marathon, but that was just how Sandy paced himself. Races always worked this way. Sandy and Linc would lead the pack—far out in front—but Linc would be in the lead for most of the race. Sandy allowed this because his friend always burned himself out near the end. And Sandy always had a reserve of energy to pour on the speed during the final three miles.

So, he wasn't worried. He knew he would win.

But, he was worried about why he couldn't hear or see Linc. He should have been in range by now. Sandy continued glancing from side to side as he raced along, ducking under branches that seemingly popped up just to challenge him.

He looked down at his watch. Okay, time to make his move.

He willed his legs to push harder and leaned his body slightly forward. Arms pumping, fists clenched, the long sprint to the finish line was now officially under way. His body was a finely-tuned machine, and finishing first was now the only thing on his mind. Well, that and deking around pesky branches.

He rounded a bend in the rough path and saw the tree he knew signalled that the end was near. This tree was his landmark. It had a thicker trunk than most of the others in the forest.

But…it was a bit different this time from what he remembered. A large branch extended outward over the path. Must have partially split off during a storm.

Sandy ducked as he approached the branch.

But, the branch moved downwards with him, matching his move.

Sandy hunched down even lower at the last second, but, it was too late.

The thick branch moved slightly backwards and then swung right towards him, colliding with tremendous force against his forehead.

He went down hard, and was aware of the outlaw branch falling down beside him along the weed-laden path.

He lay on his back, unable to move.

His eyes were able to move, though, and they followed unexpected motion from behind the trunk. A familiar figure raced out from the protection of the tree, and headed off in the direction of the finish line now only a couple of miles ahead.

Sandy's vision was blurry, but he was able to make out a strong jaw line, muscular frame, arms and legs pumping with newfound vigor, and short blonde hair contrasting sharply with the forest green.

Sandy whirled around and grabbed Linc's hand, removing it roughly from his shoulder. He thrust it down to his side and bent it backwards at the wrist.

Linc winced, but then just as quickly smiled in that sardonic way that Sandy remembered so painfully. That smile that said, without words, that nothing could touch him, nothing could hurt him, and he could do whatever he pleased.

At one time, his best, most trusted friend. A friendship that was short-lived after a series of episodes betrayed Linc's true character. Character traits that seemed to be encouraged by the special unit they were both attached to at West Point.

The chosen ones.

Known as the Honor Guild.

Sandy let go of his hand and quietly chastised himself for showing emotion, for losing control. He knew that Linc preyed off that. In fact, he remembered that it always seemed to give him pleasure.

"Thanks for giving me my hand back, Sandy. So nice of you. Kind of like how you gave that medal back to the general. You've disgraced yourself again, as you always did. You never could cut it, never could accept the code of honor, could you? You couldn't just suck it up like the rest of us. Always had to be holier than thou. You deserved what happened to you. And, because of your high and mighty attitude, you missed out on being with us. Being in a position to make a difference."

Sandy shook his head, and growled. "Why are you here—in front of me—after all these years? And why the hell are you trying to dredge up old memories? What's the fucking point?"

Linc raised his right hand to his forehead in mock salute, and clicked the heels of his shoes together with military flourish. "I came here today to watch you receive your medal. Wanted to congratulate you, try to bury the hatchet."

"Well, I guess you wasted your valuable senatorial time." Sandy turned away once again and began his lonely, angry walk down to the carpark, mindful of the fact that the cold-hearted bastard hadn't once mentioned any regret over the loss of Sandy's family.

This time there was no heavy hand on his shoulder, nothing to trigger more painful memories. Although, they were all there, just below the surface of his consciousness.

That code of honor that Linc referred to had been a unique one just for the elite cadets of the Honor Guild. A totally different code than the one the normal population of West Point Academy was subjected to.

The secretive Honor Guild had a purpose, and essential to that purpose was redefining what the word "honor" really meant. Honor for the HG was a subjective thing, and a moving target. And the purpose of the HG was long-reaching, with brutally strategic implications. Honor had to be a moving target for a unit like that.

Lincoln Berwick had graduated HG with flying colors.

Sandford Beech had flunked out in disgrace.

And, as far as the media and public were concerned, he had disgraced himself once again. His unpatriotic display up on that stage would follow him. He knew that, and the first hint was the flock of reporters he could see up ahead who were no longer being held at bay by the senator's security team.

4

The house was blue. As blue as the sky. It stood in all its majesty on a corner lot in downtown Lexington, Massachusetts, an area of the city that featured older character homes, but not too old. Most were built after 1940, though designed in styles that gave tribute to the area's history.

Some were Georgian, and some were Cape Cod. But, most were the colonial style which was appropriate for the legacy left behind by the trials and tribulations of the greater Boston area.

Lexington was known as the birthplace of American liberty. The breakaway from England along with its onerous taxation and arrogant rule. The very first shot of the American Revolution was fired in Lexington and the first blood of the battle was shed there as well.

The population of the city sat at 35,000 and it was only eleven miles northwest of its giant neighbor, Boston, which now had bragging rights of almost 700,000 souls.

Sandy got out of his Lexus, dragging his heavy briefcase along with him. Even though he had a three-car garage, he usually left his car in the driveway. Sarah's Mustang was still parked inside; he hadn't found the strength in his heart to sell it yet. He never drove it either, which was a shame for a Mustang, which was built to be driven. And driven hard. Sarah had always loved speed, and he remembered that cute little smile that came over her face every time she fired up the powerful engine. He always knew she was going to let it rip as soon as she got it out on the highway. And she would do that at least once a day—even if she had no reason at all to go out. She would just power down the roof and let her hair blow in the wind. That was her therapy. Not that she needed therapy—it just made her feel good. Like how some people liked to plant stuff, or knit things—Sarah just enjoyed speed. That was her vice. Her only vice. And Sandy had loved that side of her.

As he made the walk up to his elegant front door, he admired the princely look of his house for probably the thousandth time. It was colonial style, just like most of the others on his street, but it also had some Cape Cod features—the dormer windows being the most prominent. It set his house apart from all the others on the street just by its hybrid appearance.

Like the Mustang, he hadn't allowed himself to sell the house yet either. Most people would have, after losing their entire family. But he just couldn't. Something was holding him back from doing that. The house had a strange pull on him, and he wondered if it was because it had taken him and Sarah five years to find their dream home. It had been such a long ordeal—nothing had satisfied them until they saw this house on Fair Oaks Drive.

Maybe that was why he was still living there. They had put so much time and effort into finding it, that perhaps it was a betrayal of sorts to Sarah if he sold it. He didn't cry anymore when he wandered the rooms. Now he just smiled when he pictured her sitting in the little window seat in the study, her legs curled up in that girly way that she liked to do. Or when he walked by the baby grand piano in the music room. He could almost hear the tunes that rolled off her fingers and could clearly picture little Whitney sitting beside her, pounding her index finger randomly on whatever key struck her fancy. Sarah smiling at her, encouraging her, making her think that she was actually enhancing the tune.

Sandy walked into the kitchen and tossed his briefcase onto the table. Then, as was customary, he glanced out the window at the backyard. He smiled. He could see them in his mind. Swinging on the swings together trying to see who could reach the greatest height; Liam always letting Whitney win and feigning frustration in the process.

Then, there she was climbing to the top of the slide and pushing off with a squeal, big brother waiting at the bottom to catch her. And he always did. He never let her hit the ground as most big brothers would have done.

Next was the climbing gym—they'd always loved to move through it as an obstacle course and time themselves. Laughing, screaming at each other happily, trash-talking—and, once again, Liam always letting Whitney win. Sandy was pretty certain she knew, just by the suspicious little smirk on her face whenever she came inside to proclaim, "Dad, I won again!"

Just like the Mustang and the house, Sandy hadn't found the strength to sell the playground equipment or the piano yet, either. There was no good rationale for keeping any of those things, but, he knew they were there to stay. Nothing could motivate him to sell them. They were a part of his life. An important part of his life. A connection to the past, a wonderful past.

The house was far too big for him. At 6,000 square feet, it was a monster. A dream house, one that he and Sarah had actually imagined in their minds before they'd even seen it. They'd drawn sketches of this house, fiddled with the dimensions, dreamt of finding the perfect lot and just building the damn thing.

And then they saw it. It was probably the happiest day of their lives, after their wedding day and the births of their little angels.

He found himself wandering aimlessly around the house quite a bit now. Restless, whenever he had time on his hands. Even though his job at the Lincoln Laboratory was demanding, he still had far too much time to spare. He knew he had to find ways to fill that time, and he did have a couple of projects on the go. But, he needed more.

He heard the distinctive thump of the evening newspaper landing on his front porch. He opened the door, waved at the paperboy, and picked up the paper. He always enjoyed catching up on the day's news after a hard day at the lab.

He brought it inside and stretched out on the soft leather couch in his living room. Removed the elastic band and unfolded the paper.

The headline and photo made him gasp. There the man was, in full living color, under the heading: Senator Lincoln Berwick Declares Candidacy for President.

Sandy dropped the paper onto his lap and closed his eyes. He couldn't bring himself to read the article. Instead, his mind was overcome by a memory.

Excitement in the halls and in the classrooms. It was autumn, and election time. A chance for the boys to prove their leadership skills. Sure, in the grand scheme of things, it was small potatoes. But, at West Point, in that little world, it was a big deal. Future leaders were being groomed, and school election time was the opportunity to taste the thrill of victory, to outsmart your opponents. Just the way you would have to do it in the real world one day—the world they wanted you to be ready for. It was just another test. An important one.

The Honor Guild was engaged in an election campaign, and there were three candidates who had won the Guild's version of primaries. It was down to three: Sandford Beech, Lincoln Berwick, and a preppy kid named Jonathan Aldersyde.

They each had their campaign teams, kids who worked hard lobbying for votes, making signs, shaking hands, and promoting their candidates. All good fun, but serious fun. Because this stuff had the word "future" written all over it. And they all knew it. And winning at West Point was everything. They'd been taught that in the short time they'd been there. They'd been told what they were being groomed for, and it was an awesome responsibility for kids their age.

According to all of the reputable polls, Sandy had the lead. All of the speeches had been made, and they'd each done well. But, Sandy was the best—the most electric, the most charismatic of all three. And he was the candidate who was also best liked as well. The likeability factor was a big one in elections. They all knew it.

Linc was nipping at his heels. Close behind in almost every category except that elusive likeability factor. But Sandy knew the election was now his to lose. Unless he did something stupid, there was no way that Linc was going to catch him. And he had no bond of friendship standing in the way anymore, either. He was all out for victory with no concern at all for how Linc felt. Their relationship had become strained since that marathon when Linc had knocked him unconscious with one swing of a branch. He'd confronted him afterwards, but Linc just laughed in his face.

Sandy had considered reporting him, but it would only have been his word against Linc's, so there was no chance of winning that fight. And, there was also the honor code that he knew he had to consider. If he broke that code, he'd be out. So, he had no choice but to suck it up, accept that his best friend had literally knocked him out of the race.

This time he would beat him. And he wouldn't feel bad about doing it. They weren't friends anymore. Sandy would become the newly elected Honor Guild Commander.

Then one morning it all changed.

He remembered several of the brass crowding around his locker, searching inside—pulling out a package and opening it. Sniffing it.

Grabbing him by the arms and hauling him off to the one office no one ever wanted to visit. Being told that he was going to be disciplined for possession of marijuana. He'd be assigned harsh duties, lose his free time, and be grounded to the campus for six months. And, needless to say, he'd be ejected from the election campaign for violation of honor.

But, he was expected to be grateful that he wouldn't be booted from the Honor Guild program, because, of course, the honor code worked both ways. This was his opportunity to learn important lessons in honor, redemption, and forgiveness.

And, a few days later, he had the pleasure of watching Lincoln Berwick elected Commander of the Honor Guild.

Another one of his lessons.

Sandy threw the newspaper onto the coffee table. Jumped to his feet and began pacing the room. He couldn't read that damn article right now, he knew that would be the wrong thing to do. He would leave it until he'd calmed down.

Almost as if programmed, he opened a door in the hallway and headed downstairs to his basement lab, which was where he went when he was feeling particularly restless—or angry.

Right now, he needed a diversion. Needed to focus his brain on something else, anything else.

Sandy's basement was huge. Totally unfinished, which was just the way he liked it. Perfect for storage and for experimenting with his various creations.

Most of the work he did at the Lincoln Laboratory was highly classified, and he really wasn't supposed to have any data or re-creations in his home. But, he'd broken that rule a long time ago. The honor code only went so far. He'd learned that lesson the hard way.

He chuckled to himself as he pondered how ironic it was that he worked at a lab named Lincoln, the same name as his long-time nemesis. The man who might now become the next president of the United States.

Sandy enjoyed his work at Lincoln. It challenged his mind, even though the things they played with there were scary as hell and had a purpose far beyond what morality would dictate. That part always bothered him, but the work challenged his genius IQ and he needed that stimulation. Even if it caused conflicts from time to time in his brain—and in his soul.

The project that he was heading up right now, and the one that had occupied him and his team for the last several years, was a sub-category of Directed Energy Weapons. Those types of weapons had already been developed and he'd been involved in ironing out some of the faults since he joined the Lincoln Lab seven years ago. The weapons had proven to be troublesome, and, consequently, had been used only sparingly in conflicts so far.

He'd been developing a new version over the last couple of years. The large prototype was back at the Lincoln Lab, but, he had his own smaller prototype right there in his own basement. There weren't enough hours in the day back at the lab to do things properly—he needed his spare time at home as well to move the project along.

So, he had a miniature version of his own. A miniature version of a Pulsed Energy Projectile, otherwise known as PEP. It was advanced weaponry of the highest order, and top secret. Which made it even riskier for him to have his own version at home. If it was ever discovered, he could only imagine what would happen to him.

Leavenworth, for the rest of his life. Or worse.

The basic principle of the PEP was the emittance of an infrared laser pulse, which created rapidly expanding plasma directed at the chosen target. It was a directed energy weapon in the extreme, because Sandy had perfected it to exceed the speed of light.

The weapon would fire a stream of plasma—basically an excited state of matter consisting of electrons and nuclei. Sandy had developed it to become most lethal at longer distances, because his engineering of the weapon allowed the plasma to expand to an unlimited mass the farther it traveled.

When it hit its target, the result was immediate. Immediate destruction, absolute collapse of whatever mass it collided with.

For objects with denser mass, it was desirable to fire the weapon from a farther distance. For lighter masses, short distance was fine.

What Sandy and his team were struggling with right now were the issues of sound and visibility. The Pentagon needed the weapon to be quiet and invisible, and they just weren't there yet.

Which was one of the reasons why Sandy had a miniature working prototype right in his own basement. The challenges with the weapon needed more hours than he could devote at the Lincoln Lab. He needed the privacy of his own home, and his own thoughts, to perfect the weapon. He had a good team, but sometimes they just got in the way.

Sandy walked to the end of a long corridor and stacked a metal box on top of a storage rack. Then he walked back to his PEP device and activated the camera. He focused it on the metal box and took a photo.

Next, he pushed a button on the machine that instructed it to recognize the pixels of the object in the digital photo, search for it with its sensors, then simultaneously calculate and program the distance.

Then the PEP would automatically line it up.

Sandy didn't even have to aim the damn thing.

Dr. Sandford Beech, PhD in experimental nuclear and particle physics, donned a pair of ear mufflers and took a deep breath.

He pictured his old friend Lincoln Berwick—and punched the little red button.

5

The esteemed senator from Dallas, Texas, sat at the head of the table as he normally did.

Which, in reality was more symbolic than anything else.

It just made him feel good. He didn't really belong at the head.

He rubbed his distinctive cleft chin—the one that made him look somewhat like the iconic actor, Kirk Douglas—and looked around the table at his team.

Well, it wasn't really his team, not people he chose himself—but they were at least all humming the same tune. If he'd tried to pick his own team, they would have just changed it on him before he'd even had the chance to host a welcome cocktail party.

Didn't matter. They were good folks. Talented folks. Sharks. The type of people he would have hired himself.

He glanced at his campaign manager, Bob Stone.

"Well, where do we stand, Bob? Give us a status report."

Bob smiled. "We're looking good. Polling well, and the primary season hasn't even started yet. You're commanding good audiences at your rallies, and the media, so far, are giving you a wide berth."

Lincoln Berwick nodded and gazed out the window at the Dallas skyline. He smiled inwardly when his eyes landed on the old Texas School Book Depository building.

"Now, there's a piece of history."

One of his team members, Meagan Whitfield, a shark in her own right, asked, "What piece of history are you talking about?"

"Well, the assassin's nest, of course. I look at that building almost every day. It's a cold reminder of what measures have to be taken from time to time. For the good of country."

Meagan frowned. "That's not a piece of history we should be talking about here, Linc. Not while we're planning your presidential campaign."

He glared at her and jabbed his index finger in her direction.

"You would be well served to remember it. That was the most momentous event in U.S. history, even more so than the American Revolution. I wasn't even alive in 1963 when Kennedy was killed, but that day still shaped my life. And it will shape my future, too. November 22 will always be a day in my mind for celebration. It's a symbol of the brave steps that Americans must take once in a while to protect the sanctity of this country."

Meagan glared back. "He was a hero to most citizens and was loved almost universally. You would be wise to remember that as you campaign for the job he held for only a few short years. If you're not careful, your career could also be short."

Bob Stone jumped in. "Okay, okay, we're getting a bit off topic here. Let's all agree that Kennedy was loved, and let's also agree that he needed to go. Fair?"

Linc wasn't finished yet. He hadn't had the last word.

"Yes, he was loved. But, that was just a smokescreen. He was weak, wanted to pull out of Viet Nam, planned to dismantle the CIA—and do I need to remind you, Meagan, what his plans were against the oil industry here in Texas? The state's economy would have been decimated if that prick had been allowed to live. The brainpower and guts that it took by some of our bravest patriots to take that menace down, is worth remembering and worth celebrating."

Meagan wasn't going to let him have the last word.

"Think what you want, I'm not disagreeing with you. I'm just stating a fact. The fact is, he was a popular president, and if the American public ever finds out that his own country killed him, there's no telling what might happen. The same is true about 9/11.

"You can pontificate all you want, Linc, but it would be wise for you to shut the hell up and concentrate on the task at hand. Watch your mouth, show the respect that the citizens expect you to show, and stick to the script. And the script on the Kennedy issue is that he was loved, admired, and, despite being a Democrat, we in the Republican Party loved him too. Got it, hotshot?"

Linc's blood was boiling—he could feel it in his face, and with the blurriness in his eyes.

Through the film that was now covering his eyeballs, he studied Meagan Whitfield with disdain.

She was older, in her sixties, old enough to be his mother if she'd gotten knocked-up at a tender age. But, he couldn't imagine who would ever want to fuck such a witch to begin with.

He knew her background well. A Wall Street lawyer, and one of the biggest corporate wheeler-dealers on the planet. Wealthy beyond anyone's wildest dreams, she only served on his team out of dedication to the cause. She wasn't paid for her time and neither were any of the other eight people sitting around the table.

Not even Bob Stone, industrialist, major shareholder of the nation's largest defence contractor. He was the official campaign manager, but his role was more of trying to keep the peace between Linc and the other members of the team; particularly Meagan Whitfield.

Linc took a few deep breaths, and felt his adrenaline rush slowly drop off. This wasn't the time for a fight, especially one he couldn't win.

He mumbled, "Okay."

She wasn't finished yet. This time it was her finger jabbing in the air.

"You would be wise to remember some other history, Senator Berwick. Where you came from, what the Honor Guild meant and still means. What that program has cost most of us around this table, many more outside of this room, as well as the countless others who came before us.

"Your destiny was chosen for you over twenty years ago—you were bought and paid for. You wouldn't have risen the way you did in your career without us, and you certainly wouldn't be in this prestigious position you're in right now if it wasn't for us.

"You don't get to think on your own—we tell you what to think. We can't afford screw-ups, can't afford to show our cards—and if you allow some of your radical thinking to become public, this will all have been for naught. We may all agree with your thinking, but sharing those thoughts with anyone outside this room, even with Republican Party officials, would result in disaster. It would be stupid. None of this should be a surprise to you."

Linc felt his blood pressure rising again.

"Of course, I know what it all means. But I didn't get this far just because of you and the Honor Guild. My genius IQ, good looks, and charisma, can captivate the country. Without me, you and your backers would be nothing. I have the talent to run this country and I probably would have made it to senator without your help. And maybe all the way to the White House, too, without your help. And, don't pretend to be loyal Republican Party supporters. You could care less about the party. You're just using it as the most desired vehicle for your agenda."

Meagan smiled. "Yes, Senator, that's right. They have no idea that we've hijacked their agenda and their platform. And you, Mr. Handsome Charismatic High IQ Man, are our way in. You're our Trojan horse. The first wave of Honor Guild students are just now reaching electable age. And you're part of that first wave. There will be a lot more behind you. And there are quite a few beside you as well, in other key roles in Congress and elsewhere.

"So, you're not the only one we have at our fingertips to choose from. Get over yourself. And, we've infiltrated the Republican Party because their basic official platform is closest to the values we believe in. But, yes, they'd be horrified if they found out they've been hijacked by our special…group. Our role has to remain secret. Because, without a Party, we can't attain power. And, power, after all, was the original purpose of the Honor Guild."

Bob Stone got up from his seat and walked over to the coffee machine, poured himself a cup and returned to his seat.

"I think we've heard enough, Meagan. You've beat our boy up quite a bit for one day. Can we move on to campaign stuff?"

Meagan nodded and waved her hand in exasperation. "As long as he got my message loud and clear."

Bob looked at Linc, and asked softly, "Senator? Are we good to move on?"

Linc folded his arms across his chest. "Message received. You don't have to worry about me. This whole thing started off from my just expressing how I felt about that stupid Book Depository building. I didn't mean anything by it."

Meagan leaned back in her seat and pointed out the window. "I agree with the symbolism of that building. But, some things we have to keep to ourselves. I worry about loose cannons like you—worry that you'll express that view to others who don't want to hear it. To reporters, on talk shows, at your rallies. I'm sorry if I was tough on you, but I prefer to nip things in the bud before they become uncontrollable public relations nightmares."

Bob raised his hand. "Enough, Meagan. I think Linc understands. You've made your point."

Linc leaned forward and rested his elbows on the table. "Yes, let's move on. We're here today to talk about my competition—within the party, and outside. What handle do you folks have on that?"

A youngish dotcom billionaire at the end of the table raised his hand. His name was Boris Malkin, and, while he was on the shy side, he always had important things to share. Linc liked him, mainly because boy wizard showed him respect. More than he could say for a few others around the table.

"Yes, Boris?"

"I'm in charge of that process, Senator. We have things covered pretty well. There are five other candidates who have declared so far for the Republicans. We think that will be the extent of it. The primary season starts in a couple of months, so it's a bit late for anyone else to jump into the race now.

"Out of the five contenders, three of them are our folks—just token candidates that we've put into the race to give you some pretend competition, make it seem legit. Their orders are to do poorly in the debates and drop out after the first few primaries.

"The other two are wild cards—you know them. Governor Maitland of Florida and Senator Dixon of Ohio. Those two are your real competition, and we can't do anything about them except hope that your charisma and intelligence carries the day."

"You can dig up some dirt, can't you?"

Boris nodded. "Of course, that goes without saying and we're already digging. And, if we don't find anything, we'll just make it up and leak it through the usual channels. But, that may not work—they have some loyal followers. So, we still need you to shine, just in case."

Bob was writing notes on his pad. He raised his head and looked in Boris' direction. "How about the Democrats? We have to look ahead, past the primaries. What's your assessment of their candidates, Boris?"

"We know most of them, of course. Popular, but not rocket scientists by any stretch of the imagination. Linc should make mincemeat out of them in the general election."

Bob nodded in agreement. "Yeah, hopefully, but what I meant was—what can we do about them?"

Boris smiled. "Well, our plan is to destroy the strongest of their candidates during the primaries, to make sure the one Linc eventually runs against is the one we want him to run against. So, we'll hold back our best dirt until that guy I'm thinking about gets the Democratic nomination. Then, we'll take him out just a few weeks before the election with a shocking revelation that will make it impossible for them to defend against in the short time left."

"What if you can't find anything shocking enough to destroy him?"

Boris smiled again, more sinister this time. "Well, we can just create it out of thin air, or if all that fails, we do, of course, have other ways of taking people out."

Linc rolled up his shirtsleeves. "Well done, Boris. We can always count on you to have your ducks in order."

Bob nodded. "Yes, keep at it, Boris. We'll look forward to updates as we move along."

He pointed at Linc.

"Now, we need to vet you in advance. If we're able to find stuff out about you, you can bet the press will find it too. And, your competition will as well. So, I'd rather we know about it up front so we can deal with it, manage it, bury it."

"We already know a lot about you, of course—you've been our boy for a long time. But, I try not to be naïve about these things—that Sarah Palin dingbat was a perfect example of how we can all be blindsided by style and bluster."

Bob clasped his hands together. "So, cleanse your soul, Linc. Is there anything we need to know from your past that we don't already know? Even as far back as your West Point days? The Honor Guild? Anything we don't know that we should know?"

Linc felt a sudden pressure in his chest, as his heart began to race.

He scratched his head, feigning surprise at the question. "Well, no, Bob, nothing I can recall. At least nothing worth mentioning."

6

"Isn't there too much regulation right now, anyway? I mean, do we need the government interfering in every little aspect of our lives, Professor Beech?"

Sandy smiled at the curly-haired student. Kind of a nerd, one of those high-tech geniuses who would probably end up inventing video games one day. But, he was a good kid and Sandy liked him.

He couldn't remember his name, nor any of the other half dozen students who were sipping coffee with him in MIT Lecture Hall 5K.

He'd just finished a lecture on aeronautical physics, with particular emphasis on the world's latest innovation—and nuisance—known as Unmanned Aerial Vehicles. More popularly referred to as drones.

Even though Sandy's primary work was at MIT's Lincoln Laboratory, he still lectured once or twice a week at the main MIT campus in Cambridge.

He was a popular professor, probably because he got to pick the topics that he wanted to lecture on. His emeritus status gave him certain privileges and, as long as he lectured on topics that were related to the students' general curriculum, he was as free as a bird.

Also, after each lecture he did something that most professors never bothered to do—he held informal chat sessions with any students who were able to hang around for a while before their next classes.

One of the kids would always run out and get coffees for everyone—or tea, if that was their vice of choice—and they would all just chat together.

The students loved it; loved the informality of it, and really enjoyed the chance to just have a conversation with a famous and esteemed professor.

Professors were usually seen as being above such frivolity, but not Sandy. He loved young people—their energy and even their naivety—and it was stimulating for him to interact with such curious brains. He fed off it—got his motivation from it. It helped convince himself that he was doing something worthwhile.

"Sorry, son, I don't remember your name."

"It's Jonah, sir."

Sandy took a sip of his coffee, and scanned the six pairs of enthusiastic eyes that were hanging on every move he made.

He crossed his legs and gestured with his hands.

"Well, Jonah, look at this lecture room we're in. It has structure, design, a certain discipline to it. You're used to that, and you'd probably be lost here at university without some kind of structure. You call me sir or Professor, but I'm a normal guy just like you. Our lives are full of regulation and protocol, and without those things we'd wander around aimlessly. And—it would be a very dangerous world indeed, wouldn't it?"

Jonah nodded.

An attractive blonde girl raised her hand.

Sandy laughed. "You don't have to raise your hand anymore. We're just chatting here."

She blushed. "Sorry, Professor. I'm Janice, by the way. These drones you were talking to us about—aren't they just toys, though? Can't we trust common sense without a whole bunch of rules? I was going to buy one, but then I read the regulations and changed my mind."

"What I tried to share with you guys in the lecture today was the technology itself, how far it's come. It's one of the examples of physics at its most sophisticated state. But, while you may just use a drone as a toy and fly it around in a field, not everyone would be that responsible. And, believe it or not, regulations are still not set in stone. States are involved, the FAA is involved, and they've just recently released draft regulations that have taken ten long years to prepare. Can you imagine? Ten years to prepare a draft on equipment that has been in use for that long already?

"Amazon is frustrated, and they should be. They were planning to launch a home delivery program using UAVs, but the new regulations are clear—there has to be an operator who can keep the vehicle in "line of sight." Which, of course, completely screws up Amazon's plans to have a fleet of drones operating across the country using remote operators."

Janice frowned. "But, doesn't the military use remote operators for their drones?"

Sandy nodded. "Yes, they do. But, that's a different category entirely. Intensive training, and the technology in the drones that the military uses is far more advanced than the commercial or backyard drones that are being sold on the wide market. Personally, I thought Amazon's plan was stupid. I couldn't even begin to imagine a bunch of unmanned drones delivering parcels across the country. A recipe for disaster, and right out of The Jetsons."

"The whats?"

Sandy chuckled. "Sorry, I'm dating myself. It was an old TV show, before your time. Futuristic nonsense, but, fun."

A preppy young guy, dressed in a suit and tie, jumped in.

"Professor, I've been reading and seeing a lot on the news about drones lately. It seems to have become an election issue—how they're being used in Afghanistan, Yemen, and other shit-holes like that. Sorry—excuse my language."

"That's okay. What's your name?"

"Kyle."

"Well, the first thing I would say, Kyle, is that those places aren't "shit-holes." They're important cogs in the history of the world, and if they're in a sad state right now it's because we've made them that way. We've destroyed them; interfered with their governments, economies, and their religions. We've made all sorts of excuses—mostly lies—to wage war against these countries, and the agenda has far more to do with economics and global power than it does with Islamic terrorism, believe me.

"Secondly, it's only natural that drones would become an issue in the election. They're causing horrific casualties wherever they're being used, and it's not only a foreign relations issue now, but, a moral one as well.

"Each of the two main parties will try to differentiate themselves on issues like the Middle East. You've probably been watching the speeches—the Republicans tend to be the war party, defending interventions everywhere. The Democrats, on the other hand, concentrate more on diplomacy and domestic issues.

"And, Republicans also believe in less government, fewer regulations. It's no surprise that their laxness over bank governance led to the Great Recession of 2008. That happened on their watch.

"They believe in de-regulation, favoring Wall Street, inadvertently allowing sloppiness to creep into the system. They're the ones who also believe everyone should be allowed to run around with machine guns.

"The Democrats, on the other hand, believe in tighter regulations, bigger government, and less war.

"If the Republicans win the election, chances are that drone regulations here in the U.S. will become non-existent. So, Amazon will be very happy. You can probably guess who their CEO is supporting."

Kyle frowned. "I think all politicians are crooked. They all seem to lie, say whatever it takes to get elected. I find it hard to follow this stupid election cycle. It's confusing, and it's so long. It goes on forever, and I'm sick of hearing about it. I guess students who take political science understand it, but to me it all seems nuts."

Sandy laughed. "That's because you're studying to be a scientist, Kyle. To your mind, everything has to be logical. Politics is the most illogical process in the world. And, yes, it goes on forever here in the United States. The only word that could be used to accurately describe it is marathon. It's an endless marathon that actually starts right after a president is elected. Both parties begin posturing for the next election four years hence. It's ridiculous. They spend more time trying to grab power, or hang onto power, than actually governing. That's one of the reasons why the country is in such a mess right now. No one's paying attention."

Jonah leaned forward. "I have to admit I haven't been paying attention all that much, either. When is the actual election, Professor?"

"Next November. But, primary elections start, state by state, in February. That's the process that each party goes through to select their eventual nominee for President. That takes several months and concludes in the summer. Then, the two main parties' candidates square off for the remaining three months to actually compete for president. In addition to that, there are primaries and elections that take place to choose senators and congressmen."

Jonah shook his head. "Ridiculous, and what a waste of money."

Sandy nodded. "Yep. Billions are spent every four years on this. Think how far that money could go for other things."

"How many senators are there?"

"A total of 100. Each state gets to have two senators. And, the House of Representatives has 435 members—those are allocated state by state based on population."

Janice crossed her legs. Sandy noticed Jonah stealing a sneak peek, which didn't surprise him. He had to admit she had shapely legs, and he suspected that Jonah might have stuck around for this coffee chat just because she was there.

She pursed her lips, apparently pondering something to say.

"What is it, Janice?"

"You seem to know a lot about politics and the world. We've all noticed that, just from chatting with you or listening to your lectures. Have you ever thought of running for senator or—president?"

Sandy quickly shook his head. "No, Janice, I haven't. I think I'd be frustrated. Too much of an idealist."

"But, you're so smart, and you speak so well. It seems that these days public speaking and image are the only skills they pay attention to. After every speech from a candidate, the journalists seem to be totally obsessed with how well they spoke, what they wore, how loud they were, or how they gestured. They seem to ignore what they actually talked about. It seems so silly—and so shallow to me. No substance."

"Yes, you're right."

She persisted. "It seems to me that for a smart, honest person like you, who also speaks far better than any of those other clowns, you'd be a shoo-in."

Sandy smiled. "Aww…that's so nice of you to say. I appreciate it, I really do. But, no, politics isn't for me. I enjoy what I do too much to jump into that circus. And, I don't think I'd even have the energy for a brutal marathon like that."

Janice pouted slightly, just before a frown crossed her face. Sandy knew she wanted to say something else.

"What is it? What's troubling you?"

She sighed. "I don't want to insult you, but in the short time I've been exposed to you, I've seen you as kind of a father figure."

He smiled. "That's a compliment, not an insult."

"Can I ask you a personal question?"

"Well…sure. If I don't want to answer it, I won't. So shoot."

The young woman was turning beet red. "I lost my father when I was very young, so, because of how I felt about you—uh, I'm so embarrassed—I read up on you. I know what happened a couple of years ago. You lost your family in that terrorist attack. You're a father, who's no longer a father. I really felt terrible about that. I'm a daughter without a father, and you're a father without your children."

Jonah looked at her curiously. "I didn't know that."

A cramp was starting to form in Sandy's stomach. He shifted in his seat. "That's okay, Janice. What was your question?"

She paused for a second to bite on a fingernail.

"I've seen the campaign ads from that candidate—I forget his name—Washington?"

"Close. It's Lincoln. Lincoln Berwick."

"Right, that Lincoln guy. He's using you in one of his campaign ads. It shows a clip of you from a few months ago, on a stage, throwing a medal at some soldier. Uses a caption something like: "A disgraceful excuse for an American." Then the ad goes on to show bombs dropping in some country and soldiers being taken away on stretchers."

Jonah's mouth was hanging open in shock. "God, I better watch TV more often. I haven't seen that ad yet."

Sandy glanced at his watch and stood. "Guys, I have to get going. Have another lecture in a few minutes."

Janice stood as well. "I'm so sorry, Professor Beech. I've upset you, I think."

"No, you haven't, Janice. It is painful to remember, but I'm okay."

She touched his forearm. "Can I still ask my question?"

"Sure."

"Can't you sue that bastard? How can he do that to you? Using you in his ad, dredging up the horror you went through? I don't blame you for not accepting that medal. They were so rude to you, so insensitive."

Sandy grimaced. "No, Janice, I can't sue him. That was a public event, and I made a spectacle of myself. I should have expected that clip would pop up somewhere in someone's propaganda. My speech was all over the news after I did that event this past summer, and things eventually died down. But, now, with this presidential campaign, I should have expected it would come back to haunt me. It's just the type of thing these war-hawks would use."

"It hurts me to see you being used that way. Isn't there anything you can do?"

Sandy slouched slightly and lowered his head for a second, hoping to hide the sadness in his eyes. Then he pulled himself together, stood erect, and clapped his hands.

"Okay, kids, we're done for today. Get along to your next classes."

As they were leaving the lecture hall, Kyle stopped and looked back at him.

"What are you, Professor? Republican or Democrat?"

Sandy opened his briefcase and stuffed his tablet and phone inside.

"I'm a registered Democrat, son. But, in reality, more of an Independent."

Kyle smiled. "Good."

7

John Nichols fired up his computer, then sat and waited while the old machine took its usual five minutes to come to life. He knew he needed to replace the damn thing, but that would cost money—and he didn't have any.

He googled the restaurant where his meeting would take place tonight. Well, it wouldn't be in the restaurant itself—instead it would be outside the front entrance. Nice and public. Nice and safe.

John had asked for $200,000. Been second-guessing himself ever since, though. Should have asked for more. But, he wanted to make it easy for the prick to pay him. Didn't want any delays and didn't want to risk asking for too much, either. He was pretty sure he was safe, but you never knew. He had kept his address a secret, and since he didn't have a credit card or anything like that, he wasn't easy to track down. And he'd rented his basement apartment under a false name—same with his phone and utility payments.

That kind of money was going to change his life. Sure, he wouldn't be rich, but he'd be able to live in a better place than the shit-hole he lived in right now. Might be able to pay off some debts, buy a car, and have enough left over to travel a bit.

And, most importantly, give a lot of it away to two special people.

What the hell, maybe also stock up on some good whisky rather than the cheap stuff he was drinking tonight.

The same cheap stuff he drank every night.

He poured himself another full glass of the poison. Then guzzled half.

It didn't even sting any more. He remembered when he first started drinking heavily a lifetime ago, the strong liquid used to take his breath away. And burn his throat. Now, he didn't feel a damn thing.

He knew full well that it had affected him in other ways, though. His brain just didn't think as fast as it used to. Things took a lot longer to process now. And, because the stuff didn't have the same drunken effect on him as it had years ago, he ended up drinking more in one sitting than he used to. Which meant his brain was taking more of a beating with each session, because his natural braking system had long since failed. There were no brakes anymore.

John glanced at his watch. A couple of hours to go. Judging by the google map, it would take him an hour to get there—one bus ride, followed by a short stint on the subway.

He sighed, pushed his wheeled chair back from the computer, and looked up at the mantle. Two pretty faces smiled down at him from behind the glass of a picture frame. His ex-wife, Judy, and daughter, Cynthia. They were both long gone now, and he hadn't seen them in at least a decade.

He'd phoned them many times, but that had been the extent of it. Judy wanted nothing to do with him. Cynthia, however, was always pleasant enough to him over the phone, and he always made sure to send her a birthday card each year.

She'd be fifteen in a couple of months.

John grabbed a pen and wrote out a reminder to himself on a sticky note.

He still loved them, but the damn booze had ruined everything for him. Judy urged him to get help, and he'd tried real hard, too. But…every time he climbed onto the wagon he just fell right off again. She finally gave up—packed some suitcases, took his daughter and left. They still lived in New York City, but he'd been respectful enough not to visit them.

Many times over the years he'd tried to persuade Judy to let him visit, but she wouldn't have it. Probably because he always told her the truth. Every time he asked if he could come by, she always answered him with a question of her own.

Always the same question: "Have you stopped drinking?"

And he always answered the same way: "No."

John was never able to lie to her, and he'd never been violent with his family. Even though he'd been trained in skills that would curl the toes of even the most hardened soldier, he'd never used those skills.

He knew their address—they'd moved a couple of times and Judy trusted him enough to always let him know. They lived in Queens now. He lived in the Bronx.

She still loved him. He felt that. And he loved her, too. Always would.

A few hours ago, he'd sent her a package in the mail. Even though his brain wasn't working all that well anymore, he'd remembered to cover his bases. The package was one of those padded envelope thingies with a note and a cassette tape contained inside. The note was a short one—just long enough to tell Judy that he'd have some money for her and Cynthia shortly. Enough to make their lives a little better. Actually, a lot better.

But, in case something happened to him, he told her in the note to keep the cassette tape safe and sound. He didn't want her to listen to it, but instead to get in touch with an old friend from back in his West Point days. He wanted Judy to give him that cassette tape, a recording that had been made without a certain other person being aware.

In his note, he told Judy that in the event he died, the cassette had to get into his old friend's hands. Without delay.

It was the original. The copy he had in his pocket, ready to exchange tonight for $200,000. He wondered if the asshole would come in person. He doubted it. He was an important senator now, so John was sure he had "people" who did this sort of thing for him.

The cassette recorder had been stashed out of sight in his dorm room twenty or so years ago. John couldn't remember actual years anymore. It was just a damn long time ago.

The machine had been whirring away silently, while he talked frantically with his classmate. And that classmate never knew that their conversation was being recorded.

More than a classmate actually—the one and only Commander of the Honor Guild.

Lincoln Berwick. Now, Senator Lincoln Berwick, and a leading contender for President of the United States of America.

While that clandestine machine was recording, John and Linc were discussing the events of a certain fateful night. Lincoln tried to calm him down. And ordered his silence. Warned him of what would happen if he broke the code of honor.

John still had the cassette tape after all these years, even after a special friend tried to blow the whistle for him. The same friend who he'd instructed Judy to send the original of the tape to. A courageous friend who'd removed the burden from John and went to see the Honor Guild Dean on his behalf. Didn't even disclose John's name. Kept him out of it, because he was probably unsure at the time how far they'd allow the query to go. And, John never told his friend that he had an actual recording. Was afraid to. Didn't want that to slip out, and make him or his friend targets. He'd save that for later if the school decided to take it further.

It didn't go far at all. The honor code was upheld. And, soon after that, his friend was expelled. Demoted back down to the regular population of West Point, ousted from the Honor Guild. Ordered to observe the code and keep his mouth shut. Told that they would exact their own form of justice upon Lincoln Berwick, but that was as far as it would go. Some things were meant to stay "internal."

But, because his friend had violated the honor code, he had to go. A promising student kicked out of the leadership program.

A program that at one time had included John Nichols as one of the promising ones as well. He'd only lasted one year longer than his friend.

When he was finally ousted, it was for being a drunk.

But, despite the memory-challenged state his brain was in now after too many alcoholic years, he could still remember what had caused him to start drinking. John closed his eyes and drifted off…

The van cruised along slowly. It was a panel van, owned by one of the guys. Two captain's chairs in the front, bare floor in the back. Well, bare except for a mattress. John was sitting on the floor along with two other guys. Up front was the driver, and in the passenger seat sat Lincoln Berwick. He was the scout—on the lookout.

It was "wild oats" night. They had these wild excursions usually once a month. Always in a different town, or one of the suburbs of New York. Usually not too far from campus.

They were all brilliant students at West Point, privileged to be in the secretive elite division known as the Honor Guild. And Lincoln was the newly elected Commander of the Honor Guild—the student leader, the one who had authority over the others. The school had made it clear to all of them that the Student Commander had to be respected. That was just part of the honor code.

John and the others in the van were subservient to Lincoln; in fact, they felt it quite an honor just to be allowed to hang out with him, be his friend. Being loyal to Lincoln could only augur well for their standing in the leadership program. They knew their destinies were being determined with every single test, every athletic achievement, and every grade they aced. They'd also witnessed what usually happened to students who had fallen out of favor with Lincoln.

Ostracized, humiliated, and sometimes even expelled.

He had power. He was a leader and the most favored one in the Honor Guild.

Lincoln seemed to look at life as being just one big entitlement. No one fucked with him.

John remembered the words that started the nightmare.

"There's a hot one. Slow down, Hank."

Then the sound of the van door sliding open.

"Hi there, darlin. Wanna party with us?"

A soft voice answered. "Maybe. What's in it for me?"

"There's five of us. Be a good payday for you."

The soft voice again. "Okay, then."

She reached her hand up. Lincoln grabbed it and pulled her into the van. He gave her a rough shove and she landed on the mattress.

Sliding the door shut, he called up to Hank in the front. "Okay, drive, find a good spot to park and then you can have a go, too."

Linc pointed. "Okay, John, you first."

John looked down at the girl on the mattress. She had a pretty face, but was wearing lots of makeup. Tight little skirt that had hiked itself up almost to her crotch by her positioning on the mattress. A halter top, which was low-cut enough to display her ample breasts. She was definitely hot, and John felt a stiffness forming in his crotch.

"C'mon, John. We haven't got all night. Are you going to fuck this one or just get your usual blow job?"

John had the urge to fuck her, for sure. He'd wanted to fuck all of the girls they'd picked up. But something always stopped him. They were just hookers, after all, and probably saturated with every infection you could imagine. He'd discovered that he had the willpower to resist. Restricted his part in the exercises to just blow jobs, even though those carried certain risks as well. But, he figured the small risk was worth it.

"No, Linc, I'll just do the blow job thing."

Lincoln laughed, followed by cackles from the other guys.

John dropped his pants and she crawled over to him. Wrapped her mouth around his erect penis and went to work. He watched her face as she sucked away. Suddenly she looked so innocent, so—young.

In less than two minutes it was over, and unfulfilling. The longer he'd looked at her innocent face, the limper he became. John simply pulled out and yanked his pants back up.

Linc just laughed mockingly and spun the girl around, forcing her back down onto the mattress.

"You're a wimp, Johnny boy. My turn. Watch how it's done."

As Linc began pounding away relentlessly at the slender body, John stretched out on the floor. He was dying for a cigarette, but had forgotten to bring his. Suddenly, he noticed the girl's purse. It was unzipped, and there was a pack of Winstons poking out of the top. He reached over and pulled them out.

Along with the cigarettes, out came a laminated library card.

Curious, he looked at it in the dim light. Her name was Monica Hartwell.

He caught his breath as he noticed her birth date. Quickly did the math.

Yelled out at the exact moment that Linc arched his back and sighed, blowing his load inside her. "Linc! Stop! She's only fourteen!"

Lincoln pulled out and faced him. "What?"

John waved the card in the air. "Look! Her library card! Fourteen!"

Linc turned his gaze back to the girl. "Is that true?"

Monica looked scared. She nodded.

In a fit of rage, he slapped her across the face, causing the side of her head to slam hard against the van's metal rib cage. As he jumped to his feet, pulling his pants back up around his waist, he screamed down at her, "You little bitch!"

He zipped up his jeans and glared at John. "Christ, she looks twenty! How were we supposed to know?"

John just shook his head, not knowing how to respond to his friend. Then his attention was drawn back to Monica lying on the mattress. He noticed that her eyes were closed and there was blood flowing out of the right temple area of her forehead.

He knelt down on the mattress beside her and shook her gently. "Monica, are you okay? Monica?"

Then the twitching started. Hardly noticeable at first, just around the corners of her mouth. Followed quickly by her shoulders and her chest. Suddenly Monica's entire body was shaking, and her arms and legs began flailing in the air.

Her eyelids opened, but John could only see the whites of her eyes. She was breathing heavily, and her mouth was opening and closing rapidly.

Suddenly the mouth closed, teeth clenched together tightly, followed by a cracking sound that reminded John of the time one of his teeth was destroyed in a football tackle.

She was choking now.

"My God, she's having a seizure!"

John's four friends were standing in a circle around him and the girl. Hank yelled, "What do we do?"

John called out, to no one in particular, "Hold her legs and arms still! Does anyone have something flat, like a popsicle stick?"

Linc's voice. "Here's a comb. Maybe that'll work."

John fought with his fingers to get her mouth open. Her teeth were clenched together in a vice grip. He managed to just barely shove the comb in and then quickly slid it towards her tongue. He pressed down. "I think her tongue's choking her!"

Her breathing seemed to improve almost immediately. John looked up at Hank. "Drive, Hank. To the nearest hospital. We have to hurry."

Hank whirled around and headed towards the front of the van. But, Linc stopped him. Grabbed him by the shoulders and pulled him back.

"We're not going to any fucking hospital. Are you crazy? We'd have to take her in and identify ourselves. She's a minor. My cum's in her. We'd have to explain what we were doing, and when she comes around she'll tell them herself."

Hank raised his hands, confused. "Well, what are we going to do?"

"She'll be okay. John has things under control. Once she's herself again, we'll just drop her off somewhere."

Suddenly the convulsions increased in intensity. John was struggling with trying to keep her tongue depressed while her body was twisting from side to side. He panicked. "She's not okay! She's going to die! Drive, for fuck's sake!"

Just as suddenly as they started, the convulsions stopped. Monica's body went still and the whites of her eyes stared blankly up at the roof of the van. John felt her neck for a pulse, then her wrists. Frantic, he began CPR.

He cycled in the dead silence of the van for around five minutes until finally giving up. Bent over and rested his head on the mattress. He was breathing hard, and could feel tears running down his cheeks.

Monica Hartwell was dead.

He looked up at his friends. "We did this."

Linc folded his arms across his chest. "No, we didn't. She pretended to be older than she was. How were we supposed to know? And she had a seizure; what could we do about that?"

John jumped to his feet and smashed his fist into Linc's jaw. "You bastard! You hit her—crushed her temple! That's what brought on the seizure! And if we'd rushed her to a hospital, we might have been able to save her."

He braced himself for the fist that he thought would be hurled back at him, but it didn't come. Linc just rubbed his jaw and pointed over at Hank. "Start driving. Find a remote spot on the highway where we can dump her."

Linc glared at John. "She was just a whore. No one's going to care or miss her. And we couldn't take a chance on ruining our lives over her."

Then he pointed at all four of them, dramatically, one by one. "This is a test for each of you. I'm your Commander. The honor code has no bounds and no expiry date. No one breathes a word about this, ever, to anyone. If you want to talk about it, you talk to me and me alone. I'll give you the strength to deal with it."

As the van resumed its journey, this time looking for a dumping spot instead of a tramp they could fuck, all John could think of was that her name was Monica Hartwell, she was just fourteen years old, and probably a sweet girl deep down inside. Desperate and despondent, and—for some reason that he would never know—had lost her innocence and self-respect somewhere along the way.

And, now her life.

When Hank finally found the perfect spot, he pulled over and Linc heaved her lifeless body out of the side of the van onto the soft shoulder of the highway.

As if she were a sack of garbage.

Then, he jumped out, and, with one foot, rolled her down the side of an embankment into a ditch.

The last thought that entered John's mind before the van started its journey back to campus was that the only semen inside of Monica Hartwell was Lincoln Berwick's.

John snapped out of his trance and glanced at his watch. Time to go. Finally, the nightmare that had changed his life oh so long ago was going to change his life again. This time for the better. A candidate for President would want this skeleton from the past to stay buried.

He picked up his house keys, flicked on the outside lights, and opened the door to the stairs that led outside from his basement apartment.

Suddenly he was thrust backward, hard.

Two figures entered the apartment and shut the door quietly behind them. One of the well-dressed men rushed him and before he could cry out, some type of material was stuffed into his mouth.

Muscle memory from his training decades ago reacted automatically in his body.

He swung around, grabbed the man's arm and flung him over his shoulder. Then he spun as the other man advanced, catching him with a well-placed kick to the chin.

But, they were strong and he wasn't anymore.

Within seconds, John was on the floor.

One man frisked him and found the cassette tape in his front pocket.

"Here it is."

The other guy walked over to the dining room table and came back with the bottle of whisky.

The material was pulled from his mouth and some kind of brace was rammed inside to take its place. It felt like one of those brackets that dentists inserted during a root canal.

His mouth was now propped wide open. John tried to scream, but the sound that came out was guttural.

They put the whisky bottle between his lips and tilted. The liquid poured down his throat, unrestricted. He gagged, they pulled the bottle back, then tilted it again.

When half the bottle was gone, they poured the rest over his clothes.

The men yanked him to his feet, dragged him down to the bathroom, and threw him into the tub.

His head was spinning; the sudden rush of liquor into his bloodstream was definitely working its magic on his senses.

John was puzzled, because booze never usually affected him all that much. He wondered if it was because it was so much at once, with very little chance for oxygen to interfere.

Then he wondered why he was even bothering to analyse that at this moment—this moment when he was going to die.

And he knew he was going to die.

He had no fight left—and hadn't really—since that night in the van so many years ago.

Back then when he was a young man, with his entire life in front of him.

He heard two words.

"Left wrist."

He didn't resist as they rolled up the left sleeve of his shirt, preoccupied instead with picturing Judy and Cynthia in his mind's eye. At least the way they'd looked in that picture frame. He had no idea what they looked like now.

He hoped and prayed that Judy received his package in the mail, and that she would do what he'd asked her in his note.

As he watched the sharp blade of the knife slide across his wrist and the red torrent of blood surge down over his lap, he pictured a sweet little face in his mind.

Not the way he'd last seen her, but, instead, the way he would have *preferred* to have seen her.

Not on her knees sucking his dick.

Instead, in a pretty pink prom dress, with a white corsage wrapped around her wrist.

Her proud parents taking pictures, kissing her on the cheek, telling her how lovely she looked.

Her boyfriend, taking her soft hand and escorting her out to the car, holding the door open for her like the lady she was. Kissing her gently on the lips while she beamed with pride.

Then, later in the evening up on the gymnasium stage wearing a crown.

Monica Hartwell, Prom Queen.

John Nichols' chin drooped onto his chest now and the extremities of his body felt completely numb, freezing cold.

And it suddenly occurred to him how they'd been able to find him.

Despite being so careful with the fake name, unlisted phone number, and secret address.

But, he'd forgotten one thing.

They'd traced him through the internet, his IP address.

How could I have been so stupid?

8

Lincoln Berwick's flight was leaving in about ten hours, and he still didn't know if he'd have a travel companion.

He paced the length of his massive kitchen, and then, for no particular reason, wandered into the front foyer. He was trying hard to control his temper, and he always found that pacing was an effective way of exhausting the adrenaline rush. Punching walls also did the trick once in a while.

He marched back into the kitchen again, opened the French doors to his patio, and stepped outside. It was another bright and sunny day in Dallas, even though it was late in November. Linc was glad that the oppressive heat of the summer was long behind them.

He paced back and forth across the patio, glanced upstairs at the master bedroom window, and wondered if she'd started packing her bags yet.

Linc shielded his eyes as he gazed across the expanse of backyards in his neighborhood. All of the lots were a minimum of two acres, so the privacy was great. And fences weren't allowed, so as not to detract from the aesthetics of the most expensive area in Dallas.

Yes, Highland Park had it all. Homes that fetched into the multi-millions and some of the best schools in the country. And, if truth be told, the schools were the main reason why Highland Park was so expensive. The quality of both public and private schooling was top-notch, and the well-heeled oil executives wanted their little darlings to have the best of the best.

Linc and his wife, Melanie, lived in the neighborhood because it was just the place to be. The place to be seen and the place to brag about if someone asked where you lived. Eyes always lit up as soon as Highland Park was mentioned. It was a status symbol, bragging power for those who felt they needed it—almost the same as driving a Bentley.

Linc didn't really care about the fact that there were great schools where he lived. As far as he was concerned, he'd never need those schools.

Kids were not in his plans. They had, however, been in Melanie's plans when they first got married ten years ago, and he'd led her to believe that he wanted them, too. But, that was a lie. He needed her in his life, and it was easy to convince her that he was excited about being a father one day.

Linc was a lawyer then, and Melanie helped him launch his senatorial bid.

She was the classic trophy wife—blonde, beautiful, and smart. Sweet and caring as well, but Linc didn't give a shit about that side of her. All he cared was that she looked good, talked good, and walked good. Melanie was the perfect image for him.

She'd never seen it coming. Melanie actually thought he was one of the good guys—the silly girl.

Linc inherited his father's law practice after he died. He'd been one of the most successful corporate lawyers in Texas and a specialist at mergers and acquisitions in the oil industry. It was a practice that set Linc up perfectly when he decided to take a run at the Senate. He had an instant network of rich donors, folks that he'd taken care of quite nicely in the years since he won his seat. And, they'd continued to take care of him.

He sat down on the chaise lounge on his patio, waiting impatiently for Melanie to get over her crying fit and pack her fucking bag.

He had a busy week ahead of him, and he needed her by his side. Speeches at rallies in three different cities. A private jet at his disposal. Adoring followers waiting to hear him speak. And the smiling trophy wife was essential. People needed to see that he had a loving wife, wanted to know that he was happily married and planning a family one day. That's the façade that Linc carried with him to every rally, and Melanie was expected to do her part. Back him up every step of the way.

He thought back to his father, pictured him in his mind. A smart man. Linc admired him, and was thankful for the fact that he'd left him one hell of a legacy. It served to put Linc on the launch pad for his political career.

The law firm was also something he could go back to one day if politics failed him. He'd left the firm in the capable hands of his partners, and his own shares in the firm were now in a blind trust. It was nice to know he had that to fall back on, but he didn't think he'd need it.

He was going to be President—could feel it in his bones.

His father had always treated Linc as if he were his own biological son. A sterile man, but willing and able to be a doting father despite the fact that he was shooting blanks.

His dad's connections and money made it all happen.

A very exclusive sperm bank in New York City, which supplied the wealthy elite with the most high-grade sperm available. Guaranteed to have come from the strongest stock—strongest not only in terms of health and longevity, but also in terms of gray cells.

The little buggers were future geniuses just waiting to be inseminated.

And the bank had rules—the sperm would only be sold to the wealthiest and most influential families, only to American parents, and it had to be proven that the maternal recipients came from similar stock.

Linc was lucky that his mother was also a genius and a southern lady with a heritage that went back further than the Alamo. She had the "right stuff."

So, Lincoln Berwick was born.

And, as far as he was concerned, he was a gift to the world.

And that world might one day thank Legacy Life Ladder Incorporated for making it possible for the birthing of the greatest leader the free world had ever seen. Well, that gratitude really couldn't be expressed, of course, because the company was an invisible enigma. Only those "in the know," had any idea what it was all about. And, it would remain that way.

In those elite circles, it was nicknamed Triple L. A private company, controlled by an exclusive alliance of influential corporations. In fact, some of the same corporations that were represented by the eight people on Linc's campaign team.

Linc shook his head and pushed Triple L out of his mind. He had more important things to do today than reminisce about his immaculate conception.

He was rapidly losing what little patience he had.

Time to check on Melanie, dry her eyes, and say the tender little words she needed to hear.

Linc went back inside, and made the long climb up his grand staircase to the master suite. There she was, sitting on the edge of the bed, head resting in her hands.

Linc didn't see a suitcase.

He sat down on the bed and wrapped an arm around her shoulders. With his free hand, he softly touched the purple and red welt that was blossoming under her chin.

She jerked her head back and shoved his arm away.

"I'm not going with you. And, when you come back I'll be gone."

Linc stood. His tender approach wasn't working.

He glared down at her. "You are coming, and you're going to play your role as you always do. You're my loving wife, and you'll show that."

Melanie shook her head. "I can't do this anymore. It's a nightmare."

"I'm running for President. The stress of it all gets to me sometimes. I'm sorry for hitting you. I really am. A little make-up will hide that bruise easily. Pack your bag."

She shook her head again. "I want a divorce. You always apologize after hitting me, and then you just hit me again. This time you hit me where it shows. It never ends. I can't hide how I feel any more than I can hide this welt."

Linc picked up a vase sitting on the night table and threw it with all of his might into the dressing table mirror, smashing both.

Melanie shuddered and started crying again.

"You've picked a fine time to ask for a divorce. Here we are on the threshold of making it to the White House, and you want a divorce?"

She rubbed her eyes with her tiny fists. "I've asked you before, and you just ignored me. I asked for a divorce long before you decided to run for President. But, stupid me, I gave in. You promised you'd change, but, it never lasted long. I'm serious this time. I've already talked to a lawyer."

Linc reached down and grabbed her by the hair, pulling her face up to meet his. "You did what? Are you crazy?"

Tears flowed down her cheeks, and Linc was happy to see her wince at the pressure he was exerting on her scalp. She whispered, "Please don't hit me again."

"I'll tell you what you're going to do. You're going to call that lawyer and tell him you've changed your mind. And that you expect him to keep it confidential. That I'll sue his ass if this gets out to the press."

Melanie just stared up at him, body trembling. In a shaky voice, she replied, "You can't stop me, Linc. I'm entitled to a life, and I don't want you in it."

He grabbed her by the throat, shoved her back on the bed, and climbed on top of her. With his hand still on her throat, he growled, "Yes, I can stop you. Unless you pack that bag and come with me now, and then stay with me until I win the White House, you'll have an unfortunate accident. Do you understand what I'm saying? You won't get that divorce, and you won't live to see anything from me. You'll die. And, you know what? The voters might like me even better if that happened. I'd get the sympathy vote. The poor lonely widower, losing his loving wife in a car accident."

He released his hand from her throat.

She took a deep breath and sighed; a sigh filled with a combination of sadness and resignation. Stared back at him through teary eyes.

Linc could see the fear in those gorgeous green orbs, and he was confident she believed him. Believed that he was capable of arranging such a thing, and wouldn't hesitate to do so. He'd made his case, just as if he were back in the courtroom.

Melanie pushed up on his chest.

"Get my suitcase out of the closet, please. And my make-up case."

*****

Linc glanced at his watch. "Okay, Jason, we'll have to be quick. Melanie and I have to be at the airport in a couple of hours. So, cut to the chase."

They were sitting in Linc's study, a room segregated from the rest of the house down a hallway off the front foyer. He'd made sure the room was completely soundproofed when the mansion was built. Perfect for meetings such as the one he was having right now.

Jason Reid was ex-Secret Service, and head of Linc's private security detail. Linc kept this security team totally separate from the one provided by his campaign handlers. Because there were just some things that needed tending to from time to time that the others didn't need to know about. Linc believed in keeping information compartmentalized, and some information was best kept to a small trusted circle.

And he trusted Jason Reid. As well, the man and his team were paid handsomely. As far as Linc was concerned he owned their souls.

Jason pulled a cassette tape out of his suit pocket and handed it to him.

"Here it is. My recommendation is that you destroy this thing. Burn it. Don't delay."

Linc nodded in agreement. "Any problems?"

Jason shook his head. "No, went smoothly. I have a question for you, though. What about the ex-wife and kid? Do you think those are loose ends?"

Linc scratched his chin. "I doubt it. They've been divorced for a long time. Probably haven't kept in touch, since he was a hopeless drunk. But…might be worth keeping an eye on them, anyway. Some electronic surveillance maybe? Put someone on her tail for a bit?"

Jason jotted some notes down on a pad. "No problem, boss."

Linc leaned forward in his chair. "Let's hope there's nothing to worry about. If they both happened to die right after John Nichols' suicide, it might draw attention."

Jason nodded. "I agree. We'll just do some snooping for now. There's probably nothing to worry about. But, you have to be concerned about whether or not there's a duplicate of that tape somewhere. That would be worrisome."

Linc took a long sip from a bottle of Perrier. "Yeah, might lose a bit of sleep now thinking about that."

"Senator, it's time to move on to those other friends of yours who were with you that night. I know that Nichols was the only one trying to blackmail you, but if the others hear about his death they may step forward if they knew what he was doing. Chances are they probably didn't know—Nichols was so down and out that they probably never kept in touch with him. But, my recommendation is that you don't take the chance. And, all of them are so unrelated to each other, except for the West Point connection, that it's unlikely anyone will connect the dots. That was a long time ago, and a lot of young men attended West Point."

Linc crossed his legs and folded his arms over his chest.

"Yeah, I guess you're right. Might as well clean house completely. Okay, write these names down: Hank Price—he's the chief engineer at Boeing in Seattle; Lloyd Franken—a senior astronomer at NASA in Houston; and, Bill Tomkins—CEO of Tomkins, Hatfield Inc., a large investment banker on Wall Street."

"How would you like them done, boss?"

"I'll leave that to you. Mix it up a bit—can't have too many suicides."

"Will do. Once these are done—aside from Nichols' ex-wife and kid who probably won't be necessary—all the loose ends from that little adventure of yours will be tied up. You'll be able to campaign without all that junk floating around in your brain."

Linc stood. "That would be nice. It has been troubling for me since that prick tried to blackmail me, and I'm sure I haven't been as effective campaigning as I could have been. I shouldn't have to deal with annoyances like that; I have far better things to do. But, that's the kind of world we live in now, Jason. Everyone wants a piece of the pie and they're prepared to make threats in order to get what they want."

The senator from the great state of Texas grimaced in despair, and shook his professionally-coiffed head from side to side causing a strand of blonde hair to fall down across his left eyebrow. "You know, Jason, it's a sad and greedy world we live in now. But, I'm already starting to feel better now that you've got things under control."

Jason Reid flashed a big smile. "Thanks for your confidence, Senator. And, once you're elected President, the world will start to look better. I'm sure of that."

9

"I have no interest in getting you busted. I only want what I want."

The wooden park bench felt cold on his bum, and even though there was no snow on the ground yet, Sandy was pretty certain that it would appear any day now. After all, it was early December.

It sure looked Christmassy, though, with the fir trees in the city park adorned with red and green icicle lights. Snow was the only element missing.

Not that he gave a shit about Christmas anymore, anyway. It was just a light show for him now; nothing more, nothing less.

He glanced at his watch, then turned his attention back to the man sitting next to him. It was 10:00 at night, and he just wanted to get home. But, first, he needed to get this over with.

Sandy spoke again to the silent figure wearing a dark black trench coat accented by a woolen toque pulled low over his forehead. "Did you hear me? Hand it over."

The man grasped a manila envelope tightly in his left hand. He turned his head and faced Sandy—the first time he'd looked him in the eyes since their rendezvous.

"How do I know I can trust you to keep quiet?"

Sandy's fists clenched as he stared into the eyes of the crooked politician. Boston's deputy mayor, Christopher Clark, was nervous, he could tell. But, that was the least of his concerns. The information in that envelope might answer some of his questions, and if Clark didn't hand it over in the next few minutes Sandy was just going to take it from him. Which he knew he could easily do.

"Coming from someone like you, that's pretty funny. Is trust an important thing to you? Does the mayor trust you? Do the citizens trust you? I know I did, until the trail of my investigation led to you."

Christopher shook his head. "Things just got out of hand; I got in too deep. I don't like it, but I'm past the point of no return now."

Sandy raised his voice slightly. "I'm not your priest. I couldn't care less about how you feel. You can carry on and do your dirty work, I don't give a shit. All you politicians are the same. If I tried to bust you, the mountain would be a high one indeed. One I wouldn't live long enough to climb. So, carry on doing your shit, I don't care. I just want my answers."

"You never told me how you connected me."

Sandy shook his head. "No, I didn't. I have my connections. You forget who I work for, which is just a division of the Pentagon. No surprise, then, that I have lots of shadowy people I can call upon to open doors. So, don't fuck with me. There are certain people who know I'm meeting with you. If something happens to me, something will happen to you."

He nodded. "Okay, I get that. But, my Mafia connections that you seem to know about, it wouldn't take much for me to set them loose on you. You're aware of that, aren't you?"

Sandy laughed. "That's pretty funny. And, you'll find this even funnier. We found out a thing or two about the Boston Mafia—the Ferrara crime family, run by Paolo Marino. A violent history, mostly amongst other crime families. They tend to leave the average person alone, but somehow, they're able to sniff out insects like you who they can pay off. My connections run in some of the same circles, but on the right side of the law. They have somewhat of a—symbiotic relationship, shall we say? Your friends in the Mafia work both sides of the street, Mr. Deputy Mayor."

"What do you mean?"

"They're not stupid. They know that bread sometimes has to be buttered on both sides. And, you do stand out like a sore thumb. Someday, someone else is going to be puzzled about how you can afford that large house, cottage, and three cars on a deputy mayor's salary, which I believe right now is exactly $120,000. A nice salary, but not nearly enough to cover what you own. So, I'd be more careful if I were you. Maybe downsize a bit."

Christopher crossed his legs and leaned in closer to Sandy. "Are you saying they actually volunteered me to you?"

"Not to me. To my people. The Mafia may be paying you, but you don't know them all that well, do you? Sure, all you see are the things they do—the drugs, the prostitution, strip joints, union influence.

"Your job is to smooth the waters, pave the way for them. You probably look down on them as being the lowest of the low, but you're more than willing to take their money. And they're tapped in, Mr. Deputy Mayor; tapped into information. The Mob survives on information—sometimes they use it, sometimes they don't. But, information is always their trump card so they can play both sides of the fence."

He whispered. "Are you trying to warn me?"

Sandy shook his head. "No, I wouldn't do you that favor. I'd rather just kill you myself. In my mind, people like you are as low as human beings can get. The Mafia has far more class than you do, and they have a certain honor that they uphold. I admire them for that. I'm accustomed to honor codes myself—sometimes they can be insidious, but in the Mafia's case there's a certain regality to it."

The deputy mayor shifted farther down the bench. "I shouldn't be talking to you. And, you shouldn't be talking to me, either. You know who I'm beholden to, obviously, and those aren't people you can fuck with. One call from me and you're history, Professor Beech."

Sandy chuckled. "You just don't get it, do you? Let me spell it out for you. The Mafia knows about all sorts of things. The Kennedy assassination, for one—who did it, who was behind it. And, contrary to popular belief, it wasn't them.

"They also know about 9/11. They know that one day it might blow up, but in the meantime, it's information they hold in their hip pockets. Keeps them safe.

"As I said, they use information like currency. They've been leveraging those things for decades, in all the right circles.

"And they know about something else, too. But, this something else they know about hit too close to home, right here in Boston, and it was far too brutal even for them. More than half of the victims were children, for Christ's sake. The Mafia is very family-oriented.

"They picked up rumblings about the Quincy Market massacre. And there's an anger burning in their collective belly over that one. Their intelligence network told them you paved the way for some things to happen. That you know more than you'd be willing to admit. And that you're a prostitute who also works both sides of the street yourself. You were paid off handsomely, by all accounts. By someone. You probably don't even know who was behind it. But, I want to know."

Sandy could see that the deputy mayor was now licking his lips. A dry mouth was usually the first clue to an anxiety attack.

"Yes, Mr. Deputy Mayor—I was never able to let this go. For over two years I've been digging, as I'm sure even someone like you would have been doing if your entire family had been slaughtered. We were banging our heads into brick walls until we made the Mafia connection. And it was apparent that they didn't approve. They gave you up—yes, your secret employers gave you up. They sympathized with my cause, supported it, and led us in the right direction. Because, they have this honor thing going on, and it's what's allowed them to prosper for at least a century.

"And, all you elected assholes did was try to give me a medal. You make me sick."

Christopher swallowed hard. "Am I in danger?"

"I'll be honest with you, even though I don't give a shit. I don't think they would have hesitated to kill you over the Quincy Market attack, because it makes them want to puke. But, since information is currency, I'm guessing that's the only thing that will keep them from doing that. Once we came knocking, though, they felt an obligation to help. Because of their honor code. So, they tipped us off to you. That you might be the conduit to what really happened.

"They told my people that if for some reason you didn't cooperate, to let them know. I don't know what that means—maybe they'd just have a donut and coffee with you."

Christopher stood. "I've heard enough. You're shaking me

down, making this shit up. I don't believe that you or your operatives have talked with the Ferrara family. You're just taking a flying leap. Somehow, you got a tip about this and you're trying to scare me. You know nothing."

Sandy got to his feet as well. "I have a few specifics that they've allowed us to use against you. A certain union leader who you've made payments to, money laundered from the Mafia. Transactions traceable to you with the use of a little muscle. Also, a condominium project on the east side which bypassed construction codes, and for some reason missed having safety inspections done during its various stages of erection. Should I go on? You see, they despise you so much, they're willing to give up certain things, things that can't be traced back to them, but can be traced back to you."

The deputy mayor's face went white, yet he still clutched tightly to the manila envelope.

Sandy held out his hand. "Give it to me."

Suddenly Christopher raised his right hand and gestured with his index finger. Then, he whirled around and ran like a scared rabbit through the deserted park.

But, not as deserted as Sandy thought.

His invisible antenna went up and he spun around just in time to see a figure hurling towards him out of the darkness. Pulse pounding, he leaped on top of the bench to get a height advantage.

The dark figure lunged, something shiny in his hand swinging in an arc. Sandy danced down the length of the bench, but the knife managed to catch his jacket, slicing an opening at waist level. Sandy's foot lashed out at the man's head, catching him square in the forehead knocking him to the ground.

He jumped off the bench, bringing one foot down on the wrist of the hand holding the knife. But, the man didn't stay still. He arched his back and brought both knees up into Sandy's crotch.

The pain surged through his groin as he fell back against the park bench.

The assailant was on his feet now, swiping the knife in an arc—towards Sandy's throat this time.

Despite the crippling pain in his groin, Sandy's forearm reacted on pure instinct, knocking the man's hand upward. Then, with his other hand, he grabbed the thug's forearm and bent his arm backwards. Working both hands in unison now, he jerked the arm violently, pulling the shoulder out of its socket.

The attacker screamed, but only for a second. Sandy's lightning punch to his Adam's apple silenced him. The man went down, clutching at his throat.

Sandy left him there. He had something more important to do.

He turned and ran down the park pathway. The deputy mayor had a bit of a head start, but not that much. The fight hadn't lasted long. And Christopher Clark was a bit on the dumpy side, so running probably wasn't his strong suit.

Sure enough, once Sandy rounded the bend in the path he saw Clark. In less than a minute he was right behind him. He could hear the fat man huffing and puffing. Sandy shot the palm of his hand out and pounded him hard between the shoulder blades. That was enough to send the politician down, flat on his face.

He leaned down, ripped off his toque, and grabbed him by what little hair he had. Yanked him up and flipped him over onto his back. The deputy mayor was sputtering some nonsense, but Sandy just ignored him. He reached down and pulled the manila envelope out from under his arm.

Giving a two finger salute, he stared down at the bureaucrat in disgust.

"Don't forget that I've lost my family, Mr. Clark. Nothing will stop me from getting to the bottom of this. I want justice. It sounds like you were just the paid gopher in this, so you're not important to me. Don't make the mistake of *making* yourself important to me.

"And you may want to check on your loyal bodyguard back there. I think he's choking to death."

10

"I have to be back in Washington tomorrow. A couple of important votes in the Senate that I need to be present for."

Meagan Whitfield smiled knowingly. "Any issues that we'd be excited about?"

Linc nodded. "Yeah, one's a defence appropriations bill. Some new stealth fighter jets that are long overdue. I'll vote in favor of that, of course. And the other one's that namby pamby bill the Democrats have been pushing hard for—free tuition for first year university students. I'll nix that one, or, at the very least, vote in favor of tying it up in amendments."

Meagan nodded. "Good. Well, the defence bill should pass easily—polls show that fear about terrorism and Russia are way up there still. Congress has no choice but to pass spending bills on defence right now."

Bob Stone interjected. "Yes, but we need to do more. The number one concern from the latest polls we're getting is the economy. Security is number two and fading fast. Needs some stoking."

Linc gazed out the window. As always, his eyes landed on the Texas School Book Depository. He loved that landmark—motivated him to do whatever was necessary.

It was only the three of them meeting in his Dallas office this time. There was no need for the other six members of his team at every meeting. Meagan and Bob were the key players, and the rest deferred to them to represent the entire team at occasional ad hoc meetings.

Linc nodded at Bob. "I agree. The Democrats are making the economy the boogie man. And, it's an easy case for them to make.

Stock market's been tanking, unemployment is way up, and interest rates are still crushingly low. People are feeling it. They're talking about tax increases on the upper five percent, something the middle class just loves to hear."

Meagan stirred some cream and sugar into her coffee. "The Dems are gaining traction. And even your Republican opponents are starting to hum the same tune. They're starting to sound just like Democrats, for God's sake. We've branded you as the candidate of safety, security, and intolerance of the Middle East. We started stoking that mood about three years ago now. The trouble is, once things calm down for a while, the average simple-minded voter starts forgetting how terrified they were. They forget the images, start worrying instead about their jobs and their mortgage payments."

Bob played with his pen, and Linc could tell that the wheels were turning in his head. "How did your speeches go over the last two weeks?"

"I was pleased. Big crowds, lots of noise. The press were out in full force. As you know, I hit three cities the first week and five last week. I'm exhausted, but it was worth it."

"I've seen the transcripts of your speeches. You're still using Tanya as your writer?"

"Yes, she's really good."

"Well, she's gonna have to get better. You're jumping around a lot, straying from the terrorism theme. You need to stick with that as your main message. You're the only candidate who's had that in his arsenal, and we need to keep strengthening that brand."

Linc shook his head. "I disagree. While that's important, I notice the eye rolls and yawns in the audience when I go on about that too much. I can't just talk about that alone. As Meagan said, that's not the number one worry for people right now."

Meagan rapped her spoon on the table. "You misunderstood me, Linc. I was only stating the obvious. It doesn't mean we can't change that, bring the terror threat back up to the top spot again."

"True. But, I'm feeling some pressure from the Republican executive, and a few high-profile members of Congress. They're afraid that the Republican Party is going to continue to be branded as the 'war party.' They want to move away from that and recreate the perception that we're the party of economic prosperity—bring back those Reagan years in voters' minds."

Bob shook his head. "The economy's fucked. The only thing that will keep the country from collapse is defence. This global economy nonsense was a mistake right from the get-go. It'll only work in our favor if we control the monetary supply and natural resources. This globalization crap has forced us to play the war card. We need perpetual war, war without end. And if things don't happen that cause us to go to war, we have to make those things happen. I hope you understand this.

"Are you aware of what would happen to us if the world became a peaceful place? If we didn't control what other countries did, how they spent their money, how they sold their resources, who they traded with? Do you recall the predictions of disaster that came out with Libya's preparations to start using an Arab currency for oil trades? All the Arab nations would have followed if we hadn't put an end to that.

"And this BRICS Bank crap started by Russia? If we hadn't worked with the Saudis to collapse world oil prices, that bank would have become a reality. Containment is the key to America's prosperity, and if we let up on that it will be a disaster for this country. Our economy is far too fragile and our $20 trillion debt is crushing us."

Meagan nodded. "He's right, Linc, you know he is. So, get back on the program. Fear is the only way we can keep the economy going. It's a house of cards ready to collapse if we pause to take a breath.

"And, remember this, while the Republican Party has some noble ambitions, we're using them only as the vehicle for your election. You're not a Republican. You know who your backers are, and the party is as oblivious to that as they are to most things. We're hijacking the party for the good of the country."

Linc clasped his hands together. "I know—you both make a lot of sense. And, I'm a loyal soldier in the cause. But, remember that old saying: "First, get elected." That's what I'm trying to do, and we have to be realistic about our tactics. Once I'm in office I can do whatever the hell I want. But, I have to get there first."

She rubbed his shoulder; a rare sign of affection which Linc knew was forced.

"We're on the same team. I know where you're coming from. But, you need to be differentiated from all of the other candidates. Fear will do that for you. They're all humming the economy tune and, while people are listening to them, after a while that will become a tired refrain.

"If you're humming that tune, you'll just disappear in the crowd despite your charm and good looks. Our angle is fear, and we have to play it all the way to the White House."

"Okay, well, we've had some ads running. They've been focused on the patriotism thing, all that bullshit. Seems to work with a certain segment."

Bob poured himself another coffee from the pot on the table. "Yeah, I've seen those. They're good. Shows that professor guy throwing his medal back at the general. Very effective. I read that he attended West Point just like you. Did you know him?"

"Yes, I did. He was in the Honor Guild for a while, but then got demoted back to the regular student body. A weakling—couldn't handle the stress. I didn't have any use for him. Not surprised when he performed that spectacle on stage. Loved attention, loved to be different."

"Well, nothing wrong with that. But, did you light a fire by showing him in that ad? Does he have any reason to talk about you to the press?"

Linc shook his head. "Nothing to talk about. He's a loser. Anything he said about me could be countered by us talking about how he couldn't cut it in the elite of West Point. I'm not worried about him."

"He does important work at the Lincoln Lab. Would it be beneficial if we arranged to have him lose his position? Make him look like even more of a loser in case he spoke out against you? I mean, he can't be happy about how you've used him in that ad."

Linc shook his head. "No, for now I think it's best that we let sleeping dogs lie."

Meagan looked at Bob. "I think we need a new ad. More graphic. Stir up some memories. Reinforce the idea that only Senator Berwick can keep America safe, remind them of how dangerous it is out there."

She started counting on her fingers. "We've had 9/11, which most people have forgotten about, and most of the millennial voters weren't really old enough to be all that scared when it happened. Then, we had the Boston Marathon bombings, and the Quincy Market massacre. Several mass shootings in clubs, theaters, and malls. There have been horrific slaughters in Paris and Belgium. Germany, too.

"But, all of that just rolls off people. The European attacks have had very little effect on Americans. They just shrug and go back about their business. The only ones that have really had some impact are the ones that have happened on our own soil. And, the gold medal attacks so far have been 9/11 and Quincy Market. Those had the greatest horror factor. But, it's been too long. Ancient history. Quincy was over two years ago, and 9/11 was a hell of a long time ago now.

"We have to stoke the fires. In the absence of another attack soon, I think we need to do an ad which combines some graphic images of 9/11, interspersed with the dead bodies and pools of blood on the promenade of Quincy Market. What do you guys think?"

Bob gave a thumbs up. Linc nodded his approval.

Meagan smiled triumphantly. "Okay, I'll get going on that. Then we'll gauge the polls to see if it helped. If the effect is minimal, then we'll have no choice but to consider a fresh attack."

Linc stood. "Sounds like a plan. And, I'll tell Tanya to start strengthening the fear angle in my speeches. We'll be a double-threat."

*****

Sandy threw the manila envelope onto the dining room table, and removed his shredded jacket.

He cursed as he examined it, while at the same time thanking his lucky stars that the knife hadn't shredded his abdomen instead.

Walked over to the bar and poured himself a scotch neat.

He knew he was going to need it.

If what was in that envelope matched his anticipation, he knew he'd be having a sleepless night.

So, might as well be drunk.

He carried his drink over to the table and sat down. Took a long sip and broke the seal on the envelope.

Sandy drew in a deep breath, held it for a few seconds, and then pulled out the handful of papers contained inside.

He stared at the top sheet. Leafed through the rest.

His fingers started to tingle, and an annoying cramp started making its presence known in his stomach.

The pages were all blank.

He sighed, leaned his head back, and gazed up at the ceiling.

He'd been played—by people more sly than he was.

Christopher Clark had only wanted to know how much he knew, where he'd gotten his tip from.

And once he'd learned what he needed to learn, Sandy was supposed to die in that park.

Sandy sighed again and rested his head in his hands.

Astonished at how he could have been so naïve, so stupid, so careless.

He was lucky to be alive.

Then the phone rang.

11

Bill Tomkins rolled his chair back, spun it around, and gazed out the window of his twentieth-floor office.

It was a corner office, of course, because he was the boss. And while he had a massive living room area that he could stretch out in, he didn't do that very often. It was odd, he thought, that with the ridiculously large office he had—1,000 square feet, the size of an average apartment—he usually only used about ten percent of it.

This is what he'd always wanted. Or, perhaps instead, what he was told he always wanted. To be CEO of a major money firm, one of the most influential investment bankers on Wall Street. And, he was quite young—he had a long way to go still. In his mid-forties, no debts, top of his game, and one of the most aggressive arbitrage players on the planet.

Arbitrage was just the fun part. The part that made him giddy with joy.

Mergers and acquisitions, however, were the serious stuff. And he'd leveraged his firm, Tomkins Hatfield Bankers into the position of being one of the first on the list to be called whenever a deal was being contemplated. Well, he didn't even have to be called most of the time—he was so tapped into the intelligence network he usually knew what was percolating before anyone else did.

He watched as the lights of New York danced at him through his picture window. Glanced at his watch and sighed. Ten o'clock at night—and he'd started work at six in the morning. Just another typical day.

The lights were hypnotizing. He loved this time in his work day. All of the employees gone, but the city still alive. Everyone seemed to have somewhere to go, someone to be with.

Except Bill.

Studying the cityscape was like watching another world. An alien planet. Life was happening out there, and he was just an observer.

He owned a multi-million-dollar penthouse apartment only three blocks away, but he preferred instead to just sit right where he was. His office was a sanctuary to him, where his comfort zone was.

Bill also owned a beach house in the Hamptons, but, he never went there either. He let his nieces and nephews use it, because he knew they'd enjoy it more than him. And, someone might as well enjoy it, considering what it cost.

They always invited their uncle to join them, but Bill always declined. What was the point? He would just be on his tablet all day anyway, checking the markets.

There was no one back at the apartment for him to go home to. No Mrs. Tomkins, no kids, not even a budgie.

He considered the irony—yep, this was what he'd always wanted.

Bill concentrated for a few seconds on his image reflecting back from the picture window. Hair was still on the blondish side, but had gone darker over the years. In a decade or so it would go lighter again, a dignified shade of silver.

And, he'd still have no one to go home to. No one who cared whether he lived or died. Not even a goddamn budgie.

One of his nieces was taking her kids to the Hamptons this weekend. She'd phoned him earlier and practically begged him to join them. Her name was Sheila, and she was a darling. His favorite niece. And, he'd almost considered going. Thought that he might even be able to force himself to stay off the internet, just for one weekend.

But, then, he'd have to find some way to join in, have fun, and talk about fluffy funny stuff. Bill just didn't know how to do that. In fact, he didn't have a clue. In a boardroom setting he knew that he was scintillating. But, in a social environment that involved interacting with normal, nice, simple people, he was a lost soul. It made him feel inferior, insecure. Bill didn't like that feeling.

He'd been taught at West Point to shake those feelings off

when they snuck up on him. To never ever show a weakness, and to understand that insecurity was only a sign of his superiority. In other words, he would never be satisfied, he would always have to be better than the next guy—and whenever he got feelings of insecurity, it only meant that he hadn't been pushing himself hard enough. Was, instead, allowing himself to go soft if he gave in to those feelings. And that was dangerous for a leader.

But, Sheila was his favorite niece.

His big sister's daughter.

Well, his *half* big sister.

Same mother, different father, whoever the hell the father was.

Bill had been the only child in the family who'd been artificially inseminated. He was the youngest and his mother had told him that his father had become sterile, but that he'd loved Bill just as if he were the biological father.

Regardless, Bill loved his niece—or at least he thought he did.

What was "love," anyway? He'd never been in love, but he knew he felt pangs of softness and tenderness towards his nieces and nephews. Part of his brainwashed mind told him that he needed to push those pangs aside, that they were a sign he was going weak.

A different part of his mind told him that was hogwash.

Despite all his wealth and success, Bill was empty inside. He knew that, despite the fact that he'd been taught to think the opposite. He didn't used to think that way, but lately that reality had been creeping up on him more often. Was this how he wanted to live for the rest of his life?

And, while he wouldn't dare admit it to his friends and enemies at the Bankers' Club, he really enjoyed those tender feelings that he got once in a while. He loved the warm zone that came over him when he saw Sheila and her kids together.

He wanted so desperately to laugh and be silly, if only he could just learn how to do that. Maybe Sheila would help him.

Maybe—what the hell—maybe, he should join them at the Hamptons this weekend.

She was popping by to pick up the keys in a few minutes. She had her own access card to get into the building after hours, because Bill had gotten her a part-time job down in accounting on the fourteenth floor. He made sure to have her access card coded to include his floor too, the twentieth, just in case she ever wanted to pay him a visit. Which wasn't often, but once in a while she poked her head in and gave him a smile. Usually Bill didn't know what to say—small talk was hard for him. But, Sheila was so understanding. She would always guide him along with a few gentle questions.

He always got the feeling that she knew he needed that special help, and he loved her for it.

At least he thought he did. Whatever that rare warm feeling was.

Bill spun his chair around and turned his attention back to his computer. Hadn't checked his personal email for a week or so now. He had two email addresses, and the one that he checked every hour on the hour was his business email. His personal inbox tended to get ignored.

Well, he had to wait for Sheila to show up, so might as well kill some time.

Scrolled down through his messages and came across one from his alma mater, West Point. It was their monthly newsletter for the alumni—usually fluff stuff that Bill didn't care about.

He opened it up and scanned the headlines. Clicked on Obituaries out of curiosity and started reading to see if there was anyone familiar on there.

Saw a name—John Nichols—a name that immediately caused the acid in his stomach to rise into his throat. He choked for a second and took a long sip of water for relief.

Then he read the story. A suicide. The story didn't say how; it was very careful to just say that his death was self-inflicted.

The acid in Bill's stomach hadn't risen into his throat out of any sentimental memories that he had of John Nichols.

Not at all.

Sure, he knew him and they'd hung out together—but John was thrown out of the Honor Guild after only two years. He'd been an insufferable drunk.

Bill, on the other hand, was one of the fortunate ones who graduated from the Honor Guild. And from that point onward given every advantage possible, every corner cut, every influential contact money couldn't even buy—to get him to the powerful corporate position he was in today. To be able to influence world markets in favor of the good ol' U.S.A.

But, poor John Nichols had turned into a drunk.

And Bill knew why. The reason why the acid had rushed up into his throat.

Bill and the other Honor Guild graduates had been taught to block out incidents or events that caused stress or anxiety. Taught in very specific ways. Effective ways. Because real leaders could never allow anxiety to enter their lives.

That would be a weakness.

And, all of the graduates of the Honor Guild had their lives mapped out for them.

They were all destined for something, depending on their individual strengths. They were groomed that way. And, to make sure that the corporations investing in their welfare got their money's worth, their brains had been manipulated by teams of psychologists. To remove feelings and weaknesses, so they'd been told. To remove any imperfections that could cause depression, anxiety, or unnecessary conscience attacks.

The promises made to the graduates were not in the least bit vague. They were guaranteed wealth and power. In exchange, they had to simply keep quiet about what they'd endured at the Honor Guild. Even those who were expelled. They were told in no uncertain terms that their lives would be very short indeed if they ever exposed the program for what it really was.

As for Bill, he'd been promised success in the corporate world. He was flagged as a future business executive because of his natural intellectual prowess with mathematics, high finance, and marketing. Others had been labelled as future scientists, engineers, or political leaders. They all had career paths given to them when they graduated, and they all had sponsors who followed their lives every step of the way.

The responsibility of the sponsors was to remove hurdles.

He thought of John Nichols again, and inevitably the memories flashed across his brain. Which wasn't supposed to happen. He concentrated on trying to make the images go away, but he couldn't.

That poor girl, thrashing around on the floor, John Nichols gallantly fighting to save her life, doing something with her tongue. The rest of them standing there helpless, not knowing what to do, or what the implications would be if she died.

Then she died.

Her sweet innocent face, belying the slutty image that she portrayed. She was so young, and they hadn't known. And hadn't really cared, either. She'd just been a piece of raw meat for them, good for one purpose only.

Then she died.

And they just dumped her by the side of the road.

Bill could feel the acid rising again. This shouldn't be happening. He was taught to stop reactions like this. Why couldn't he now? Was he just getting old? Was it all wearing off?

That episode in the van had turned John Nichols into a drunk. And, now he'd killed himself and Bill was convinced that the two were related. The poor guy just couldn't live with the memories any longer and decided to make them go away.

Bill was shaken out of his thoughts by a familiar singsong voice.

Sheila sashayed into his office and wrapped her arms around his neck. Gave him a big kiss on the cheek. Bill tried awkwardly to return the gesture but all he got for his effort was an earlobe.

She smiled knowingly. "Uncle Bill, I told you I could have met you at your apartment. Why are you still here?"

He smiled back at her. "Lots of work to do, dear. But, I'm just about ready to leave. You've given me a good excuse. Maybe you'll let me buy you a coffee?"

"Starbucks?"

"Absolutely. Wherever you want."

Sheila straightened his tie. "What I really want is for you to join us this weekend. The kids would love it. Please? Pretty please?"

Bill nodded. "I decided just a few minutes ago that I'm going to do just that. Maybe you can teach me how to have fun!"

She hugged him again, and exclaimed, "Oh, I'm so happy! I never expected you to agree! We'll have so much fun, and, yes, I'll teach you. There's no one better equipped than me to teach someone how to let their hair down."

Bill heard the sound of a wagon being pushed down the hall just outside his office. Then a man in blue coveralls poked his head in through the doorway. "Mr. Tomkins? Do you mind if we start cleaning your office?"

Bill waved his hand. "No, not at all. We were just about to leave."

"Thanks, sir." Another man followed him into the room.

Bill was surprised to see that they were both Anglos. He'd never seen anyone other than Hispanics cleaning the offices before.

"Are you guys new?"

"Just filling in, sir. The regular crew is busy with carpet shampooing down on the tenth floor tonight."

"Oh, I see. Well, mine could use a shampoo too."

"You're scheduled for another night, sir."

"Okay, then. I look forward to it."

He turned his attention back to his niece, while one of the men walked behind him and started dusting his desk. The other cleaner turned on the vacuum and began running it along the carpet behind Sheila.

"So, shall we go out on the boat this weekend? Would you and the boys like that?"

Sheila clapped her hands with joy. "Oh, would we ever. Can we pack a picnic?"

Bill laughed. "I've never been on a picnic—ever. I might enjoy that."

"Well, I'll pack a picnic that—"

Suddenly Sheila was cut off by one big hand around her mouth, and a massive forearm squeezing her throat.

At that exact same moment Bill began struggling with a chord of some kind wrapped tightly around his neck. It was very quickly choking the life out of him.

While watching the terror in Sheila's eyes, he calmly brought his hands up to his throat and tried to slip his fingers in between the chord and his skin. But, it was too tight.

He knew what his next move was going to be.

It would be quick, and because Sheila was standing right in front of him, she would unfortunately get hit.

But, he couldn't worry about that for the moment. Nor did he even allow his brain to waste gray cells wondering what this was all about. He'd been trained to simply eliminate the threat first before considering anything else—or anyone else.

Bill stretched his strong arms over his head and behind his back. He grasped his hands tightly around the back of the assailant's head, bent over, and threw the man into the air.

The thug flipped as he went over and his feet caught Sheila square in the face. The force of the impact caused her and the attacker behind her to fall backwards onto the floor, with her on top.

Bill didn't hesitate.

At that moment, he was a robot. Everything came naturally to him. Skills long suppressed from lack of use came back to him instantly. Bill reached down and grabbed Sheila's right hand. He yanked her roughly off the chest of the assailant and flung her back towards the other side of the office.

The thug started to rise to his feet, but Bill spun him around. With a forearm squeezing tightly around his neck, and a hand grasping the side of his head, he twisted violently. There was a slight snapping sound just before the man went limp. Bill dropped him to the ground like a rag doll.

The other attacker was on his feet now, a knife in his hand. He began a mad dash over to the end of the office where Sheila was lying stunned on the floor. Bill knew what the guy intended to do. There was no way he was going to let his niece become a hostage.

Thinking fast, he picked up his Samsung tablet from the top of his desk. Holding it in his hand like a Frisbee, reacting automatically to the training he'd received back at West Point in using ordinary objects as deadly weapons, he flicked the tablet at lightning speed towards the head of the man rushing towards his niece.

It smashed into the attacker's skull, just above the right ear. Bill heard a soft grunt, just before the man's disobedient body crashed on top of the coffee table.

Bill calmly walked over to the deathly still form and checked the throat for a pulse. Feeling none, he noticed the blood quickly soaking the hair on the side of the head where the tablet had hit. He'd either flung the tablet harder than he thought, or it had connected with just the right spot on the attacker's skull.

He shook his head, disengaging himself from the fighting mode that his brain had programmed him to execute.

Then, Bill surprised himself. He crawled down onto the floor beside his sobbing niece, held her tightly in his arms, and kissed her warmly on the cheek. Over and over again.

And, while still in a state of confusion, he found himself softly whispering in a tone he'd never heard his voice use before.

"I love you, Sheila. I'm so sorry. We're safe now, and I'm here with you."

12

Sandy's first thought was to just let the machine take a message, because after the bizarre experience in the park with the corrupt deputy mayor and his hired thug he really didn't feel like talking to anyone.

But, something caused him to reach for the receiver.

"Hello?"

A sweet and vaguely familiar voice at the other end. "Hello, Sandy. It's been a long time."

Suddenly, the memories came back, and the voice was no longer vague.

He pictured her in his mind. Saw her moving across the gymnasium floor, tumbling along the mats. Tiptoeing precariously across the balance beams. A gold medal draped around her neck after she won the world championship.

The sound of her voice still made his heart flutter.

"Judy?"

"Yes. I'm surprised you recognize my voice. It's been forever."

"It has. I think the last time I saw you was at the wedding. Speaking of the wedding, how is old John?"

"That's why I'm calling you, Sandy. He's dead."

Sandy felt a sudden chill. They'd lost touch over the years, but John had been his closest friend throughout his tenure at West Point.

Sandy had been the first one to get booted out of the Honor Guild, followed a year later by John. After that, they were classmates in the regular student population of West Point, trying hard to leave the memories of the Honor Guild far behind them.

He remembered that one of the things they'd always joked about was that they were two peas in a pod. They discovered, when chatting about their families over a beer one night that they'd both been conceived through artificial insemination. They thought that was kind of a strange coincidence. Who knew? Maybe they even had the same father?

The drunker they got, the funnier the semen jokes got. But, the next day, those jokes never seemed quite as funny.

The power of booze.

"Aw, I'm sorry to hear that, Judy. I didn't know. How did he die—were you with him?"

"No, we'd been divorced for over a decade, and I hadn't seen him in at least that long. He killed himself, Sandy. Slit his wrist. The coroner said he had an extremely high blood alcohol level at the time of death."

Sandy felt his mouth go dry. "I don't know what to say. I'm shocked. I'd heard that drinking had become a bad problem for him, but I hadn't talked to him since just after your wedding. We just lost touch, I guess. I moved to Massachusetts and you guys stayed in New York."

"Yes, his drinking is what broke us up. I couldn't take it anymore. He was a troubled man, Sandy. Depressed, I think."

Sandy nodded knowingly. He had a pretty good idea why John had become depressed, but he'd sworn Sandy to secrecy about the incident and Sandy had always respected that.

"I'm so sorry to hear this, Judy. I think I heard that you have a daughter? How's she taking it?"

"Yes, Cynthia. She's almost fifteen. She hadn't seen her father in so long, so she's doing okay, I guess. And, so am I. It's sad, yes. But, the saddest part is that he wasted his life. He was such a nice man deep down inside, and had an absolutely brilliant brain. Well, you know that, of course. He could have done anything he wanted to."

"You're right. He could have. I feel so bad for not keeping in touch with him. I might have been able to help him in some way."

"Don't think that, Sandy. You can't help someone who doesn't want to help himself. I tried, believe me."

"True."

She paused for a second. "I'm the one who should feel bad, Sandy. I heard about how you lost your family a couple of years ago, and I never got in touch with you. I'm so sorry. And, now I see your face plastered all over those ads that Linc is using in his campaign. That guy makes me sick, still, after all these years. And, what he did to you and me back when we were so young, I'll never forget that."

"That's okay. I understand—we'd all lost touch, and the way my family died was so…horrid. Even people who came to the funeral really didn't know what to say."

Sandy heard Judy sigh. "It's more than that. I wanted so much to pick up the phone and call you, but I thought I would sound…opportunistic…callous. I mean, once upon a time you and I were an item, and by the time your family died I was single again. It just didn't seem right to me, almost indecent."

A scene suddenly flashed in Sandy's brain.

Judy, standing at the edge of the dance floor along with several of her friends. It was Barnard College in New York City. One of the top ten girls-only universities in the country. The West Point boys and the Barnard girls used to hang out a lot—joint dances, charity events, athletic competitions. Sandy was attending the dance along with Linc, John, and a few other Honor Guild guys.

She was wearing a long flowing green dress, and her auburn hair was accented with a red rose. He thought at the time that she was the most stunning girl he'd ever seen in his short life. His eyes focused in on her, blocking out everyone else. Her eyes locked in on his, too—and they lingered for the longest time.

But, Linc was also enamoured. He immediately stomped over to her and asked her to dance.

Sandy replayed the next images in his mind—in slow motion.

Her head shaking the answer, No.

Linc spinning around and heading back, anger blanketing the face, which had turned a brilliant shade of red.

Judy then crooking her index finger at Sandy and inviting him over.

They were together the rest of the night, and for most of the following year.

Until he broke her heart.

More correctly, until she thought he broke her heart.

"Yeah, I can see why you'd feel that way, Judy. Totally understandable. Don't give it another thought."

"Sandy, I have something to tell you. And...something to give you. It was John's last wish—he sent me a note before he died, along with a cassette tape. In his note, he said that he was hoping to come into a large sum of money and he was going to give Cynthia and me most of it. But, it was strange—he said if something happened to him, that I was to get in touch with you and get this tape to you. He insisted that I not listen to the tape, and I haven't."

Sandy felt his fist gripping the phone tighter. "I...don't know what that tape could possibly be about, Judy," he lied. "But, if John said not to listen to it, don't."

"Should I mail it to you?"

Sandy's instinct told him that would be a mistake. A voice in his head whispered to him what this tape was all about. The same ancient story that had caused John Nichols to descend into depression and transform into a hopeless alcoholic. The same story that got Sandy booted out of the Honor Guild, to be followed by John a scant year later.

"No, don't do that, Judy. Are you still in New York?"

"Yes, in Queens."

"Okay, that's only about a four-hour drive from Boston, so I'll just cruise on down the coast. It would be a good excuse to see you again, anyway. And I'll get to meet Cynthia."

A few seconds pause. Then, "Oh, Sandy, it will be great to see you again, too. I really mean that."

"It's a date, then. Text me your address. I'll text you back as to what dates look good for me, and you can let me know what works."

"Okay, see you soon, Sandy. It will be so nice."

Sandy hung up the phone and stretched his feet out on top of the coffee table.

So, John was dead and he had a tape. And was hoping to come into some money. Seemed as if he thought he was in some danger? Which sounded to Sandy like blackmail. Kind of like what he himself had just tried to do with the deputy mayor.

Maybe it wasn't suicide after all?

Sandy remembered way back to the day when John's guilty conscience forced him to confess about what happened in that van with Linc, three other guys, and the young girl. John was so afraid, didn't know what to do. Was scared about the idea of blowing the whistle on the Honor Guild Commander.

Sandy volunteered to do it for him, but promised to keep John's name out of it. He remembered how the dean listened to him intently, promised him that he'd deal with it. That justice would be served, but that it was imperative that no shame be brought upon West Point. What was done was done, and nothing would bring the young girl back. Sandy accepted that—believed that the dean would deal with it in the honorable way that the school's legacy demanded.

But, it didn't work out that way. He had no idea whether the dean ever talked to Linc about the death of the girl. All Sandy knew was that within days he was kicked out of the Honor Guild and sent back down to the regular population of West Point. And warned that he was to keep his mouth shut. Or…

He didn't know what the "or" meant and hadn't wanted to find out.

So, did John's cassette tape have something to do with that incident? Was he blackmailing Linc—timed with the launch of his presidential campaign? Had John deluded himself into thinking the bastard was easy pickings?

Judy's voice sounded exactly the same. It was as if the last twenty or so years hadn't passed by at all.

Sandy, Linc, and John had each been connected to Judy back in their university days.

Intimately.

That night of the dance was the beginning of a wonderful relationship for Sandy and Judy, but it was the beginning of something else, too.

An insidious simmering burn began that night.

Judy was Sandy's first love.

And, while he'd indeed loved Sarah with all of his heart—a love that evolved into a sort of adoration—there was just something about how he felt about Judy that was never duplicated. Something in the gut, the brain, the heart. Impossible to describe, but also impossible to forget.

Linc hated the fact that Sandy was dating Judy. He wanted her, pure and simple. He tried to intervene many times, but Judy rejected him. Told him that she was in love with Sandy.

The two of them planned to get married after graduation. They'd decided what breed of dog they'd have—even before discussing the number of kids. They would have a house in the New York suburbs, and Judy would coach gymnastics at one of the high schools. Sandy would become some sort of scientist—didn't really know which way he'd lean, but he knew he'd be doing something brainy.

Then one day Judy heard a knock on the door of her dorm room.

A knock that would change both of their lives.

The girl was wearing shorty shorts, and a revealing tank top that overtly taunted small-breasted Judy with a pair of 38Ds. She proceeded to tell Judy that her boyfriend was a hound dog, who'd enjoyed a threesome with her and her equally ample girlfriend. She uttered words that hurt, graphic words designed to create images that would break a tender heart. Gave her the other girl's phone number so Judy could check with her and verify the story. Told her that she was telling her these things because she felt she deserved to hear what a terrible boyfriend Sandy was.

Their romance ended that night. Sandy protested his innocence, but, she wouldn't listen. Said she'd called the other girl already, and that she'd repeated the same story verbatim.

Sandy said it was a lie. That he'd never cheat on her.

Her logical retort was, "Why would they lie?"

Sandy didn't have an answer for that.

Linc swooped in almost immediately to fill the void.

Judy was vulnerable, got caught in the crossfire. He charmed her.

At first, he was nice to her, but it didn't take long for her to see his dark side. She broke up with him and ended up with John Nichols on the rebound.

After she and John had been going out for a few months, he told her about what he'd learned during a night of heavy drinking. A night when Linc declared to the group of guys that Judy was just a slut and he was glad to be rid of her. Then, in a drunken stupor, bragged to the group how he'd paid off a couple of strippers to make up that story about Sandy. Gave each of them $1,000 for their bullshit. Just so he could cut Sandy out of the equation.

Sandy was proud of John for telling her that. It helped unbreak her heart. And he took a risk doing it, because there was the chance she'd come running back to him.

Which she did.

Judy came to his room and told him she was sorry that she hadn't believed him. She was crying uncontrollably, and Sandy soothed her in the best way he could. But the soothing fell far short of what they used to do together.

Too much time had gone by.

He and Sarah had been dating for a while, and he wasn't prepared to go back in time. By then he loved Sarah and wouldn't consider hurting her. He was committed.

And he'd been hurt too—hurt that Judy hadn't believed him. She knew him well enough to know that he never would have done that to her. He'd loved her.

An immature, stubborn decision on his part.

A decision that had a profound effect on several lives.

He should have appreciated how shocked and hurt she must have been when confronted by that slut at her door. He'd expected too much of her, had expected her to be stronger than any average person could realistically be.

But, back then, Sandy was just an immature, stubborn young man.

Lincoln Berwick, now the senator from the great state of Texas, and possibly soon to be the next President of the United States of

America, viciously broke the heart of the love of his life. And in the process, he'd broken Sandy's, too.

All because Lincoln Berwick wanted what he wanted.

13

The waves gently rolled in to shore, leaving the sand glistening for a second or two after the water retreated. Like magic, the sand returned to normal, waiting to be kissed once again.

Bright sunshine added extra sparkles to the grains of sand and a warm steady breeze was blowing in from the west, making this middle of December day unusually balmy. Christmas was looming, yet it felt like just a typical day in June.

Bill Tomkins kicked off his sandals and wiggled his toes into the sand—something he hadn't done in a long time.

Then he did something that for him was completely wild and crazy. He rolled up his pant legs and waded into the frigid water. It sent a shiver through his entire body, but it felt strangely wonderful. Made him feel alive. And a little bit carefree—a quality that most people would never associate with Bill Tomkins.

He walked in a bit deeper until the water was past his knees, soaking the edges of his rolled-up pants. Then he turned around and gazed back at his beach house just as a larger wave smacked him in the ass.

Sheila waved at him from the upper deck. She had the two boys with her, Fraser and Wallace. They were six and four respectively; adorable, just like their mother and, unfortunately, fatherless. Sheila had been widowed a couple of years earlier by a drunk driver—husband Sean was killed driving home from work—and it had taken her the better part of a year to get back to her normal self.

The kids had suffered a bit, although they were too young at the time to really know their father all that well. They were more upset that their mother was upset.

Bill had tried to be there for her, help her through it, but he knew he'd failed miserably. His sister and brother-in-law had done most of the nurturing. Bill had provided money—not exactly heartwarming, but it made him feel like he was at least doing something.

Still, he got the impression from his family that they knew he hadn't been capable of doing more. There'd been no resentment at his absences from family functions, no yelling or screaming, no accusations of being a cold-hearted bastard.

They knew him far too well and had long ago given up on trying to find his heart.

Bill smiled and waved back at Sheila. She was beckoning him to come back up to the house. He could see smoke rising off the hood of the barbecue, indicating that dinner was almost ready.

He'd been fiddling with the barbecue himself a couple of hours ago, trying to figure out how to work the damn thing. It was a massive unit, with a side warmer, sear burner, and a grill large enough for at least a dozen T-bones. But, he'd never used it before.

Sheila had grown impatient with him and shooed him down to the beach.

And he was glad she had—it had been ages since he'd walked on his own beach and was surprised at how much he was enjoying it.

And he couldn't even recall having a good hard look at his house from that angle before. It looked so much bigger from the beach.

The house was about forty years old and had a lower porch as well as the upper deck that Sheila was cooking on. It was Cape Cod style, clad in yellow-painted clapboard siding. One of the most impressive homes on the beach and it was way too big for Bill.

But, a great investment.

He'd bought it five years ago for a cool five million, and it was now assessed at over seven.

His private beachfront was a stretch of about 1,000 feet, which housed a seriously long dock where he kept his Boston Whaler moored. Just something else that he hardly ever used.

The Hamptons were located on the easternmost edge of Long Island. This most exclusive enclave was divided between two distinct sections: Southampton, and East Hampton. There were fifteen hamlets contained within the Southampton district and another seven in East Hampton. Bill's house was in the Southampton sector, in a distinct village called Sagaponack, which was the most expensive zip code in the entire United States.

The Hamptons' reputation as being a fashionable summer resort community began way back in the 1800s. It was actually described by the New York Times in 1893 as being comparable to everyone's idea of the Garden of Eden.

Bill picked up his sandals and walked back up to the house. Sheila was calling him now with some sense of urgency—making it known that the crown pork was ready and waiting.

He walked up the stairs and she greeted him with a hug. The little boys grabbed onto his wet legs, forcing him to drag them into the kitchen.

And he wondered what the three of them saw in him.

Was it the expensive house on the beach? No, couldn't be. His niece was the least material person on the planet.

Maybe it was because he was such a tough nut to crack. Always pleasant, but never overtly affectionate. Everyone liked a challenge, so maybe that was it.

Or, maybe they just saw something in him that he'd never seen himself. Perhaps they were the only ones in his circle who didn't look at him as being a cold-hearted wheeler-dealer. Maybe they could see through him, see his heart, feel his longing for something more substantive than money.

Dinner was wonderful.

Sheila was a great cook, and he made a mental note to get her to show him tomorrow how to work that damn barbecue. He wanted to cook for her and the boys for a change. See what he could whip up. Challenge himself. Hell, if he could string together billion dollar mergers, how difficult could cooking be?

Sheila put the boys to bed and then joined Bill in the living room.

Even though it was a warm December evening, Bill had thrown a couple of logs on the fire. Why, he didn't know. Probably because he knew Sheila would like that.

She curled up on the couch opposite him.

"I worry about you, Uncle Bill."

"Stop with the 'uncle' stuff. Just call me Bill."

"Okay, Bill, answer me this—when are you going to get a woman in your life?"

Bill laughed. "Oh, I don't have time for that. My life's a nightmare of business deals, and I travel so much. I couldn't do justice to a relationship."

"Forgive me for asking this, but are you gay?"

"God, no! Do I seem gay to you?"

"No, not at all. But, it's common and more accepted these days, so it would be nothing to be ashamed of."

Bill smirked at her. "Well, I'm not. But I want you to teach me some cooking skills tomorrow, so I hope that doesn't reinforce your suspicion."

Sheila laughed. "Okay, so you're not gay. Instead, you're a rich, handsome, and incredibly powerful international investment banker. And, you're all alone. One hell of a catch, I would say."

Bill shook his head.

"Not that great a catch, my dear niece. I've been closed off for most of my life. Unable to show another side of me—a side I hope is deep down in there somewhere, but I find it hard to bring it out."

Sheila uncurled her legs and leaned forward on the couch.

"You just need practice, and you don't realize it, but, you show that side to me and the boys all the time. And my mom says that you're one of the kindest men in her life."

"Well, she's my sister—she has to say that. And you're my niece—you're obligated, too."

Sheila shook her head. "No, I'm not obligated at all. If I didn't feel that way, why would I always look for ways to spend time with you? You're my favorite uncle."

Bill got up and threw another log on the fire.

"Maybe you just have some sense of missionary zeal. I'm a never-ending project for you ladies."

"I've seen that gentle, caring side of you many times in my life. You're being too hard on yourself, and maybe because you're so used to being a hard-nosed businessman you don't even recognize that other side of you when it does show itself."

He sat back down and nodded. "Maybe."

"I saw the caring side of you just a few days ago. In your office. You crawled down onto the floor and cradled me. I felt like a baby. You have no idea how much I needed that from you at that moment. I was so scared and kind of in shock."

Bill lowered his eyes, suddenly feeling self-conscious. He whispered, "God, I was so worried about you, Sheila. I'm glad you're okay."

Wincing in frustration, she retorted, "You're missing the point. You gave me what I needed without me even asking. That side of you came out, that side that you never give yourself credit for. I've always seen you as a caring and generous uncle. But, also, so very strong. I feel safe around you, and my mom has said the same thing. You made her feel safe when you were all growing up together. Uncle Brad never gave her that same feeling—you were different. The brother she could always count on to defend her. And you did it for me that night in your office. Bill, how the hell were you able to fight like that? I've never seen anything like it! You were like a machine; those two guys were dead in a matter of seconds. I was horrified, but...fascinated. Proud of my uncle."

Bill felt uncomfortable talking about it. Wished she hadn't seen him in action like that.

"That's a side of me that I really never wanted you to see, Sheila. You know I attended West Point. That's where I learned skills like that. That school is top notch in so many ways, and when you graduate from there you come out well-rounded physically as well as mentally."

"Maybe you can teach me some self-defence techniques some time?"

"Sure. We can start tomorrow. Good idea."

Sheila paused for a few seconds. "You never joined the army. Aren't you supposed to serve as an officer after graduating from West

Point?"

Bill took a sip from a glass of Grand Marnier that was sitting on the table.

"Well, yes and no. I was in kind of an elite division that taught all of those military skills and the art of war—all that bullshit. And, of course, all divisions of West Point give a full university education as well. But, the division I was in was more of a targeted one. We were supposed to be the gifted ones, groomed for paths in life other than military."

Bill paused for a moment before continuing. "I guess the way they looked at it was that war could be fought on many fronts—not just on the battlefield. War is simply about winning, and dominance—those can be achieved on the battlefield, but sometimes they can be achieved more effectively in boardrooms, scientific labs, manufacturing plants, and in election campaigns. The military is all about supremacy, and only a small part of it is actual combat. That's just the most visible part, the part that everyone sees on the news. But, the public doesn't consider that every time someone like me pulls off a major international acquisition providing extra leverage and power to an American company, that's also a battle won."

His niece tilted her head, encouraging him to continue.

"Or, when an engineer in a lab invents a high-tech weapon that puts extra fear into the hearts of our enemies, that's a battle won as well. And, think of strong leaders that we put into positions of power in Congress or the White House—those are soldiers for the cause, and if they're smarter and more devious than leaders of other countries—voila—another battle won. And all those battles would be fought and won without firing a shot."

Sheila stared at him, wide-eyed.

"Wow, I never thought of it that way before. So, they intended you gifted ones for the brainier battles; those battles that didn't involve traipsing around in the mud with machine guns slung over your shoulders."

Bill nodded, and replied with sarcasm dripping from his tongue, "I guess they didn't want to take a chance on having our valuable brains splattered all over the desert sands. Best to save that for the lower IQs."

"You're sounding cynical, Bill."

He shook his head. "No, just realistic now after all these years. And, reflective I guess. Wondering what all that grooming caused me to give up, or what I've sold my soul for."

Sheila got up and stood with her back to the fire.

"Why did those burglars try to kill us? Why didn't they just take what they wanted?"

Bill got up as well and walked over to the bar. Poured himself another drink. He gestured to her. "Do you want one?"

"No, thanks. I'm going to bed in a few minutes."

He walked over to the fireplace and stood beside her.

"I don't know why they attacked us. They didn't have guns on them, probably because they were afraid of the noise. So, perhaps they thought it was easier to kill us than try to restrain us. Knives are easier to defend against than guns so maybe they thought their best tactic was to just to take us down."

Sheila frowned. "But what did you have that was worth stealing? You don't keep money there, nothing of real value. Unless, perhaps, they wanted your computer for insider financial information?"

Bill hugged her. "You should head off to bed. They're dead now, not a worry anymore. Who knows what their motivation was—could be the computer, you might be right."

"Okay." Sheila hugged him back. "Goodnight, Bill. Thanks for saving my life."

He laughed. "Hey, I just wanted to enjoy your cooking for a few more years."

"Well, I owe you that now for the rest of your life."

She turned and headed towards the staircase. Bill called after her.

"And, it's about time you started dating again, my dear. It's been two years now. You're so worried about me, but I'm kinda worried about you, too."

Sheila turned around and smiled. "I might start soon, uncle dear. I have my eye on someone—I'll tell you about him tomorrow."

Bill watched her climb the stairs then sat back down on the couch.

While staring at the flames dancing in the fireplace hearth, he could feel his brain doing its own little dance.

The problem with having an IQ off the charts, was that his brain never stopped working. It always challenged, always questioned, and whenever there were dots to connect they just connected almost by themselves.

The NYPD had accepted the fact that the burglars were just there to steal. And that their easiest way to steal was to get rid of the two occupants of the office.

The regular cleaners had been found tied and gagged in a closet near the lunchroom. Stripped of their uniforms.

The thugs could have indeed been burglars. Yes, that was possible.

But, they were Anglos with expensive haircuts, while the normal cleaners at the office were Hispanic. So, if they were burglars, would they actually masquerade as cleaners? Their shoes were shiny and Italian. And, they were articulate—at least the one guy who'd done the talking.

They didn't fit the mold. They seemed more…professional.

The police found no identification on them, which was odd. They were going to check their fingerprints in the database, but Bill suspected they'd find nothing.

And, to immediately try to kill him and Sheila said to Bill that they knew something about him. Like, they knew that he wouldn't be an easy target to restrain. As if they already knew he was a lethal weapon. If so, how did they know?

And, for this to happen right on the heels of John Nichols' suicide seemed too much of a coincidence. Too hard to swallow.

There were three things that he and John Nichols had in common.

They'd both attended West Point.

They'd both been in the gifted program known as the Honor Guild.

And they'd both been in the van the night of that young girl's death.

Along with three other guys.

Bill thought about those other guys. Hank Price worked with Boeing in Seattle. Lloyd Franken was down at NASA in Houston. And Lincoln Berwick was a senator, now running for President of the United States.

Bill still kept in touch with Hank and Lloyd from time to time. But, he hadn't seen or talked to Lincoln since graduation.

Bill's brain was still churning.

He knew enough about politics to know that the profession attracted some of the biggest narcissists imaginable.

People who felt they were entitled.

And, because they spent their lives feeling entitled, they usually had skeletons in their closets.

He couldn't even count how many scandals had broken out over the last decade or so, ruining the careers of promising politicians. It was almost like an epidemic in Washington.

What happened in that van was one of the most disgusting and tragic things imaginable. It had haunted Bill over the years, and may have even contributed to his avoidance of closeness and intimacy. He'd never forgotten that poor girl and his role in her death, even though he'd tried real hard to wipe it from his mind.

He was sure the other guys had never forgotten either.

One was now dead of an apparent suicide.

Bill himself had almost died the other night.

Of the four of them still alive, which one had the most to lose if this incriminating skeleton ever crawled out of the van?

Had John Nichols been a loose end?

Was Bill a loose end?

Were the others?

Was the attempted robbery just a coincidence?

Bill stoked the fire, spreading out the embers to allow it to burn out faster.

It was time for bed.

He knew that his REM sleep would be active tonight—assembling all of the information into illogical patterns, only to be sorted out nicely by his conscious state when he awakened in the morning.

Regardless, he was pretty certain he already knew the answers to the questions.

14

"...and here it is almost Christmas, but, Americans can't even make a trip to the shopping mall without worrying about being shot or blown up. Trust me, the threats are real, and they're going to get worse. ISIS is the most well-equipped terrorist organization the world has ever seen, and they're everywhere. Don't delude yourselves into thinking they won't hit us again.

"The present leadership is not taking the threat seriously. Despite the Boston Marathon bombing, the Quincy Market massacre, and countless mass shootings at shopping malls, nightclubs, theaters and schools, we are not safer today than we were before 9/11. Your government tries to convince you that you are, but they're wrong. Dead wrong."

Senator Lincoln Berwick paused for effect, and gazed out over the 5,000 people crammed into the convention center.

He couldn't even remember the name of the place—some godforsaken facility in downtown Toledo. A decrepit city that he'd never bother to visit if he weren't running for president.

And, as his eyes absorbed the tank tops, torn jeans, and baseball caps adorning his rapt audience, he silently admonished himself for the slumming he was forcing himself to do.

These weren't the type of people that he could ever relate to, but, he was doing his damnedest anyway to convince them that he was the type of guy they could sit down and have a beer with. And, he knew this crowd probably drank beer—lots of it.

He'd made sure to dress down for this speech—which he'd actually had to do for most of his speeches. The electorate that he was appealing to were, by and large, angry rednecks.

So, he'd worn jeans, a golf shirt, and a tweed blazer. Still far better dressed than his audience and his jeans didn't have holes in them, but, he looked like he could sort of blend in while still maintaining a presidential air.

Linc was adept at relating to whatever audience he was speaking to. He had a little help from his campaign manager, Bob Stone, of course, but most of the time Linc could adapt to the audience in tune with his own instincts.

He was a skilled public speaker and in this day and age of image over substance, the ability to speak with hypnotizing charisma was the one skill that could almost always guarantee success.

Linc was in the final throes of his speech, and the audience mainly consisted of Republican voters getting fired up for the primaries, which would start in a couple of months' time. Right now, it was just a beauty contest, with Linc vying for attention and affection against five other candidates.

All fifty states and the offshore territories would hold primaries or caucuses until the summer. The winner should be evident by the time of the July convention.

He knew that it would be pretty much a cakewalk. So, he was looking ahead to the fall election campaign against the Democratic nominee, because as far as he was concerned he would be the Republican nominee.

No doubt about it.

The Republican Party wouldn't be happy if Linc were the winner—and they were also out of the loop with respect to the group of people behind his campaign. And, no doubt they wouldn't approve if they were in the loop.

It was really just a party within a party, and the tried and true Republicans had no clue whatsoever as to what was going on. They were good people, but a bit naïve. The power behind Lincoln's campaign was unstoppable. The GOP would never be the same again.

As for the five other Republican candidates, three of them were plants.

Boris Malkin had done his job well.

All three were capable, but more in need of money than power.

Numbered bank accounts in the Cayman Islands took care of that for them. Deposits made in advance and agendas provided. All three would be as rich as sin, but would voluntarily take dives.

They would campaign their little hearts out, but then begin making one gaffe after another, deliberately embarrassing themselves in the primaries. They would be toast by the time the convention rolled around.

The fix was in.

The only candidates that Linc had to worry about were the two serious ones—the real candidates. The idealistic governor of Florida and an annoyingly intelligent senator from Ohio. Ohio was the state that Linc was speaking in today—he wanted to hit the guy on his home turf.

Linc was pretty certain he could beat both of these bozos, but Boris had promised some help.

Insurance policies.

Boris wasn't able to find any real dirt on either of them, but a well-oiled machine of operatives had been working hard behind the scenes to create back-stories on each of the two candidates.

For the Florida governor, it would be a financial scandal—kickbacks and payoffs. Not real, of course, but it would sound real—real enough to derail the guy's campaign.

And for the Ohio senator, it would be a sexual thing. Once again, contrived, but damaging as hell. Those stories would be leaked over the next few months.

Drip, drip, drip…

Senator Lincoln Berwick would be the last man standing by the time the convention rolled around.

Next stop—the general election in November against the Democrat nominee. The world was unfolding as it should.

After that, the White House.

Linc pictured himself sitting in the Oval Office, commanding.

He could almost taste the power, the ability to affect events anywhere in the world where he chose to. It was downright orgasmic.

Shivers ran down his spine just thinking about it. The most overwhelming military on the planet at his fingertips, the ability to nuke countries that dared to defy the entitlement of the United States of America.

All of the pansies who'd occupied the Oval Office, in the generations since Truman, had shown nothing but weakness—a reluctance to brandish the most terrifying weapon imaginable. Well, Lincoln Berwick wouldn't be that kind of president.

What was the point of having the most sophisticated nuclear weapons imaginable and not use them? Especially since they'd been refined to be more tactical now. No longer was there the worry that radioactive contamination would devastate entire continents. They could be used selectively now, annihilate some rogue nation and leave the rest unscathed.

He had a Top Ten list—headed by North Korea and Syria.

Followed close behind by Venezuela and Nigeria.

Of course, no list was complete without Iran, and possibly Turkey.

There were lesser countries on the list, but they could wait. After he unleashed the first few attacks, they'd probably all toe the line and no longer be a problem. He'd have to wait and see.

And, as soon as these rogue nations were eliminated, America's prominence in the economic realm would become apparent. The U.S. stock markets would roar, because, in comparison to everyone else, they would be seen as a safe haven.

America would also have the economic might and fear factor to get out of its twenty trillion in debt obligations—it would simply erase all debts owed to foreign nations and banks. Who would dare oppose the country that had just nuked several of its enemies? And, the World Bank would be controlled by U.S. interests so their influence would be impotent. The United Nations, as usual, would be a paper tiger.

Power had its advantages—Linc had learned that simple fact over the years. The problem was, everyone prior to Linc, aside from Truman, had been afraid to use that power.

No more.

Linc got excited just thinking about it. America would be back in the exalted supreme position by the time he was finished.

He'd taken Bob Stone's advice and had a chat with his speechwriter, Tanya, before this event in Toledo. Told her the speeches had to hit harder, have more fear built in. Fear needed to be the theme. It was going to be the key to beating the Democrats in November.

Tanya got the message—the words she'd conjured up for this speech were scary and gut wrenching. He needed more speeches like this one.

Linc smoothly slid his eyes across to the left teleprompter, and began his closing remarks.

"We've been pushed around long enough. We're America, and we deserve more respect than the world is giving us. The economies of the world would be anemic without us. It's about time they started recognizing that. And, I'm the one who can do that for you. In fact, I'm the *only* one who can do that for you."

He paused as 5,000 people jumped to their feet, screaming and applauding. He smiled, knowing he had them in the palm of his hands. Bob Stone was right—these were the words they wanted to hear, *needed* to hear.

He raised his hands high in the air, bringing almost instant silence to the audience. He felt shivers down his spine again with the realization that the mere raising of his hands could command attention—and silence. Now he knew how Jesus must have felt on Mt. Sinai.

His steel blue eyes roamed over to the right-side teleprompter.

"With Lincoln Berwick as your President, you will no longer cower, no longer feel unappreciated. Americans will never live in fear again. And they will be respected wherever they travel in this great big world and, yes, even feared. I will make sure that our enemies understand what it means to defy the greatest democracy the world has ever seen.

"Trust me with your votes in the primaries and again in the general election. We'll never have an opportunity like this come our way again. We're at the end. America is on the verge of imploding, and we cannot let this happen.

"As your president, I will *refuse* to let it happen! Let me fight for you!"

*****

Linc was sitting in a Cadillac stretch limousine with one other passenger. The chauffeur was weaving his way through traffic in the direction of the Toledo airport. The glass privacy screen gave the two passengers the isolation they needed.

Jason Reid was sitting across from Linc and they were both sipping vintage red wine.

"Your speech went well. The crowd was fired up more than I've seen in a long time. Senator, I think the momentum is in your favor right now."

Linc took a long sip from his glass of Merlot, and stared at his private security chief. These ex-Secret Service guys were all the same, he mused to himself. Well dressed, emotionless, coldly authoritative, and always in control. If they gave out compliments, they were usually just polite practiced gestures. But, Linc didn't mind—he liked being patronized.

"Yeah, I can feel it too, Jason. Let's get down to business, though. I have the feeling that you have something disturbing to tell me. A sixth sense."

Jason nodded. "That's why you're a good politician. Yes, we struck out with Bill Tomkins. He's one tough character. He killed both of my operatives."

Linc nodded. "Any possibility of this being traced back to you?"

Jason shook his head. "No, they were 'blind' contractors. No trace as to who hired them. It will be a dead end for the police."

"Good. Well, I'm not surprised about Bill. He was trained by the same people who trained me. Next steps?"

"Well, I'm wondering if you should bring Bob Stone and Meagan Whitfield into the loop on this skeleton from your past. Might be better if they know so they can prepare responses and strategies if something does get out. This thing will kill your candidacy—and could even send you to prison."

Linc folded his arms across his chest as the car turned onto the main expressway leading to the airport.

"Absolutely not. They don't need to know. I hire you for things like this, and I want results. Tell me what you plan to do now."

"Okay, then. I was only thinking of your campaign. Those folks are on your side."

Linc shook his head. "I don't want to hear any more about this. I'm not telling them. Again, what's your plan?"

"We need to move fast on the other two. Tomkins will be on his guard now if he figures out that the attack he suffered wasn't a simple robbery. Especially if he knows now about the death of John Nichols."

"Well, when those other two die, Tomkins will know for sure something is up. So, we'll have to brace for that."

Jason pulled a notepad out of his pocket. "There's no point trying for Tomkins again right now. Best for us to wait until after the others are dead. And we might get lucky. Their deaths might just warn him off for good—scare him into silence."

"Possibly. But, he's a West Point grad, and Honor Guild. We don't scare easily."

"That's true. Anyway, I think our best tactic right now is just to get rid of the other two. Process of elimination will reduce the possibility of a leak."

Jason read from his note pad. "Hank Price and Lloyd Franken." He looked up. "We'll do these quickly and then talk about how to deal with Tomkins after that. Okay?"

Linc cracked his knuckles while gazing out of the tinted window of the limousine; the Toledo airport looming in the distance. He was relieved to soon be flying out of this shithole of a city.

"Okay. Make it fast. I'm getting one of those sixth sense feelings, and I don't like it."

15

He loved it when engineering students came on this tour. Today, it was a group of first year enthusiasts from the Bothell campus of the University of Washington. Wide-eyed, innocent, and ready to take on the world.

And, at least some of them, the best and the brightest, would graduate as aerospace engineers and perhaps even join Boeing one day. As far as Hank was concerned, they couldn't make a better choice.

Hank Price had been at Boeing for fifteen years, and had risen to the position of chief engineer after only five years at the company. He loved his job, especially this part where he got the chance to interact with young people.

Even better, being able to say that he'd been instrumental in the development of the world's newest and most famous luxury jet, the 787 Dreamliner, was something that always impressed people at cocktail parties.

Not that he was out to impress anyone, but it was a source of pride to him. It was the one jet that everyone wanted to fly on—it was pretty much on everyone's bucket list. And, it was a beautiful jet—Hank was darn proud of it, as was his team.

Fuel efficient, fast, and equipped with comfort features that were lacking in most passenger jets today. He knew it would revolutionize the world of air travel, and that was a heritage that he'd be able to take with him to the grave. Maybe his contribution to the long-running Dreamliner project would even be noted on his headstone?

Hank normally worked out of the Seattle head office, but on Tuesdays and Wednesdays of each week he conducted tours of their massive factory in Everett, only 25 miles north of Seattle.

The tour was officially known to the public as the Future of Flight, which sounded kind of space age, but, it really wasn't.

It allowed the public to see the actual construction of jet aircraft, piece by painstaking piece. They were usually enthralled with the degree of robotics that was used in the factory, which made aircraft assembly plants much more efficient than they used to be. The robotics were a highlight of the tour, for sure.

And, the advanced level of automation that Boeing employed allowed their jets to reach market much faster than they would have a mere two decades ago.

By volume, the Everett plant was the largest building in the world, at a mind-boggling 13 million square meters. And visitors could watch several varieties of famous Boeing jets being assembled: the iconic 747, the jumbo 767, the sleek 777, and of course the ground-breaking 787 Dreamliner—Hank's pride and joy.

The Everett facility was the only commercial jet assembly plant in North America to offer tours to the public, and it had been Hank's idea to initiate them years ago. These tours had played a huge role in enhancing Boeing's reputation, and they added just that little extra measure of comfort and confidence to the flying public.

The Boeing plant was one of the largest tourist attractions in the entire state of Washington, with hundreds of thousands of visitors every year.

As a result, hotels and restaurants had sprung up in the Everett area—the factory was solely responsible for an economic boom that was unrelenting.

Hank led the group of students along a catwalk, which allowed them a birds-eye view of the assembly operations.

Some jets in their infancy, and others in their final stages.

"Sir, that's a strange-looking wing."

Hank glanced over at the young man. He was pointing down at one of the jets being prepped for its final coat of paint.

Hank chuckled. "Hard not to notice that, isn't it? Yes, that's the 777, and, believe it or not, its wings are hinged. The wingspan on that jet is so wide that the plane wouldn't make it down most taxi ramps.

So, the pilot has the ability to press a button commanding the wings to bend upward at the hinge so he can taxi safely to the airport gates. Neat, huh?"

The kids all stared down in unison at the high-tech jet, mouths open in amazement.

He continued. "While the body of the 777 is aluminum, the wings are made of a very strong carbon fibre—much lighter than aluminum—which gives the jet more efficient lift and aerodynamics. We're always striving to make our planes more efficient, and, of course, more environmentally friendly. Very important these days. And, our airline clients appreciate that our plane designs help them contain fuel costs, which means they can afford to offer airfares at more competitive prices. Needless to say, more efficient jets add more to their bottom line profits as well, which of course is what it's all about in the grand scheme of things."

Hank glanced at his watch, and then clapped his hands together.

"Okay, follow me. Unfortunately, the tour's over and your bus is probably waiting for you already in the parking lot. Slack time over, back to campus to bury your noses in your books."

He laughed as a collective groan followed him down to the main concourse.

He didn't blame them for groaning—he'd always enjoyed field trips, too, way back when he was a student, and the thought of going back to class again had usually brought pains to his stomach.

These tours kind of reminded him of his university days—being able to escape the office in Seattle twice a week to make the thirty-minute drive north to Everett. He really enjoyed getting away from the office politics even just for a little while—engaging with young eager students was much more invigorating.

Hank pulled his phone out of his pocket to check his messages. The thing had vibrated a couple of times while he was with the students, but he never answered it while he was with a tour group.

They always got his undivided attention, even though they didn't always offer him the same courtesy. He noticed that several of them had been busy texting instead of paying attention, and he also had to caution all of them before the tour that no photos were allowed in the assembly plant. Basic protection against industrial espionage. The kids grumbled a bit, but they seemed to understand.

Two text messages.

One from his secretary reminding him about a meeting first thing in the morning.

He smiled at the second message—a brief one from his old friend, Bill Tomkins, on the other side of the country. All it said was for Hank to call him as soon as he could.

He hadn't seen Bill in a couple of months, back during a business trip Hank had made to New York. They'd grabbed some dinner and a few beers afterwards.

Two Honor Guild guys reminiscing about their days back at West Point.

It was always a good time whenever they got together—Bill was still the same guy, very intense, extremely serious. But, after a few drinks he managed to loosen up.

Hank considered it his personal mission to try to bring Bill out of his shell whenever they met. And, he was actually a funny guy when he let his hair down a bit, which he probably didn't do all that often.

But, it was always easier to loosen up with old friends, people who knew you before you'd achieved success.

And Bill Tomkins had sure achieved success—probably the wealthiest of all the old crowd. Sure, Lincoln Berwick was on a run for the White House now, but Hank tried not to think of him too often.

All he knew was that he definitely wouldn't be voting for that cold-hearted prick next November.

Well, he'd phone Bill back when he got home. They could have a good chat and schedule their next rendezvous.

Hank walked out through the front lobby to the parking lot, where his Cadillac Escalade was waiting for him. He loved the vehicle in some ways, but in other ways he hated it. It was a massive SUV, one of the larger ones on the market. So, it was great for hauling stuff, and there was lots of room for his wife and three kids. But, because of its size, it felt clumsy at times and the sway always bothered him when he turned corners at higher speeds. The Caddy always gave the impression that it was getting ready to roll.

But you couldn't beat the sheer luxury of a Caddy. The interior was sumptuous.

He settled into the plush leather seat and wheeled his way out of the parking lot. After a couple of short detours he was on the Interstate 5, heading south to Seattle.

It was only a couple of weeks until Christmas, so Hank made the executive decision to take the rest of the day off. Playing hooky was just one of the many perks of being Boeing's chief engineer.

He hadn't done any shopping yet, and he was perilously close to running out of time.

His wife, Kristy, wanted a fancy new blender, but Hank had already decided to ignore that and get her a diamond bracelet instead.

And the kids wanted some new computer games, but, he was going to ignore that, too. New bikes were in order for each of them, and with Seattle's spring weather all year long it was the perfect climate for cycling. He wanted his kids to begin weaning off the video games and get outside more.

He cruised along happily—Christmas was his favorite time of the year, and even though they rarely got snow in Seattle, he and Kristy always made the house look festive. Which was another reason why he was going to play hooky this afternoon—he knew she wanted to get the tree up this evening. If he went back to the office, he wouldn't get out of there until at least 10:00. There was always something brewing that would tie him to his desk. Best not to know.

Hank tuned the radio in to a holiday favorites channel and began singing along with Bing Crosby.

The highway was pretty clear—he passed through the suburbs of Lynnwood and Mount Lake Terrace without traffic of any note, even though he'd expected there would be. This time of the year things tended to bog down, and he suspected that the traffic would get worse the closer he got to Seattle proper.

Just after passing through Parkwood, a car careened around him at top speed and had to slam on its brakes due to another car in front. Hank rammed his foot down on the brake pedal and managed to slow his beast down just in time to avoid running up his bumper.

He leaned on the horn and cursed out loud, which somehow made him feel better.

But, he made a mental note to get his car in for a check-up. The brakes had seemed to take much longer than normal to react. His car was heavy, so the stopping distance was longer than most cars, but, he found it strange he'd come so close to hitting that jerk's bumper.

And, he'd have to get his steering checked too—far too much play in the wheel. Which was typical for most Cadillacs, but on this drive home it felt abnormal to him.

He made sure to leave a lot of space between himself and the jerk up front, just in case.

Hank managed to relax again, and he cranked the music up a little bit louder.

As he turned into the highway curve leading towards the Lake Union area, he could see up ahead that traffic was backing up as normal on the bridge that crossed the narrows between the lake and Portage Bay.

The Caddy struggled through the curve—the steering was acting up again. Hank found that he had to turn the wheel much farther than he normally did. It wasn't responsive.

He managed to get around the curve safely, but it was unnerving as hell. He could feel his heart starting to pound harder and beads of sweat materialized on his forehead.

Hank decided he'd better slow down—he'd have more steering control if he was going slower, and he was now on the downward slope of the highway leading to the bridge up ahead. The telltale red brake lights told him there was the usual congestion on the bridge.

He took a deep breath and applied the brakes.

His foot went right to the floor.

He lifted his foot and pumped again.

Nothing!

Frantic now, he pumped the brake several more times.

No response.

The Caddy was now picking up speed fast as it descended the hill towards the bridge. Hank steered around the jerk in front of him and just managed to avoid hitting another car heading north.

He was racing down the middle line of the highway now, missing cars in both lanes by mere inches.

He leaned on his horn and didn't let up. Drivers up ahead either heard the horn or saw the ominous sight of the oncoming Caddy in their rear and side-view mirrors. They all began moving over to the soft shoulder.

Hank kept pumping the brake, to no avail. His hands were gripping the steering wheel so tightly that his fingers had turned white. Sweat was now dripping into his eyes, the salty sting causing his vision to blur.

He slammed his foot down on the emergency brake pedal, but that too had no tension.

He considered his options. There weren't many.

In fact, there was only one.

The worst thing imaginable to him would be to take out a family. But, he had to stop this thing, and the only way to do that would be to slam into the back of another vehicle. But, it had to be a large vehicle, larger than his.

The airbags would hopefully save him.

He found his target. A transport trailer up ahead. No passengers that would be imperiled by his decision. He would just aim for it and brace himself.

He glanced down at his speedometer. The car was racing along now at 130 miles per hour, and with the way everything was whizzing by his side vision he was surprised that he wasn't going faster than that. He thought of turning off the ignition, but was afraid that he'd completely lose whatever power steering ability he still had left.

He careened around a pickup truck, and it seemed as if the Caddy had done it on two wheels.

Hank set his sights on the back of the transport trailer, only about 100 yards ahead of him now.

He turned the steering wheel just enough to aim the SUV directly into the middle of the rear end of the truck.

The Caddy didn't respond.

Hank turned the wheel again, but the damn thing just spun in his hand.

The Caddy was totally out of control now. No brakes, no steering.

He held on tight to the wheel while shoving the back of his head against the padded head restraint.

All he could do now was wait. The Caddy had a life of its own.

It missed the section of the truck that Hank had tried to aim for. Instead, it clipped the side, causing the Caddy to spin.

Then it rolled.

Over and over again. For some strange reason Hank tried to count how many times the car flipped, but he lost his train of thought once his head banged against the side window.

The air bags deployed as soon as he'd clipped the back of the truck, but they deflated almost as quickly as they had inflated. Hank wondered why.

It didn't matter.

The Caddy was still rolling, and out of the corner of his eye Hank could see the guardrail looming during one of the rolls.

The SUV smashed into the rail, then up and over.

Suddenly the rolling of the Caddy was more graceful.

Silent.

It spun slowly in the air, and Hank could see the blue waters of Lake Union quickly approaching.

But it seemed so peaceful now. No more jarring and grating of metal against asphalt, or metal against metal.

It was just blue sky and blue water with each full revolution of the Cadillac.

Then a hard smack as the car crashed into the lake. Hank banged his head once more and this time it almost knocked him senseless.

He gasped in shock as the car nestled itself into the frigid waters of Lake Union. Water was somehow finding its way inside, even though the windows were all closed.

He shifted the handle upwards and rammed his shoulder against the door. But the water pressure outside prevented it from budging even an inch.

While hopelessly pressing down on the now impotent power window buttons, he cursed himself for forgetting to open them before the impact with the truck.

That impact seemed so long ago now.

The car shifted front down and began its dramatic death dive.

As Hank Price sucked in what he knew was going to be his last breath, he was vaguely aware of a fading tune on the radio.

A familiar and soothing male voice, crooning about chestnuts roasting somewhere.

16

It was only the first week of January, but Christmas and the celebratory turn of the New Year were already a distant memory. To Sandy, those dates didn't even exist anymore. He always avoided the malls and shops in the days and weeks leading up to that painful time of the year; a time that was now erased from his mental calendar.

This had been the third holiday season without his family, and he knew now first hand that it was true what everyone said—that Christmas for some people was the saddest time of the year.

He wasn't a Scrooge about it, though. He still wished people Merry Christmas and Happy New Year, but those refrains were empty to him now. And when he saw decorated Christmas trees and happy families out for walks, he didn't begrudge them their joy. But, he couldn't help wiping tears from his eyes.

The tears just came so easily for him whenever he saw scenes that reminded him of his own Christmases past.

He would never have those days back.

All he had were his memories, but the saddest part of all was that he didn't even want those memories lurking in the recesses of his mind. Memories were supposed to be the supreme treasures of life, but for him they were like torture.

He knew that it was a paradox. Even though the festive time of the year hurt him to his core, he still lived in the same house with the same things that were around when his family was alive. He didn't really understand why that was, but the house with all its memories gave him some semblance of comfort, whereas Christmas scenes being enjoyed by other families caused him pain.

Perhaps it was just the sight of people alive and happy that caused him angst, whereas his home was still his safe place, even with all its inert memories. Life itself, with all its real-time happiness on display, was the problem for him, he guessed.

Sandy shook his head and snapped out of his daydream. Driving along the network of interstates wasn't the smartest time to be off in a trance. He squinted his eyes and focused on the road ahead.

He'd left Boston almost four hours ago. Decided to take Interstate 95 instead of the coastal secondary roads. Even though it was unusually dry and mild for January, he didn't want to take a chance on the smaller highways despite the fact that the scenery would have been better.

He took the I-295 turnoff and continued along until veering off onto I-278, which took him across the RFK Bridge. He was now in the Queens borough of New York City, which was southeast of the Bronx. He knew that John Nichols had lived in the Bronx, just a short drive away from his wife and daughter in Queens. He winced as he thought of John's death and how sad his last few years must have been, ostracized by his own family. They had lived so close to him—yet, so far.

Judy knew he was coming. He'd set the date with her the previous week, and he could tell by her voice over the phone that she was excited to be seeing him again.

Sandy was excited too, but also apprehensive.

The last time he'd seen Judy had been at her wedding, which must have been about twenty years ago, give or take. Normally, seeing an old friend wouldn't be stressful for him, but with the history they'd had together during their college days, this was a wee bit different. And, how Lincoln Berwick had lied and schemed to break them up just so he could swoop in and take his place.

She lived in the Astoria neighborhood in northwest Queens, a nice middle-class area with easy access to mass transit. Judy had told him over the phone that she was a teacher at a local high school—science and physical education.

She was also the coach of the gymnastics team, which didn't surprise Sandy in the least considering the star athlete she'd been back in her days at Barnard College. He was surprised she'd never tried out for the U.S. Olympic team, since she'd already won medals at the international level, but she told him that she had never wanted to be that competitive an athlete. She preferred teaching instead, inspiring young people to achieve beyond their expectations and just to enjoy the sport. That didn't surprise Sandy either—she'd always been a humble person and just a special kind of sweetheart.

His first love.

Sandy steered his sleek Lexus coupe down a couple of side streets into the center of Astoria, then made his final turn onto Crescent Street. He pulled up in front of number 207 and parked his car along the curb. There was no driveway or garage, but he couldn't help but admire the character of Judy's two-storey Georgian home. Glancing up and down the street, he decided in an instant that her house was the nicest on the block. Just another thing that didn't surprise him.

He walked slowly up the cobblestone pathway onto the front porch. Took a deep breath and rang the doorbell.

The door opened after the first ring, and Sandy's heart skipped a beat.

Judy stood in the doorway—well, really only his memory of Judy stood there. This was a young replica of the girl he used to love. He knew that her name was Cynthia and that she was fifteen years old, but she looked more like college age. Virtually identical to the vision of the girl he first saw standing across the dance floor, beckoning him to come over to her. He chuckled to himself—glad she'd inherited her mom's looks and not the ugly mug of his old friend, John.

Sandy held out his hand. "You must be Cynthia. I'm Sandy."

She rejected his hand. Instead, Cynthia threw her arms around him and gave him a big hug. Then she pulled back and smiled coyly at him. "Here in Queens we give hugs, Professor. Mom has told me all about you, particularly the part where you were her first love!"

Sandy felt himself blushing as she led him into the foyer.

"You look just like your mother did, Cynthia, when she was only a wee bit older than you. It's uncanny how much you look alike."

She took his jacket and hung it in the hall closet. "I love your car,

Professor. Will you take me for a spin later? Pretty please?"

Sandy laughed, more at how precocious and outgoing she was, than at her question.

"Of course I will, if it's okay with your mom. And quit calling me Professor."

"It'll be okay with mom. She'll want to go with us, but only if you open the sunroof."

"It's January, Cynthia. Hardly sunroof weather."

She shook her head, long hair swooping across her face. "No, it's perfect sunroof weather. I insist!"

"Okay, we'll be a little wild and crazy then. Deal."

She twirled several strands of hair in her right hand. Then cocked her head. "So, if I can't call you Professor, what should I call you? I know you have a PhD, so should I call you Doctor, then?"

"Absolutely not. You're a young lady now, so I want you to call me, Sandy. Okay?"

She squealed with delight. "I'd love that. Makes me feel so mature."

Sandy glanced into the front living room. He noticed it was adorned with several beautiful antique tables along with a line of plush chairs and couches. Easy on the eyes. He always knew that Judy had good taste, so this was the way he would have pictured her abode to look.

Cynthia's warm welcome and friendly banter had chased his butterflies away. His mouth was no longer dry, and his breathing was much more relaxed. He was anxious to see Judy now, no longer apprehensive.

He turned towards Cynthia. "So, where's your mom? Is she hiding from me?"

"No! In fact, don't tell her I said this, but she's been busy making herself pretty for you. She'll be down in a few minutes, don't worry."

Suddenly a voice from the top of the center hall stairway. "I heard you, dear daughter. Thanks for embarrassing me."

Cynthia squealed again, and exclaimed, "Oops!" Then she ran toward the back of the house, leaving Sandy all alone, gaping at the vision of loveliness sashaying down the majestic Georgian staircase.

Judy smiled as she got closer. "I really didn't plan this grand entrance, Sandy. You're a bit early. Now, you'd better promise that you'll catch me if my nervousness causes a misstep."

He extended his arms out wide. "I'm ready for you."

Judy swooped into his arms. They hugged for what seemed like several minutes, but was in reality only a few seconds.

Then they pulled back and gave each other the once-over.

She was still the beautiful girl he remembered. A few worry lines on her forehead, and her eyes were a bit bloodshot, but he figured she'd probably had a few sleepless nights lately knowing he was coming. She still wore her auburn hair long just like when she was in college, and the green color of her eyes was as alluring as ever.

"You're still the handsome stud you were in college, Sandy. My gosh, you've hardly aged at all. Your hair is still blonde, and your eyes are as blue as ever." She then looked him up and down. "And, no fat!"

"I was just thinking the same about you—you haven't changed much either. Despite the tough times we've both had, I guess we can be glad that life hasn't taken too much of a toll on us yet."

She leaned in and kissed him on the cheek. "Thanks for coming. So, what do you think of Cynthia?"

"She's a ball of fire, and a mini-you. When she answered the door, it took me back in time."

Judy took his hand and led him towards the back of the house, into the spacious and elegant kitchen. There was a bottle of Bordeaux on the table, along with two glasses.

"Yes, she is a handful, and full of spirit. I need to keep a close eye on that girl."

"She'll be a heartbreaker one day, Judy."

She looked up at him, and then quickly lowered her eyes. "Kinda like me, huh?"

Sandy realized that he'd struck a sensitive chord—and so early in their reunion, too.

"A slip of the tongue. You know I didn't mean it that way. But, if we're being accurate, your heart was broken first."

"True. Not by anything you did, but by what that psychopath Lincoln framed you for."

Sandy sat down at the table and picked up the wine bottle. "Can I pour you a glass?"

"Yes, indeed. Let's catch up a bit and try to avoid talking about Senator Lincoln Berwick."

Sandy grimaced. "I'd like that, but I have the funny feeling that he's going to creep into the conversation somewhere along the way."

They spent the next three hours, and two bottles of wine, talking about all that had happened in their lives since the last time they'd seen each other. And, a lot had happened.

To Sandy, chatting with Judy seemed like they'd never been apart. After all these years, it was as if they'd been away from each other for just a week or two. It was nice.

And nice that he was able to talk about the tragedy that he'd endured. There weren't many people he could talk to about that, but with Judy it was easy. She'd suffered tough times as well, and Sandy could tell that she'd still loved John right up until the day he died. She just couldn't allow herself or her daughter to be near him anymore. He was toxic and self-destructive.

She didn't know why he became that way, but Sandy knew. He didn't have the heart to tell her that part of the story yet, but he knew he would summon the courage eventually. He felt that she deserved to know, because it was clear that she blamed herself for John's depression. She thought that there was something about their relationship together that drove him down into the depths of doom.

To the point, eventually, of suicide.

And Sandy wasn't yet convinced that it was suicide. The note and the cassette tape would open the door for him, he was sure. He suspected that John had been dabbling in blackmail, which had put his life in peril.

Sandy took a long sip of his wine. "Are you ready to let me see the note and hear the tape?"

She nodded.

Judy walked over to a built-in desk on the other side of the kitchen. Came back with a padded envelope in one hand, and an old cassette player in the other.

"Here. The note and tape are inside."

Sandy opened the envelope and took out a single piece of paper. Right away he recognized John's distinctive handwriting. As Judy had told him over the phone, the note said that he would soon have a substantial amount of money to give to her and Cynthia. But that she wasn't to listen to the tape—that, instead, she should keep it safe and sound in case something were to happen to him. If something did, the note instructed her to make sure the tape was given to Sandford Beech as soon as possible.

Which was what had brought Sandy and Judy together right now, at her kitchen table, drinking wine.

Sandy reached into the envelope again and took out the cassette tape. He then plugged in the player and inserted the tape. He had a good suspicion as to what this tape was about, although he'd never known that there was a tape. John never told him about it, probably to protect him.

Sandy had spoken on his behalf to the dean, without identifying him, and told the entire sordid story about the rape and death of the fourteen-year-old girl. But, he'd had no idea there was a tape about the incident. He couldn't imagine this tape being about anything else, knowing that the guilt and horror of that incident was what had driven John to self-destruction during his short life.

He looked up at Judy, and grimaced. "Time for you to leave the room."

She pointed her index finger at him. "No goddamn way. I'm listening to that tape."

Sandy shook his head. "That wasn't John's wish. His last will and testament was that you give this tape to me and that you weren't to listen to it. We have to respect that."

"He doesn't deserve my respect. He took his own life. That act made any last wish null and void."

Sandy lowered his eyes. "I have a suspicion as to what this tape is about, Judy. I know some things you don't know. John wanted to protect you. If what I think is on this tape, it might make you sick to your stomach."

She shook her head defiantly. "He was my husband, and I'm not some delicate flower that you have to protect. I can handle whatever is on there. Do this for me."

Sandy paused for a few seconds. Then, he just nodded his head forlornly, made the sign of the cross, and pushed the Play button.

17

"Calm down. Be a man. You're pathetic."

(Sound of sobbing.)

"I'm…trying. But…I can't…get her…out of my mind."

"She was a slut. No one gives a shit about her."

(More sobbing. The sound of a slap against flesh.)

"Oh, now you're hitting me just like you hit that little girl? The all-powerful Lincoln Berwick, hitting a child. Proud of yourself?"

"Hey, John, you thought she was older too. Wasn't just me. And you didn't hesitate to stick your dick in her mouth, did you?"

(Something hard slamming down on the floor.)

"Sure, but only your cum is inside her, Linc. That could tie you to her."

(Another slap.)

"It's just cum, you jerk. Doesn't prove anything. They can't prove whose cum it is."

"They could—you never know."

"No, they can't, John. So shut the fuck up. Why the hell are you crying over a little slut? What was she to you?"

"Her name was Monica Harwell, Linc. She was a little girl, and you killed her. Why the fuck did you have to hit her so hard? Or, at all? She wasn't hurting you. So, why?"

(The sound of a punch.)

"Because she tricked us. Made us think she was older. That's why. She deserved it."

(More sobbing.)

"Deserved to die? And to be dumped like a sack of garbage in a ditch? Is Orange County Road Number Six the grave site she deserved just for being fourteen?"

(A softer tone of voice.)

"John, you were the brave one. You tried to save her. The rest of us didn't know what to do. You can't take any blame for this. You're right. I hit her, and I dumped her. I did it out of panic. But, we can't ruin our lives over her. We have to be together on this, all five of us. Buds forever."

"What if the police come here, Linc? They're going to find her body, and where you dumped her isn't that far from campus. They might assume West Point guys were involved."

"So what? There's nothing connecting us to her. Except my cum—and my cum doesn't exactly have my signature on it. If they come here, they'll ask some questions of the staff and some of the boys, and if they ask us we just deny. That's the secret to freedom, John. Denial. Deny, deny, deny. Don't crack. And, I'm your leader. I'm the Commander of the Honor Guild. I have your back. Just follow my lead."

(A deep, fitful sigh.)

"I just don't know, Linc. I'm scared."

(A rustling noise, then what sounded like a body banging against a wall.)

"Stop! Knock it off! Damn, now I've twisted my ankle, and I have track practice this aft!"

"Fuck off, John. Who gives a shit about your ankle?"

(The voice turned deep and guttural.)

"I've tried to be reasonable. That's over—here's what's at stake for you. You will follow the Honor Code and respect your Commander. If you don't, I will kill you and dump you in the same ditch as your little slut, Monica. You can be together, forever. Your choice."

(A door slamming. Then silence.)

Sandy pushed the Stop button on the tape player and glanced up at Judy. He'd forced himself not to look at her face while the tape was playing.

Her eyes were as wide as saucers, and she was covering her mouth tightly with her right hand. Her left hand trembled as she clenched and unclenched a fist—over and over again.

"Are you okay?"

Judy shook her head.

Sandy got up from his chair, walked around the kitchen table and hugged her from behind. Nestling his cheek against hers he could hear her breaths, labored and anguished. Listening to her husband's young voice on tape was probably shocking in itself, but the subject matter of the recording was no doubt more than she could have imagined. Sandy thought that maybe he should have given her an advance warning of what he'd expected.

"I had no idea, Sandy. He never told me about this—thing—that happened."

Sandy backed away from her and knelt down on the floor, taking her hand in his.

"I'm so sorry, Judy. I know this is a shock to you. But, it might explain why John descended into depression and alcoholism. You can give yourself a break, now. It had nothing to do with you."

She stared into his eyes. "You knew about this. Were you there? Were you one of the five?"

He shook his head.

"No. But, John confided in me. I went to the dean on his behalf, but kept his name out of it. I told the dean that someone had confessed the incident to me, and I identified Lincoln Berwick as the leader, the rapist, and the killer. The dean assured me that justice would be exacted, but nothing happened. Well, nothing except that I got booted out of the Honor Guild, followed a year later by John. I got kicked out for violating the Honor Code, and John got booted for being a drunk."

"What's this stupid Honor Code?"

"It's hard to describe, almost a sacred rite of passage. They take it more seriously than the law itself. You violate it at your peril, and serious offenses get overlooked for the greater good. There are some things about the Honor Guild itself that are kind of weird. It was an elite group of young men, all high achievers, all high IQs. Futures were determined for each boy, and plans would be put into place to make sure those futures happened."

Sandy took a deep breath. "After a few years in the program, high level sponsors would be assigned to each kid, kind of like career guides or—a more apt description would be like guardian angels. I didn't get far enough into the program to have a guide assigned, nor did I ever find out how each of us had been selected in the first place. We were all West Point students to begin with, but quickly got shuffled into this special Honor Guild unit. Because we were apparently 'special.' I guess if I'd lasted in the program I would have learned more about what it was all about, but I might also have been more beholden to it. I don't regret getting the boot."

Judy seemed to be regaining her composure. "So, how did they all end up being with this girl?"

"They picked her up in a van. Thought she was a hooker. John was the one who discovered she was only fourteen, by seeing her age on her library card. Warned Linc as he was in the middle of—fucking her. Linc got mad, hit her hard across the face, and her head slammed into the side of the van. Went into a seizure. John apparently tried real hard to save her, it's important you know that. But, she died. Then Linc just dumped her by the side of the road, and kicked her body into a ditch."

Judy seethed, "Bastard."

"That word is far too kind."

"Did the police ever investigate? Did they visit West Point?"

Sandy shook his head. "Not that we know of. We checked the newspapers for weeks after the incident. Nothing. Makes you wonder, doesn't it?"

"Covered up?"

Sandy nodded. "I think so."

Judy shook her head. "Unbelievable. Her poor parents, never knowing what happened to her."

"That incident shook John to his core, and he was despondent when nothing was done. He never told me he'd made a tape—kept that as his own private secret. I don't know why, maybe to protect me since I went to bat for him. It's such an incriminating thing, that he might have been afraid for both me and him. And he held onto it for all these years—maybe he thought he could use it one day."

Judy squeezed Sandy's hand. "He did try to use it, didn't he? You know something."

Sandy squeezed back.

"I know as much as you know. But, I suspect that's where this windfall of money was going to come from. Sounds like blackmail, and not in the least bit a coincidence that Lincoln Berwick is now a presidential candidate. I think John saw this as an opportunity to finally do something worthwhile with his life. Extort some money from the bastard and use it to take care of you and Cynthia. Make amends."

Judy started crying. "He was murdered. It wasn't suicide. Linc killed him."

Sandy nodded sadly. "The dots seem to connect. I doubt that the coward would have done the deed himself. He has people now for things like that. But, if this old skeleton got out of the closet, it would have devastated his campaign, let alone his freedom."

Judy stood up and started pacing.

"Sandy, listening to that tape, there was something that wasn't characteristic of John. At times, he was sobbing like a baby. And, he let Linc smack him around and didn't fight back. Instead, he just whined. He sounded pathetic."

"I think he was play-acting. John was a very intelligent man. He knew how to get as much as possible on that tape. In fact, I think he was brilliant. One time John and I were having drinks and, as we got drunker and drunker, and babbled and babbled, we discovered we had both been conceived by artificial insemination. Isn't that a weird coincidence? We joked about how smart we both were and that maybe we even had the same father and didn't know it. But, I think John's gray cells were a lot more powerful than mine. Such a waste."

"Yes, such a waste. I regret that Cynthia never really knew the man that he used to be. But, Sandy, no matter how down or depressed John was at times, I don't remember ever seeing him cry. And he knew how to defend himself—he wouldn't let anyone push him around."

"I agree. John wasn't being himself on that recording. Sly dog.

He was smart in other ways too, Judy. He made sure to get the name of the girl on the tape, her age, and also the location where her body was dumped. He took a chance doing that, but Linc didn't seem to clue in at all. I think that's why John went into his crying wimp act—to distract Linc from the specific information he was getting on tape."

Judy stopped her pacing and sat down again.

"Who were the other three?"

"I've lost touch with them over the years, and I don't think they were all that close with Linc, or John either for that matter. They were just kids out cruising around, wilding, and things got out of hand. But, I saw them at a couple of West Point reunions over the years. Hank Price became a bigwig engineer at Boeing. Lloyd Franken moved up to the top ranks at NASA. And Bill Tomkins, the guy I knew the best out of the three, became a Wall Street banker."

Judy smirked. "They did well. The Honor Guild paid off."

"Yep. All three graduated from it, along with Linc, of course. And, they're all perfect examples of what I was talking about. Linc might be the next president, and the other three are all in influential positions of power. Their careers were chosen for them, and they were guided along—or, manipulated. Who knows?"

"But, you did okay, Sandy, despite being kicked out of this—Guild thing."

"Yeah, I did. Professor at MIT and now the Lincoln Laboratory as well. Can't complain. West Point does give a good education, but I sometimes wonder what kind of power position I would have been steered towards if I hadn't flunked out of the Honor Guild."

"You might not have been as happy."

"No, but I'm not happy now anyway, so I guess the end result was the same."

Judy wrapped her arms around his neck and kissed him on the cheek.

Sandy broke the awkward moment with a question. "Do you have your computer handy? We could look these three guys up and see how they're doing?"

Judy opened a drawer and pulled out a laptop, fired it up, and passed it over to him.

Sandy searched for Lloyd Franken first.

"Here he is. Still at NASA. Says here that he's the senior astronomer, responsible for near-earth objects and defensive capabilities."

Next up was Hank Price.

"There's old Hank. A nice pic of him—still a handsome dude. Chief engineer at Boeing. Oh—what's this?"

Judy rubbed his hand. "What? Tell me."

Sandy looked at her, then back at the screen again. "He's dead. Died in a recent car accident. His vehicle rolled off the highway into a lake near Seattle. Says here that he might have fallen asleep at the wheel."

He googled Bill Tomkins next.

"There's Bill—a good photo of him, too. Still looks the same, pretty much. CEO of an investment banking firm on Wall Street. I always liked Bill. A special kind of guy, different from most of the guys at West Point. A very hard nut to crack, but once you did, he was nice to be around. We always hit it off."

He scrolled down further.

"What's this?" Sandy swallowed hard before continuing. "A news article here says that he fended off a couple of thugs in his office. Says here that it was a robbery gone wrong, and they attacked him and his niece. Bill killed them both in self-defence. Happened just recently, just before Hank's death."

Judy squeezed his arm. "John's death is recent, too, Sandy."

Sandy stood, walked over to the window, and gazed out at Judy's large backyard. "Your grass is still very green for January. Looks great."

Judy joined him at the window. "You're thinking what I'm thinking, aren't you? That these can't be coincidences? Out of the original five from that van, John is dead, Hank is dead, and Bill would be dead if he hadn't killed the attackers instead. There are only two left who haven't been killed or attacked—that Lloyd guy at NASA and Lincoln."

"Yes, and John was the first to die. Clearly, he was trying to blackmail Linc."

"Linc decided to take out all the other loose ends? Just in case?"

"Maybe. And that means that Lloyd will be next, and very soon. They'll probably leave Bill alone for a while. It might look too obvious if they tried again so soon with him. And he'll be on his guard, too."

Sandy could sense that Judy was shivering. He wrapped his arm around her shoulder and gave it a squeeze.

She turned her gaze away from the backyard and ran her fingers through Sandy's hair.

"You have such nice thick hair. Did you notice that all three of those men you googled had blonde hair just like you?"

Sandy laughed. "Yeah, I did. Well, mine's a little bit darker than theirs, more dirty blonde."

"John had blonde hair, too."

Sandy nodded.

She continued fingering the hair on the back of his head.

"And, so does Linc."

He nodded again, then reached back and grabbed hold of her wandering hand, stopping it in its tracks.

Judy tapped the fingers of her free hand against the windowpane. "Don't you think that's weird, Sandy?"

18

It was located on the tenth floor of a rather normal looking office tower on West Street in Lower Manhattan, appropriately only a block away from Goldman Sachs.

Appropriate, because the motivations of the two companies were similar.

Power and money.

But that's where the similarities ended.

Goldman Sachs was high profile and always in the public eye. You couldn't ignore Goldman Sachs, and it would have been negligent for its executives to allow it to be ignored. Publicity was what it thrived on, and its business model was based entirely on being top of mind and first at the table for any mergers and acquisitions that needed money and expertise.

The tenth floor of 400 West Street, on the other hand, was low profile. It only had a handful of employees, and its business model required it to remain low profile, and secretive to all except America's richest and most powerful.

Even though companies like Goldman Sachs prided themselves on planning for the longer term, in reality that wasn't the case. Not with the demands placed on executives by shareholders. Fortune 500 companies could pretend all they wanted to, but long-term thinking was not the reality for their business models. Instead, short-term shareholder value was paramount.

The occupant of 400 West Street, however, was a behemoth in long-term thinking, and its impact on the corporate, scientific, military, and political worlds was immeasurable. In fact, if anyone attempted to place a value on the company in the interests of an IPO, it would be virtually impossible to measure or quantify.

The company was, in a word, priceless.

Legacy Life Ladder Incorporated took deposits.

And they sold those deposits only when the time was right, and when the buyer was right. But, different from any other corporation, the selling price of its deposits was immaterial. In fact, even profits were immaterial. It only charged enough to cover expenses, because margins meant nothing in its business model.

In some ways, the company was like a charity, just without the tax advantages. Its view of the world was decades in advance. In fact, deposits sold today wouldn't see a payoff until forty or more years down the road.

After more than half a century in existence, it was only within the last few years that the guardians of the corporation were finally seeing the first fruits of its labors. In fact, some of the original founders of the company hadn't even lived long enough to see this wonderful payoff.

Legacy Life Ladder Incorporated was a cumbersome name, albeit describing the purpose of the company perfectly. But, it took far too long to say. So, for those in the know, it was simply referred to as Triple-L.

Triple-L was a sperm bank.

The practise of donating sperm for human conception dated as far back as the eighteenth century. But, it took until the early twentieth century for efforts to begin on freezing and storing sperm.

Then, science took it all to a new level in the 1950s when research led to cryobiology innovations, resulting in the launch of the world's first sperm bank after a successful birth from cryopreserved sperm.

It's not easy for men to make money from sperm donations. Most banks require that the man be between eighteen and forty years of age, must be willing to commit to at least six months of jerking off in a controlled environment, provide two or three generations of medical history, and have no chronic health problems. Some banks require that the man have a college degree, and be at least of a certain height.

If a man qualifies on those basic counts, he then has to provide several sperm samples for testing. If the sperm count is high, the candidate is then tested for sexually transmitted or genetic diseases, and even has to undergo an interview and medical examination. Serious business.

Usually the screening takes about three months, and less than five percent of applicants are accepted by the typical sperm bank. Successful candidates sign a contract and consent to ongoing health checks. Pay rates range from $100 upwards per donation. Lucrative, particularly for students.

But, it's not as secret a process as some are led to believe. Donor profiles are made available to potential recipients, including family history, recordings of the donor's voice, as well as childhood and adult photos.

Semen samples are treated with a solution that protects them from damage during freezing and thawing. Then they're placed in vials, sealed up, and slowly put through a freezing process in liquid nitrogen vapor. The frozen samples are maintained at a mind-numbing temperature of minus 320 degrees Fahrenheit.

The only real difference between fresh and frozen sperm is the time of survival. Frozen sperm only lasts for about twenty-four hours in a woman's uterus, whereas fresh sperm can survive for up to five days.

Most people would be surprised to know that frozen sperm has no expiration date, providing that the storage environment is stable and uninterrupted. Reports from the recognized sperm banks have recorded normal conceptions and births from sperm frozen for almost thirty years.

Triple-L, which enjoys the luxury of not having to report to any regulatory body whatsoever, has recorded births from sperm frozen for over sixty years.

Meagan Whitfield pushed the button for the elevator that would take her to the tenth floor of 400 West Street. When she exited on that floor, there would be no signs, or logos, or even the name of the company displayed on the directory board. Nothing to welcome her except a heavy wooden door blocking entrance or visibility to anyone not having a magnetic security card.

She left the elevator and inserted her card in the reader. The door clicked and Meagan entered the antiseptic hallway that led to a row of offices. She knew which office she wanted—the corner one at the end of the hall. She walked along, waving to several people along the way. They all knew her. She was one of the owners of Triple-L.

She knocked on the corner office door and entered without waiting for a welcome.

Dr. Derek Schmidt was the managing director. A geneticist with German roots, he was now seventy years old. Meagan knew that in a few years he'd have to be replaced, but for now he was still as sharp as ever. And committed. Meagan liked commitment.

They shook hands, and Meagan sat down in the guest chair across from Derek's desk.

"How are you, Derek?"

"Doing just fine." He chuckled. "Business is as good as ever."

"Yes, and we have a lot of work still to do. You must be excited, though, seeing our first creations finally making their marks in the world."

He nodded enthusiastically. "It is exciting to watch. Sometimes I feel like Dr. Frankenstein. The pride of knowing that all of our work decades ago, and all of our nurturing along the way, is showing itself now in leadership positions. And, Christ, now we even have a presidential candidate!"

Meagan smiled. "Yes, I share your excitement. As you know, I'm on the campaign team for Senator Berwick, and, while he's a bit of a handful at times, we do a good job of keeping him in line. Hopefully, though, he won't be our only hope. We have to have...fallback plans."

Derek laughed. "No surprise that you'd have contingency plans. And, knowing you, Meagan, I'm sure you're up to the task."

"I am. Anyway, I wanted to ask you if you'd thought any more about our conversation a couple of weeks ago—about expanding and modernizing our donor supply."

Derek clasped his hands together, and his voice suddenly took on a more serious tone.

"I have, and for now I would recommend we just stay the course. The human stock in the last couple of decades has shown significant decline and dilution. Our stock right now consists of about 200,000 samples, taken from only fifty elite donors. The sperm ranges in age from thirty to sixty years old, and it far exceeds the quality of any samples we could take today from younger populations. I'm not telling you anything new here, by emphasizing that the younger populations don't hold a candle to their ancestors. The human species has declined dramatically, not only in health, but in gray cells."

Meagan grimaced. "I suspected you'd say that. It was just an idea, but I respect your opinion. As long as we have sufficient supplies to last us a few more years, then we probably shouldn't try to fix what ain't broke."

"I'm glad you agree. Those fifty donors come from Danish, Austrian and German pure stock. It's very hard to find pure stock anymore, so we're lucky to have the best of the best here."

Meagan stood, signalling that their meeting was over.

"Alright then, Doctor. We're done for today. We have a board meeting next week. Are you prepared?"

Derek stood as well, and held out his hand. "As always. And, I'll fill the board in on what you and I have discussed today."

Meagan shook his hand. "Good. We'll just have to warn the board that we'll continue to have leaders with blonde hair and blue eyes for the foreseeable future."

Derek laughed and ran his fingers through his blondish hair. "And, what's wrong with that?"

19

He raised his right hand to his forehead in salute. Which was the way he always ended his meetings—well, at least those meetings that went well.

Those who knew Lloyd Franken, also knew that was his signal that a conference was over. He saluted them as his little way of saying thanks and also just a polite way of telling them to get the hell out of his office.

"Okay, folks, see you all tomorrow—we'll meet at 9:00 a.m. sharp. And, Todd, remember that I need those projections desperately."

Todd Blake smiled and nodded. "Don't worry, boss, I'll have them. But, if they're not ready, I'll treat to the donuts and coffee."

Lloyd laughed and patted him on the back. "Correction. If they're not ready, you'll have lots of free unpaid time for donuts and coffee."

Todd smirked. "Luckily, I know you're really just a teddy bear under that Roman emperor exterior."

Lloyd closed the door behind them, then poured himself a glass of water. Sitting down at his desk, he removed his shoes, swiveled his chair around, and rested his feet up on the windowsill.

His office at NASA's Johnson Space Center faced west. Which was nice, because he could look clear across the five-mile expanse to where his home was in the quaint town of El Lago, one of the Houston area's most exclusive communities. His days were long, but the reward for him was being able to relax in the evenings on the dock at his waterfront home on Taylor Lake. "Dock" was an understatement, of course. The dock itself was just the floating extension of a full-fledged boathouse just fifty feet away from his mansion.

Lloyd's wife, Cassidy, was a bit overwhelmed with the home—said it was too big for them and too much work to keep up with. But Lloyd had finally convinced her to hire a gardener and a housekeeper. She felt sheepish about such extravagance, but agreed that as long as they were going to be living in the lap of luxury, she needed some help.

Lloyd had to agree to something too, though. She wanted children and he'd resisted that for years. Yes, it would be nice, and they certainly could afford to give them a good life.

The expense of having kids had never been the reason for his inertia. No, instead it was the uncertainty of it. Because he just didn't know his own background, and he'd never told Cassidy that he'd been the product of artificial insemination. She asked him if he'd been adopted, because she knew neither of his parents had the Nordic looks that he possessed. He just explained it away as some kind of recessive gene.

When he was a young man, he'd confronted his parents on his wish to know the ancestors on his biological father's side, and who the sperm donor was. They told him the name of the sperm bank—Legacy Life Ladder Inc.—but also told him that it wasn't a normal sperm bank. While most of those types of establishments would give details if the donors allowed it, at this particular bank there was a strict policy of no background information except for the donor's country of origin.

Lloyd's donor was from Denmark.

He'd contacted the Legacy sperm bank himself, and they simply confirmed what his parents had already told him. No information whatsoever would be provided.

It felt strange to Lloyd not to know his own history, and he felt guilty not being able to assure Cassidy that his background had no surprises. So far, she hadn't pushed on it, but he had no idea how she'd react if she knew he was the product of a sperm gift. All she knew about him was that he had movie star looks and the IQ of a genius. Maybe those two things would keep her curiosity at bay?

Lloyd figured that his donor father, though, would no doubt be proud of his unknown offspring. He glanced up at his framed degrees mounted on the wall. Two PhDs—one in astrophysics and the other in aeronautical engineering. And he was recognized at NASA as the chief astronomer, which carried with it the added responsibility of overseeing the most disturbing project of all—searching for, documenting, and preparing defensive plans, for near-earth objects.

That responsibility had also thrust him into the role of director of the Orion project, a massive undertaking that would propel NASA into a new age of human space travel. Orion would take humans farther into space than any of the previous Apollo, Gemini, and Mercury programs, and would certainly be more impressive than the now defunct space shuttle program. It would be the safest and most advanced spacecraft ever built and had its eyes on Mars. Of particular interest to Lloyd, it included a plan to land on one deep space asteroid that posed a future danger to Earth.

Orion's first test orbit was successfully launched back in 2014. In fact, it was two full orbits, not just one, and the mission took only four hours. It was a complete and total success, and the future looked promising. He knew Orion would keep him busy for decades to come.

Which reminded him of his last meeting of the day. He looked at his watch—his guest should be arriving any minute now. They were heading out to dinner at a country manor restaurant called The Greenhouse. It was a bit out of the way, but his guest mentioned that he'd heard good things about it and, well, dinner was the man's treat so Lloyd wasn't going to complain. Even though he'd prefer instead a local restaurant so he could get home early to his dock on the lake.

His meeting was with an executive from Virgin Galactic. A senior vice president by the name of James Whitehead, apparently based out of Virgin's Long Beach, California, research facility. Back in 2011, NASA had signed a cooperation contract with Virgin for joint research projects, but nothing of any value had resulted so far. In fact, as far as Lloyd was concerned the relationship had just been one big yawn. Virgin had suffered several launch disasters, and investors were clamoring for results. Their dreams of being able to provide space tourism and satellite launches was rapidly fizzling.

But Lloyd was confident that Richard Branson would eventually get his act together. The delays were reportedly due to his legendary concern for perfection and safety, and Lloyd couldn't fault him for that. He'd met the man once, and who couldn't be impressed by Sir Richard?

This James Whitehead guy had requested the dinner meeting a couple of days ago. Said it would be the impetus for a proposed increase in their contract work with NASA. Wanted to engage NASA's help with their new Launcher One orbiter, and some innovative ideas for their Newton 4 rocket engine—something to do with their attempts at creating a new plastic fuel.

Lloyd had no problems working with other space entities—Elon Musk's SpaceX was another organization NASA had close ties with, and as far as he was concerned the more cooperation the better. And the extra side income to NASA was always appreciated, considering budget constraints.

So, he'd have dinner with James Whitehead and see where it might lead. As long as he was home in time for martinis on the dock with Cassidy, he'd be a happy man. Tonight was one of the nights she told him she'd be in her prime fertile zone. Baby-making was in her plans, and there'd be hell to pay if Lloyd was too late. Maybe they could get a bit wild and crazy and conceive the child on the dock?

Lloyd turned his mind reluctantly to the strange call he'd received the other day from his old school-mate, Sandy Beech. He hadn't talked to Sandy in years, and then, out of the blue, there he was on the phone.

He didn't know what to make of the call. It was nice to hear from Sandy, but it was disturbing as hell.

First of all, he'd had no idea that Sandy knew about that ancient incident with the fourteen-year-old girl. Lloyd had blocked that girl's death—and his role in it—out of his mind over the last couple of decades. He didn't like having to revisit it again. His mind had been trained to block out unpleasantness.

Sandy told him about the deaths of John Nichols and Hank Price, and the attempt on the life of Bill Tomkins. Said he was phoning him out of the utmost concern. Told him about a tape that John had left for him and that he suspected the deaths were a result of John attempting to blackmail Lincoln Berwick—the esteemed Senator Lincoln Berwick—and probably soon to be President Lincoln Berwick.

Lloyd was taken aback. While he'd trained his mind to block it out of his consciousness, deep in the recesses he'd always wondered if that skeleton from the past would come back to haunt them.

But it was so long ago.

And Sandy's warning sounded so much like a conspiracy theory. Would Lincoln really resort to murder to bury this scandal? While John might indeed have been blackmailing Linc, Lloyd hadn't talked to him since graduation from West Point. Lloyd wasn't a threat to him and wouldn't even consider resurrecting that horrible incident. He just wanted it forgotten, buried, erased.

But his powerful brain cautioned himself. Two who were involved in that girl's rape and death were now deceased within mere weeks of each other. And a third was almost killed in his own office. Sure, with the two who died, one was an apparent suicide and the other was a car accident. So, could have just been coincidence. But the fact that Bill Tomkins was attacked around the same time led Lloyd to wonder. What if what Sandy was saying was true? If so, Linc was tying up loose ends fast. It was like a movie script.

Lloyd was shaken out of his pondering by the ring of his phone.

"Franken, here," he said, then recognized their receptionist's voice with the news that his appointment was here. "Sure, Mary, tell James I'll meet him in the lobby."

Lloyd forced the unpleasant thoughts out of his head, and positioned his brain back into business mode. Time for dinner, and hopefully some new revenue for NASA.

He took the elevator down to the lobby and walked over to greet the only one waiting at this late hour of the afternoon. James Whitehead looked the part of an executive. Well-dressed and poised like he was ready to take on the world. Well, maybe at least outer space.

They shook hands and headed out to the parking lot.

Lloyd led James to his Lincoln Navigator, and he drove out onto the country road which would lead to The Greenhouse—about a thirty-minute drive north.

They made small talk about Virgin's ambitious plans and James seemed to be well-informed on all aspects of their successes and failures so far. As a senior executive, he gave the impression he'd been empowered to make deals. Confidence practically oozed from his pores.

"So, you're looking to increase your activity with NASA, James?"

"Absolutely. We need some help on our new engines and fuel source, and we think you guys might have the answers for us. Of course, we'll share any discoveries together for equal benefit."

Lloyd nodded. "I think we can talk. While I'm not a particular fan of the new plastic fuel concept, it might have some merits if we can test it properly under controlled conditions."

James pointed to an intersection up ahead.

"Turn left at that junction, Lloyd."

"No, that won't take us anywhere, James. I know the way. The restaurant is straight along this road—another ten miles or so."

James voice suddenly turned cold. "Turn left, Lloyd."

Lloyd's stomach did a turn. He looked over at James. The executive's face was now a cold mask, and the large pistol in his hand was pointed at Lloyd's head.

In an instant, a myriad of thoughts went through Lloyd's mind. Not the least of which was Sandy's ominous warning, jumbled together with an image of Cassidy waiting for him on the dock with a pitcher of martinis.

But the one thought that was paramount in his quick brain was the car's accelerator. He slammed his foot to the floor and the powerful engine roared. The vehicle lurched forward and within seconds the speedometer indicated they were hurtling along at 140 miles per hour.

James yelled. "I'll put a bullet in your head right now! Slow this sucker down!"

Lloyd yelled back as he held his foot to the floor. "Fuck you, asshole!"

Then, with the steely determination that had been pounded into his brain back at West Point, he steered the car off the road, down an embankment, and directly toward a massive oak tree.

Eliminate the threat before anything else.

Lloyd flung his right hand to his side, and pushed down on the red latch release on his attacker's seatbelt, hearing the reassuring click. He was vaguely aware of the man's frantic attempts with his gun-free hand to slip it back into place.

As the tree loomed ahead, he saw the face of a child.

A young girl lying dead on a mattress, blood pouring from her forehead.

He could even smell the scene—the sickening, sweet odor of semen mixed with horny boy-sweat.

For the first time in years, Lloyd Franken felt tears in his eyes.

Tears that clouded his vision of the crash.

20

It was pouring rain in Lexington. The entire Boston area was under the angry shroud of a January storm, threatening to turn itself into a blizzard by evening.

Sandy waited in the dry comfort of his house foyer until he saw the car pull up in front. Then he made a mad dash out to the curb, holding yesterday's newspaper over his head for protection.

The door opened magically and he ducked inside, pulling shut the heavy bullet-proof shield of metal behind him.

The windows of the black stretch limousine were tinted, casting the interior of the massive vehicle in a dark gloom.

Cigarette smoke drifting up from the occupant sitting across from him only added to the atmosphere and served as a sober reminder of who he was meeting.

The custom-made Cadillac pulled away from the curb and cruised slowly down the street. The movement of the vehicle prompted the first words from his host.

"Feel free to crack the window open if the smoke bothers you, Dr. Beech."

Sandy shook his head.

"No, thanks. I'd rather not be the subject of gawkers. This car does draw attention. That's why I asked that you just meet me somewhere discreet instead."

"I had some business in downtown Boston this morning. Meeting this way was just more quick and convenient. I hope you don't mind."

Sandy pulled on the handle of the footrest, and stretched his legs out in the cavernous cabin.

"No, it's okay. I'm glad you agreed to meet."

The man poured himself a cup of coffee from a thermos resting in a side stand.

"Would you care for a cup, Doctor?"

"Yes, that would be fine. Thank you."

As the man poured, Sandy studied his expression. He seemed calm and relaxed, despite being formally dressed to the nines. A custom-tailored black suit, with matching vest. High collared starched shirt adorned with a pink silk tie.

Only real men wore pink.

Cool, calm and dapper was the essence of the man Sandy knew as Vito Romano. Consigliere to Boston's Ferrara crime family, reporting directly to the Godfather himself, Paolo Marino.

The man's demeanour oozed the same confidence as his appearance.

He had a dark "film noir" quality about him, reminiscent of gangster movies from the '50s. Broad shoulders, slim and trim build, perfectly coiffed dark hair, and a face that reminded Sandy of Tony Bennett in his early years.

Despite who he worked for, Sandy liked Vito. Had known him for several years now and, although their relationship had always been mutually helpful and friendly, it had remained formal and respectful.

Which was exactly the way Sandy wanted it.

Vito was the type of guy who could be comfortable at the race track, the opera, the occasional gangland shooting—or standing in front of a jury, which, being the Mafia family lawyer, he'd had to do on many an occasion.

He hadn't lost a case yet.

Vito took a long sip from his coffee cup, then broke the silence with his smooth velvety voice.

"Before we get into the reason for our meeting, I wanted to pass along thanks to you for that information on MIT admissions guidelines. Those changes were good for us to know in advance. We have several family members trying to get in there, and that inside track you gave us will be helpful."

Sandy nodded sheepishly.

"Glad to be of help."

Vito laughed.

"No, you're not. But, thanks for being polite and saying so. At least you can console yourself in knowing that those little secrets aren't anything related to national security. Like, you didn't exactly tell us about all those secret weapons you're working on at the Lincoln Laboratory, right?"

Sandy smiled.

"I'm not working on any secret weapons."

Vito returned the smile.

"No? You have nothing to do with something called the Pulsed Energy Projectile—the PEP?"

"Don't know what you're talking about, Vito."

Vito shrugged his shoulders. "Okay, we can do this dance together—as we usually do. Someday, maybe over a glass of expensive scotch, you'll tell me all about it."

"That will never happen, Vito."

The Mafioso placed his right hand over his heart and nodded.

"I respect you, Doctor. Just jazzing with you. You've never sold out to us—never taken a dime. Our relationship has always been one of just information exchange. That's admirable, compared to most of the people we know."

"Thanks."

The man opened a briefcase that was resting on the seat beside him and withdrew some papers.

Then he extinguished his cigarette and looked straight into Sandy's eyes.

"We're still sickened by what happened to your family, Doctor, and all the other families. I want you to know that our hearts were broken that day, and I can't imagine how you've managed to go on. I don't know if I could have been that strong."

Sandy lowered his eyes and nodded.

"We heard that the deputy mayor tried an ambush on you. And that you left his bodyguard in pretty bad shape—ended up in the hospital with a punctured larynx."

Sandy poured himself another cup of coffee from the thermos.

"Yes, and all I got for my trouble was an envelope with blank pages. I think he thought I was bluffing, shooting blanks."

"Mr. Christopher Clark has been on our payroll for a few years now, as you know. He's been a useful idiot, paving the way with certain city contracts and projects. We've paid him handsomely and, on a deputy mayor's salary, our offer was too tempting for him to ignore. But, as we alerted you, we heard through the grapevine that he's been on the payroll for others as well. We didn't really care all that much until we heard that he might have had some involvement with that Quincy Market affair. Nothing specific, just some rumblings about him."

Sandy leaned forward in his seat.

"I told him that I knew about his Mafia contacts. And that you folks had given me a hint of his involvement. I guess I was a bit on the naïve side, thinking that if he knew I was on to him, he'd just tell me what I needed to know and be assured that I'd leave him alone after that. He'd be just a small fish to me—a conduit to the ones I really need to know about."

Vito smiled. "First, let me correct you. We don't like the word, Mafia. Prefer Cosa Nostra, okay?"

Sandy smirked. "Okay, Vito. From now on, you're the Cosa Nostra to me."

Vito fingered through some of the papers in his hand, stopping at one, running his index finger down the side of the page.

"Mr. Clark arranged permits for three horse-drawn ice cream wagons that day, for a company known as Boston Party Pleasures. We checked—that company doesn't exist. Mr. Clark also signed the orders to have the road barriers temporarily removed and for the Boston Police to allow full access to the promenade for the wagons."

Sandy's mouth was hanging open. Then he blurted out, "Why wasn't this ever disclosed as part of the terrorism investigation? The official report said that the barriers were compromised and that the police were confused as to what their orders were."

"Well, you are indeed naïve, aren't you, Doctor? It shouldn't surprise you how easily things can be covered up, glossed over, particularly when the public is more concerned with the actual horror itself. The World Trade Center investigation was another joke, as was the Warren Commission on JFK's killing. The Boston Marathon attack was another one full of inconsistencies and cover-up. This is what makes the world go round."

Sandy was aghast. "But how were you able to find this out?"

Vito laughed. "As I said earlier, maybe we can do some more information trading one day over a nice scotch. We're tapped into most things, Doctor. And, we keep quiet on most things as well, because, to us, information is currency."

"Is that why you're telling me this?"

Vito's face took on a serious mask.

"No, not at all. We consider you a friend, one of the good guys. What happened to your family makes us sick. And to all those children that day. Children are sacrosanct. We don't intend to trade on this information. You owe us nothing for this."

Sandy crossed his arms. "Who paid him?"

"Before I tell you that, it's important for you to know that you've rattled our fat little friend. He's been making some discreet enquiries about you with one of our contacts—basically a "handler"—the guy we use to make payments to him and arrange for the help we need from him from time to time.

"The two of them have become pretty close over the years, and I guess Clark trusts him. Anyway, our foreman played along with him and kicked it up the pyramid the way he's supposed to. We told him that you're hands-off, and that he's not to entertain any discussions about you. Anyway, you should know that Clark asked if something could be done to you."

Sandy felt goosebumps run up and down his spine.

"You have nothing to worry about from us, Dr. Beech. But I would suggest you perhaps buy yourself a good watchdog and an alarm system for your house. Desperate people will sometimes do desperate things. Clark feels vulnerable now, and you're the reason. While he'll get no help from us, with the amount of money we pay him he can afford his own little army. Be on guard."

Sandy clenched his hands together and cracked his knuckles, the sound reverberating through the cabin.

"Okay. Thanks for the warning. So, who paid him?"

"We have some of the best forensic accountants and internet chasers on the planet. We discovered that Mr. Clark has a numbered bank account in Bermuda. Two deposits were made by separate entities three months prior to the Quincy Market attack. Large amounts. Both of those entities were shell companies. But we tracked back to the principals."

Vito glanced down at the papers in his lap.

"The first deposit was made by a company traced to a Meagan Whitfield. She's a high-powered mergers and acquisitions lawyer on Wall Street. The second deposit was traced to a guy named Bob Stone, a defence contractor, also of New York."

Sandy's back stiffened.

"What connection could these people have with the Quincy slaughter?"

"Your guess is as good as mine. But they do have some things in common. They're both shareholders in an exclusive sperm bank thing in New York called Legacy Life Ladder Inc. Only for the rich and powerful—very much under the radar.

"We also tied them together with that senator running for president right now. That Lincoln Berwick character? At the time of the Quincy attack the presidential race hadn't started yet, but they were both involved at that time in a consulting capacity with his senatorial office.

"And, now, lo and behold, they're both shown on official registration records as being players on his presidential campaign team."

It felt as if all of the oxygen had just been sucked out of Sandy's lungs. As he struggled to catch his breath, he saw ghosts dancing in front of his eyes.

The happy faces of Whitney and Liam holding out their little hands. Excited for the ice cream money that they knew their loving dad would never refuse them.

21

The damn beeping sound wouldn't stop. Every four seconds it beeped and it was driving him crazy. That, and the fact that he couldn't move. He'd tried but it was impossible. He was strapped to the bed, his body on a slight incline.

At least, he thought he was strapped in.

Couldn't really tell. The only parts of his body that could move were his eyeballs, and even they were restricted by the wrappings that covered his entire face. His nose was uncovered, though, and there seemed to be a slit where his mouth was. He could feel that there were bandages on the top of his head too. Tubes ran from his arms and a couple of other wires ran from—somewhere—towards that damn beeping machine.

He concentrated on rolling his eyeballs downward. Yep, strapped in at the chest, pelvis and lower leg areas. Concentrated on moving his head slightly to the side, but that was impossible. Instead, shifted his eyeballs back and forth, side to side. Could see that some kind of wire cage surrounded his head, extending down to his chest area. Reminded him of the contraption that Hannibal Lector was forced to wear in Silence of the Lambs, but what he was wearing was more like a cage than a mask.

Two nurses were whispering to each other in the corner. The room seemed small, from what he could tell with the limited range of view he had. And, it looked as if he was the only occupant.

Neither of the nurses seemed interested in approaching the bed. They just kept watching him. And whispering.

The door opened and a uniformed police officer poked his head in. He said something to the nurses and they just nodded in return.

Then the door quickly closed again, and he could see through the little window that the officer was standing right outside the door.

Standing guard, he presumed.

No one else was in the room watching over him. No wife, kids, or friends.

And he didn't really expect any.

His head was still a bit foggy, but getting clearer with each minute that went by.

They'd been in the car together, driving towards a place called The Greenhouse restaurant. There had been a left-hand turn coming up, but they missed that.

Instead, they raced against the wind. He remembered hearing it whistling outside the window, feeling its pressure of resistance against the massive vehicle. The car had sped along so fast that the trees along the side of the road were just a blur, a swath of green with no distinctive features.

Then they went down. Over an embankment, bouncing along the rough gopher-holed landscape. Shockingly, the car seemed to pick up even more speed as it tore through the underbrush, with a thick old oak tree dead ahead as its apparent target.

The Lincoln Navigator drew a bead on the tree and didn't waver.

He remembered the seatbelt sliding across his chest, going in the wrong direction. Caught it with his left hand, and tried to ram the clasp back into its bracket. He couldn't remember if he'd succeeded or not.

And he couldn't remember hitting the tree, either. But, clearly, they must have.

Two other things were suddenly unsettling to him—as if being strapped to a hospital bed wasn't unsettling enough.

Had he succeeded in his assignment?

And—had they found his gun in the wreckage?

*****

His parents had died ten years ago in a car accident. Driving through the countryside of upper New York State, they'd lost their lives in a one-sided duel with a moose. The massive animal came right through the windshield.

Sandy was told that they'd died instantly. Cynically, he knew the authorities almost always said that, in a pathetic attempt to give solace to grieving relatives. But, once he saw the havoc that the antlers of the beast had wreaked upon the head and throat areas of his mom and dad, he knew they hadn't been lying to him.

Sandy was an only child and while he and his father had not been biologically related, the wonderful man had raised him as if they were blood-relatives. He wished he'd had at least one or two siblings, but that wasn't to be. He guessed that it was because his father was sterile, and it was enough of a gamble to go to a sperm bank once. Twice might have been too much for his parents to roll the dice against.

It certainly wouldn't have been the expense that stopped them from having more than one child. They were wealthy and well-connected. One of Boston's power couples. His dad had been a successful investment banker and hedge-funder. He'd been clever in choosing all the right moves throughout his career. Street-smart, and even somewhat of a street fighter, too, when he had to be.

But, Sandy's mother was the genius in the family. One of the nation's most celebrated neurosurgeons. She practised medicine right up until the day she died.

As he sat on his front porch with a four-foot-high pile of file folders on the floor beside him, Sandy pictured them in his mind. He missed them every day, but more so today than ever. Looking through old records and photos had taken him back in time, to lives well-lived and lives well-documented. His parents had suddenly seemed real and alive again.

Sandy had never cared about being conceived by artificial insemination. For some strange reason, it had never bothered him. His parents had talked to him about it, but he always shrugged it off. Probably because he'd had such a great relationship with his dad, and didn't really care to think that some other unknown person had actually fathered him anonymously.

They'd pushed him towards West Point, even though he'd wanted to attend Boston College. Thinking back now, he remembered how insistent they were. He never thought about it much at the time, but now it seemed weird. Why had they been so insistent? They talked some nonsense to him about how they'd been offered a full scholarship for him to attend. He never challenged that. Never asked them why, with the wealth they possessed, they'd even need a scholarship to afford his education. But, they also made the case that his dad had attended there, and it would be nice for Sandy to carry on the legacy.

So, he relented, and went to West Point.

A few days ago, when he was visiting Judy in Queens, she'd made the observation that all five of the boys involved in that wilding incident with the fourteen-year-old girl, were blonde and blue-eyed.

Just like Sandy.

He'd always been aware of that, but never gave it much thought before.

Sometimes the obvious is staring you right in the face, and you don't see it.

Funny, when he thought back upon it now, the "special" ones like him and the other five, who'd each been chosen for the Honor Guild, were indeed similar to a lot of the other boys in the Honor Guild. They tended to have that look—blonde, sandy blonde, or light brown hair, and almost exclusively blue-eyed. There had been no dark complexions in the Honor Guild, and certainly no ethnics. Only white Anglo-Saxons.

Coincidence? Maybe. Sandy was a scientist. He knew that nature offered coincidences, and, because he was a scientist, conspiracy theories didn't normally rest easy in his mind.

But, his mind was changing. The information that Vito had shared with him about the deputy mayor's involvement with the Quincy Market massacre had twisted his thinking in a different direction.

And the involvement of two influential people who were part of Lincoln Berwick's campaign—both of them shareholders in a private elitist sperm bank called Legacy Life Ladder Inc.

The fourth of his parents' files that Sandy had leafed through caused him to pour himself a stiff scotch. He sat on his covered porch sipping it. The January rainstorm had given way to mild weather. It felt like spring, although cool enough that he still needed to wear a light jacket. But, at this moment he wanted the fresh air, and was willing to pretend it was spring to achieve that.

Buried way down in that fourth file was the contract his parents had signed to enable Sandy to enter into the big wide world.

With a firm named Legacy Life Ladder Inc.

Also referred to in the contract documents as Triple-L.

The contract stipulated that after he graduated from high school, he was required to attend West Point. But it didn't state what the consequences would be for his parents if they changed their minds later.

He began to connect more dots.

Christopher Clark, the fat sleazy little deputy mayor, cleared the way for horse-drawn ice cream wagons to enter the promenade at Quincy Market that fateful day. The three terrorists in those wagons committed the most horrific act since 9/11.

The two operatives—Meagan Whitfield and Bob Stone—from Lincoln Berwick's presidential campaign, had made sizeable deposits to Clark's numbered bank account in Bermuda three months before the terrorist attack. At that time, those two operatives were consultants to Linc's senatorial office.

That terrorist attack had horrified America and just like 9/11, the after-effects of fear and trepidation had worked their way into the psyche of the majority of Americans. The propaganda of fear had continued for the two years since the attack, non-stop from certain politicians and the media. Just as it had after 9/11, resulting then in several Middle Eastern wars and severe restrictions on personal freedoms. Politicians attracted votes just from talking tough, because who didn't want to feel safe?

And now, more than two years since the Quincy attack, Lincoln Berwick was a presidential candidate, with those same two operatives working on his campaign. And in Linc's speeches as a senator over the last two years, Sandy recalled that his theme had always zeroed in on the fear element.

His speeches since becoming a presidential candidate had ramped things up even further. He'd focused on the fear theme ad nauseum, and people were buying into the image. He was clearly the tough guy in the race, the one the media and the population at large were supporting as the "one who would keep them safe."

He'd even used the image of Sandy in one of his campaign ads, showing him throwing that medal back at the general—denouncing Sandy as a bad and weak American.

All of Linc's ads had shown horrific images of 9/11, the Boston Marathon attack, and the Quincy Market slaughter. All designed to foster the fear that his campaign revolved around.

Fear was clearly Senator Berwick's hook-line.

Sandy drained the rest of his whisky in one quick slug, then poured himself another from the bottle waiting patiently on the table beside him.

He couldn't get the images out of his mind.

All five had blonde hair and blue eyes, just like Sandy. That connection had always been there in the recesses of his mind, and he'd never challenged it—not just with those five, but with the vast majority of his classmates in the Honor Guild. It had taken Judy to point it out to him and drive it up to the surface of his consciousness.

Sandy knew that John Nichols had been the product of a sperm bank, and he knew that Linc had been, too. They'd joked about it back in the early days when they were jovial friends.

He wondered now about the other three—Hank Price, Bill Tomkins, and Lloyd Franken. Hank was dead now, so he'd probably never know about him. But, he'd have to ask Bill and Lloyd. He'd just talked with Lloyd the other day, warning him about what had been happening and about the tape recording of John's that he had. They promised each other they'd catch up in a few days when they chatted again.

In the meantime, Sandy's curiosity was on fire. He knew what he had to do.

He picked up his cordless phone and punched in a number that he only ever dialed reluctantly.

"Romano here."

"Hi, Vito. It's Sandy Beech."

"So soon? We just talked yesterday, Dr. Beech. What a pleasant surprise."

"I need your help with something, Vito."

A pause. Then, "For you, I'll listen."

"I need a cover identity. New name, passport, driver's license, all verifiable. Available online, that if checked will be seen as air-tight."

"We can do that."

"I need to be well-connected—in a power position of influence."

"Easily done."

"I'll also need your help with changing my appearance—can't take the chance on looking like me. I've been too public."

"We have pros who do that all the time. Easily done. If you don't mind my asking, who are you trying to deceive, Dr. Beech?"

"I need an appointment with that New York sperm bank, Legacy Life Ladder Inc. I want to make a pitch for sperm and see what I can find out."

Vito sighed into the phone. "Are you sure you want to do that?"

"Yes, I'm sure, Vito."

"Well, for you, we can do all these things. But, what do I get in return?"

Sandy took a deep breath and clenched a tight fist with his free hand.

"You were interested in a certain weapon."

Vito chuckled. "The Pulsed Energy Projectile?"

"Yes."

"Well, that would be sufficient payment. I'd love to hear about it—out of curiosity only, of course."

Sandy lowered his voice to almost a whisper. He didn't know why, he just did.

"If your people can make me fool-proof, I can do better than just tell you about it. I can give you a live demo. In my basement."

22

"Don't move, dear. Just relax—I'm here with you, and I'm not leaving."

Lloyd Franken gazed into the hazel eyes of his gorgeous wife and was instantly comforted. Her eyes always had that effect on him. That magical combination of confidence and girlish sparkle. He was glad to see her.

But, where am I?

She reached over to a side table and retrieved a bottle of water with a straw. Easing it towards his mouth, she urged, "Here, take a sip."

The cold water rushing down his throat was instant relief. He hadn't realized how dry he was until that precious first sip.

Cassidy stroked his forehead with one hand and squeezed his shoulder with the other.

"You're very lucky, Lloyd. It could have been a lot worse."

Lloyd gazed around the room for the first time.

"I'm in a hospital. How long?"

"Since yesterday. You were in a car accident out on the highway. No other vehicles involved, thank God. The police said it appeared as if you lost control and crashed into a tree."

The highlight reel was now playing in Lloyd's brain. Gun pointed at him, accelerating the car down an embankment, taking direct aim at a large tree trunk.

"James! His name is James!"

Cassidy slid her fingers through his hair. "Stay calm, darling. It's okay. Your friend is alive. He's not in very good shape, though. Your seatbelt and airbag saved you, but James apparently wasn't wearing his belt. Went through the windshield. I'm sorry. Maybe you can see him later."

Lloyd was about to blurt something out, but a little voice in his head told him not to.

Cassidy was still talking, tears in her voice this time. "You called from the highway. Phoned 911, and then you called me. I could hardly recognize your voice. I was so scared. But, you were alert enough to tell me where you were. I drove out, got there just after the ambulance. By that time, you'd gone unconscious. Followed the ambulance to the hospital. Another ambulance took your friend. He was in terrible shape, but you only had a few cuts and bruises. And, a minor concussion."

Lloyd swallowed hard, then took the glass out of Cassidy's hand and treated himself to another long sip.

"How long have I been out?"

Cassidy shook her head. "After you got to the hospital, you regained consciousness. You've been awake ever since, but not really with it. Not aware. You seem fine now."

She leaned over and kissed his forehead. "They want you to stay until at least tomorrow, just to be on the safe side."

"Okay."

She leaned in close, nestled her cheek against his, and giggled in her girlish way. "Lloyd, you know I'm in my peak time right now, don't you? I know you weren't anxious for us to have a baby, but don't you think having an accident is a bit extreme?"

Lloyd humored her with a laugh of his own, even though he didn't feel like laughing. He wrapped his stiff arm around her shoulders and kissed her on the lips.

"I'll make it up to you next month, okay? Promise. And, Cassidy, I do want a baby with you. I'm excited about it—just took me longer than you to get used to the idea. But, after this, I'm going to want a baby more than ever."

Cassidy's face broke out into a big smile. "Okay, we'll set a day and time next month. Until then, maybe we can just practice?"

"You bet we can."

Making babies was the last thing on Lloyd's mind right then. All he could think of was the phone call from Sandy Beech, advising him of the deaths of John Nichols and Hank Price. Apparently, a suicide for John and a car accident for Hank.

But there had also been that attempt on Bill Tomkins' life, right in his own office.

And Sandy had told him about the tape recording—the one that John had made of him and Linc discussing the rape and death of that young girl.

John, Hank, Bill, and Linc—and Lloyd himself, had all been in the van that night.

Two were now dead, and two others had suffered attempts on their lives. The only one who had escaped unscathed so far had been Texas Senator Lincoln Berwick.

Coincidence?

Lloyd eased Cassidy off of his lap and stretched his long arms.

"I think I'm ready to go home today."

"No, no—the doctor said that would be a mistake. You've had a concussion, Lloyd."

He raised himself up into a sitting position.

"Okay, this is what we'll do. Let me wander around a little, see how my legs and everything work, and then we'll decide."

Cassidy held out her hands. "I'll only agree to the wandering around thing right now. Let's see how you do."

Lloyd grabbed hold of her hands and eased himself to his feet.

Suddenly Cassidy snapped her fingers. "I almost forgot. There was a detective here before. He wanted to chat with you. I guess about the accident. He's waiting out in the lobby. Do you want me to go get him?"

Lloyd shook his head. "No, show me to the room where my friend is. I want to check on him first."

"He's just down the hall. I peeked in through the window a few hours ago. He looked in really bad shape. In fact, he's so bandaged up you can't even tell whether it's a man or a woman."

"Maybe I can cheer him up a bit."

Cassidy held onto his hand, led him out the door, and slowly down the hospital corridor.

She squeezed his hand tightly and watched him carefully as he walked. "You're doing really well. I'm proud of you…and relieved."

"I'm a tough old fart, hon."

"Yes, you are. I'm glad. Hey, when I was down at James' room before, there was a policeman standing outside the door. I don't know why. A bit strange."

Lloyd nodded.

Not so strange. Apparently, the police already knew something about the man named James Whitehead, or they'd found his gun at the scene of the accident.

They reached the room, no policeman in sight. Lloyd gazed through the glass pane and saw a figure that was unrecognizable. His entire head and face covered in bandages, with some kind of a halo or retainer around his head. The bandages had slits for his eyes, nose, and ears, and Lloyd could tell that the man's eyes were open. His eyeballs were flitting back and forth, following the activity of the two nurses.

"Stay here, Cassidy. I want to say a few words to James alone. Hope you don't mind."

She crossed her arms and examined him up and down. "Are you sure you're okay?"

He gave her the thumbs up sign. "I feel great. Nothing to worry about."

"Alright, then. I'll go down to the cafeteria and get us a couple of coffees. Back in a sec."

"Make mine double-double. I need the energy."

"Enjoy the time with your friend. He'll be glad to see you."

Lloyd grimaced as he watched her head off down the corridor, then opened the glass door and entered the private room.

One of the nurses came over to him right away. "I'm sorry, sir, you can't come in here."

He put on his most charming smile. "It's okay, dear. I'm the friend that was in the car accident with him. I just want a few minutes. Just to give him a smile and a few encouraging words. I promise I won't touch anything."

The nurse hesitated, then looked over at her partner. She nodded.

The young attendant lifted her clipboard and took a pen out of her jacket pocket. "What's your name, sir?"

"Lloyd Franken."

"Okay, I see that your name is cross-referenced here on his chart. I guess it's okay. But, please don't upset him. He's doing better, but still not completely stable yet. He broke his neck."

"Thanks. Could we have some privacy for a few minutes?"

The nurse motioned to her friend. "Okay, we'll be right outside the door if you need us."

As they moved towards the door, the figure on the bed suddenly started making noises. Not words, just sounds. Utterings. Almost animalistic.

The man's pupils were like the balls in a pinball machine, bouncing around, trying desperately to convey something to the nurses. The noises coming from his mouth were supposed to be words, but fell far short. He couldn't move his body, because he was strapped to the bed. Couldn't move his head because of the halo contraption. A tube was attached to his arm, and there were electrodes and wires connecting his bandaged head, fingers and chest areas to a machine beside the bed.

All he could move were his eyeballs and his dysfunctional mouth and tongue.

In response to the guttural sounds, the nurses hesitated at the door.

Lloyd waved them on with his hand. "He's just excited to see me. It's okay. He'll calm down."

They didn't seem too convinced, but, reluctantly left the room anyway, leaving Lloyd alone with the man who had attempted to kill him.

The noises became more frantic the closer Lloyd got to the bed. He leaned his head down and glared into the man's frightened eyes.

"Shut your fucking mouth, or I'll shut it for you."

Suddenly there was silence, and Lloyd thought he could see some rationality in the man's eyes. Some kind of reckoning with the reality he was facing.

"Okay, here's how things are going to go. I won't kill you if I get some answers. You obviously can't talk, so I want you to blink your answers. Your answers will remain with me—I won't tell the authorities. One blink for "no" and two blinks for "yes." Do you understand me? Blink twice if you do."

Two blinks.

"Do you work for Virgin Galactic?"

One blink.

"Were you hired to kill me?"

Two blinks.

"Was it related to industrial espionage?"

One blink.

"Was a political campaign involved?"

James hesitated for a few seconds.

Two blinks.

Lloyd then named several politicians as a control experiment, and got one-blink answers to each name.

Then he dropped the bomb. "Was it related to Lincoln Berwick's campaign?"

James paused again. Then his eyes started darting from side to side. He didn't blink. He just kept rolling his eyeballs, avoiding Lloyd's glare. Lloyd could tell that there was something wrong. The man's breathing was becoming labored, and for a second or two his eyeballs rolled up out of sight into his forehead. Stress and anxiety were taking their toll. And, perhaps Lloyd's last question.

Lloyd knew he didn't have much time left.

He raised his voice slightly and asked again. "Was it Senator Lincoln Berwick?"

James just stared up at him. Eyes glazed over and unblinking.

"Okay, James, or whoever the hell you are. I think I've got my answer."

Lloyd raised his hand up close to his chest, hidden from view in case someone was peeking in through the window. He squeezed his outstretched fingers together tightly, mimicking the shape of a dagger. He pointed them downward towards James's throat, teasing him.

Taunting him—to death.

"I lied. Now I'm going to kill you."

That was all it took. His eyes rolled up into his forehead for the last time, and James Whitehead let out a fitful gasp. The intermittent beeping of the monitoring machine stopped, replaced by a steady forlorn hum. Clearly, the man's heart had given up the fight. Scared to death.

The nurses, accompanied by a doctor, rushed into the room and pushed Lloyd out of the way. He didn't protest. They had work to do.

But he knew it was too late. And he didn't care.

*****

"So, you're saying you'd never met or seen this man before?"

Lloyd shook his head emphatically. "No, never."

The two detectives sat in front of him, clipboards in hand. Lloyd was sitting on the edge of the bed and now fully dressed. To avoid Cassidy having to listen to their line of questioning, he'd sent her off to the carpark to bring her Subaru around to the front of the hospital. She would then just wait for him there. Better for her not to hear his answers.

One of the detectives, a guy named Derik, checked his notes. "The name on his identification was James Whitehead. He also had business cards with Virgin Galactic logos. But we checked, and that was all bogus. We've run his fingerprints through the national database—no luck there either. We have no idea who he was."

Lloyd shook his head. "I don't know what to tell you."

The other detective, Chris, scratched his forehead, clearly puzzled. "We found his gun in the passenger side of the wreckage. His fingerprints were on it, not yours, which is why we posted an officer outside his door. Do you think he was planning to kill you? Did he threaten you that way?"

Lloyd folded his arms across his chest. "No threats. He just wanted me to turn down a deserted road, which is when I accelerated and sent us into that tree. That was my only hope. I had no idea what he was planning, so I wasn't going to take any chances."

"He wasn't wearing his seatbelt."

"I undid it before we hit the tree."

Chris nodded. "Very smart, very cool thinking on your part. We see from your records that you're a graduate of West Point."

Lloyd nodded. "Yeah. They teach you to be cool at that school."

Derik smiled. "Nice to see your training paid off."

Chris wrote something down on his notepad. "Tell me, what do you think he wanted with you?"

Lloyd grimaced.

"I don't know. Could have been industrial secrets—maybe he wanted to threaten me to get some information. At NASA we've had some serious technology hacks over the last few months, and several scientists have been shaken down with blackmail for certain information regarding specialized components. None of those scientists are employed with us any longer, but there were a few holes we had to plug afterwards. There are numerous private and public scientific corporations out there, as well as high tech companies, that would benefit from the specialized knowledge we have."

Chris grunted.

Derik leaned forward in his chair. "Why were you in his hospital room, pretending to be a friend?"

Lloyd leaned his imposing frame forward as well, matching the detective's move. "Wouldn't you? If someone had tried to take you at gunpoint, wouldn't you have wanted to know why?"

"Well, yes, but you could have left that to the police."

"I'm a take-charge guy. Couldn't help myself."

Chris lowered his voice for the next question. "Did you…do anything while you were in there?"

Lloyd used the full power of his piercing blue eyes and stared the detective down. "What are you implying?"

Chris fidgeted. Lloyd was fully aware of the effect that his blue-eyed stare had on people. It conveyed absolute dominance—and, strangely enough, a sort of innocence.

After a few moments of silence, Chris persisted. "Well…did you touch him? Was that your intention? To cause him harm?"

Lloyd shook his head. "No, detective. He was a virtual vegetable. Posed no danger to me any longer. All I wanted were a few answers if I could get them."

Derik closed the cover of his clipboard and stood. Chris followed his partner's lead.

"Did you learn anything from him?"

Lloyd sighed. "No. Nothing at all. The man couldn't talk, so I gave up."

He lowered his eyes, feigning regret. "Then…he just…died."

23

Their flights came in to La Guardia within an hour of each other. Lloyd from his home in Houston and Bill from Bermuda where he'd been setting up a new off-shore captive. Sandy had driven down from Boston to meet them and got there with ample time to spare. Time enough to have a decadent breakfast at the airport and several cups of rocket fuel coffee. He hadn't slept well for the last several nights, so the coffees were mandatory.

They looked good. He hadn't seen them in several years, but those years had clearly been kind to them—as they had to Sandy as well. But he could see that Lloyd's face hadn't yet completely healed from his accident—well, "accident" was a kind word for what had happened to him. Still a few cuts and scrapes that were gradually turning into scars—and within a few days he'd probably look as good as new.

Bill bore no signs whatsoever of the attempt on his life and his niece's. The thugs had barely laid a finger on him before he made sure they met their demise. Bill was still Bill. No outward emotion, no signs of concern. Just a hearty handshake, the kind you'd expect to get if you were meeting him in a boardroom for the very first time. Sandy knew that Bill would take a while to warm up—small talk was not his forte. Never had been.

At first, not much conversation in the car as Sandy drove them to Judy's house in Queens. Sandy kept his eyes on the road as the other two men absently glanced out the window.

Then Lloyd broke the silence.

"Thanks for warning me, Sandy. I should have listened to you, been more on guard."

Sandy winced at the reminder. "I really didn't expect you to take me seriously. It's hard even for me to believe now, even after all that's happened."

Lloyd folded his arms. "Sounded like a crazy conspiracy theory. And, as you remember, back in West Point we were all taught to be fearless. I guess even after all these years it's hard to forget those feelings of invincibility."

Bill spoke up for the first time from the back seat. "Poor Hank and John. They didn't see it coming, did they? I phoned Hank just before it happened to him. Asked him to give me a call. I guess I didn't make it sound urgent enough. Should have included a warning in the voice mail message. I think I was afraid of sounding too alarmist—or too crazy."

Sandy shook his head. "Should have, could have—we could all say that about a lot of things, Bill. Don't beat yourself up over it."

"Sandy, I just saw Hank a couple of months ago. We had dinner and a few drinks. He was in New York on some business, and we always tried to connect when he was in town. He looked really good... and really happy. His family was everything to him—seemed to have his priorities straight. More than I can say for myself."

Sandy was surprised at the rare moment of introspection from Bill. The untimely deaths of their two old classmates must have activated a nerve, one that had been numb during all the years that Sandy had known him.

Sandy decided to change the subject. "I don't think you guys ever met Judy. She attended Barnard College, which some of us at West Point arranged joint parties and dances with. You two ran in a different circle when we were in school together."

Lloyd chuckled. "My God, there were so many damn cliques back in those days, it was hard to remember which circle you were supposed to be in."

"Ain't that the truth? Anyway, I dated Judy until Linc sabotaged our relationship. He stepped in and took my place, until Judy realized what an asshole he was. She then moved on to John, and they got married. Depression and booze eventually killed that union, and they divorced about ten years ago. A daughter, Cynthia, around fifteen, spitting image of her mom. Judy works as a teacher and gymnastics coach. She was a world-class gymnast in her day."

Lloyd asked a question, in almost a whisper. "You mentioned she has John's tape, the tape that was meant for you. Did you let her listen to it?"

"Yes."

"How did she react?"

"Not well, but better than I expected."

"You told her that Bill and I were in the van that night?"

"Sorry, but—yes."

"Oh."

"She's a big girl, Lloyd. What's past is past. We have to be concerned now about the future and making sure we all *have* a future. She's in the same peril as you guys. She knows too much and now, with that tape, I know too much."

Sandy turned down Judy's street and pulled up in front of her house.

"Okay, guys, get your bags out of the trunk. She knows you're going to stay here for a few days, and she's perfectly okay with that. In fact, right now she's so scared she welcomes the company of strangers with skills like yours for a while."

24

After getting Bill and Lloyd comfortable in their guest rooms, Judy played hostess for the afternoon. Sandy would be staying just for the one night and agreed to take the couch in the living room.

Small talk dominated the afternoon. The disturbing reason why they were all together had been left for later.

Judy was heartened by how pleasant the strangers were. She knew and had loved Sandy, so he wasn't a surprise at all. But Bill and Lloyd were charming and respectful, and she found that to be in sharp contrast to the knowledge she now had of how the two of them were involved in the rape and death of a fourteen-year-old girl decades ago.

A secret that neither of them relished, but one that must have haunted them incessantly over the years. They were now successful adults; one with a family, and the other no doubt wishing he did have a family.

Judy was enchanted watching how easily Cynthia interacted with the men. And how they charmed her in return. But, she couldn't push the thought out of her mind that Cynthia was about the same age as the girl whose death they'd caused back when they were wilding in a party van.

The paradox was striking, as was her own acceptance of their bad judgement so many years ago. And the bad judgement of her own husband as well, in that same van.

She consoled herself with the thought that for John, Bill, and Lloyd, the consequences were unintended. And, that John had tried valiantly to save the poor girl's life.

Judy was also fully aware of the contrast, that the boy who had callously caused that girl's death was the one and only Lincoln

Berwick. The others were just innocent—sort of—and had been weak bystanders. But, she hoped, weak no more.

She'd cooked a delicious roast beef dinner, which they all enjoyed along with a few glasses of Zinfandel. Cynthia had gone over to a friend's house after the meal; a sleepover with ten of her closest buddies.

The adults were now sitting in the living room, relaxing.

"Later" had arrived.

Judy studied the three men. Now that the small talk had subsided, Cynthia was gone, and all of their bellies were full, she had the chance to comprehend how astounding—and spooky—this rendezvous was.

"I'm sorry, guys, but, this is just too weird. Do you not see it?"

Sandy scratched his chin. "See what?"

"You could all be brothers. Look at you. Blondish hair, blue eyes, all around the same height, athletic physiques. Goddamn, it's uncanny. And weird."

The three men, as if on command, glanced at each other, then quickly looked back at Judy again.

Lloyd took a sip of his wine. "Can't deny it, Judy. You're right."

"Now, to make things even weirder, just add John and Linc. And with the photos I've seen of Hank Price, he was in the mix too. What's the deal? All six of you!"

Sandy rubbed his forehead, then stood. "I was the product of artificial insemination. I know that both John and Linc were too. What about you two? Do you know?"

Lloyd nodded. "I was too."

Bill folded his arms across his chest. "So was I."

Judy gasped. "Excuse my language, but, what the fuck?"

Sandy talked as he paced the room.

"I dug up some old files that my parents kept in their archives. The sperm bank that they used for me was a place called Legacy Life Ladder Inc., located right here in New York. The contract had my parents agree that I was to attend West Point when the time came."

Lloyd stood as well. "Jesus, my parents told me the same thing. Same sperm bank."

Bill jumped in. "I knew my parents used a sperm bank, but I had no idea which bank it was."

Judy chuckled. "I would bet a year's salary that it was the same place."

Bill nodded and lowered his voice. "The coincidence is too much, the fact that we were all products of a sperm bank. Wondering if the same bank was used for John, Hank, and Linc as well."

Sandy poured himself another glass of wine.

"It gets weirder, folks. I've been connecting a few dots along the way. And Linc seems to be in the center of the dots. There's a deputy mayor in Boston, Christopher Clark, who was on the payroll of two people who are high up in Lincoln's campaign, not just the presidential campaign, but while he's been a senator—Bob Stone and Meagan Whitfield. Both of whom are also shareholders in this secretive sperm bank, which apparently is referred to as Triple-L."

He could see he had their full attention.

"You all know I lost my family in that Quincy Market terror attack. Well, I've been doing some digging. Mr. Clark was paid off, money deposited in an offshore bank account by Whitfield and Stone. Paid off to allow the security detail to back off, and paid off to allow those ice cream wagons to enter the promenade the day of the attack. And these two characters are now running Linc's presidential campaign, as well as being shareholders of the sperm bank that we probably all came from."

Bill raised his voice for the first time, to an angry level that Judy hadn't heard since he arrived. "Are you saying that the Quincy terrorist attack was set up? Planned? A false flag?"

Sandy nodded. "Seems that way."

"Why?"

"Have you listened to Linc's speeches over the last couple of years? Have you seen his campaign ads? It seems as if he's been creating paranoia, a climate of fear. And presenting himself as the only candidate who has solutions. Could this be a case of creating a crisis and then offering solutions? The birth of a brand?"

Lloyd wrung his hands together and cracked his knuckles, so

ferociously that the sound reverberated around the room. "This is nuts! Sick! Can't be possible, can it?"

"It is sick," Sandy agreed. "But, we seem to be in a sick world right now, where power is everything. Let's face it, these connections and coincidences are too hard to ignore. Follow the crumbs."

Bill took another long sip of his wine.

"Sandy, you were booted out of the Honor Guild, but Lloyd and I are well aware of how we were controlled. Pushed along career paths that we had no say in. Consultants were assigned to us, who guided us, mentored us, and then cleared the path for our...rather spectacular careers. Without their help, we probably wouldn't have succeeded.

"I know that Hank had the same special help, and no doubt Linc did too. His path was carved out in politics, and ours were carved out in the sciences and business worlds. Seems like fate was simply manipulated for all of us."

Judy jumped in. "Sandy, how do you know about these Whitfield and Stone people?"

"I have a contact in the Mafia...or, as they prefer, Cosa Nostra."

"Jesus!"

"I know. But, they do know things, and, tit for tat, they are more than willing to help out."

"What's the cost to you?"

"Hopefully not much more than mutual respect. I do respect them, in a perverted kind of way. But, hear this. My family was slaughtered, and by hook or crook, someone is going to pay for that. I have very little else to live for now."

Judy nodded sadly. "I understand."

"No, I don't think you do. Beneath my calm, cool, West Point-engineered exterior, I have a burning rage. And it has to be extinguished. There's only one way I know of to do that."

Bill rubbed his forehead, massaging his temples. "What's next?"

Sandy was silent for a few seconds. Then, he walked over to the window and gazed outside, keeping his back to the group.

"I've asked my Cosa Nostra contact to arrange a meeting for me with Triple-L. I'm going to be disguised, with a fake online identity. I need to find out more about this secretive sperm bank. I'll let you all know what I find out, if anything."

"What then?"

"I don't know. But in the meantime, we have to realize that we're all in danger. I think Linc and his people are trying to pick all of us off, one by one. This skeleton from the past has the potential to bring him down, ruin his plans for power. And maybe even send him to prison. More importantly, I think it fucks up the plans of his handlers. I wonder how much Linc is really in charge."

Lloyd whispered, "I've arranged twenty-four-hour security for my wife."

Bill nodded assent. "Same for me. My relatives are all protected right now, and for the foreseeable future. No point taking any chances here."

Judy pulled a blanket up tightly around her chest. "And I want you two guys to stay with me until we figure this out. Okay? Best we all stick together right now. Please?"

25

"Who the hell are you people, anyway?"

Meagan Whitfield laughed at him in such a mocking way that it made Linc's blood boil.

"I think that in all the years we've known you, that's the first time you've asked that question. You are slow, aren't you?"

Linc pounded his fist on the table, causing the coffee mugs to vibrate.

"Don't talk to me that way, Meagan! I'm not some little puppet you can jiggle up and down!"

Meagan shook her head slowly, then turned towards Bob Stone. "You talk to him, Bob. I think our boy has a problem with strong women."

Linc could feel the blood rushing to his face. His cheeks were red hot and the collar of his white Givenchy shirt felt moist around the neck. He loosened his tie and undid the top button.

"Yes, do that. Talk to me, Bob."

Bob sighed. "I sure wish you two could get along better. Meagan, you need to choose your words more carefully, and Linc, you need to grow up and get your ego in check.

"And no, Linc, you are not our puppet. But, we do own you. We allow you considerable latitude to think on your own, but this whole thing is much bigger than you. We'll make you a success, we'll put you in the Oval Office, but you have to do things our way."

Bob's words had their usual effect. Linc started breathing easier, and he nodded his understanding. "Okay, but, answer my question—who are you, really?"

Bob glanced over at Meagan, and she gave a slight nod.

"Meagan's right. I don't think you've ever asked us that question before. We've been part of your life and your career for a very long time now. And, having attended West Point and as part of the Honor Guild, you knew that mentors like us would be involved in making your career a reality. You can't deny you didn't know that."

Linc looked away, out through his boardroom window at his favorite landmark, the Texas School Book Depository. Once upon a time a sniper's nest, now a simple museum. But still a powerful sight to behold.

"Yes, I knew that. But everything just started happening so fast. And, while you guys may have been pulling some strings for me, I gave myself a lot of the credit as to how well I was succeeding in life. As I said, I'm not some little puppet."

Meagan spoke up, softly.

"We removed hurdles for you, Senator. Every step of the way. Hurdles that normal people have to deal with in life, you didn't have to. We didn't tell you about most of them—you didn't need to know. Now, I wish we had told you every time we did something for you. I think your success has gone to your head."

Linc glared at her.

"No, it hasn't. But, I resent being told that what I'm doing isn't enough. You called this meeting today because you feel I'm not being passionate enough in my speeches. I asked my speech writer to change direction, and I think Tanya has done a great job for me. As for my speeches, my audiences are always mesmerized. I doubt that I could do any better."

Bob cracked his knuckles. "You'll have to do better. More anger, and, as Meagan says, more passion. The polls are stagnant. The damn economy is still number one, and your task is to make fear number one. If the economy remains the biggest worry, you will lose against the Democrats, and that's as blunt as I can be. We've come too far to lose. Losers seldom get second chances."

"I'm not a loser."

"Then, show us."

Linc nodded. "Okay, okay, I'll show more anger. I'll get them riled up. But, you still haven't told me who you people are. I've just taken your help over the years thinking that all of you were just political operatives, but it feels like it's more than that. You engineered that Quincy Market terrorist attack, which set the stage for my political fortunes. For a while after that, fear was the number one concern. Now I'm talking it up again, reminding voters of the horror, and, over time, my speeches will have their effect. But, I'm feeling like I'm just a front for you people. So, who are you? About time you told me."

Meagan clenched her hands together. "Bob and I arranged this meeting today to advise you of a trip we want you to take. We'll call it sort of a spiritual revival for you, nothing more than that. But, before we tell you about that, I will bring you in on the picture a bit more. It's probably time for that, and it might make you less resistant to the control we have to exert," she said.

"Your destiny started getting mapped out the day your parents agreed to have your mother artificially inseminated. A group of us are shareholders of that sperm bank, Legacy Life Ladder. It's exclusive, you know that—only the wealthy and well-connected. And the mothers being impregnated must have the best genetic match to the superior product the sperm bank provides.

"Your genetic composition, and that of your colleagues from the Honor Guild, are all of incredible superiority. All of the students from the Honor Guild are products of Triple-L. And all of the graduates have mentors, like you do, guiding them through their lives."

She flicked a glance at Bob. "And all of us mentors belong to an elite group, a very secretive group. We represent some of the largest corporations in America, and we take our responsibilities seriously."

Linc raised his hand to stop her. "How did you get into this group in the first place?"

Meagan shook her head. "That's above your pay grade. Let's just say it's a 'legacy' thing, just like the name of the sperm bank. Can I continue?"

Linc nodded.

"We call ourselves the Aufsteigen Group."

"Where the hell did that name come from? Sounds German?"

"It is German, even though hardly any members of our group have any direct heritage from Germany. We just like what it means and what it stands for."

"And that is?"

"The word *aufsteigen* means ascension. Which is—to rise up, to soar."

"I know what ascension means, Meagan. What are you rising up and soaring against?"

She shook her head. "Not *against* anything, per se—more being *for* something. Superiority, dominance. We feel we can accomplish our goals with leaders who are genetically superior—in politics, business, health sciences, technology, the military. We're solely an American group, committed to America."

Linc stood and walked over to the window. Stared out at the Depository building, and felt a smile begin to cross his face. He liked the word superiority, and loved the fact that they saw in him a specimen who was—genetically superior.

He turned around and faced them. "Thanks for answering my question. So, that's who you really are. Not just my campaign advisers, or my mentors. You're something called the Aufsteigen Group."

Bob smiled. "Yes. And you're our ascendant."

26

After they cleared away his dishes, Linc pushed the magic buttons, transforming his first class seat into a first class bed. Across the aisle from him in the adjacent pod, his escort did the same thing. Some guy by the name of Horst, a combination bodyguard and translator provided by Meagan and Bob.

Linc closed his eyes and thought back over the meeting in his office a couple of days ago.

He'd learned a lot.

His ego had been reinforced by knowing that he was thought of as superior, although that really wasn't a surprise to him. But he still needed to hear it once in a while, and he was pretty certain Meagan and Bob knew he needed to hear it. Clever of them, and all part and parcel of their desire to manipulate him.

He'd also learned who his handlers really were. Part of a mysterious clan called the Aufsteigen Group. Inspired by the objective of an ascension. And he was their ascendant. Linc liked the sound of that. He wanted to know more, but from the reaction of Meagan and Bob, he knew that at least for now that was all he'd be permitted to know.

Well, if they got him to the White House, he was fine with it. They could control him until then, but after that he figured he'd be able to break out and be his own guy. He'd be the most powerful man in the world. How much control did they really think they'd have over him then? As far as he was concerned, the Aufsteigen Group could then go find someone else to manipulate. He'd play along in the meantime.

Right now, he was en route to Buenos Aires, Argentina. An eleven-hour flight from Dallas, and a loss of two hours on the time difference when he arrived. He and Horst would stay at a hotel in the city that night, catch up on the jet lag, then head out for a long drive across the country. A sixteen-hour trek to some godforsaken place called Salta, in the far northwestern corner of Argentina. It actually would have been faster to fly to Chile, and then drive from there to Salta, but Meagan felt that security was better if they simply stayed within Argentina. He didn't know what she meant by that.

Linc closed his eyes and began to ponder who this mystery man was that he would be meeting. Meagan said that he was not part of Aufsteigen, but that he was aware of the group and supported it. She told him he was a very old man. Linc asked how old, but, she didn't answer him.

He tried to pin her down on why this visit to a very old man in Argentina was so important. She was vague, saying only that he was spiritual inspiration to Aufsteigen and that Linc would find him motivating. Now that Linc was poised to take over the reins of the United States government, meeting this wise old man would be an important step, and the timing was right.

Linc smiled. Pictured himself sitting behind the Resolute desk, reveling in the knowledge that it had been a gift from Queen Victoria to President Rutherford B. Hayes way back in 1880. Imagine, President Lincoln Berwick being one of the favored few to be able to make life or death decisions sitting behind such a relic of history. He wondered if he could launch his first nuclear strike from that desk.

Senator Berwick drifted off to sleep with a big smile on his face.

*****

Horst didn't talk much. He concentrated on the drive. Linc offered to take over to give the guy a break, but he wouldn't hear of it. They left Buenos Aires at 3:00 a.m., and it was now 6:00 p.m. Stopped along the way for three quick pee breaks and a sandwich by a roadside stand.

They were now on the outskirts of Salta. Linc could feel how thin the air was—the travel brochures that Horst had given him described this area as being in the foothills of the Andes, almost 4,000 feet above sea level.

During the drive, Linc had asked Horst several times who it was they were meeting. All he'd answered was, "Soon."

Linc guessed "soon" had now arrived. Horst had pulled over to the side of the road and taken a long sip of his bottled water.

"The man's name is Herman Braxmeier. He speaks only German—I will translate for you. We'll be having dinner with him and his wife, Angela, and stay the night as well. We leave tomorrow."

Linc shook his head. "That name doesn't ring a bell. I know the names of most of the important people in the world. Why is he important?"

Horst allowed a rare chuckle. "You'll see. And, you will show respect. Understand?"

"How old is this fellow?"

Horst put the car into gear, and pulled back out onto the highway. "He's 129 years old."

Linc choked. "That's impossible. The longest living person in the world died twenty years ago, and she was 122!"

Horst frowned at him. "Maybe she didn't hold the record after all. And Herman has had excellent care over the years. Taken good care of himself, and had lots of help. You'll see."

Horst seemed to know his way around. Cruised the circumference of the main population center and headed out into the country. Quite isolated now, but Linc could see a large structure off in the distance, at the top of one of the mounds of the foothills.

As they approached, Horst turned off the radio, and reminded Linc once again to let him do the talking—and to show respect. *Annoying.*

The large white cement structure could just barely be seen behind the high walls that surrounded the property. And there were armed guards patrolling the exterior. Linc counted four men just at the front of the property alone, each with side arms on their hips and rifles slung over their shoulders.

Horst pulled up beside a booth and extended his hand out the window in some kind of salute. The guard seemed to know him. He nodded and pushed a button on a remote unit. The iron gates opened and they drove through into a large courtyard.

Another guard met them, and Horst handed him the keys. Then

the guard pointed to the front door indicating they could proceed inside.

Linc followed Horst up the steps and through the front door into a large foyer. It was dark inside, very few windows in this front section of the house.

He felt insecure, out of control—and a deep sense that something ominous was about to happen. Linc didn't like that feeling. For this entire trip, Horst had been in control, and treated Linc as if he was just a little kid, didn't have the right to know anything. This was unsettling, and not the way Linc was accustomed to things. He was a U.S. Senator, for God's sake and the future President of the United States. Horst didn't seem to give a shit about that, and he got the feeling that this Herman character wouldn't care either. Unsettling.

Another guard appeared and motioned them to follow him into a salon room. This area was cavernous, and the wall was lined with photos hanging from chains.

Linc walked around the room and examined the pictures. They were all World War II era, mostly of the infamous Nazi leader, Adolf Hitler, speaking to crowds, mingling with crowds, and saluting crowds in the familiar Nazi extended arm gesture.

None of the photos showed Hitler alone, always just as the prominence in the crowd. Linc could relate to that. He enjoyed seeing photos of himself that way.

The sound of rubber wheels running along wooden floors interrupted his thoughts. Linc turned away from the wall and watched as an elderly woman entered the room, pushing an even more elderly man in what looked like a gold-plated wheel chair.

Linc remembered Horst's warning to show respect.

But he couldn't hide his astonishment.

The elderly man, who was presumably Herman, smiled up at him from his wheel chair. A kindly smile. Or maybe the smile just looked kindly because he was so old and, at this point, so harmless as well. Old people always looked harmless and kindly, no matter what horrors they had committed in their younger lives.

Linc knew that his mouth was hanging open. But no words came out; no sound whatsoever.

Though, he wanted to say something, anything.

Even just a warm, "Pleased to meet you, Herman."

Linc glanced back up at the ancient photos hanging from the wall, then back down at the smiling old man in the wheel chair. He did this several times—couldn't help himself.

And, then he just knew. He didn't know how he knew, because it was too crazy to comprehend.

But, somewhere deep down in the recesses of his soul, he knew.

27

With his customary morning tour of the laboratory and refrigeration units completed, Dr. Derek Schmidt headed back along the corridor towards the office section of the massive tenth floor complex.

He popped into one of the preparation rooms along the way.

"How's the latest batch, Imre?"

A short bespectacled man in a white lab coat smiled and nodded. "Everything's just fine. I think our client will be happy. Three good embryos to choose from, all male."

"General Maitland?"

"Yes, these are his. We'll be doing the implant to Mrs. Maitland on Thursday."

"She'll be one happy lady."

Imre took off his glasses and rubbed the lenses on his lab coat. "This was a challenging one. Her eggs weren't easy to get. And, that poor couple has waited a long time for this. Now, a baby is on the way. A happy day indeed."

Derek patted the scientist on the back. "You can be proud. Another happy customer, and, of course, another worthwhile addition to the world is on his way." He was proud of the fact that his facility was proficient in all aspects of birth challenges. Whether it be artificial insemination or in vetro fertilization, they were capable of performing the procedure successfully.

Derek resumed the walk back to his office. He enjoyed making the rounds every morning and also enjoyed the exercise it gave him. At seventy years of age, it was good for him to move his legs as often as he could. Sitting behind a desk for too long always caused them to stiffen up on him.

He flashed his security card against the magnetic reader and pushed open the heavy door that led to the office corridor. Two men stood sentry on the other side of the door.

The laboratory section of Triple-L was heavily secured with alarms, not only for burglary or fire, but also for freezer and refrigeration temperature controls. The fate of no less than 200,000 precious sperm samples depended upon the temperature being maintained at the perfectly prescribed level.

And every accessible doorway was secured both by magnetic controls and by unarmed security personnel. They didn't wear uniforms; they didn't need any. Their demeanour and bulk spoke volumes about who they were and what they were capable of.

"Top of the morning to you, gentlemen!"

The guards smiled back at Derek, and one of them spoke. "You're looking particularly chipper today, Doctor. Anything you need from us right now?"

"No, but thanks for asking. How's the family, Jim?"

"Oh, not bad. Well, our little guy has ADHD apparently, according to our family doctor. A bit of a worry."

Derek frowned, and dismissively waved his hand in the air. "Oh, poo on that, Jim. These quacks over-diagnose that nonsense. And then they just drug them up—that's their solution. I'm guessing they've prescribed a regimen of Ritalin, right?"

Jim nodded. "Yeah, we haven't started him on it yet, though. Kinda scary to think what it might do to his personality, but we need to do something."

"It'll suck the life out of him, Jim. You won't recognize him. His spirit will be smothered. Tell you what, bring him in to see me."

"Really?"

"Yes. I'd be glad to help. No family physician can compete with even the most junior scientist we have on our staff. We'll help him. You won't need any drugs."

Jim put his hand over his heart. "I don't know what to say, Doctor. Thanks so much. But, I'm afraid to ask...what will this cost?"

Derek patted him on the shoulder. "Nothing at all. My pleasure to help you out. But, promise me, no Ritalin, okay?"

"I promise, Doc. My wife will be so happy to hear this."

Derek laughed as he resumed his walk down the hall. "Just consider it one of the perks of working at the most advanced genetics lab in the country."

Back in his office, Derek sat down in front of his computer, put on his glasses, and began scrolling through the day's itinerary. Saw that he had an appointment at 10:00. Checked his watch—only ten minutes.

He clicked on the man's biography, package of financial disclosures, and reference letters. Derek had already reviewed the file in detail a few days ago, but wanted to refresh his memory.

The man's name was Stuart Manning, from Chicago. An investment banker, with a net worth of approximately 100 million. Was determined sterile a couple of years ago, but his wife, Alexandra, was a perfectly healthy host. Her medical records, heritage tree, and IQ tests all looked superior. Derek nodded, and muttered, "A good candidate."

He scanned over Stuart's financial disclosures. No debts, an annual income of twenty-five million, give or take. Reference letters from several high-placed sources. All looked good.

He re-read the email from Stuart. His American Airlines flight from Chicago was due in to JFK last night at 9:00, so he had every reason to expect that he'd be on time for their meeting.

A stickler for detail and caution, Derek clicked on his email address book and sent a query off to his contact at American Airlines.

There was a knock on his door and his assistant, Molly, poked her head in.

"Doctor, Mr. Manning is here. Can I bring him in?"

Derek waved his hand. "Yes, yes, of course. Thanks Molly."

She backed away from the door and ushered the man in. Derek walked from behind his desk and greeted his guest with an outstretched hand.

"So pleased to meet you, Mr. Manning. I'm Derek Schmidt, the managing director here at Triple-L."

"Call me Stuart. Thanks for seeing me, Doctor Schmidt. I hope you received my package?"

"Yes, I sure did. Very complete. And, you can call me Derek. Please, have a seat."

Derek poured them both cups of black coffee and sat down once again behind his desk. Stuart seemed to him to be the consummate executive. Tall, trim and athletic, dark hair, stylish slightly tinted glasses, expensive suit, Italian leather shoes. A good-looking man, and for a moment Derek thought what a shame it was that the man was sterile.

"How was your flight last night? On time, I hope? American Airlines I think you said?"

"Yes, thanks. Landed almost bang on 9:00. That doesn't happen too often with American these days."

"Time is precious, so we'll get right to our discussion if you don't mind. How does your wife, Alexandra, feel about your pursuit of a contract with Triple-L?"

"She's excited, Derek. We've both been very frustrated the last few years, and when I finally discovered I was shooting blanks, we decided we had to do something. Your name came up in the circles I run in. Triple-L seems to come highly recommended."

Derek smiled. "We are very special. And we only deal with special customers. Your credentials seem impeccable, and your wife seems like the perfect candidate. In the scheme of things, of course, she's far more important than you are. We'll have to do extensive background checks on both of you, you understand, but, on the face of it we should be able to do business."

"Can you explain the process to me, Derek?"

"Yes, of course. I trust that what I tell you will remain confidential, even if we don't accept you?"

"You have my assurances on that."

"Well, that's good. Because, just to get an unpleasantry out of the way early, if we found out that your assurance was not honest, we would be in touch with you."

"What do you mean by that?"

"We don't like publicity, Stuart. If your mouth happened to be loose, we might have to shut it for you. Is that blunt enough?"

Derek noticed that Stuart swallowed hard at that comment.

"Understood."

"I hope so. It's best I be honest with you up front, as we expect you to be with us."

"Okay, can you tell me what's involved?"

Derek rolled his chair back and crossed his legs.

"Here at Triple-L, we are committed to producing the most superior physical and mental specimens. When you purchase sperm from us, you are receiving quite simply the best. We have been in business for over fifty years now and we only have fifty sperm donors, with almost a quarter million specimens frozen. Some of those have been frozen for decades. Most of them come from German or Danish donors.

"Our philosophy is that the most genetically superior humans will make the best leaders, whether they lead in politics, science, business, or the military. And our philosophy is also that the humans we produce from our sperm must be male. We will not produce female babies."

Stuart frowned. "Why is that?"

"Because this is meant to be a man's world, and we want it to stay that way. While we do have some women in our ownership group and on our board, even they agree with this philosophy. In leadership positions, there is no room for emotion and sensitivity. Leaders must lead. Period."

"How the hell do you accomplish this? Is genetics that advanced now that you can determine only male offspring?"

"Yes, we can. A little basic science lesson. The father always determines the sex of the baby. The mother will always have an X chromosome in her egg. The father's sperm can either have an X or a Y chromosome. If the sperm has an X, the baby will be XX—female. But, if the sperm contains a Y chromosome, the baby will be XY—male."

"So, how do you know?"

Derek folded his hands behind his head and continued.

"A sperm has twenty-three chromosomes. One of those will be an X or Y. The remaining twenty-two chromosomes are called autosomes, and have nothing to do with the gender make-up of the baby. They determine other things like health, longevity, intelligence, etc.

"The egg from the mother contains twenty-three chromosomes as well, but the gender chromosome for the mother is hard-wired at X. Only the sperm has the wild card of being either X or Y.

"So, a normal human being will end up having forty-six chromosomes in total, twenty-three from the man, and twenty-three from the woman. These chromosomes contain the entire genetic composition of a human.

"Sperm can be pre-screened as to whether or not it contains the X or Y chromosome, because each time sperm is produced it will be random. So, tests have to be performed on the actual sperm sample. But, this pre-screening isn't fool-proof. Only sixty-percent effective.

"So, we use what's called a Pre-implantation Genetic Diagnosis. Several eggs are extracted from the mother, kept in a refrigerated state, and then fertilized with sperm from our donor. After three days in the lab, several embryos will have developed from this fertilization. Our scientists then determine the gender of the embryos.

"The strongest male embryo is then chosen, and the others are simply discarded. The chosen embryo would then be implanted into your wife. At that point, we've done our job and you and Alexandra can look forward to the birth of your healthy baby boy."

Stuart shook his head. "Astonishing. While, at the same time, quite simple."

Derek nodded. "Yes, I guess one could say it is simple. Really, anything is simple if the objective is honorable. Because, the task is made simple by determining to just overcome any obstacles. Without obstacles, anything is simple."

"So, at that point, your involvement ends?"

Derek chuckled. "Well, not really. First of all, we charge no fees for our service. We only ask you to reimburse our expenses, which are around $100,000 per specimen. And before we perform the service, you must sign a contract agreeing that certain mentors will be involved in your child's life. Not much involvement until college age, though. At that point, your boy must attend West Point, and if proven to be as superior as we expect, he will be chosen for an upper echelon group at West Point called the Honor Guild.

"From that point on, his future will be determined for him. You and your wife will have no say in his future. He will be guided along a career path that will guarantee wealth, power and success."

Stuart leaned forward in his chair. "What if we don't agree to that when the time arrives?"

Derek mounted his elbows on the desk, and rested his chin on top of his clenched fists.

"You don't want to contemplate such a thing."

"What?"

"You're clearly a clever man. A contract is a contract. There is no way out of your contract with us. Well, that's not entirely accurate, there is a way out, but it's not one you'd wish to choose."

Stuart frowned. "What are you saying?"

Suddenly there was the sound of a little beep on Derek's computer.

"Excuse me for a second, Stuart."

He clicked on the email reply that he'd just received from his contact at American Airlines. He read to himself: "Derek, no one named Stuart Manning was on our flight last night, nor this morning or any other flights from Chicago to New York in the past week. I trust this information will be helpful to you."

Derek looked up at Stuart and smiled. Then he slid his hand underneath the top of his desk and pressed a little red button. Within mere seconds, two burly security men burst through the door of the office.

The geneticist commanded, "Take him."

28

From that moment on, time for Sandy flew by in a flurry of motion and pain. The two men grabbed him from behind before he'd had a chance to react. They yanked him out of his chair, and one of the men slammed a thick fist into his belly.

As Sandy doubled over in pain, his hands were pulled behind his back. Then they were restrained by plastic handcuffs around his wrists.

Derek calmly walked over while the two men held him erect. Strangely, he was smiling at him, but the smile betrayed something else under the surface. Confidence, for sure, but also a certain kind of evil.

"Who are you, Stuart Manning?"

Sandy stared blankly at him, still out of breath from the punch to his gut. He wondered what had blown his cover. Everything seemed to be fine—right up until Derek had excused himself to look at his computer. Had he received some kind of alert?

"I'll repeat the question. Who are you?"

Sandy spit out the words. "I gave you my name."

"No, what's your real name?"

Derek crooked his finger at one of the men and another punch landed in Sandy's mid-section, this time around the kidneys. Sandy gasped.

"We can do this all day, if you want."

Sandy's mouth was as dry as sandpaper, and he felt weak in the knees. If one of the thugs hadn't been holding him up he was sure he'd be lying on the floor by now.

He sputtered. "My name…is…Stuart Manning."

"Okay, we're getting nowhere on the name thing. Let's try another question. Why are you here?"

All of a sudden Sandy felt faint. His chin drooped onto his chest, and, as he gazed down at the floor, it started spinning in tight little circles.

Almost like background noise, he heard Derek address the men.

"Can't do any more of this here. Take him to our place in the Bronx. I'll follow shortly in my car. Use the stretcher to take him down in the elevator to the garage. Cover him with a blanket so no one sees that he's been bound. I'll give him a light sedative so he keeps his mouth shut in the elevator. And put on white lab jackets so you'll look like emergency personnel."

The next sensation Sandy remembered was the jab of a needle in his right forearm.

Then...blackness.

*****

When he came to, everything was a blur. His eyes felt like there was some kind of film over them, but gradually they began to focus.

His captors had taken off his fake glasses, presumably because they intended to start working on his face now that his belly was mush.

He noticed the glasses sitting on a little table beside him. Sandy was actually glad to have them off—they were annoying, even though the lenses were just clear glass.

Vito had given them to him, saying they would help disguise him a bit more, particularly with the tinted lenses. They would hide his distinctive blue eyes.

He was sweating from his scalp, either from stark fear, or maybe because of the black die in his hair. Ever since Vito's men had applied the die, his head had felt sticky and hot. He hoped that with his scalp dripping moisture that the die wouldn't drip along with it.

For the moment, he was relieved to know that he was still somewhat disguised, particularly with the molds that Vito's men had applied on the insides of his cheeks to puff out his face a bit. Sandy prayed that once these goons started punching him in the face, he wouldn't choke to death on the mold stuff.

He glanced around the room he was in. It was clearly some kind of storage warehouse, although quite small, maybe around 1,000 square feet at the most. One wall had several filing cabinets stacked against it, and another wall had boxes piled high to the ceiling.

The floor was cement, and the ceiling was unfinished with exposed pipes and beams. There were four windows, but they were blacked out. There was a double metal door on the window side of the room, and a single door at the back. He recalled hearing Derek mention the Bronx, so he presumed that was where he was now.

The handcuffs were off. Instead he was now duct-taped across his chest and over his thighs, holding him tight to a chair. His ankles were also taped together.

There was no possibility of him being able to use either his hands or his feet in defense.

Made Sandy wonder if they knew what skills he had. Whether they knew that if he was unencumbered he would be a lethal weapon. He thought back to Derek's sudden change in attitude after looking at his computer. There must have been some warning about him.

Although, he didn't think that Derek knew yet who he was—otherwise, he would have no further use for him. He wouldn't be sitting in this chair right now. No, the man wanted to know why Sandy had scammed him. Why he went to such trouble to get an interview.

And, Sandy began chastising himself for taking such a chance. What was he thinking? Curiosity, at times, was a dangerous game to play. And he'd played himself right into danger. These people obviously didn't fool around. When Derek said that everything about Triple-L was strictly confidential, he wasn't kidding.

Sandy knew he was in serious trouble.

The front door opened and in walked the two goons who had accosted him back in the Manhattan office.

The sunlight beamed in through the doorway, so at least he knew it was still daytime. He wasn't sure, however, how long he'd been out. So, it was possible, he guessed, that it was already the next day.

The men pulled up chairs and sat down several feet away in a corner of the room.

Then the door opened again, and in walked Derek Schmidt himself. Clearly, the good doctor didn't mind getting his hands dirty.

He calmly strolled to the corner where his men were sitting, and dragged another chair over, placing it directly in front of Sandy.

Derek sat down and crossed his legs. He pulled a pack of cigarettes out of his shirt pocket and lit up. He held it out to Sandy.

"Would you like a puff?"

Sandy shook his head.

"Good for you. A terrible habit. I must give it up one day. Funny that a doctor like me would smoke, huh? But, you know, life is short, and I know all the genetic probabilities of contracting cancer from smoking. In my case, the chances are slim, so I'll indulge."

Sandy said nothing, which he figured was his best chance of staying alive.

"I'm a careful man, Stuart, or whatever your name is. I know that you didn't fly in on American Airlines to JFK last night."

Sandy thought, *At least I know now that it's still the same day.*

He decided to talk a bit, to buy some time.

"Did I say American Airlines? Sorry, I meant United. And you must have misunderstood me. I flew in to LaGuardia, not JFK."

"Ha, ha. You're a funny man. Nice try. After my men escorted you here, I checked United as well. No sign of you. Any other airlines you'd like to suggest?"

Sandy swallowed hard. *Should have kept my mouth shut.*

"Now, here's where we're at, you and I. You must have had a reason for conning your way into an appointment with me. Whatever that reason is, I'd like you to just tell me so we can get this over with.

"We're not killers, Stuart. My men aren't even armed. We create life, we don't destroy it. We go to great lengths to keep our facilities secretive, because the American public just wouldn't understand what it is we do. I'm sure you can understand that what we do is special, and important. And, it's work that must continue. I would like your support for that secrecy."

He continued. "I'm guessing that you're an investigative journalist. Am I right?"

Sandy kept his mouth shut.

"You're doing a story, right? Somehow, you heard about us. And, of course, it would indeed be one hell of a story, probably Pulitzer Prize material? The biggest thing since Watergate, but even bigger."

Sandy tried moving his arms. Could feel cramping starting in his shoulders.

"Uncomfortable, are you? We could cut you loose if you'd just clear this up for us. You wouldn't be the first reporter who came after us. We've had several over the years. And, we've paid each of them off, quite handsomely.

"We know full well that reporters have their bases covered—usually other associates who are in on the story, too. So, I'm sure you're smart enough to have done that. Killing you, if that's what you're afraid of, would do nothing for us. Because, we don't know how long the trail is. We're better off coming to an agreement with you, giving you enough money that you'd be motivated to kill the story and use that money to pay off your associates, editors, whoever. Make sense?"

Sandy nodded.

"Good. So, let's try this again. What's your real name, and what media outlet do you work for?"

Sandy had no idea what came over him, but he regretted it as soon as he opened his mouth.

"Joseph Goebbels, of the Third Reich Journal."

Derek's face turned beet red. His cruel little mouth opened and closed, with no words. Instead, he turned and motioned to one of the two thugs sitting in the corner.

The man rushed over, and Sandy braced himself.

A fist hit him square in his left eye socket, knocking both him and the chair over onto the floor. The man grabbed the chair by the slats and slammed it upright again. Then, another fist, this time into the right eye.

Sandy felt the ache in his eyeballs, radiating outwards to the top of his head and to the tip of his chin. For a few seconds, everything was a blur. But suddenly, his sight was clear again, but he could sense the encroachment of swelling around his eye sockets. His vision was gradually being blocked by the swelling, slowly but surely.

"Thanks, Jim."

Derek turned his head and called to the other man.

"Alfie, get over here. I think it's time we did a tag-team on our friend here."

Through his narrowing vision, Sandy saw the bulk of Alfie arrive to stand beside the man named Jim. Both stood with their fists clenched, awaiting their next orders.

"Stuart, be reasonable. Do you really want to suffer like this? Tell me what I want to know."

Sandy thought that perhaps he could buy some time. Give him a phony name of a reporter at the *New York Times*, or something. But, he knew that would only buy him minutes. Derek would simply check the validity of that answer on his computer.

Easy to google anyone and anything these days—answers within seconds. Just like how the evil geneticist had had the good sense to double-check Sandy's account of the airline and airport.

In other words, it was hopeless. There seemed to be no way out of this.

Then suddenly, there was.

The locked metal double doors burst open.

Four men rushed in, one of them holding some kind of battering ram. The other three had very large pistols in their hands, made even larger by the silencers attached to the barrels.

All four were dressed in jeans and sweatshirts. Sandy's quick brain told him these weren't cops. The silencers were dead giveaways.

Derek jumped to his feet and raised his hands. His two thugs did the same.

One of the mystery intruders pulled out a knife and cut away the duct tape that surrounded Sandy's body. The other three walked over to Derek and his men, and rammed the long barrels of their guns against their foreheads.

They said nothing. Without hesitation, two of them pulled the triggers of their pistols sending Jim and Alfie to the ground. Eyes and mouths open wide in shock, perfectly shaped circles in their foreheads.

After they hit the ground, just for good measure, the killers put one extra bullet into each of their brains.

Derek just stared down at them, stunned by what had just happened, as the third killer held his gun steady against the good doctor's temple.

Then this third killer spoke for the first time.

"You're the lucky one, Dr. Schmidt. Your life will be spared today. We might collect at a later date. Bye."

One of the men gently helped Sandy up out of his chair, but he immediately crumpled to the ground. Just like a fireman saving someone from a burning building, the giant of a man picked Sandy up, slung him over his shoulder as if he were a sack of potatoes, and jogged with ease through the door and out into the parking lot. The other three men followed.

He carried Sandy over to a black stretch limousine. The door magically opened, and Sandy was carefully placed inside. The man then joined his three friends in a black SUV parked in front, which quickly drove out of the parking lot.

Sandy slumped sideways across the plush leather seats, as the limousine also pulled away.

He heard a familiar voice. "Well, Sandy, you're quite the sight for sore eyes."

Sandy pushed himself up into a sitting position, and stared into the eyes of the one and only Vito Romano.

Exhaustion and pain were taking their toll, but he found the strength to ask, "How did you find me?"

Vito laughed. "Those eyeglasses I gave you. They contained a micro GPS tracking chip. You didn't think I'd let you venture out unprotected, did you? You're a valuable friend. Those glasses also had a miniature video camera mounted in the bridge of the frame. Isn't technology wonderful? They transmitted your entire audio and video conversation with Schmidt to our van that was cruising around West Street within Wi-Fi range. We have it all recorded—useful stuff. And once they took you to the Bronx, the GPS tracking chip allowed us to follow to where they were keeping you."

Sandy carefully touched one of his swollen eye sockets. "Geez, then, what the hell took you so long?"

"We decided to stop for a little pasta along the way."

Sandy chuckled, despite the arrows of pain shooting across his face.

"Where are you taking me?"

"Back to your girlfriend's house in Queens."

"She's not my girlfriend."

"Sorry. Correction. Your ex-girlfriend."

"How do you know about her?"

"Oh, Sandy, Sandy. We make it our business to know things."

Sandy winced as he rubbed the other eye. "Well, thank God for that."

Then something occurred to him.

"Vito, you're in the Boston Cosa Nostra. This is New York. What are you doing here? Isn't this a violation of…I don't know…some kind of code between you guys? This isn't your turf."

Vito smiled. "Things have changed a lot since Michael Corleone and *The Godfather*. We're not as territorial as we used to be. We scratch their backs, they scratch ours. It's the way of the world now."

"I guess it must be. Tell me, why didn't your guys kill Schmidt back there?"

"No need. Not necessary. His two thugs were expendable. But, Dr. Derek Schmidt might prove useful to us, especially now that we have him on video. We never squander opportunities, Sandy."

Sandy nodded knowingly. "Kind of that 'information is currency' thing again, huh?"

"You got it, my friend."

Sandy leaned forward in his seat and held out his hand. Vito took it and they shook.

"Vito, thank you for saving my life. I owe you."

Vito pulled a glass of red wine out of the console holder and took a sip.

"You're very welcome, my friend. And, yes, you do."

29

Linc snuck up behind Melanie and gave her an affectionate slap on the bum. He did these little things from time to time, just to show her that once in a while he could still be a wee bit frisky.

She was standing at the kitchen counter, slicing up some carrots and other assorted veggies for dinner.

No reaction at all to his sign of affection, so Linc decided to take it a step further. He slid his hand up her skirt, and brushed his fingers against her crotch. No panties—he liked that.

She wriggled uncomfortably, and pulled his hand down.

Linc nestled his chin against her neck, and whispered, "You look sexy when you're cooking."

"I'm not cooking, I'm slicing. And, you might want to re-think getting so close to me while I have this in my hand." Melanie waved the knife in the air to emphasize her point.

Linc laughed. "Oh, that turns me on even more. If you want to play rough, we can do that."

"No, Senator, I don't want to play rough—I don't want to play at all."

"Aren't we formal? Calling me 'Senator' now?"

Melanie turned around to face him, holding the knife in front of her.

"I've decided that I'm going to call you that from now on. That's all you are to me, now. A senator. You're not my husband. We're just playing pretend until you win what it is you want to win. Then, as you promised, I expect you to set me free. I'm holding you to that promise, Senator."

Linc backed away from her. "Well, alright then. Call me whatever you want, I don't care. Just make sure you play your role to perfection."

Melanie placed her knife on the counter. "Where is it you're forcing me to go next week?"

"We have to head to Iowa. The first presidential caucuses are being held, and all indications are that I'll win. Iowa is the first on the schedule, and in five months' time I should have locked up enough delegates to win the nomination. And make a mental note that from Iowa onward, you'll be a busy lady. The New Hampshire primary follows Iowa, then South Carolina and Nevada. After that, seven states are up for grabs on Super Tuesday. And we continue until all fifty states and territories have voted."

"Do I have to smile and land fake kisses on your cheek?"

Linc chuckled. "Yes, that's part of the job. And you need to make it look like you're enjoying it. While you're at it, remember that virtually every woman in America wishes she were in your place."

"Every woman in America doesn't know you like I do."

Linc sneered at her, then flung his hand out and grabbed her by the hair.

"We may be pretending here, but it's a long haul ahead, lady. I don't have to put up with your insults. If you want me to leave you alone, treat me the way I expect to be treated."

Linc relished the look of fear that suddenly crossed her face. She said nothing, but he noticed that she'd swallowed hard the instant he grabbed her by the hair.

Now he wasn't faking, or patronizing. All of a sudden he really was horny.

With his free hand, he undid his jeans and let them fall to the floor.

"Well, sweetheart, since you insist on calling me Senator, I think you need to also start acting the part of a staff member." He laughed. "Get down on your knees."

*****

Linc was resting comfortably in his sound-proofed office. He loved this section of his mansion. It was his sanctuary, and it gave him the complete solitude that he needed from time to time. In fact, lately more than usual. It was a handy place to hold meetings as well, one of which he would be having very shortly.

Meagan Whitfield and Bob Stone were coming over for dinner. But first, they would meet in his office so they could discuss things that Melanie wouldn't be allowed to hear.

As for Melanie, after she'd finished giving him a half-hearted blow job, he left her to clean up the mess. Told her also to put on a decent dress and some damn panties. And to behave herself during dinner. Part of her role in this was to convince his handlers that their marriage was a happy one.

He stretched out in his leather recliner and reflected on his trip to Argentina. He was still in a state of shock, but for a guy like Linc, with his innate ability to control his emotions, you would be hard-pressed to tell.

On the trip back to Dallas, he tried to pump Horst with questions, but the man basically ignored him. Linc figured he'd been given orders and was simply doing his job. But, Linc hated being ignored. It really bothered him.

The man who officially went by the name of Herman Braxmeier hadn't talked very much over dinner. His wife, Angela, said that he was suffering from the early stages of Alzheimer's. Linc thought that was kinda funny, considering he was apparently 129 years old.

But, when he did talk, and Horst translated—assuming the translation was correct and not faked—he had some powerful things to say:

"Once in a while comes a man of destiny. One who is misunderstood by people of lesser intellect. I was that man, and I understand you might be too. We will find out if that is true or not. One thing you cannot do is collapse under criticism or assaults on your being. You must always prevail and, above all else, win and survive. One thing you must also remember—stay at least two steps ahead of everyone else."

There were a few other mumblings from the old man, but that one statement was what Linc remembered most. Herman tried to talk about Germany, but his eyes kept misting over every time he mentioned the Fatherland.

And, while he recalled a few of his trusted Nazi officers, he struggled to remember most of their names.

The old man was clearly overcome with emotion when he talked of his most trusted comrade, Hermann Goering. Said that was one of the reasons why he had chosen the name Herman for himself, though he had made the spelling slightly different out of respect for his friend.

But he flew into a surprising rage when he mentioned Heinrich Himmler, the one who had betrayed him by holding secret peace talks with the enemy when it was clear that the war was going to be lost. Linc was astonished at the quick outburst from the man, because, considering his age, mustering up that much emotion must have taken some real effort.

However, at that moment of anger, Linc felt goosebumps run up and down his spine. Even at such an advanced age, the inflection in his voice and the violence on his face were a surreal reminder of the old newsreels of the Nazi leader giving speeches. At that moment above all other moments, Herman Braxmeier was Adolf Hitler.

At least five times during dinner, Herman just simply nodded off. Angela would prod him from time to time, and insert another spoonful of food in his mouth. Linc could tell that she cared about him a lot.

All she said about their time together was that they'd been married in Argentina about fifty years ago. Linc asked what Herman had done since arriving there from Germany. She just shrugged her shoulders in response. Either she thought it was none of his business, or he'd had enough wealth that he had no need to do anything at all. Linc wondered if it was possible that such a man could be content to do nothing.

Linc had done some research when he returned from Argentina. The official story was that Adolf Hitler had killed himself by gunshot through the roof of his mouth on April 30, 1945. He was hiding in his bunker in Berlin as the allies were closing in.

His wife, Eva Braun, was with him at the time, and she matched his act by ingesting a tab of cyanide. His prior instructions to his aides were that their remains were to be burned, which apparently, they were. The Soviets recovered the remains when they arrived in Berlin.

But, over the years, the accounts of how Hitler died had become controversial. Some historians discounted the records as just being Soviet propaganda. Others said that the truth was covered up.

Then, in 2009, American researchers performed DNA testing on skull fragments that the Soviets had long insisted were those of Hitler, recovered from the burnt ashes. Those tests revealed that the skull was actually that of a woman, not a man, and that she was younger than forty years old when she died.

Linc discovered that there was a voluminous amount of information about Hitler's death on the internet, some believable, some outrageous.

But the one theory that he found credible was that once Hitler realized that the war was lost and it would only be weeks until he was captured, he'd planned his escape. The exodus became essential in his mind once he'd discovered that his close friend, Heinrich Himmler, had betrayed him.

That exodus was accomplished by submarine. A submarine just for him and his closest aides, after he'd killed his wife, Eva. He'd grown tired of her and saw her as an unstable risk.

As well, a fleet of several more submarines carried cash, precious jewels, and artwork, most of which had been stolen from the wealthy Jews he'd ordered exterminated.

The reports indicated that the submarine fleet landed under the cover of darkness on the shores of Brazil, but maybe that had been wrong. Maybe, instead, it had been Buenos Aires, Argentina. Either way, authorities in at least one of those South American countries had enabled him and had continued to enable him for the following decades. Linc surmised that there must have been enough riches in those submarines to spread around.

He thought back to the words of advice that Herman had offered to him: "Stay at least two steps ahead of everyone else."

Senator Lincoln Berwick was convinced beyond any reasonable doubt, that Herman Braxmeier was Adolf Hitler. He felt honored to have been entrusted with this history-shattering secret.

Linc chuckled to himself when he realized how insightful Herman's words had been. He had indeed kept himself at least two steps ahead of everyone else.

30

"So, what did you think of him?"

Linc winced. "I was astonished. I thought I'd lived a momentous life up until that moment, but after meeting him and being privy to this secret, I'm humbled."

Meagan smiled. "Good to hear. Did you glean any kind of spiritual revival from him?"

Linc shook his head. "No, nothing of that sort at all. He's certainly not one of my historical heroes. But, I'm astounded by one thing. His ability to survive against all odds."

Bob nodded. "Yes, it is incredible, isn't it? While most of us may not agree with his master plan and how he executed it, one thing that can be said about him is that he was probably the most powerful leader the world has ever seen. He had the ability to convince anyone of anything. And he did it with masses of people at a time. Hitler was the perfect example of the power of oratory. The power of image. Even if he was a cruel asshole—and a twisted thinker—the one and only ability that was needed to lead and influence people, he had in spades."

Looking his protégé square in the eye, Bob wrapped up the lesson. "I'd like you to take that thought with you as you enter the primary season, Linc. Doesn't matter what your policies are, how wrong they are, or how impractical they are, your ability to fire up the masses is the one skill that will give you victory. This is the point we were trying to get across to you the last time we met. The need for more anger. The need to stoke fear. These are the things that Hitler did so well—and look at the power it gave him. But he wasn't humble enough to know when to stop. He pushed his agenda too far, too fast."

Linc leaned back and rested his feet on top of the desk.

"I get the message. Thank you for bringing me in on this secret. I'm indebted, and actually quite titillated by the knowledge."

Meagan smiled at him, the warmest smile he'd ever seen from her. But her words betrayed the smile. "Good. Just keep that secret to yourself, or you'll be killed."

Linc lowered his feet to the floor. "There's no need to say that to me, Meagan."

She immediately changed her demeanor. Had made her point, in the brutal way she always did, and was ready to move on.

"We have another issue to talk about. Another attack is in the early stages of planning, once again in Boston."

"Why Boston again? Isn't that a bit of overkill? Maybe we should pick a different city this time around?"

She shook her head. "No. Boston is particularly terror-sensitized right now, after the Marathon bombings and the Quincy Market attack. Our polling indicates a swing in favor of Republicans, which, for a Democratic stronghold like Massachusetts, is nothing short of a miracle. We need to capitalize on that fear sentiment. The Democrats are weak on security, and your messages are starting to take hold across the country, but, surprisingly, also in Blue states like Massachusetts. If you can swing states like that, you're guaranteed to win the White House."

"Okay. Tell me something, did you get your ideas about false flag attacks from Hitler's legacy? I studied the guy in history classes back in college, though not in too much detail. But I did a lot of reading after getting back from Argentina. It seems as if the little man arranged for the arson attack on his own Parliament building, the Reichstag, back in 1933. He used that event to blame the Communists, resulting in the arrest and execution of sympathizers and liberals.

Linc was on a roll. "But more shocking than that, he used it to deny journalists freedom to speak or write anything critical of the Nazi party. Personal freedoms were taken away after the Reichstag burned down, including freedom of protest. And, largely, he managed to do this with very little opposition, because somehow, he convinced the people of Germany that the Communists were on the verge of an overthrow of their government. And, within a few short years, the purge on Jews began."

Bob shifted uncomfortably in his seat. "I don't like to talk about things that extreme. That's not what we're trying to accomplish. Right now, we just want to win and grab power. But, I agree with Meagan about the fear angle, and, you're right, Hitler's act against the Reichstag was definitely a false flag. It's been used many times since, of course, but that was a terrific model of what could be done to sway public opinion."

Linc crossed his arms over his chest. "I know you guys paid off an elected official to get access to the promenade the day of the Quincy attack. But how did you get those three idiots to become assassins?"

"We used 'cut-outs.' People who were connected to the ISIS terror movement, but not committed to it. For money, they'll act as organizers, to recruit fools who actually believe all that Islamic fundamentalist crap. We paid them, they recruited these three fanatics who thought they were acting for the cause, and they carried it out to perfection. They weren't even from the Middle East—these jerks were American-born."

"I see."

Meagan jumped in. "We do, however, have a slight problem."

"What's that?"

"You went to West Point with that man we've been using in some of our ads—Sandford Beech? A professor and scientist at MIT, the Lincoln Laboratory?"

Linc flinched. "Well, yes, you knew that. And we decided that our ads could use his medal-tossing stunt at the ceremony as a means of attacking anti-American behavior."

"Let me get to my point, Senator. Yes, he's a bona fide American hero and clearly a rebel. And he lost his family the day of our attack. What you don't know is that we paid off the deputy mayor of Boston, a greedy little prick named Christopher Clark. He's also taking payments on the side from the Cosa Nostra, for things they want done from time to time."

Linc was listening.

"Well, apparently, Clark received a threatening visit from the one and only Sandford Beech. Tried to extract information from him. Told him he knew that he was involved in the Quincy Market attack—apparently, from a tip received by Beech from the Cosa Nostra. He, no doubt, has friends there, too. Clark is in a bit of a panic now. He asked his controller at the Cosa Nostra to put out a hit on Beech. They never got back to him. Nothing but silence. He knows the mob is working both sides of the street, so he feels he can't trust them anymore. Shows how stupid he is, thinking he could trust gangsters." Meagan shook her head, looking disgusted.

"He's asked us to do something about Beech. Feels the man may be getting too close to the truth, and, of course, Beech is motivated by revenge due to the loss of his family. So, we have some decisions to make. Is Beech as dangerous as he sounds, and could he be trouble? And, while we still need a paid-off stooge in the Boston hierarchy, is the deputy mayor now a liability for us? Should we dispense of him?"

Linc stood up and walked over to his bar. Poured himself a Scotch neat. Didn't offer any to his guests. He felt an unfamiliar pang of conscience, and, strangely—nostalgia. Sandy Beech could be killed if he gave the word here and now, in this room. But, for some reason that he couldn't explain, he hesitated. Sandy had always been there, as a friend at one time, an adversary, and now as an enemy. He was part of Linc's history, part of his identity, and a symbol of a victory that Linc had achieved over the only person he'd ever felt was a worthy opponent.

"Leave Sandy alone for now. We'll talk about him later. As for that Clark fellow, kill him."

31

All were still safe and sound back in New York.

And all was quiet in Boston.

Sandy had been home for a couple of weeks and had just finished chatting with Judy over the phone. Bill and Lloyd were still staying at her home in Queens, all hunkering down together. Judy told Sandy that she was enjoying their company, and that they all felt much safer staying in one spot right now.

Bill was able to head into his office each day, since he worked in New York. But, each night he returned to Judy's house.

Lloyd had hired twenty-four-hour security to watch over his wife Cassidy in Houston, and the excuse he'd given NASA for his absence was recovery from the car accident.

He hadn't told his wife that the car accident had been a deliberate act on his part to avoid an attempt on his life. He'd tell her eventually, after all this uncertainty was out of the way. For now, she didn't need to know. She didn't know about the security detail either. They were pros and knew how to conduct surveillance without being noticed. But she was always in their sight and in close range. Lloyd was comforted by that.

Their mission to conceive a baby would just have to wait for a while.

Sandy was happy to sense a relative calm in Judy's voice. Having two capable guys like Bill and Lloyd staying with her for the foreseeable future, was no doubt reassuring for her.

She'd gone into a panic when Vito had dropped Sandy off at her house after his ordeal with the thugs at Triple-L. He knew he hadn't looked too good—in actual fact, more like death warmed over. Face bruised and cut, eyes swollen up like baseballs, and walking hunched over from the multiple punches to his gut.

Judy and Cynthia nursed him back to health, while Bill and Lloyd largely stayed out of the way. When he was in the mood to talk, though, they were all ears.

All were astonished to hear of what he'd learned at Triple-L, and horrified at what they had done to him after discovering he was an imposter. Sandy just thanked his lucky stars that he had a special friend like Vito Romano. Not many people could brag of the Cosa Nostra saving their lives. The world worked in strange ways sometimes.

But they were all in a strange place in their lives right now.

Judy and her daughter Cynthia were at risk because of the amateurish attempt by John Nichols at blackmailing Linc. And Judy had now heard the tape recording John had made back at West Point, the tape that he'd been using for blackmail. If Linc, or his thugs and handlers, got the notion that perhaps John had made a copy of that tape, then Judy and her daughter were in peril.

Bill Tomkins had survived an attempt on his life, and the life of his niece, in his very own office.

And Lloyd Franken had survived the hit on him by deliberately slamming his car into a tree.

John Nichols was dead, from what was most likely a faked suicide.

And Hank Price was dead from an apparent car accident in Seattle, but all suspected that was a hit as well. Too much of a coincidence.

Of the five boys who were in the van that fateful night decades ago when the underage girl was raped and lost her life, only three remained alive. And one of those three appeared likely to be the next President of the United States. He was the one who had everything to lose if the truth about that night were disclosed.

If that tape ever surfaced.

If Linc's DNA were ever connected with what happened to that fourteen-year-old girl.

Senator Lincoln Berwick was the only one who had the motive to kill John and Hank, and to have attempted to kill Bill and Lloyd. And now, there was reason to fear he had the motive to kill Judy as well and possibly even her daughter as collateral damage.

Sandy, on the other hand, believed that, for now, he was relatively safe from the murderous motives of his arch-enemy and former best friend.

Ironically, though, he'd created his own perils lately.

His disguised visit to Triple-L had clearly been a bad idea, and he was lucky to have escaped with his life. Thanks to Vito.

It was a good thing he'd had a well-documented fake ID that day to go along with his disguise. Since Triple-L was linked to this whole strange story, if he'd been identified he would also be on the hit list now.

He'd also created his own peril with the attempted shakedown of Christopher Clark. That was another little covert operation that had gone south. Clark had been more careful than Sandy, with one of his thugs hiding out in the park that night.

And now, according to Vito, Clark had tried to get the Cosa Nostra to kill him. Thankfully, the mob had ignored the crooked politician's request, but Sandy figured that wouldn't stop the fat little man. Clark was clearly worried that he was a threat. Not necessarily a threat physically, but a threat to his livelihood.

In reality, though, Sandy was a threat to him for a significantly more noble purpose.

Sitting in the lonely confines of his study, Sandy remembered back to that day.

That day when a bloody hole appeared without warning in the forehead of his lovely wife.

He replayed in slow motion the sight of the horse collapsing on top of his two wonderful children, crushing the life out of them.

And discovering that Deputy Mayor Christopher Clark, out of pure greed, accepted money to clear the way for it all to happen. Arranged permits for Boston Party Pleasures, a company that didn't even exist, to run three horse-drawn wagons onto the promenade that day—wagons that contained cowardly assassins waiting inside, waiting to slaughter hundreds of innocent people.

Christopher Clark, the official who'd ordered the barricades taken down to allow those wagons to enter a pedestrian area where they never should have been.

Christopher Clark, who had received untold sums of money deposited into a numbered Bermuda bank account three months before the terrorist attack.

Money deposited by Meagan Whitfield and Bob Stone, two top officials with Lincoln Berwick's presidential campaign. A campaign that was doing its level best to instill fear in the hearts of Americans, angrily preaching of the evils that lurked around every corner. For the sake of votes, and only votes, propagandizing people to believe there were terrorists hiding under every bed.

And it was working.

Lincoln Berwick had just waltzed to victory in both the Iowa and New Hampshire primaries. His message was getting through.

Sandy's family, and hundreds of others, were slaughtered so that Lincoln Berwick could garner votes.

The more he thought, the more his hands trembled with rage.

Vito Romano had given Sandy two things when they'd last met a few days ago.

First, was a gun—a "throwaway" as he had described it to Sandy. Untraceable.

Second, was the address and directions to the lakefront cottage that Christopher Clark visited every weekend without fail.

Sandy poured himself a drink and walked out into the living room. Stared at the piano that he still hadn't had the heart to sell. Saw his wife and daughter sitting together on the bench, pounding away at the keys, singing duets totally out of tune. Laughing, tickling each other.

He wiped a tear from his eye.

Then Sandy whispered the names of his family.

"Sarah, Whitney, Liam."

Over and over again he whispered their names, and eventually there were just too many tears to wipe away. The front of his shirt was soaked, and he collapsed to his knees on the floor in front of the piano, sobbing uncontrollably.

Sandy raised his head and gazed up at the framed family photo sitting on the ledge of the piano.

Once again, he whispered in the deathly silence of the room, and brought his hands together as if in prayer.

"I'll make things right, I promise."

32

Sandy was enjoying the usual coffee clutch with his students after one of his lectures at the MIT Cambridge campus. The usual suspects, the most vocal being Jonah, Janice and Kyle.

Over the last few months they'd each been doing political research, due to the presidential primaries being in full flight right now.

"What's your opinion so far, Dr. Beech?"

Sandy stirred some sugar into his coffee. "Well, Kyle, I try not to pay too much attention to it. The process is so long, and I don't like who's winning the Republican primaries so far."

Janice passed the cream over to Sandy. "You mean that Senator Berwick guy?"

Sandy nodded. "Yep. He's already enjoyed landslides in Iowa and New Hampshire. South Carolina and Nevada are next, and it looks like he'll win there too."

"He scares me, Doctor."

"He scares me too, Janice. And I know him personally from back in our West Point days. He's always been kinda scary."

Jonah stuffed his books into his knapsack. "I have to get going. Class in five minutes. But, I wanted to ask you. Is what that Senator's been saying in his speeches true? Someone like him should be in the know, which makes me think I had better listen to him."

Kyle turned to Jonah. "You mean all that stuff about new terrorist attacks and sleeper cells in every city?"

"Well, yeah. Makes me wonder. Is he right? We've already had a lot of mass shootings. He makes it sound like more are being planned and ready to happen. I mean, he's a senator. He should know, right?"

Sandy shook his head. "I don't think so, Jonah. It seems to me that Lincoln Berwick is trying to whip everyone up into a frenzy, just for votes. And it seems to be working. Yes, we've had some terrible massacres in this country, but the vast majority of those were committed by home-grown Americans, not terrorists. Usually they're just garden-variety nutcases who never should have gotten their hands on guns in the first place."

"Yeah, but they did."

Sandy finished his coffee, then picked up his briefcase. "I have to get going, too. My classes are done for the day, so time for me to run some errands. All I'll say, Jonah, is this—if Senator Berwick were that concerned about the safety of the American people, he'd be proposing changes to the gun laws. But he's not. He'd rather just scare people into voting for him, and terrorism is his flavor of the day. He's shrewd, as are his campaign folks."

Janice stood. "You're right, Dr. Beech. There doesn't seem to be any consistency. Do you think he'll be the next president?"

Sandy shrugged. "Don't know. I try not to think about it too much. See you at next week's class, kids. Gotta run."

He started for the door, but then felt a gentle tug on his jacket. Turning, he saw Janice scurrying to keep up with him.

"Could I get a lift from you, Doctor? I'm done for the day, too, and I only live a couple of blocks from here. Would that be okay?"

"Well, sure. Follow me."

They headed out to the parking lot together—Sandy's car was not far from the main campus entrance. He held the door open for her and she hopped in.

As he steered out of the lot, he turned to her and said, "Point the way, Janice."

"Just straight ahead, first left, then first right. Halfway down the street on the right."

They drove in silence for a minute, then Janice crossed her legs and leaned towards him. "You really should go into politics, Doctor. We need smart people like you. That Berwick guy is really scary."

Sandy laughed. "I'm flattered, Janice. But, politics is not for me. Thanks for saying so, though."

He made the last turn and pulled up to the curb halfway down the street.

"Thanks so much, Doctor." She unsnapped her seatbelt and leaned in closer. "Do you mind if I give you a hug?"

He didn't have a chance to answer. Her arms wrapped around his neck, while at the same time caressing his lips with hers. He didn't know how long the kiss lasted, but it was long enough for both of their tongues to get acquainted. And it was long enough for Sandy to experience the tug and pull of wanting it to continue, but commanding himself to end it.

The command won out. He cradled her cheeks in his hands and pushed her face back.

"No, Janice."

"It's okay, Dr. Beech. I'm an adult. I won't tell anyone. Come up to my apartment with me."

He shook his head and continued to cradle her face. "You're a lovely girl, but I'm old enough to be your father. And I'm one of your professors. It's not right."

Janice flashed him a half smile, half smirk. "You really are one of the good guys, aren't you?"

Sandy grimaced. "No, not really. But, considering who I'm saying no to, I sure must be one of the stupid guys."

Janice cocked her head and planted a kiss on his cheek. Then she opened the door and got out of the car. Leaning in through the window, she said, "I'm sorry if I was forward. I just wanted you. If you ever change your mind…"

Then she was gone. Sandy watched as she walked up the path to her townhouse, and he caught himself undressing her in his mind.

33

It was Friday afternoon and wonderful weather for a drive to the lake. Not just any lake, though. Sandy was driving to Lake Webster, one of central Massachusetts' more popular recreation spots and only about an hour's drive from Boston.

When he'd met with Vito Romano a few days ago, they'd mapped it all out. Vito gave him exact directions to Christopher Clark's cottage, which was on an isolated stretch of shoreline on the west side of the lake. Good that it was isolated. Gunshots wouldn't be heard.

But to be on the safe side, Vito had given Sandy a silencer to go along with the Beretta "throwaway" pistol.

Sandy patted the insides of his jacket—silencer on one side, Beretta on the other. He'd already practiced screwing the silencer onto the threaded barrel, which served to actually double the size of the pistol.

Deputy Mayor Clark didn't have any family, so no one would miss him. Well, they might miss him at City Hall, but that would probably be the extent of his mourners. The selfish little man had kept all of his bribery money to himself, spoiling himself with a monster house, three cars, and a cottage on the lake. Not to mention, of course, the secret Bermuda bank account. But not so secret that Vito wasn't able to track it down.

Sandy couldn't really enjoy the drive, thinking instead of what lay ahead on his latest covert adventure. So far, those gambits hadn't worked out too well for him.

But he was on a mission, and he could feel the adrenaline rushing through his veins. Today would be a crucial cog in his wheel of justice and revenge. It might just work.

Arriving at the lake, he drove along the county road to the west side. Saw the sign for Meadow Lane, which led down to Clark's lakefront cottage. He drove part of the way down the lane, then turned off along a dirt path and parked the car in a dense thicket of trees. He jumped out, locked up, and began the mile-long hike to the lake.

Meadow Lane was a well-kept road, really just a long driveway because there was only one cottage at the end. An easy hike.

He could smell and feel the lake before he saw it. That fresh scent that bodies of water always betrayed their presence with, along with a progressively stronger breeze the closer he got.

Then he saw it.

A large A-frame cottage, nothing fancy. But it was right on the lake which meant it would sell for big bucks.

Sandy walked along the decking to the front porch, which partially hung over the water. A splendid sight: water glistening in the afternoon sun, shoreline on the other side of the lake heavily forested with fir trees. It wasn't even officially spring yet, but there was no snow on the ground any longer. If you were good at pretending, it looked like a typical summer day in Massachusetts.

He pulled a tool out of his pocket and picked the cheap lock. The door creaked as he pushed it open. He closed it behind him and gazed around. It was an open concept cottage—one large bedroom in the loft above, and two other bedrooms opening off the large living room. On one side of the wall was a desk, and beside the desk was a heavy steel safe sitting on the hardwood floor.

Sandy walked into the kitchen, opened the fridge, and pulled out a can of beer. He then walked over to the side of the cottage that looked out over the back driveway. Collapsed into the supple leather of an inviting recliner, stretched his feet out, and calmly sipped his beer.

Stared out the window and glanced at his watch.

If Christopher Clark was true to his apparent schedule that Vito had informed him of, he'd be here in less than a couple of hours for his leisurely weekend at the lake.

*****

Sandy had dozed off into a light sleep, but awoke to the sound of a car engine. He rolled off the recliner and dropped to his knees on the floor. Peeked up just high enough to get a view of the driveway.

A black Ford Explorer pulled up behind the cottage. This wasn't Clark's car—Vito had told him that Clark drove Cadillacs. The driver hopped out at the same time as one of the back doors opened. A large man exited, then reached back in and dragged out a reluctant passenger by the collar. He pushed him forward towards the house and the two men followed close behind.

The reluctant passenger, hunched over and stumbling nervously along the path, was Deputy Mayor Christopher Clark. The two men following him were dressed in suits, and strode along with the self-assured swaggers of dudes with plenty of notches in their belts.

Sandy dashed across the room to the spot he'd already picked out for himself. A large louvered closet that looked out over the entire expanse of the living area.

He stepped inside and shut the doors.

Next, he pulled the Beretta out of one pocket and the silencer out of the other. Screwed it onto the barrel, flipped off the safety, and held the gun down at his side.

Then he peered through the slats of the closet and waited.

The sound of a key in the lock; then the turning of the door handle.

The door burst open and Clark was shoved roughly into the cottage, followed by the two suits.

Clark stumbled and fell to the floor. One of the men chuckled. "You are a clumsy little fool, aren't you?"

The other suit shut the door behind him. "Okay, we haven't got all day. You gave us some stuff from your house, but it wasn't enough. You have another laptop, because there wasn't much on the tablet at your house. Where is it? It's either here or at your office, but I doubt very much you'd keep a hard drive at your office with what we're looking for on it."

Sandy could see that spittle was coming out of the corners of Clark's mouth.

"It's…in…the safe."

"Open it. Now."

Clark crawled over to the safe, spun the dial, and pulled open the heavy door. He reached in, and pulled out a laptop. He started to close the safe door, but was stopped by one of the men yelling out, "Don't shut that! Pull everything out of there!"

Clark did as he was told, and piled documents and cash onto the floor next to the laptop.

Suddenly the ring of a cell phone. One of the suits reached into his pocket and clicked on.

"Yes, Ms. Whitfield. We're here now. We got some things from his house, and now we're at his cottage. There's a laptop here, which may have what you need, plus some money and stuff. What? Okay, I'll ask him."

The suit put the phone against his chest and directed his attention to Clark, who was still sitting on the floor. "I have Meagan Whitfield on the phone, you know, the one who's been paying you a fortune? She wants to know the password for the laptop."

Clark wiped the sleeve of his shirt across his drooling mouth. "It's 'Quincy.'"

"Well, isn't that appropriate."

He talked into the phone. "He says it's Quincy, ma'am."

The man chuckled. "Yeah, real creative, huh?"

"Oh, okay, I'll ask him that, too."

He put the phone against his chest again. "Mr. Clark, she wants to know the password and PIN number for your numbered Bermuda account—you know, that account that Ms. Whitfield and Mr. Stone have been depositing money in for you."

Clark stammered, "Why…does…she want that?"

He raised the phone back to his ear again. "He's resisting on that, ma'am."

He sighed. "Oh, okay, we won't bother then."

Clark yelled out from the floor. "Let me talk to Meagan! I don't know what's going on here! I've done everything asked of me!"

The suit shoved the phone back into his pocket. "She's already hung up. Doesn't want to talk to you."

"Okay, okay, I'll give her the bank account info!"

"Doesn't matter anymore. She'll find out another way."

He nodded to his partner. They each pulled pistols out of their waistbands, and promptly pointed them at Clark's head.

"We're sorry, Mr. Clark. Nothing personal. You're just a loose end."

Clark screamed "No!" Lowered his head and wrapped his arms around it in a last pathetic defense.

Sandy kicked open the closet doors, raised his Beretta, and fired two precise shots. Both men collapsed to the floor. Sandy rushed over and aimed two more shots at the chest areas of each man.

Clark was expecting by now to feel the force of bullets slamming into his head, but instead all he heard was the soft spitting sound of Sandy's silenced Beretta.

He slowly raised his head and stared up in astonishment at Sandy.

"You!"

Sandy unscrewed the silencer and stuffed it and the pistol back inside his jacket pockets.

"Yes, me. I came here to talk to you. I didn't expect you to have company. Right now, you're still in deep trouble. I despise you, but I don't want you dead. They did, apparently under the orders of some rich friends of yours. I know who they are, and I know all about your connections to them."

Clark struggled to get his chubby body back on its feet again.

"I don't know how to thank you, Dr. Beech."

Sandy pulled his cell phone out of his pocket and punched in a speed dial number. "I don't want your thanks. But right now we have to get you to a safe place fast."

Someone picked up at the other end. Sandy asked, "Is that address still available for me to use? Okay, great. Be there soon. Same combo? Good."

Sandy clicked off and directed his attention back to Clark, who was staring at the still figures lying on the floor.

"Christopher, pick up all that stuff on the floor, as well as the laptop, throw it all in some kind of bag and let's get going. My car's parked about a mile up in the forest. On the way out, we'll get that stuff those men took from your house. It's in their Explorer, right?"

Clark nodded and dashed into the kitchen. Pulled a couple of cloth shopping bags out of a drawer and collected all of the things off the floor.

"Okay, I'm ready."

Sandy opened the door. "Let's go."

Clark pointed. "What about those guys?"

"Least of your worries."

"Where are we going?"

"A safe house in Boston, owned by our mutual Cosa Nostra friends. You'll be safe there until you figure a way out of this shit you're in."

*****

They waited ten minutes, laying as still as could be. Just in case Beech and Clark came back for some reason. Then the two "dead" men got to their feet, brushed themselves off, and headed out the door. One of the men took a tool out of his pocket and carefully locked the door behind them. No point in leaving this nice cottage unprotected while the owner was away for an indefinite period. It would be waiting for him, safe and sound, when he finally returned one day.

The suits hopped into the front seats of the black Explorer, and the driver pulled out his cell phone again.

"Hi Vito. All is well."

He chuckled. "Oh, it was a beautiful con. We all played our roles perfectly, Oscar performances all around."

The suit turned on the ignition while he continued to chat with his boss. "Yeah, I think we're in good shape for the next stage."

He shifted into gear and backed up the Explorer. "Well, they left about fifteen minutes ago, so they should arrive at the safe house in about an hour."

The man laughed again. "Yeah, we'll make sure to steer clear of them. Can't run the risk of ruining good theater."

34

It was a gorgeous day in South Carolina. Just perfect for being out on the golf course. Even more perfect because Linc was leading his two partners by five strokes. And they were only on the tenth hole.

Of course, he'd done some creative cheating here and there. Shot five, carded a four. Didn't count his whiffs. No penalty stroke for landing in the water. Kicked his ball out of the rough a couple of times when no one was looking. Shifted his ball to a better lie in the sand trap.

All little things, but they added up. Linc enjoyed golf, but he thought some of the rules were just darn silly. And when rules in life were silly, Linc just ignored them. He also hated to lose—at anything, even golf.

He didn't think his two partners noticed the corners he was cutting, but his security guy did. All he did each time was give him the thumbs-up. The guy clearly knew who was buttering his bread.

Meagan Whitfield and Bob Stone were his golfing buddies today—one of the few times the three of them were actually doing something social. But, Linc knew it wouldn't be all fun—they had told him before the match that they wanted to talk to him sometime during the game. Sounded serious, but, with those two, it was always serious.

They had three golf carts. Each of them in a cart with a security officer. While they didn't anticipate any incidents, you couldn't be too careful any longer. Linc had just won two primaries, and he had two more coming up this week. Liberal protests followed him everywhere and even some conservative rabble-rousers as well. It seemed as if his Democratic and Republican detractors finally had something in common—they hated him with a passion.

Senator Lincoln Berwick was an equal opportunity asshole, and, right now, the most divisive politician in the country. That was by design, of course, and as far as his campaign organizers were concerned, his ticket to the White House.

His base consisted primarily of people who loved guns; were against immigration unless the arrivals were mostly white Anglo-Saxon; and believed every Muslim was out to kill every American.

Linc chuckled every time he thought of how gullible and easily led people could be. But he didn't care. As long as they voted for him, that was all that mattered. Linc held tight to his old touchstone: "First, get elected." He fervently believed in that maxim, and he knew that once he had the keys to the Oval Office he could do whatever the hell he wanted.

So, when out in public, Linc always had security details with him. Meagan and Bob normally didn't have to worry about that, because they were mostly behind the scenes. But when they were out in public with him, Bob always arranged for the campaign to provide extra security. Just in case.

Today, they were golfing at the private Spring Valley Country Club, just outside South Carolina's capital city, Columbia. Columbia was also the largest city in the state, with 135,000 people, only slightly larger than the better-known city of Charleston.

Columbia was named after the historical icon Christopher Columbus. But Linc wasn't impressed by that. In his opinion, Columbus was highly over-rated by history, and by all accounts, a phony. Most of the honors bestowed on the pompous prick were never even earned. Compared to a real icon, like Adolf Hitler, Columbus was a joke.

Hitler's place in history was ruined, unfairly, as far as Linc was concerned. Sure, he was brutal and misguided, and lost control of his own vision. But his accomplishments and victories were nothing short of spectacular; now forever overshadowed by The Holocaust.

He thought back to his short trip to Argentina, and meeting the great man up close and personal. Goosebumps tickled his spine as he recalled his first image of him, rolling up in his golden wheelchair. A moment he would never forget.

Spring Valley was a private country club and none of them were members. But, because Linc was a Senator, and a presidential candidate, the club made an exception for them to play today. As they should. They also agreed to clear the course with a three hour start-time window, to make sure they had privacy during their match. Bob cut them a cheque for $20,000—out of campaign funds, naturally.

Linc chuckled to himself. Donors should be glad their hard-earned dollars were going to a worthy cause such as a day's relaxation on a golf course, a course most donors could only dream of being able to afford to play.

The three carts pulled up to the eleventh tee box, and the golfers and their security team jumped out. Meagan motioned to the security guys, kind of a wave action with her hand. They immediately got the message and walked away from them, down the pathway along the fairway.

Linc pulled a Big Bertha out of his bag and began his practice swings. Meagan and Bob walked over to him.

"We need to talk now, Linc."

"Can't it wait until the nineteenth hole? Over a drink?"

"No, this is nice and private here."

Bob took the club out of Linc's hand. "We need your attention, Senator."

"Alright, alright. I thought you guys wanted me to relax today. This is South Carolina primary day, and it looks like I'm going to win my third in a row. Need to unwind so I can deliver a rousing speech tonight at the convention center."

Meagan smiled. "We're confident you'll be fine. And, yes, you'll win today and in a few days, you'll take Nevada, too. We're on our way. But, we have some loose ends."

"Okay, I'm all ears."

Meagan leaned against the side of her golf cart. "I was talking with Dr. Schmidt a few days ago. It seems we had an incident at the Triple-L offices in New York. A man pretending to be a prospective customer infiltrated our screening. Was pretending to be someone else, and we suspect he was disguised as well.

"Schmidt had him hauled away to a different location, in an attempt to convince him to spill the beans as to who he was. Anyway, long story short, they must have been followed, because the warehouse was penetrated by four men. Schmidt's two guards were shot dead. Schmidt was told by one of the men that his life was being spared and that they might 'collect' later. We're thinking the plan must be extortion or something down the road."

Linc winced. "Jesus, he's lucky. What kind of extortion could they use?"

"The imposter might have been wired or something. Schmidt didn't think to check him over to see if he was wearing anything."

"Who do you think these people were?"

Meagan folded her arms across her chest. "A couple of tell-tale signs. They killed the guards execution-style. Bullets to the head, then extra shots for good measure. They seemed like pros. Also, Schmidt said that they fit the stereotype of Mafia. Big guys, dark Italian looks."

"Mafia?"

"Yep, that's his guess."

Meagan pulled a photograph out of the pocket of her jacket.

"This photo was developed from the office security cameras. We think the visitor was disguised, but we wanted to know if you've ever seen him before. He doesn't ring a bell with us."

Linc took the photo and stared at it. He gulped.

Then he nodded slowly. "I know him. He has dark hair and glasses in this photo, and his cheeks look kinda puffy, but I'm 100% certain who he is. Some things can't be disguised, not from people who have known him a lifetime."

"So, who?"

"Sandford Beech. My old West Point classmate."

Bob took the photo from him and looked at it. "You're sure?"

"Yep."

Meagan had been leaning casually against the golf cart. She pushed herself off and moved closer to Linc. "We talked about him with you the last time we met. Told you about how Dr. Beech had shaken down the deputy mayor, Christopher Clark, trying to get information about the Quincy Market attack. He told Clark he'd been tipped off by the Mafia—who Clark also has a relationship with.

"You told us to kill Clark, but leave Beech alone. That might have been poor judgement on your part, Senator."

Linc lowered his head and nodded. "Might have been."

"Something else we have to tell you. We sent a man out to take care of Clark the other day, in line with what you wanted. Clark's disappeared. No one knows where he is—no sign of him at his house or cottage. He's just gone. We phoned his office and were told that he's away for a week attending a funeral for an aunt in New York. We did some research—he has no living aunts or uncles. So, there's something very fishy going on here, Linc. And what's most coincidental is that the men who raided the Triple-L warehouse sound like Mafia, and we know that both Clark and Beech have connections to the Mob.

"And now you're telling us that the imposter at Triple-L looks like Sandford Beech. I think we can connect some dots here. Does someone have Clark in their custody? Protecting him? Interrogating him?"

Linc shuffled his feet. "I don't know what to say."

Bob threw a golf ball into the air and caught it behind his back. "We may have a serious problem here, Senator. Making matters worse, Clark was already involved in the early stages of our next false flag attack. Our plan was to eliminate him before he knew too much, but he knows enough. We may have to move up the timetable. And it looks like we now need to eliminate Beech as well as Clark. Assuming, of course, we ever see Clark again."

Linc's brain was working at warp speed now. Yes, the dots were easy to connect. He should have ordered them to kill his old friend. And he thought to himself that while all this was bad, it wasn't as bad as the part that Meagan and Bob didn't know about. They had no idea that he'd raped and caused the death of a fourteen-year-old girl back in his West Point days. They had no idea that there had been a tape with his voice on it, and maybe even a copy somewhere. They had no idea that Linc had already arranged through his own private security to kill John Nichols and Hank Price, and attempted to take out Lloyd

Franken and Bill Tomkins.

They had no idea, and he wasn't going to tell them, either.

35

It was a modest house on Queensberry Street in downtown Boston. Nothing fancy, but comfortable. Two stories, a nice front porch, green lawn, picket fence, private backyard.

To the uninformed observer, it was a nicely kept family home, probably occupied by dutiful parents, two well-behaved kids, a dog, and maybe a cat. There was even a bicycle strapped to the front porch railing, and a swing set in the back garden—just to complete the mirage of a family home.

But instead, it was a Cosa Nostra safe house, occupied from time to time by some of the most despicable characters imaginable.

Vito Romano had told Sandy that they had several homes like this throughout the Boston metropolis. But he liked this one best because it was only a few blocks south of Fenway Park.

Which meant the neighborhood was fairly busy—not isolated by any stretch of the imagination. Which made it safer.

And, when he wanted to see a Red Sox game, it was ideal for him as a place to sack out after a few beers with the boys. He could do the leisurely stroll to Fenway from the house, and then stagger back again after he was shit-faced.

So, while the house occasionally hosted shady criminals and dishonest politicians, once in a while it was simply a ball game landing pad for the executives of Boston's Ferrara crime family.

Christopher Clark had been a "guest" at the house for several days now. Guarded by two burly guys who were adept at not only keeping the house clean and tidy, but also at cooking great pasta.

Clark was not a prisoner—there was no need for that. He wasn't handcuffed or restrained in any way. The man was scared out of his mind, and relieved to have escaped from what he'd understood to be certain death.

To him, Sandy was his savior, even though the man knew that Sandy had ulterior motives. He didn't care. Which didn't surprise Sandy in the least—once a sell-out, always a sell-out. Clark would probably sell his mother to the highest bidder.

And the fat little man was thankful that he'd cultivated his Cosa Nostra contacts, particularly with the powerful consigliere, Vito Romano. Up until now, they'd only paid him to make projects pass through red tape faster in the painfully slow bureaucracy that was the city of Boston. And he'd enabled them to cut corners below code on construction sites.

All worthwhile for the money they'd paid him, but now they were sheltering him. His cultivation had paid off.

On Monday morning, first thing, one of his guards gave him a satellite phone to use. Clark phoned his assistant and told her that his beloved aunt had died over the weekend and that he would be taking a leave of absence for a week to attend her funeral in New York.

He didn't have an aunt or uncle any longer, but he knew that no one would check. The Mayor's office trusted him, only God knew why. If they knew the things that he'd done, things that had now apparently caught up to him.

Sandy knew the chubby man was somewhat remorseful, as remorseful as a sociopath could be. But, he was only remorseful because he thought his deeds had almost cost him his life.

The charade that Sandy and Vito's men had performed back at the cottage had convinced Clark that he was now a "loose end" to the Berwick Presidential Campaign; that the things he had done to make the Quincy Market slaughter happen were now a liability.

He'd been duped into thinking he'd heard one of Vito's men back in the cottage talking to Meagan Whitfield over the phone when it was actually just Vito chuckling on the other end. But Clark was convinced that Meagan had ordered his death right then and there. Right in his own cottage.

Then, like a commando, Sandy Beech had come bursting out of

the closet, saving Clark's ass with deadly accurate shots from a massive Beretta. It was so sudden, unexpected, and terrifying, that the deputy mayor hadn't even noticed that there wasn't any blood.

Right now, Christopher Clark must be thinking that his entire life was in question. He'd been worried about his job, and phoning in to his office with a fake story about a funeral had been important to him.

But Sandy wondered if he'd considered the probability that he would most likely never be able to return to that job again. He figured that hadn't sunk in to his selfish little brain yet.

It probably would once he and Vito gave him the lay of the land.

If Clark was lucky—and cooperative—he might be fortunate enough to escape prison time. He'd been complicit in the slaughter of hundreds of people, including Sandy's entire family. But Sandy didn't give two hoots what happened to Clark. He wanted the ones at the top, not this little man at the bottom.

Sandy parked in front of the house and saw that Vito's black limousine had beaten him to the meeting. He and Vito were going to have a little chat with Clark today, which would set the stage for what he hoped would come next.

He walked into the house and saw that Vito and Christopher were already chatting in the living room. The guards were busy cleaning up in the kitchen. To Sandy, that seemed a paradox of the highest order. Men who had probably killed more people than he could count were actually domestic darlings.

Christopher greeted Sandy with an appreciative smile and nodded. "I wanted to thank you again, Dr. Beech." He turned his head towards Vito. "And you too, Vito. I wouldn't be alive right now if it wasn't for you two."

Sandy swallowed hard. "Fuck off, Christopher. I don't give a shit whether you're alive or dead."

Vito smiled and drained a glass of cognac. "I won't be as crass as Sandy, Mr. Clark, but I really don't care either."

Clark lowered his head and shook it from side to side. "I sure have screwed up my life, haven't I?"

Vito patted him on the back. "Yes, you have. You've done lots of favors for our family businesses over the years, for which I'm grateful, but you crossed the line when you helped arrange a fake terrorist attack.

"We in the Cosa Nostra may be bad in a lot of ways, and perhaps some think we have no integrity or compassion. But, they'd be wrong. Death and suffering of the innocent is not something we can justify. It makes us sick. That's not who we are. I want justice on this almost as much as Sandy does. He lost everything because of what you and your corrupt politician friends did, and we're on his side, not yours. This one's a freebie."

The consiglieri fixed Clark with a cold stare. "This time I'm not talking to you about arranging favors like in the past. I want nothing more from you. And there will be no more payments from us. You disgust me. What I'm offering you this time is a chance for you to gain some redemption and maybe save your miserable life. The people who arranged for that terrible massacre must pay. And my friend Sandy has a particular interest in this because of the deaths of his family," he said, turning a kinder gaze on his ally.

"The people who did this can't get away with it. You're just small fry. We don't care what happens to you. And even your benefactors from the Berwick campaign don't care about you. You're a walking dead man—you must know that by now. They tried to kill you at your cottage, and they won't give up."

Clark cracked his knuckles and whined, "What the hell do I do?"

Sandy jumped in. "You need to talk. To the authorities. Come clean and throw yourself on their mercy. Once that's done, and your story is told, you'll no longer be someone they need to kill. And, the authorities may offer you some kind of immunity, you never know. We can't promise anything; you'll have to strike your own deal. But, even if you end up doing time, at least you'll be alive."

Clark sputtered, drool dripping out of the sides of his mouth. "Who will listen to me? Who can I trust? That Berwick guy and his handlers are well connected. Look what they pulled off—one of the most horrific terror attacks ever, and they got away with it."

Vito nodded. "Yes, they did. With your help."

Clark suddenly started shaking. His shoulders, hands, knees.

Sandy leaned forward. "Are you okay?"

He was sobbing now. Shook his head back and forth. "No. They're gonna…do it again."

36

The unbearable memories of Quincy Market rushed through Sandy's brain. Like a movie trailer, but in fast-forward. The three horse-drawn wagons, dozens of kids hurrying over with money in their hands eager for ice-cream, the doors of the wagons bursting open, machine guns spraying the crowd without discrimination.

He saw lovely Sarah, still in her chair, falling backwards, mouth open in shock, a tell-tale hole in the middle of her forehead. His adorable children, Liam and Whitney, desperately running away from the gunfire, crouching down beside one of the horses. The horse falling over on top of them, crushing them to death.

Just those last words from Christopher Clark's ugly little mouth brought the images back, so vivid that Sandy thought his skull would burst from the pressure. His face felt like it was on fire from the adrenaline rush. And for the first time in his life that he could remember, he lost complete control of himself.

He lunged from his chair, and with both hands around Clark's throat, yanked him from the couch and sent him airborne into the wall. The man crumpled to the floor, and Sandy was on him in a flash.

Grabbed him by the collar of his shirt and yanked his head up to within inches of his own. "Another one? You've helped them again?"

Clark started sputtering, with more of that same sickening drool coming from the corners of his mouth.

Two strong hands lifted Sandy up and away from Clark. Followed by firm but soothing words.

"That's enough, Sandy. Leave him be."

Sandy turned around and faced Vito. He pointed to the quivering man on the floor. "Did you hear what he said?"

"Yes. But beating the shit out of him isn't going to help. Let him talk to us."

Sandy took a few deep breaths and felt the rage begin to recede.

Vito directed his attention to the man on the floor.

"I'm not going to help you up, Christopher. Get off that floor and start talking. And wipe your mouth, for God's sake. You're making me sick."

Clark rolled over onto his knees, but didn't try to stand. He rested back on his haunches, and wiped the sleeve of his shirt across his mouth.

Sandy saw sweat forming on the man's brow. And his face was redder than a bad sunburn.

Clark stayed on the floor and looked up at the two men. Breathing heavily, hands shaking, he began to speak in almost a whisper.

"A few weeks ago, they asked me to do a couple of things for them."

"Who asked you?"

"The first request came from Bob Stone. And then a week or so later I heard from Meagan Whitfield."

Vito nodded. "Okay, continue. What did they ask you to do?"

"Can I have some water?"

Vito walked over to the bar, took a plastic bottle out of the mini-fridge and threw it to Clark. He missed, and it bounced onto the floor near his knees. The deputy mayor twisted off the cap and guzzled.

Vito scowled. "Just don't drool anymore. Are you going to get up off the floor?"

Clark shook his head. "Rather stay down here right now. Feeling weak in the knees."

Sandy noticed the man's hands were still shaking, causing some of the water to drip down the front of his shirt. Clark poured some into his hand—splashed it onto his forehead and along his cheeks. His face was still red and blotchy.

"Stay down there, then. Just hurry up and tell us what we need to know."

Clark looked down at the floor. "What protection will I have?"

Sandy felt the rage building again. "Just do the right thing, for fuck's sake! Innocent lives are at stake!"

"But, what happens to me?"

Sandy took a step towards him. "Right now, you should just be concerned about staying alive. Because, in a moment or two, I might just kill you myself."

Clark recoiled. "Okay, okay. But, what happens next?"

Vito put his hand on Sandy's shoulder and eased him down onto the couch. Then he knelt on one knee and glared at Clark.

"Listen carefully. To keep you alive, the authorities will have to be involved. We told you that already. I don't know what they'll do about the tale you have to tell about the Quincy Market attack. They might not believe you. You'll have to show them whatever evidence you have on paper, in your hard drives, things like that. Just you saying that Whitfield and Stone instructed you on what to do won't carry much weight. Because we are talking about a presidential candidate here. Serious stuff. I can't be involved with you any longer once you decide to talk to the authorities. I'm Cosa Nostra—I don't have the cred. Sandy can make the connections for you, put you in touch with a top federal prosecutor. If they believe you, I'm guessing they'd want to compel your testimony in a deposition, then put you under witness protection. Otherwise, you'll be a dead man."

Christopher opened and closed his fists, as if trying to loosen up his fingers. Then he slid his right hand up to his chest and patted it. "Feels like a fluttering in my heart."

"Just stress. C'mon, sit in one of the chairs and get comfortable."

Clark shook his head. "No, I'm...more comfortable down here."

Sandy leaned forward in his seat. "Christopher, back to what you were telling us. What did those two people ask you to do?"

Clark stared at the floor. "Stone asked me to provide them with a city vehicle. I drove one out of the compound and left it for him in a plaza parking lot."

"Doesn't someone take inventory of city cars?"

He nodded. "Yes, the van was reported stolen after dispatch checked inventory. It went through the system, I tracked it down, and deleted it from the records. So, there's no record of it being stolen or even in existence now."

Sandy shook his head in disbelief. "You cover your tracks well, don't you? Do you know the license plate number?"

"Yes, it's in the hard drive of my laptop. The vehicle is a Ford Econoline van, and it says Boston Public Works on the sides."

"What were you paid for this?"

Clark took another sip of water. "They deposited $200,000 into my Bermuda account, which was for both things they wanted."

"Killing people is pretty lucrative for you, isn't it Christopher?"

"I don't kill people. I never ask what they intend to do. Even with the Quincy Market attack, I had no idea what they'd planned. I only arranged for the permits and access."

Sandy lashed down with his hand, like a dagger, right into Clark's throat. The man choked and rolled over onto his side.

"You cowardly piece of shit! Don't pretend innocence. You knew what you were doing was wrong. Even after it happened—and you knew that you'd helped to make it happen—you were more than happy to keep your money, and certainly didn't try to turn them in."

Clark struggled back to his kneeling position and scurried backwards a bit, just enough to be out of the reach of Sandy's hand. He was still holding his throat, and his breathing was becoming more labored.

The words came out in a rasp.

"About a week…after I gave them the van, Meagan met me. She…wanted me to approve the business license…for a restoration company. I pushed that through. It was a start-up company, no prior experience on the record, Muslim connected. And she wanted me to arrange to award the bid for a project to them, instead of the other bidders. We were handling the bidding process for an institution and ensuring work was done to code, etc. We do that from time to time for important city institutions. So, I arranged for them to get the project."

"What's the name of this restoration company?"

"New England Restorations."

"And they don't really exist, just like that Boston Party Pleasures at Quincy?"

"Well, they exist now, they didn't before, and they probably won't after."

"Can't this all be traced at City Hall to you?"

"I got smart this time. After I arranged the business license and the bid award, I changed the records to show another official's name, someone who passed away recently. It'll look like he did these approvals. I wasn't so careful on Quincy, but nothing was ever investigated anyway. It was white-washed for some reason. Labeled as terrorism, and left at that. I found that kind of puzzling, but counted my lucky stars. This time, though, I didn't want to take a chance."

"You're just getting real good at this, aren't you?"

Clark finally decided to stand. Slowly, he got to his feet, and leaned against the fireplace mantle. His breathing was getting more labored by the second.

"I'm not feeling too good, guys."

Vito put his hands on his shoulders and guided him over to the couch. Eased him down, and passed his water bottle to him.

"Tell us what this project is, and then we'll call a doctor for you. Looks like you're just having an anxiety attack."

Clark took a long sip and several deep breaths.

"It's the church, the cathedral."

"Which one?"

"Cathedral of the Holy Cross. Re-doing…some of the floors and pews, as well as some needed restoration work…on the pipe organ. A few weeks of work. They've…started already, should be finished in… another week or so."

Sandy gasped. "That cathedral holds a couple of thousand people at a time! It's massive!"

Vito grabbed Clark's face in his massive hand and turned it to face him, squeezing his cheeks hard in the process. "You must have some clue as to what they're planning. What are your thoughts?"

"I don't…know. But, that Senator Berwick's speeches are all about…the terrorism threat, trying to scare people about…Muslims. A prominent Catholic cathedral would probably be…a good target for them this time. That's my…guess."

Sandy jumped to his feet. "Christ, a couple of thousand people crammed into that church would be sitting ducks. Could be a bomb or some kind of gas? And what's the purpose of the van? What do they intend that for?"

Clark shook his head. "Don't know. Might not be related."

"I think you know more than you're saying. Better tell us. If the authorities are going to consider witness protection for you, you're going to need to tell them everything about this thing, as well as the Quincy Market attack."

Clark leaned forward and clutched his chest. He looked up at Sandy and gasped. Then his heavy upper body suddenly seemed to lose the ability to hold itself up. He rolled forward off the couch and crashed to the floor.

Vito dropped down beside Clark and flipped him over onto his back. Began CPR repetitions.

After fifty or so, he sighed and leaned back on his haunches. He did one final check for pulses in the city official's wrist and throat, and then just slowly shook his head.

"He's gone. Heart attack."

"Jesus."

Vito made the sign of the cross and closed Clark's eyelids. Then he called out to his two men who were upstairs in the second floor den.

They bounded down the stairs and quickly took in the scene. Didn't seem surprised. It was as if this was the type of thing they saw every day—and Sandy thought that maybe it was.

One of the men spoke. "What you want, boss?"

"Need a clean-up. The usual."

"Where?"

"Boston Harbor would be a good choice. It always is. Wait until dark, of course."

37

Sandy was driving aimlessly. Through the main streets and side streets of Boston, some of which he'd never even been on before. Normally he'd enjoy exploring new areas, but not today. Today he was looking for a Ford Econoline van, with the words Boston Public Works on the side.

And, of course, they were everywhere. With no license plate to identify the orphan van, he had very little to go on. Before Christopher Clark died, he'd said that the license plate number of the stolen vehicle was in the hard drive of his laptop. But, when Sandy entered the "Quincy" password that Clark had blurted out to the thugs back at the cabin, a prompt came up on the screen for a secondary sign-in.

So, his computer was locked up like Fort Knox, and, while Vito said one of his people could probably get into it given some time to work, they didn't have the luxury of time. Whatever was going to happen, according to Clark, was imminent.

And Vito warned that since Clark was a deputy mayor, the laptop probably had several more levels of security to get past. In other words, it was probably a lost cause. And probably also irrelevant. Vito suggested that even if they succeeded in finding the license plate number, the plate had probably been replaced by now.

Sandy knew he was right.

In frustration, he'd fled the Cosa Nostra safe house and left Vito and his men to deal with the disposal of Clark's body. Sandy knew that it would be dumped in Boston Harbor, but that was already more than he wanted to know. These guys were all so calm and matter-of-fact about it, which meant that it was probably a regular occurrence for them. To Sandy, it felt like he'd fallen through the looking glass into a world of madness.

He appreciated all of Vito's help, including the way he'd saved his life back at the Triple-L facility, but all that help had only brought Sandy kicking and screaming closer to an underworld that up until recently he'd only flirted with. Shared information with them here and there, got a little help from them here and there. But now it felt like the Cosa Nostra's fingers were squeezing his balls.

Of course, Vito hadn't actually demanded anything yet and had only acted, so far, as a concerned friend, but Sandy still wondered if his fears were real or imagined. Could the Cosa Nostra actually do anything heroic without expecting payback? And, as well, he now owed them his life, and while he liked and respected Vito Romano, he wondered when the gangster would come to collect.

Where would this lead? He didn't know. All he knew was that he needed to drive. Feel useful. Pretend that he could actually find that Ford Econoline, even though he knew that in a big city like Boston it was virtually impossible.

At the very least, though, he was blowing off steam as he drove around. Starting to think more clearly.

After a couple of hours and a couple of confrontations with the drivers of two public works vehicles, he weaved his way around Boston's maze onto Washington Street.

He parked on a side street and grimaced as he remembered one of the public works drivers yelling at him, challenging him to commit an impossible sex act. He'd yelled it loud enough that several people stopped and stared at the commotion. Luckily, it seemed as if no one had thought to raise their cellphones to snap a photo of a well-dressed man who just happened to have a middle finger shoved in front of his face by a guy in coveralls. Would have been a good one and might have gone viral.

Sandy sat in his car and stared at the impressive spire of the Cathedral of the Holy Cross.

Then he saw it. The other piece to the puzzle that Clark had confessed to.

A white sprinter van parked in a side driveway of the cathedral, with the words New England Restorations emblazoned in red.

The front doors of the church were open, and several men were lingering inside the foyer.

Sandy donned his sunglasses, got out of his car, and opened his trunk. Grabbed a Boston Red Sox cap and pulled it down low over his forehead. He then sauntered up to the front entrance.

Tried to be nonchalant, to make it look like he belonged.

Shoved his hands in his pockets and entered the building. Nodded at the men standing there, ignoring their curious looks, and made his way into the church.

All of the men seemed to be of Middle Eastern descent, which didn't surprise Sandy in the least. If there was a false flag being planned here, designed to strike fear in the hearts of Americans, the dots were connecting in his mind.

Radicals hired, given an assignment, convinced of the opportunity for jihad, destined to be caught or killed, but mission accomplished.

A Muslim firm would do the work, and the predictable disaster would happen once again. Most Muslims would be horrified, but in the dark alleys of America there were always radicals to find and manipulate for terrorism, and maybe this fly-by-night contracting firm was just one of many organizations that were willing and able. Muslims at large would be blamed once again for convenient political agendas.

Sandy's stomach was doing flips as he pondered what might be going on here.

Several workmen were straining to re-install heavy pews, and several more were on their hands and knees power-sanding a section of floor near the imposing altar.

Standing close to the altar, with his hands folded across his chest, was a man wearing a clerical collar.

Sandy took off his baseball cap and sunglasses out of respect and headed straight for him. He looked to be the man in charge of access to the cathedral and by his body language, gave the impression that he was annoyed at having to spend his day watching over workmen.

The priest smiled as Sandy approached. Sandy held out his hand.

"Hello Father. My name's Bill Brunton." Sandy had no idea how that phony name had popped into his head, but he felt better right now being Bill Brunton than Sandy Beech.

"Pleased to meet you, Bill. I'm Monsignor Flaherty. Are you with the restoration firm?"

"No, I'm just a nosy businessman. I live around the corner. Wanted to pop in and see what all the fuss was about here. Seems like you've had some major work done. I love this cathedral and couldn't resist being nosy."

"Well, I'm glad you didn't resist. Nice to talk to someone who doesn't grunt replies. These guys have been at it for two weeks now, and they're almost finished. I'm the building superintendent here at the cathedral, so it's been my job to watch over them every day."

Sandy nodded. "Pretty boring for you, no doubt."

The priest chuckled. "Yes. I'd rather be golfing, for sure!"

"So, they're almost finished?"

Flaherty grimaced. "If you've been in the cathedral before, Bill, you probably don't notice much difference. A few pews refinished, some floor sections re-done."

He looked up to the loft area at the back of the cathedral and pointed. "And we still don't have our iconic pipe organ back yet. They're supposed to be delivering it today, but I won't hold my breath. The project involved doing some aesthetic work on the decorative aspects of the organ, but these clowns work so slowly and sloppily, I'm kind of worried. A few bad pews we can live with, but that pipe organ is everything to us."

Sandy followed his finger with his eyes. "They're going to raise it back into place?"

"Yes, they'll be using a lift, just like when they struggled to get it out of here."

Sandy frowned. "Why didn't they just do the work right here? Why haul it away?"

Flaherty shook his head. "I asked the same question. They grunted and gave me an answer that I couldn't really dispute. Said they had to do the work offsite. I don't know anything about these things, so I agreed. Wish I hadn't."

Flaherty glanced at his watch. "Walk with me outside, Bill. We'll chat in the sunshine. The pipe organ ordeal should be about to begin, if they're still on schedule."

They walked up the aisle together, out onto the promenade. Sandy donned the Red Sox cap once again and pulled the brim down low. Slipped his sunglasses back into place.

And sure enough, there it was. It had arrived. In all its glory. Sitting on a flatbed truck parked along Washington Street was the 1800s pipe organ, dismantled into four large sections.

A team of four men were disconnecting the chains that had been holding it safely in place on the truck bed. Behind the flatbed was another smaller truck, with a mobile hydraulic lift being backed down onto the street along a ramp.

With his eyes fixated on the pipe organ, it had taken Sandy an extra few seconds to notice another vehicle. The one he'd been driving around Boston all day hunting for. A white Ford Econoline van with the signage Boston Public Works had pulled in right behind the hydraulic lift truck.

Sandy caught his breath and felt a pain in the pit of his stomach. The dominos were falling into place for this insidious plan from Lincoln Berwick's demented campaign.

He didn't know what the plan was, didn't know when it was supposed to happen, but all the pieces were there. The stolen van, the rigged contract to New England Restorations, the Muslim workers—all confessed to from the pathetic lips of Christopher Clark.

Another setup just like the Quincy Market massacre that had stolen Sandy's family from him. All designed to strike fear in the hearts of voters, to stoke prejudice against a race and a religion that always seemed to be the convenient boogey-man. And all designed to get people to vote for a narcissistic lunatic.

He knew his options were limited, but he also knew he had to act. He had to do something. Only he and Vito knew what this was all about, courtesy of the now dead deputy mayor. And he couldn't tell the Monsignor or even the authorities what he knew, or how he knew it. A feeling of utter and complete impotence washed over him as the few lousy options flashed through Sandy's quick brain.

And then, out of the blue—out of the interior of the Ford Econoline—an opportunity burst onto the scene.

The driver's door to the public works van popped open and a man apparently on a mission rushed up to them. He had a clipboard in his hand, and was distinguished from the others by the fact that he was white.

He smiled a big wide smile that seemed as phony as a three-dollar bill.

"Hello, padre. I'm Mason. I'm here to oversee the installation of your…pipe organ." He pointed at the Muslims. "Those guys over there will do the work, but we at Public Works will make sure everything is done safely. Electric hook-ups, etc. You know the routine."

The Monsignor seemed at a loss for words for a few seconds. Then he responded, with fire in his eyes. "I'm not a 'padre.' I'm a Monsignor. Monsignor Flaherty. You will show respect, please."

The man laughed. "Okay, sure. Well, how the hell would I know that? Just sign these sheets here, and then get out of the way. We'll need all hands on deck, and I don't think you'll be of much help." He laughed again. "Sorry, padre, but that's quicker for me to say than 'monsignor.' No offense intended."

Sandy turned his head towards Flaherty. "If I were you, I wouldn't sign anything right now. Call the diocese lawyer to review these documents before you let them do anything else."

The priest nodded in agreement.

Mason turned his attention to Sandy. "Who the fuck are you?" He waved his hand. "Get the hell out of here."

Flaherty held out his hand in the stop sign. "Hold it right there. This is God's house. I would ask you to show some respect and restraint. And my friend is right—your attitude makes me think our diocese lawyer should be here." He pulled his phone out of his pocket. "I'm going to call him right now."

Mason swore. Then, without warning, swung the clipboard at Sandy's face. Sandy ducked just in time.

He spread his feet apart and assumed a still familiar West Point stance. "You don't want to do this."

Mason laughed. "Yes, I do." He aimed his right foot in a vicious kick towards Sandy's groin.

Sandy caught the foot in his right hand, and twisted it in a 180-degree arc. Mason let out a yelp and went down, his face smashing onto the cobblestone promenade.

Several of the Muslim workmen were milling around now, puzzled as to what was going on. Mason jumped to his feet and charged Sandy. But he only managed to advance about a yard before a spin-kick from Sandy's right foot directly into the man's chin sent him to the ground for the last time.

Sandy glanced over at the Monsignor. "Better phone the police, too."

Flaherty nodded agreement.

Sandy slipped his belt from his pants. "Take off your own belt, Monsignor."

With two belts in hand, Sandy knelt down and flipped the prone Mason over onto his stomach. He secured his wrists and ankles tightly, and managed to link the belts together in a hog-tie effect.

"Okay, he's not going anywhere. When the police arrive, we can tell them what happened. But if you'll excuse me for a second, I have to make a phone call. I'm late for an appointment."

"No problem, Bill. Thanks for your help. I don't condone violence, but you did what needed to be done. You're coming back, I hope?" The priest chuckled. "And, while we wait for the police, maybe you can tell me how you learned to fight like that?"

Sandy smiled warmly—and then lied. He silently prayed that God would forgive him.

"Yes. My phone's in the car, so I'll be back. In the meantime, I would advise you not to let them unload that organ until your lawyer has a chance to review the papers this clown has."

"I won't."

Sandy jogged down the street to his car and hopped in. Pulled out from the curb, and headed in the opposite direction. As he was driving, he speed-dialed a now familiar number.

And a now familiar voice answered on the first ring.

"Vito. It's happening. I need your help again. Are you able to make a phone call on an untraceable device? Okay, good. Phone 911 and issue a threat. Say that there's a bomb installed inside the pipe organ sitting on a flatbed truck in front of the Cathedral of the Holy Cross."

38

Lincoln Berwick was enjoying his drive in the country. All by himself. Without his bitch of a wife whining about all the duties she had to perform on his behalf.

Linc didn't get it. Melanie had a wonderfully rich lifestyle, all due to him. They owned a dream home, drove expensive cars, traveled anywhere they wanted without having to pay a cent. Virtually everything was eligible to be written off as a campaign expense. She was married to one of America's most powerful politicians, a man who most women would donate their left tit to be in bed with. But did she appreciate any of these things?

No.

Linc sighed as he cruised along the Texas interstate. He forgot which one he was on, but it didn't really matter. All the interstates looked the same. All boring, all devoid of scenery, snaking their way across the country avoiding attractions that would distract the typical driver. He could have taken some country roads instead, but that would have meant downgrading the speed on his Porsche, and speed was more important to him than scenery.

Today he needed speed. And the feeling of power. Because power was in his hands to take now. He'd just won two more primaries, and was now the sure-fire favorite to lock up the Republican nomination for president. He had the world by the tail now, and the world wouldn't know what hit it when he was finally enshrined in the Oval Office.

There was already strong chatter to the effect that the remaining candidates for the nomination were running out of money. That they'd be dropping out soon. Which meant that Senator Lincoln Berwick would be acclaimed as the official nominee at the summer convention.

He smiled, shifted into fifth gear, and gunned the accelerator to 140 miles an hour.

But Linc's smile was short-lived, which was a shame because he didn't smile very often.

His cell phone rang.

"This better be important."

"Senator, turn on your TV."

It was that bitch, Meagan Whitfield. Always eager to bust his balls and ruin his day.

"Can't. I'm in my car."

"Well, get home, or pick up a newspaper. We have a problem."

Linc swore, and clicked off.

What the hell was wrong now?

He saw a gas station coming up ahead. Pulled into the parking lot and jumped out of his Porsche. Ran up to the newspaper boxes, deposited his change, and pulled out a copy of *The Washington Sentinel*.

As he walked back to his car, he noticed two scumbags lurking around his car.

He opened the driver's door and threw his newspaper onto the passenger seat.

The two guys looked to be in their thirties, both wearing baseball caps and sleeveless undershirts. They were each holding cans of beer, and their body odor was overpowering, even from a distance.

Both of them smiled at him—smiles that basically said, "Aren't you the asshole. Pulling in to this spot in a Porsche."

One of them did a little hop and landed his ass on the hood of the car. Sat there, staring at Linc, sipping his beer, daring him to do something.

Linc closed the driver's door and in a soft voice, said, "Get off my car."

Both of them laughed. The one sitting on the hood asked, "How much you pay for this machine, dude?"

"More than you'll earn in a lifetime. Get off it. Now."

"I don't think so. It has such nice curves. Soothing my bum. Might just pull down my pants and take a shit on this thing. Won't go well with your silver color, though."

Both men laughed. Linc felt the blood start to boil in his veins.

He tried to calm down. Reason with them. "Okay, guys. I don't want any trouble here. Let's just cool it. Get off the car, bud, and we'll call it a day."

The other guy sneered and leaped into the air. Landed beside his friend, both feet pounding onto the hood. Then he stomped his right foot hard onto the metal.

"Oh, I'm sorry. Left a footprint. Let me clean it off for you."

He drained his beer can and then rubbed it with his left foot. "Oh, no, another footprint. And my beer is empty. Why don't you go get me another beer, chief? Same brand, please?"

Linc opened the driver's door again, hopped in, and fired up the sports car's powerful engine.

He yelled out the window. "Get off the car, boys, or you're going for a ride."

They just laughed. The younger one held up his middle finger and thrust it up close to the windshield.

Linc slipped the shifter into first gear and powered forward. The sudden acceleration pulled both men into the windshield. Faces planted against the glass, blood oozing out of broken noses.

He pointed the car towards the ramp onto the highway and slammed the gear shift into second. Accelerated again. Both men grabbed onto the windshield wipers for dear life. Then Linc slammed on the brakes. The powerful little Porsche had a braking system far superior to anything else on the market. The car came to an almost instant halt.

Predictably, both men went flying off the car onto the pavement in front. Unceremoniously tumbling for several feet.

Linc opened his door and jumped out. Not to check if they were okay. He didn't care if they were okay.

The thugs struggled to their feet. "You're a dead man," one of them sputtered.

Linc sneered at them. "Yeah? We'll see about that."

Years of intensive training at West Point came back to his brain in an instant. Muscle memory, the kind of memory that is seldom forgotten when drummed into a body at an impressionable and athletic age.

The men were standing side by side, feet apart, fists clenched. They both advanced at the same time.

And with the speed of Linc's response, they both also went down at virtually the same time.

Linc leaped into the air, twisting his body into a 360-degree spin. His right foot was extended, power coming from the thrust of the airborne twist and from his suddenly hardened abdomen.

One foot, and one kick, was all that was needed. The same foot curved in a balletic display, one chin at a time, within milliseconds of each other. The men grunted as they were hit by the same foot, unable to react to the blur of the man they thought was an easy mark.

Linc just stared down at them as they rolled around on the ground, arms folded and cradling their bruised and battered faces.

He jumped back in the car, pulled around the two thugs, and sped out onto the highway.

As he drove away from the scene, he cursed at the beer stain insulting his beautiful aircraft silver finish.

And then he just laughed out loud. Thinking to himself how ironic it was that rednecks like those two guys were the types he saw at all of his rallies. The types of people who thought he was their savior, their excuse to come out of the closet. And, yet, these scum hadn't even recognized him.

Yes, Senator Lincoln Berwick, and soon to be *President* Lincoln Berwick, was romancing people like these two losers. Voters like these guys would no doubt push him over the top in his masquerade as their Messiah. The irony of it caused Linc to choke on his laughter as the $200,000 Porsche roared down the open road—some decrepit interstate that he couldn't even remember.

*****

He pulled into his driveway, grabbed the newspaper without looking at it, and headed inside. Went straight to his study, poured himself a scotch neat, and settled down behind his desk.

Linc had been isolated from the news, the Internet, and all social contact the entire day. He'd wanted to savor his latest primary victories on his own, without distractions. Wanted to enjoy his own company, which is the only company he ever really enjoyed anyway.

Then that bitch Meagan Whitfield had to phone and ruin his mood. And, as if that wasn't enough, he'd had to pummel a couple of rednecks that resented the fact that he was driving a Porsche. Sometimes life just wasn't fair.

He took a sip of his drink, sighed, and opened up his copy of *The Washington Sentinel.*

It was right there on the front page. Linc's stomach rushed to his throat as he saw a photo of the Cathedral of the Holy Cross under the headline: **"Terror Attack Thwarted at Famous Boston Cathedral."**

Linc took a prolonged swig of his whiskey, and read:

> **"An apparent terror attack planned for Boston's Cathedral of the Holy Cross was stopped in its tracks yesterday by local authorities.**
>
> **"Details are sketchy at this point and officials are saying very little. However, we are reporting that bomb components were discovered in a pipe organ that was to be re-installed in the church. It had been dismantled and taken away to be refurbished and was delivered back to the cathedral yesterday.**
>
> **"The pipe organ was reportedly still sitting on a flatbed truck outside the church when the bomb squad arrived in response to an anonymous call. Authorities have confirmed that a threat was received from an untraceable phone. Police would not confirm whether the caller was an actual suspect in the case.**
>
> **"The mystery behind this plot was made even stranger by the fact that a man was found hog-tied in front of the church when police arrived. This man was apparently a Boston Public Works supervisor, but**

upon further investigation this reporter discovered that he was not known to the City of Boston utilities commission.

"Sources have revealed that the cathdedral's spokesperson, Monsignor Flaherty, is being consulted for a police sketch pertaining to a person who assisted at the scene, a man who reportedly gave his name as Bill Brunton. Police confirm that Mr. Brunton is being sought as a person of interest, and not considered a suspect.

"Police have inspected the apparent utility official's vehicle, which bore the identification of Boston Public Works.

"Inside were several canisters.

"The bomb squad was called to the scene, as well as inspectors with the Hazardous Materials division. Several officers could be seen dressed in hazmat suits, removing the canisters from the public works van. A video of the operation can be seen on our website, www.washingtonsentinel.com

"This has not been confirmed by authorities, but sources inside the Boston Police department have disclosed to this reporter that deadly sarin gas was detected within the cylinders. More details to follow."

Linc drained the rest of his drink before reaching for the phone.

39

It had been four days since the attempted terror attack on the cathedral. Media networks around the world were carrying the story. Boston authorities and the FBI were being tight-lipped about details and wouldn't confirm that sarin gas was found in the canisters recovered from the public works van.

However, they didn't deny it either.

The media were relentless. The story was so sensational, it was front page magic. Just the mere thought of one of the world's most majestic cathedrals—one that could hold up to 2,000 people at a time—being the target of a brazen attack, captured the imagination of rubberneckers everywhere.

And on the heels of the Boston Marathon and Quincy Market attacks, this case was an unusual one. Headlines screamed attention-grabbers like, "Boston Under Attack" and "Citizens Under Siege."

Naturally, politicians took full advantage, even though the attack was thwarted. The Democratic Party urged caution, as did most of the candidates running for president under the Republican banner.

Except for one.

Senator Lincoln Berwick, true to form, gave a speech in Houston two days after the event, and threw all caution to the wind. Talked about how a bomb had been installed in the pipe organ, and that sarin gas canisters were going to be connected to the device. He didn't care that the authorities had not confirmed anything about sarin gas. No, that would be too tame. Fear was the weapon of choice, and Lincoln Berwick was armed and dangerous.

To the thundering roar from his crowd of supporters, he urged immigration reform. The complete ban of all Muslims entering the country and the deportation of existing Muslim citizens. He didn't care that it was illegal, he only cared about the applause. And neither did he care that no connection to Islamic terrorists had yet been made by those investigating the incident.

Sandy had watched the speech live on TV. He cringed at every word, clenched his fists at every cheer. Felt undeniable hurt and shame every time the word Muslim was invoked, knowing full well that the politician was simply taking full advantage and broad-brushing an entire race just for political gain from a segment of racist voters who loved every word that was uttered from his dishonest mouth.

But Lincoln Berwick had the podium almost non-stop now, and he had public attention. He was a force of nature and seemingly unstoppable. With the man's recent primary victories he was now the odds-on favorite to win the Republican nomination. To make matters worse, Sandy knew full well that the Democratic roster of candidates was weak—the weakest in a generation. Linc had momentum in his favor, the wind at his back.

Sandy could feel in his bones that Lincoln Berwick would be the next President of the United States.

In yesterday's papers, and viral online, there was another complication that Sandy felt gnawing at him in the pit of his stomach.

The sketch of him was everywhere. Monsignor Flaherty had given a good description to the police sketch artist, and it was now splashed all over the news. Sandy didn't think it gave him away at all, but he admitted to himself that the sketch was pretty good. It showed him in a Boston Red Sox cap and sunglasses, but the shape of his face and jaw-line was bang on. Even though he'd had his sunglasses and cap off while he was in the church, it had been dark, and the Monsignor must have felt uncomfortable attempting to give a description without those two items. So, luckily the sketch was tainted by a cap and glasses.

But to those who knew him, it was admittedly a sketch of Sandy. And, Linc definitely was one of those who knew him. By now he would have reconciled in his mind that Sandy had intervened once again—as he had with the Triple-L sperm bank, and with Christopher Clark.

Three times a charm? Or, three strikes and you're out?

The news reports described him as being some kind of a folk hero. Someone who had just wandered into the cathedral and chatted with the Monsignor. Outside the church when the public works imposter had disrespected the Monsignor, the hero had gone into action demonstrating fighting skills that the Monsignor stated had taken his breath away. Then the stranger had mysteriously left the scene, but only after hog-tying the imposter and advising the priest not to allow the pipe organ to be unloaded.

The Monsignor, as well as the police, were very complimentary about the heroic stranger. They merely wanted to talk to him, which was why the sketch was being publicised so widely. They invited tips from the public.

They wanted to talk to the stranger.

They wanted to thank him.

And they wanted to find out what he knew—and how he knew.

Sandy shuddered, then closed his eyes and thought about what he had to do next—or perhaps more appropriately, what he might be forced to do next.

He was stirred from his daydream by the ring of the house phone.

"Hello?"

"Sandy. It's Judy."

"Hey, Judy. How are the house guests doing? Bill and Lloyd still with you?"

"Yes. And, we're getting along great. It's such a comfort having them here. Cynthia just adores them, and we both feel so much safer having them around.

"But they can't stay here forever, Sandy. We need to bring this to a close. The tape recording. What are we going to do about it? I feel so vulnerable having the darn thing, and I'm worried that someone will guess that I have a copy. And you know who I mean. I've been watching the news—the more powerful and popular he becomes, the more danger we're in with the tape."

"I hear you. I'll drive down there tomorrow and we'll talk about it. We need to contact the authorities about that young girl's death, see if the case is still open or if it can be reopened. The tape is powerful, but I think we need more. I agree, we're all in a vulnerable spot right now."

"Especially you, Sandy. I've been watching the news. You were there, weren't you? At the cathedral? That was you in the sketch, wasn't it?"

"Yes."

"My gosh! I'm worried about you. As soon as I saw the sketch I knew it was you."

"That's only because you know me, and you know that I'm up to my neck in all of this stuff. Most people wouldn't have a clue who that is in the sketch."

"Bill and Lloyd recognized you right away, too."

"Well, the same as you, they know me and we're all involved in this together. Not to worry. I'm not in any jeopardy."

Sandy heard Judy sigh at the other end.

"How did you happen to be there?"

"A long story. I'll bring you guys up to date when I see you. But, the short version is that with a little help from my friend, Vito, I managed to extract information from that deputy mayor I told you about. He was involved in the terror attack that killed my family, as you know, and he confessed that another false flag attack was being planned by the Berwick campaign folks. One thing led to another and, luckily, I followed up on what I'd learned. Happened to be in the right place at the right time. So it wasn't brilliant detective work on my part."

"That was brave of you, Sandy. I'm so proud of you—you stopped what might have been a horrific attack. I just worry about you more now because of that sketch. It's so weird seeing your face plastered all over the news."

"Judy, don't worry. It's not my face. Just the image of a dude in a ball cap and sunglasses. A few hundred thousand men in Boston look just like that on any given day, particularly when the Red Sox are playing."

"You're not making me feel any better. Just hurry and get down here to New York. We need you."

"I will."

*****

They came during dessert.

Sandy had finished off his delectable meal of roast duck with all the trimmings. To cap off the meal, he had just settled down to a treat of Crème Brule.

While raising his glass of wine in a tearful toast to the family portrait resting on the dining room side stand, he noticed it out of the corner of one eye.

A movement outside. It was dark, but the movement had made it even darker in one spot for just an instant. Then the shade of dark changed again, indicating movement. Movement was what Sandy specialized in. As a physicist, movement was everything to him. Movement of matter, movement of particles, plasma in motion.

He stood up and walked over to the living room window. Couldn't see anyone outside, but he knew without a doubt that someone had passed in front of the window mere seconds before. He glanced up and down the street. The only vehicle parked on the road was a dark SUV, several doors down; one he'd never seen before.

Then he saw movement again. Behind the large oak tree on his front lawn. It was subtle, someone less observant wouldn't have noticed it. But, it was undeniable.

Sandy took one last look at the black SUV, then rushed over to the alarm panel installed on the wall in his front foyer. He didn't want to overreact, but better to be safe than sorry.

He flipped open the cover, and poised his finger ready to punch the panic button.

The screen was dark. The alarm was inactive. Sandy pushed the main power button, but nothing happened. He cursed to himself that he hadn't purchased the line security option. If the line had been cut or disconnected, a signal would have been sent to the alarm company. But, without line security, he was on his own. There was no way for the alarm company to know that he'd gone dark.

He knew now that he wasn't overreacting. Something was happening.

Sandy rushed over to his landline phone and picked up the handset. Dead.

Ran over to his jacket and pulled out his cellphone. Punched the power button, and then 9-1-1. No signal. Nothing but static. Clearly, a jammer was being used.

Feeling the panic rising in his stomach, Sandy tried to remember what he'd done with the Beretta that Vito had loaned him. Then he remembered. He'd given it back. Silly boy.

He ran over to the circuit panel and flipped the main power switch. The house went dark, at the very instant that he heard a thundering crash at his front door.

They were in. From the dim light of the moon and the streetlights, he saw the outlines of two men crouching as they entered the foyer, one of them still holding the battering ram that they'd used to take down the door.

He dropped to the floor and quietly took off his shoes. Then crawled slowly over to a corner of the kitchen behind the center island. Thought about a knife, but he'd have to open one of the drawers to get one, which would give away his position.

Lying behind the island, Sandy considered his options—which weren't many. He could yell out, or scream, but the houses were far apart. No one was likely to hear him. He could make a run, or crawl, for the back door, but they would likely cut him down before he could even grab the door handle.

His eyes were adjusting to the light now, which meant that the intruders would be adjusting too. Looked from side to side, for something, anything.

Then he saw it. Sitting on an open shelf along the side of the island. A long butane barbecue lighter, which was a back-up in case the ignition on his barbecue failed. It had an adjustment feature which lengthened the flame, making it into a mini blowtorch. Wasn't much, but it was at least something. Sarah had bought it for him years ago, assuring him that he would need it one day, despite Sandy's insistence that the barbecue he'd bought was top of the line and would never fail.

Sarah was wiser than he was. She knew that so-called man toys had their limitations.

Now, he said a silent prayer of thanks for her foresight. But she never would have imagined he'd be using the torch for something like this.

He slid the lighter off the shelf and adjusted the flame switch to full length. Then prayed once again, this time that this torch that he'd never even used would work. It was his only hope, and a slim one at that.

Sandy listened. They were quiet, but not that quiet. He could hear them cautiously working their way across the dining room in the direction of the kitchen.

Where he was lying on the floor.

His senses were on full alert. He knew his only chance was the element of surprise. There were only two of them, from what he could see when they came through the doorway. So, while he might have luck with one, the other would be the man's backup. Whatever he did, he'd have to move fast.

Sandy focused once again on his senses. Remembered back to his training at West Point, which had drummed into his head over and over again exercises in "blind execution." Eyes weren't needed, only awareness was needed.

He focused. Listened. Gauged their distance.

Then he acted.

Pure instinct and awareness drove him from his prone position into a lunge. He threw his body upward and around the corner of the island. He could barely see the man, but he sensed him. And Sandy's lunge had taken the man by surprise.

He aimed for where he sensed his face was, and then tempted fate by using the only weapon he had.

Clicked the switch on the butane torch.

The flame surged out of the unit and extended itself to a good six inches. Sandy's senses and gauge of distance had been perfect. The flame licked the face of the intruder right around the upper nose area. Sandy slid it quickly to the side, tearing into the man's right eye.

The thug screamed in pain as he raised his rifle. Sandy knocked it out of his hand with one hard chop to the wrist. He heard the weapon crash land over in a corner of the kitchen, but decided he couldn't risk taking the time to dive for it. Instead, he went back to his safe harbor behind the island just as he saw the man's partner rushing around the corner from the living room.

Sandy slid around to the back of the island, and decided once again that the element of surprise was on his side. He heard the commotion on the other side. The man he'd burned was moaning in pain, and the other man was trying to shush him up.

Time to act.

With an athletic move that belied Sandy's age, he leaped into the air and landed his feet squarely on top of the island. The other thug whirled around at the sound, but it was too late for him to raise his gun and aim. Sandy leveled a kick directly at the man's head, sending him down on top of his friend.

Sandy was on the move again. He stretched himself into a hurdle and cleared both men who were quickly stirring themselves back into action. He knew he had no time to find the errant gun, and he decided that trying to disarm the other man held very little margin for success.

He had no time for anything other than running for his life.

Sandy headed for his safe sanctuary. The basement. Hopefully the would-be killers would just exit the house, now that it hadn't gone as smoothly as they'd counted on.

Despite the darkness, Sandy knew the house like the back of his hand. He could be blind and still find his way around.

He dashed down the hallway and yanked open the basement door. Took the stairs two at a time, guided by a flashing red light on a machine sitting in a corner of the basement.

The corner of death.

This corner of his basement had never killed anyone yet, but if those men dared to venture down into the bowels of his home, tonight would surely be a first.

Sandy spun the machine around and pointed it at the bottom of the stairs. Normally, under planned circumstances, a photo would be taken by the machine and memorized. However, it could be operated by aim as well, without the automatic recognition sensors.

This miniature version of the Directed Energy Weapon, was an exact tiny copy of the one Sandy and his team had been developing at the Lincoln Laboratory. In recent weeks, he'd perfected the objective of making the PEP both silent and invisible. It was an infrared laser pulse that forced rapidly expanding plasma at whatever target was chosen. In the absence of a photo dictating to PEP what the target was to be, it would hit the objects—or people—in closest proximity to the direction in which it was aimed. Sandy had perfected it to now be faster than the speed of light.

The PEP was the most advanced weaponry in existence, and as yet untested in combat conditions. It had its own power source, which was integral and portable. The fact that the power was shut off in the house would not affect this baby's performance.

Sandy heard footsteps upstairs. And the creaking sound of the door to the basement stairs.

He pulled a tiny remote control from a slot in the PEP, then pushed the power button. The machine emitted a subtle whirring noise, indicating it was ready. He marveled at its ingenuity and silently patted himself on the back. The thing also had night vision, and the remote control unit in his hand had its own screen. He could see on the remote exactly what the PEP was seeing.

Footsteps on the basement stairs.

Sandy dashed over behind a wall and stared at the remote.

The men appeared, crouching. Only one was holding a weapon—the other guy's gun was probably still lying on the floor in the kitchen. The armed man started firing, right in the direction of the PEP. He must have noticed the light on the weapon, which was flashing red every two seconds. Sandy ducked his head and cursed under his breath. Then, knowing time was running out on him, he quickly pressed the button of death.

The PEP gave one final whir—then activated.

No noise, no beam of light. Nothing but deadly quiet.

Just eerie silence, as the high-tech weapon emitted a pulse of energy that completely obliterated its targets in a millisecond.

If there were ever to be a sales brochure produced for the PEP, it should state: "The result will be immediate destruction and absolute collapse of its target matter."

The silence was deafening.

Sandy punched the Deactivate button on the remote, and confidently stepped out from behind his protective wall. He reached over and turned on the spotlight feature of the weapon.

Strode over to the bottom of the stairs and studied the outcome. Two large piles of dusty residue were all that was left of the two men who had come to kill him.

Sandy glanced over at an old broom and dustpan leaning against the wall. He'd clean up the mess before calling it a night.

40

The glitz, the glamour, the history.

Palm Springs, California, had it all. Strangely, it even had more caché than Beverly Hills. Because this was where the stars of the Golden Era came to party, unwind, relax. Palm Springs was their "cottage country."

Beverly Hills was fake, Palm Springs was real. The stars were able to escape to Palm Springs and just be themselves, pretend to be normal people. It had a laid-back lifestyle, one that catered to simply letting hair down and chilling. No style requirements, no behavior stipulations. Stars could wander around in jeans and T-shirts, and no one cared.

Palm Springs was blessed with one of the best climates on the planet. It was built on an oasis, but there was no denying this was desert country. The unrelenting desert encroached on the town from all corners, and there was no escaping the reality of it.

Perhaps the lack of fakery was part of the appeal to celebrities whose lives were normally consumed by it. The mandatory green grass of Beverly Hills was supplanted in Palm Springs by the acceptability of having sand yards and cactus.

Simply beautiful, in an ugly kind of way.

Some of the most famous stars in Hollywood had either called Palm Springs their getaway, or, just as often, their real home. Not a home away from home, but just their preferred place to live. Truly live.

Such was the case with one of the most famous of them all—Frank Sinatra. He'd owned a couple of properties in Palm Springs, but the one that he loved the most and where he'd lived out the majority of his final years, was located on what is now known as Frank Sinatra

Drive.

Situated along the seventeenth fairway of the Tamarisk Country Club, it had evolved into a sprawling compound by the time he was finished with it. A large main house and several charming bungalows. A couple of swimming pools, tennis courts, a restaurant-sized kitchen, theater room, gymnasium.

The compound was spread amongst almost three acres of desert-landscaped property. No grass, just sand and cactus. None of the buildings were lavish from the outside, but once inside you could easily tell that a man accustomed to the finest things in life lived there. It was, in a word, plush.

Even after he sold the property in the late '90s to a Canadian billionaire, he couldn't bring himself to leave. Hung around with the permission of the new owner until the reality of his failing health forced him to leave. Reportedly, a good portion of his dedicated house staff of twenty-six, cried uncontrollably as a limousine chauffeured the icon out through the imposing estate gates for the last time.

Meagan Whitfield stood in front of the main house and soaked up the history. She could almost hear the great man crooning one of his famous tunes. As far as she was concerned, no one could carry a song the way Sinatra could. He was a legend.

She could tell by the number of cars in the parking lot that quite a few of her colleagues had already arrived.

This was the annual retreat of the reclusive and publicity-averse Aufsteigen Group.

There were twenty-six permanent members, representing a solid cross-section of corporate America. There were also a dozen or so associate members, who hadn't totally earned their way into the club yet—but most of them would, some day, some year. Membership wasn't handed out eagerly. Stripes had to be earned, and usually the hard way.

Although the workings of the group were private and behind closed doors, its very existence was a badly kept secret. Certain media were clued in, and usually trolled their meeting spots with regularity.

The name of the group wasn't widely known amongst the general public, but rumors persisted and it had been disclosed in news reports from to time. Not that the subject of a group of corporate titans meeting in secret was a rip-roaring story line. Most Americans would just yawn and go back to amusing themselves with something more salacious.

Some media outlets had tried their level best to create conspiracy theories, but the Aufsteigen public relations machine deftly countered those stories by discrediting reporters. And sometimes, when deemed necessary, through outright threats.

The media were no doubt obsessed with the meaning of the word, Aufsteigen—the German word for Ascension. No surprise that they'd be curious, because the word, indeed, at least in Meagan's mind, spoke volumes about what the group was all about. And the fact that it was a German term most likely spurred conspiracy theories.

The Aufsteigen Group believed in superiority and dominance. And part and parcel of that was genetic superiority. That was the basic premise. If it didn't start there, it wouldn't start at all. Consequently, at least half of the permanent members were shareholders in Legacy Life Ladder Inc.

The group was dedicated to the inverse pursuits of power through money—and money through power. In Meagan's mind, the mission statement of Aufsteigen was really quite simple.

The leanings of the group were to the far right, and they were collectively fed up and frustrated with what they saw as the fruitcake preachings of the extreme left. Liberal immigration attitudes were killing the country and infecting it from the inside out. Permissive attitudes towards the gay and lesbian communities were reaching the boiling point, as well as the cry-baby coddling on the refugee resettlement subject.

The Aufsteigen Group wanted a lot of things, but certain subjects brought out their passion more than others. They wanted borders closed, and gays and lesbians ostracized. And don't even get them started on Blacks and Hispanics, which they had no hesitation in referring to as Niggers and Spics.

Their whisperings were behind closed doors, of course. Amongst themselves. They were an astute enough group to recognize that in order to effect change, the Trojan Horse tactic needed to be employed at all times.

Senator Lincoln Berwick was their Trojan Horse of choice at the moment. He had the pedigree, the brains, the looks, and the charisma to worm his way into the hearts and minds of fearful Americans. Although, they were also realistic enough to have more than one horse if need be.

But for now, he'd earned his status charmingly and his messages of fear and hate were starting to register. The disaffected members of society were coming out of the woodwork in droves, gleeful that they finally had a leader who spoke their language.

Of course, the dregs of society were not at all what the Aufsteigen Group wanted to be associated with. They were just needed to propel Lincoln to victory. "First, get elected" drove the agenda.

Senator Berwick was the ultimate Trojan Horse. Tell them what they need to hear, engage them, enrage them, and then get them out to vote.

The irony of it all was delicious. These people who had so little, and were so uneducated that they'd probably always have so little, were going to elect a human being who was genetically and socially superior. And that entitled person was being backed by other entitled people who possessed wealth and resources beyond the imagination of the inferior people who would be voting for Aufsteigen Group's ascendant.

Yes, for now, Senator Lincoln Berwick was the chosen ascendant, who would be manipulating genetically inferior people into voting for the genetically superior. Meagan chuckled at the irony of it all—and the sheer genius.

She looked at her watch. Two hours to kill until the opening night dinner. This Sinatra complex was perfect for their annual meetings. It was the tenth time they'd held it here. Nice and private, good security, and all of the attendees had private accommodations within the compound.

As far as she knew, no one had lived here since the Sinatras left.

The Canadian billionaire rented it out now for corporate retreats and conventions only, and Meagan knew that with the amount it cost her group to secure the place for just three days, he was making a small fortune over the course of any year. Her kind of guy.

Lincoln Berwick was the keynote speaker at tonight's dinner, and he'd also be attending tomorrow's morning workshop session, answering strategy questions from the membership. The group was very excited at the moment. Linc's momentum in the polls was impressive and getting stronger by the day. The members could almost taste the Oval Office now.

He was the first ascendant to come out of the Triple-L gene pool who had made it this far. Sure, there were plenty of other successes in the business, military and high-tech ranks, but this was the first time one of theirs was knocking on the White House door. Shareholders of Triple-L were finally seeing their investment pay off in the big leagues. The White House was the ultimate goal of the group, and it wouldn't be an exaggeration to say that some were drooling just thinking about it.

But Meagan needed to meet with Lincoln, just one on one. Bob Stone wasn't able to attend this year's session in Palm Springs, so Meagan would just wing the discussion on her own. She'd fill Bob in later.

It was an important discussion she had to have with Linc. Things were going so well, but, in another sense, they weren't. She was worried. Something was nagging her, in addition to the disturbing things that had happened. She hated thinking that defeat could possibly be snatched from the jaws of victory.

The closer they got to their ultimate goal, the more stressed she became.

It was like the underdog in the Super Bowl. No pressure going into the game, but all that would change if the underdog actually started winning. By the time the fourth quarter rolled around, and victory seemed actually possible, nerves became fried. Because, to taste power and victory, and then to lose it, was, in Meagan's mind, the worst torture possible.

She entered the foyer of Sinatra's main house, picked up the internal house phone, and dialed Linc's room number.

"Meet me down in the lounge. We need to talk."

*****

"Sandford rushed out of his house with a rifle," Meagan told Linc. "Right towards the vehicle, gun extended. Our driver—who was just a driver, not an operative—panicked and drove off. In other words, Sandford Beech survived. I don't know how, but he did."

Linc scratched his chin. "Hmm...didn't you have your best people on this?"

"Yes, we did. Two former Green Berets. Should have been easy."

"Well, that would be naïve, don't you think? Sandy was West Point, in the Honor Guild. The training in self-defence and killing techniques was extreme at that school. When you graduated from there, you were a lethal weapon."

Meagan scoffed. "That was a couple of decades ago! There's no way he'd still be a killing machine today."

"Clearly, he is. Did you hear from the two operatives?"

She shook her head. "No."

"Then, he killed them. He's still a killing machine."

"What is it with this guy? He harassed our stooge Christopher Clark—who has now just disappeared. Probably dead, but chances are he spilled the beans before he died." Meagan stirred some sugar into her coffee. "Sandford then impersonated a client at our Triple-L lab, and escaped within inches of his life with some help from a few of his friends. Two of our men died at Triple-L as well."

She shook her head. "And you admitted that the sketch of that man at the cathedral—the guy who fucked everything up and just vanished into thin air—looked a lot like your friend Sandy. Now, we try to kill the bastard, but he seems to have turned the tables on us—and two more of our men have disappeared. People just tend to die around Dr. Beech—and the man seems to have nine lives!"

Linc frowned. "He's brilliant, and resourceful. As well, he may feel he has nothing to lose now after the deaths of his family in the Quincy attack."

Meagan stood up and stretched her arms, from side to side, and across her chest.

"I'm feeling stressed, Linc. I feel like certain things are out of our control now. We don't know whether Clark is dead or alive. If dead, he may have talked before he died. If alive and stashed away by Sandford somewhere, he may be talking still. Either way, we have to assume that Sandford knows that your campaign engineered the Quincy Market terror attack, and, if that indeed was Sandford at the cathedral, then that was no coincidence. Clark must have told him that the church was our next target. Connect the dots."

Linc nodded. "Yes. And if he knows all those things, particularly the Quincy thing, then he blames me for the deaths of his wife and kids. As I said, he has nothing to lose now. Which makes him dangerous as hell."

Meagan chewed on one of her fingernails and then pointed it at Linc as she asked her next important question. "Does he have anyone else in his life that he cares about?"

Linc went silent for a few seconds. "The only one I can think of, and it's really ancient history, is a lady by the name of Judy Nichols. He dated her during our university years. I dated her too. She was his first love. He might turn to her now that his wife is gone. Her ex-husband, John Nichols, also from West Point, committed...suicide...a few months ago, so they're both free as birds."

Meagan uttered an "Ah-hah," as she wrote the name down in her notebook.

"Where does she live?"

"New York City. Queens, I think."

"Okay. Leave that with me."

She paused for a few seconds and stared unblinkingly into Linc's eyes. "Is there anything you haven't told me? Anything that happened between you and Sandy back in your West Point days that I don't know about? Something else that might have caused him to have such a hard-on for you?"

Meagan noticed that Linc gulped hard before he answered.

He shook his head. "Nope. Nothing."

"Are you sure? No skeletons in your closet that you're afraid to tell us about?"

Linc raised his voice. "No! I just told you that. Stop talking to me like I'm some kind of child. I'm the next President of the United States, for God's sake!"

Meagan furrowed her brow into the schoolmarmiest look she could muster. "I hope so. And, for both our sakes, I hope you're not lying to me. We'd rather know up front about a problem than have it sprung on us by surprise. If the media or some other source, splashed it out in the open and we had to react, we'd sound defensive and you'd be crucified in the court of public opinion."

Linc jumped to his feet and glared down at her. "I'm weary of your preaching and lecturing, so just leave me the fuck alone. I'm racing to the finish line. You take care of Sandy; stop him from getting in my way."

Meagan smiled to herself as he stomped off. He was clearly wrapped around her little finger. Fearful of his old West Point rival and reliant on Meagan to protect him from Sandy's intrusions. Yes, she loved theater. Manipulation was child's play when paired with good acting.

41

Lloyd's frown made its appearance only seconds after Sandy began his story, and he still couldn't wipe it off his face even though the story had now come to an end.

"That's one hell of a weapon. Is it legal?"

"Of course, it isn't—not for the common man, anyway. It's never been tested on a battlefield yet, either, but there are really no legalities as far as military weaponry anyway. Some types of weapons are banned by the UN, or through treaties, but those stipulations are all, by and large, ignored.

"What I have in my basement is a miniature prototype of what I've been developing at the Lincoln Lab. And, as you know, the Lincoln Lab, while being a division of MIT, is really a secret division of the Pentagon. I've told you that, but the general public really doesn't know it. I even carry Pentagon credentials in addition to my university identification."

Bill chuckled. "Forgive me for laughing, but that's quite the world you run in, Sandy."

Sandy grimaced. "Sometimes I laugh too, Bill. It's pathetically funny, isn't it?"

Judy had remained silent throughout Sandy's story, with her hands masking her mouth in shock. But, now she jumped into the conversation. "That darn PEP thing saved your life, that's all we should care about. If you hadn't had that machine in your basement, you would have been dead."

Sandy nodded. "Yes, that's a fact."

She inched herself along the couch until her leg was brushing against his. Judy took his hand in hers and kissed it. "Thank God you're safe. But they won't stop, you know that. You've been a thorn in their side, and with Linc running away with the presidential race, they can't let you screw things up."

"I know. Trust me, I'm worried too."

Bill stood and started pacing. "We need to go public."

Lloyd rested his feet on the coffee table and folded his arms across his chest. "C'mon, Bill. With what? What the hell do we have that we can prove?"

"We have a tape recording."

"That was from twenty-five years ago, when John and Linc's voices were barely outside puberty. Linc's voice might not even be recognizable. The only thing close to proof on that tape is John sneakily using Linc's name, and mentioning Monica Hartwell's name, but that could have been recorded today. Using his name isn't proof, and John isn't even alive to testify that he recorded the damn thing. So, it's useless."

Sandy shook his head. "It's not useless, Lloyd, but I agree that it has limited legal use. Consider this, though—a lie detector test also has limited legal value, and it can't generally be used in a court of law. But what it does do is send investigators in a certain direction, towards a target. Puts the pressure on. A tape recording would achieve the same purpose—would allow an investigation to focus on a target. And that target in this case is Linc. And the murder victim, Monica Hartwell—well, her name is mentioned in the recording. So, this recording is kind of explosive in a couple of ways. Which is why they killed John and made it look like suicide. They can't take a chance on that tape reaching public ears and creating some level of reasonable doubt about Linc's character. They'll do anything to get Linc elected, and they'll sweep away anything in their path."

Lloyd nodded agreement. "Consider this, though. If Linc and his campaign have this kind of power now, able to fabricate two terror attacks and carry out a brazen attempt on your life, can you imagine how impossible this will be once he's elected president? He'll have ultimate power at his fingertips. If you somehow manage to survive during this campaign, your life will be short indeed after inauguration.

A loose end that they'll eliminate for sure once Linc is the most powerful man on the planet."

Judy ran her fingers through her hair. "You and Bill are also loose ends, Lloyd. They've already killed John and Hank, they tried to kill both of you, and now they've tried with Sandy. The only reason they haven't tried again with you two is probably because they don't know where you are."

Bill replied in a whisper. "You're right, Judy. And when they killed John, they thought they got the only copy of the recording. If they conclude that you have a copy, you and your daughter are also in danger."

Sandy stood and started pacing the room, rubbing his chin as he thought about all that had been said by his friends.

Then he spoke, slowly, using his professorial style. "There's something out of order with all of this. John was killed because of the tape recording and because he tried to blackmail Linc. They don't know there's a copy, and they haven't bothered Judy—probably because they know that Judy and John had been divorced for several years and that John was a hopeless alcoholic," he said.

"We then connected the dots from that recording and from the death of Monica Hartwell. There were five people in the van that night. Two of them are now dead, and Bill and Lloyd had attempts made on their lives. The fifth, Linc, was the one responsible for Monica's death, and to our knowledge, no attempt has been made on his life. If it had, it would have hit the news headlines. So, our conclusion has to be that Linc is behind the murders of John and Hank and the attempts on Lloyd and Bill. Follow me so far?"

All heads nodded.

Sandy continued. "As for me, I'm in a different category. I wasn't in the van that night, and as far as Linc is concerned, I know nothing about the rape and death of that girl. So, I'm not a loose end for that skeleton in his closet like you guys are. And, even if he suspects that John or one of you guys had eventually told me about it, I wasn't in the van that night. I'm not a direct witness, so I'm not really a threat about that incident. The attempt on my life was the other night, not at all close on the heels of the attempts on you two and the deaths of the other two. You were all in the van that night. If he'd thought that I was a loose end on that, an attempt on me would have been made earlier, probably around the time you guys almost died."

Bill drained his coffee, then walked over to the pot and poured himself another cup.

"Where are you going with this, Sandy?"

"I know I'm being a bit repetitious here, so bear with me. I'm kinda just thinking out loud right now. Something's not right, or consistent. They tried to kill me the other night for a different reason. Only because I've been getting in their way, not because I know about the rape and death of a fourteen-year-old girl."

Judy jumped back in. "Well, that's not quite right. This wasn't the only time they tried to kill you. You said you were jumped that night in the park when you accosted the deputy mayor. And when you impersonated a client at the Triple-L sperm bank, you were hauled away to a place where you were going to be tortured and probably killed. If Vito's men hadn't arrived, you would surely have been dead."

Sandy nodded. "You're right. But those were unrelated. Christopher Clark had his thug jump me in the park because I was shaking him down. He was just trying to protect himself. I doubt that had anything to do with the campaign. And when that Doctor Schmidt guy saw through my cover at Triple-L, that was a spur of the moment thing. He saw me as an imposter and acted on his own to find out what I was doing there. He was going to torture it out of me, and, yes, I probably would have died if not for Vito."

Sandy paused for a few seconds before continuing. "By now, I'm certain that video footage from Triple-L has been seen by Linc and his campaign leaders. They know it was me, and they know I had friends who saved my ass. And they certainly know that I shook down Clark to find out about the Quincy massacre. As well, that sketch of me intervening in the Holy Cross Cathedral terror attack is probably a dead give-away. If you guys recognized me, so did Linc. They know that was me."

Sandy's gaze scanned the faces of his friends. "So they know that

I'm responsible for the disappearance of Clark and that he probably told me everything. They know that I know about how Linc's campaign engineered the Quincy attack, which resulted in the deaths of my family in addition to hundreds of innocents. If they recognized me as that Bill Brunton guy at the cathedral, they know that I had inside knowledge that they were engineering that attack also. They know I got that info from Clark. In other words, they know a lot."

He gave a rueful laugh. "Not so coincidentally, then, they tried to knock me off the other night. I'm a royal pain in the ass to them. But, here's the kicker—I'm a pain in the ass for a different reason than you guys are. It's obvious."

Bill cracked his knuckles. "But, if true, does that matter?"

"I think it does, because the perps are probably different," Sandy reasoned. "The things they think I'm a pain in the ass for, are campaign-related. The things I've messed up have been campaign-related. Triple-L produced all of us, as we've now discovered. We're all their products, their superior little creations. Including Linc. Anything to do with Triple-L is beyond his pay grade. I would suggest also that the Quincy Market terror attack and the Holy Cross Cathedral attempted attack were beyond him as well. He no doubt signed off and approved, but the organization of these and the monies paid to Clark came from two top campaign officials—Meagan Whitfield and Bob Stone. They organized those atrocities."

Sandy could see from their expressions that his friends were following along. "But the rape and death of a fourteen-year-old girl is decades-old history. Do you think for a second the campaign would have invested in Lincoln Berwick if they'd known that a skeleton like that was in his closet? I don't think the coward who we all know so well would have told them about that. I suspect that the deaths of John and Hank, and the attempts on you guys, were private operations carried out by thugs hired by Linc personally. He wants to keep that scandal quiet, not only from the public, but also from the campaign. Linc knows they'd probably drop him like a hot potato if they knew. Maybe they wouldn't drop him now, now that he's so ahead in the polls. But back in the early stages of the presidential race, when these attacks on you guys happened, I think he would have been history."

Lloyd slammed his right fist into his open left palm. "My God, Professor, I think you've nailed it. It all makes sense. Different attacks, from different sources, for different reasons."

Judy sighed. "I agree. But, what can we possibly do about it? If we go to the authorities about the recording, to try to implicate Linc, do you think they'd do anything about such a prominent politician? Could we trust them? Might that not just put us in more danger? Bill and Lloyd would have to offer themselves up as witnesses to the rape and death of Monica, which would put them in jeopardy. They'd be charged with being accessories. And now that Christopher Clark is dead, we can't prove that the campaign engineered these terror attacks. We can't prove anything."

Sandy continued his pacing. "Yes, we have a dilemma. But we can think this through. It seems to me that public exposure is the best way to go, if we can pull that off."

Bill picked up his phone, scrolled through his notifications, and cursed. "The prick just made another speech—a victory speech. He's won yet another primary."

Lloyd glanced over Bill's shoulder and shook his head in despair. "We know too much. This man cannot become president. But he's looking unstoppable. Virtually all of his Republican opponents have dropped out, and the Democrats have lost most of theirs. I think only two or three remain in the race, and neither of those have a chance at beating Linc's momentum in a general election. It looks like it's going to be an acclamation. A runaway train."

Suddenly, a voice from the front hallway. "Well, not quite. There is a solution. He can be stopped."

All heads whirled around in shock.

There, leaning against the doorway to the living room was the one and only Vito Romano, looking confident and resplendent in a black cashmere suit, white starched shirt, and red silk tie.

Sandy stood. "Vito, what are you doing here?"

"I figured you'd be here, Sandy. Heard you had a little incident at your house the other night, and wanted to check up on you and your friends."

"How'd you hear about that?"

Vito chuckled. "Sandy, Sandy, you should know me by now. Nothing escapes our scrutiny, particularly pertaining to people we care about. I'm glad to see you're in one piece. You can fill me in on the details later. But, for now, Judy needs to get better security for her house. The lock on that back door is child's play. I've been listening in for quite a while now. Intriguing stuff."

Judy laughed. "I'll deal with it, Vito. But, I'm glad it was you who broke in."

Vito bowed and flourished with his hand. "Thank you, dear lady."

Bill walked over and held out his hand. Vito shook it with his usual powerful grip.

"Good to see you again, Vito. But, you just said there was a solution to stopping Linc. Care to elaborate?"

Vito grinned in his knowing Cosa Nostra way. "Glad to, Bill. The solution is this—Dr. Sandford Beech needs to run for President."

42

"What? You must be joking!"

Vito sauntered over to the coffee table and poured himself a cup. Took a sip, and sighed with appreciation. "Great coffee. Nice and strong. I need that kick today."

Then he sat down in the armchair across from Sandy. "No, I'm not joking at all. I think you should do it. In fact, I think it's your obligation to do it. For your country and for what happened to your family. Not to mention the looming danger of a lunatic poised to occupy the Oval Office. I don't think you'll be able to live with yourself if you don't do it."

"I'm not qualified. As well, I'm not a politician and have never had the urge to be a politician. It's not for me."

Vito held up his massive hand in the stop sign gesture. "Calm down. Think about it. No one is qualified these days. The current president, who's retiring none too soon, was never qualified. He was an oil executive. Hell, we've had candidates who were brain surgeons, pizza tycoons, real estate magnates, military officers—the whole gambit. Being qualified doesn't matter anymore. Being passionate does matter, however, and you have every reason to be passionate. And angry."

"I'm a bloody physicist! A widower! And, now, a killer!"

"You killed in self defense. Doesn't count. And, no one can connect you to it, either. As for being a physicist, well, at least you have the brainpower, which can't be said about most of the prior occupants of the Oval Office."

"Vito, this is crazy. Just for the mere fact that, while I'm wealthy, I don't have the kind of money that can finance a campaign. These things cost big bucks, which I don't have."

"Hmm…sounds like a 'buying statement' to me. It's pretty early in our conversation for you to bring up the money part."

"Well…it's a fact."

Vito leaned back in his chair and crossed his legs.

"Here are some more facts. You're brilliant, and you were educated at West Point, which checks off the patriotism box. You were the product of an elite sperm bank committed to only the best human specimens. You were one of the chosen few, and while you're doing great work at the Lincoln Lab and MIT, your life deserves more than that. Most Americans can't compete with your pedigree. You were meant for greatness, and this is one of the greatest things anyone could ever anticipate having on their resume."

Sandy just stared at Vito, feeling the blood rushing to his face. Couldn't find any words.

Bill broke the silence. "I'd like to hear more, but, I kinda like the idea. You'd have my vote."

Lloyd jumped in. "Listen to Vito, Sandy. I'm shocked hearing his idea, but as the seconds tick by, it occurs to me that you'd be a fabulous candidate. And, Bill and I both have great connections and lots of money between us. We could be a big help."

Judy giggled. "I have nothing to offer, except maybe a friendly face to accompany you at your campaign speeches. As for Vito's idea, if you can stop Linc in his tracks, even if you don't win, that would be a victory. Someone else might come up the middle, but at this point I don't care who's president as long as it's not that dangerous man."

Vito smiled. "I'll tell you all a little secret. Have you heard about a cabal of powerful people called the Aufsteigen Group?"

Sandy nodded. "Yes. They meet in Palm Springs every year, no media, although the media try their best to cover them. It's some kind of a secret society, isn't it?"

"Yes. Probably have secret handshakes and human sacrifices too." Vito chuckled. "All joking aside, the word Aufsteigen means Ascension—signifies 'to rise up' or 'to soar.'"

"Okay."

"They're the backers of Senator Berwick. They believe in supreme corporate power and American domination over the world. Between them, the members probably have a net worth in excess of the GDP of most European countries. They want a puppet in the White House, someone they can own and control. Someone who will be beholden to them and work their agenda."

"Does the Republican Party know who's backing their leading candidate?"

Vito shook his head. "I don't know. Maybe they do, maybe they don't. Doesn't really matter. Both the Republicans and Democrats want power any way they can get it. They'd probably just look the other way. And, of course, corporate titans fit nicely within what both parties want to do anyway, so they'd probably just brush it off."

"But, I find it hard to believe that either party would support terror attacks to scare Americans into voting for them."

"No. I don't think so. I hope not. But that's a tactic that Aufsteigen have chosen to use with Berwick, and he's benefitting from it in spades. At least from Republican voters."

"So, what makes you think I could beat him, if Republican voters are giving him victories in the primaries?"

"Those are just Republican voters. They're less than fifty percent of the voting population of the United States. You'd run as either an Independent or a Democrat."

"I'm a registered Democrat."

Vito chuckled. "Sounds like we're having an actual conversation here. That's good."

"Well, I'm just trying to keep an open mind, Vito."

Vito stood and started pacing the floor, talking with authority as he walked.

"You'd run as a Democrat. They have the party machine that could propel you, and of course party funds to support you if you win their nomination. Not one of their candidates is running away with the primaries. It's still anyone's game, and several have already dropped out due to bad results and lack of funds. You could slip in as the fresh face and be welcomed with open arms."

"How could you know that?"

"One thing you forget, Sandy, is that you're a national hero. You saved countless lives on that horrific day at Quincy Market—you're exactly what Americans want as their leader. If you had nothing else at all to offer, voters are shallow enough to vote for a hero alone. You are indeed a bona fide hero."

Sandy shook his head. "I'm being shown in Lincoln's ads as an example of someone who's shamelessly unpatriotic. He's been running footage of me refusing the Citizen Honors medal, and throwing it into the face of a general, for God's sake."

Vito winced, and waved his hand in dismissal. "A good campaign can use that to their advantage. Position it as a sign that you're someone who can't be bought, a person with integrity and bravery, able to refuse the pomp and ceremony that other phony candidates embrace. In other words, you're real."

"Again, how do you know that the Democratic Party would welcome me as a candidate at this late stage?"

"Because they've said they would."

"You've talked to them about me already? Without asking me?"

Vito laughed, a big belly laugh that shook his body all the way up to his jowels.

"I didn't talk to them personally, Sandy! I'm Cosa Nostra, remember? Not the right image. We deal with politicians through cut-outs. People who we use as fronts, who are indeed the right image. Your name was floated as a possible solution to their candidate woes. They love your pedigree, love your look, and your image. And love the fact that you're a recognizable hero who apparently has a mind of his own."

Sandy shook his head, while his friends sat in stunned silence.

Vito sat down again, rested his elbows on his knees, and cradled his chin in his clasped fingers.

"I listened out there in the hall for quite a while. You and I have talked over the last few months about the Quincy attack, the corrupt deputy mayor, the Triple-L sperm bank, and just recently the near-attack on the cathedral. But, I heard you guys talking about the rape and murder of a young girl, and a possible recording that exists. You never told me about that. Lincoln was involved, by the sounds of it, which would be one damaging piece of information if it ever came out."

Sandy sighed. "Yep, it's a horrible piece of history. The poor girl died, which was tragic enough, but Linc has been closing loose ends in the last few months. We're pretty sure he's got his own goons doing this dirty work for him. Doubt that the campaign knows about it. Two of our colleagues from West Point were murdered, and attempts were made on Bill and Lloyd as well. Judy may be at risk now, if he finds out she has a copy of the recording."

"I see. Well, we can talk more about that. I'll need to listen to the recording and you can give me more details about what happened that night."

Sandy tapped his fingers on the table as he pondered Vito's words. "We were thinking that maybe we could give the tape to the authorities, hopefully get them to re-open the case. Or, somehow go public with it."

Vito grimaced. "At this stage, you can't trust the authorities. He's too prominent, and you don't know who's been paid off. The recording could just disappear. And, as I heard you guys saying—the recording alone isn't proof. To re-open, they'd need DNA evidence, assuming they collected it when they found her body. *If* they ever found her body. And the instant you start enquiring about it, you and your friends would be targets. I understand that Bill and Lloyd were there that night. They'd be in peril. You don't want to take that chance."

Sandy looked over at his friends. "No, it's not worth the risk."

"The best plan would be to pick the opportune time to release the recording for public consumption."

"But the media probably wouldn't do anything with it. They'd probably bury it, too."

Vito shook his head. "With the right connections, the thing will go viral. And we have the right connections."

Sandy frowned. "Sounds like you'd be involved if I decided to run?"

"Only in the background, Sandy. The Cosa Nostra can't be associated with a campaign for public office. We hide in the background for these things. The Mob learned from the Kennedy election. JFK would never have become president without the help of the Cosa Nostra, and then after the election he snubbed us and sent his brother on a campaign to destroy us," Vito said, shaking his head as if at a sad memory.

"Kennedy and his father were so desperate to wash their hands of the help my predecessors gave him that they went on a rampage against them. We don't want that to ever happen again. We just want to be involved in helping a candidate who has honesty, integrity, and family values, get elected. If we're too prominent in the picture, that would either turn off the electorate or cause the candidate to be so embarrassed as to lash out. So, ever since the JFK fiasco, we're far more discreet."

Sandy scoffed. "Vito, you're the Mob. And you want a candidate who has honesty and integrity? Are you fucking with me?"

Vito cracked every knuckle of his massive hands, the noise resonating menacingly around the room.

"No, if I was fucking with you, you'd know it. I like you, Sandy. And I hurt over what happened to your family. We want honest politicians, because, quite frankly, with the power elected officials have, we don't need the competition. And, as you know full well, family values come first and foremost with Italians. So, please, don't insult me. We may be a paradox, but we're an important part of the fabric of America, like it or not."

Sandy shook his head. "I'm sorry. That was insensitive of me. You've been a big help to me in all of this, as well as saving my life. I consider you a friend, although we are strange bedfellows."

"I understand. We in the Cosa Nostra do have an image problem, which is our own fault. One day we'll be able to put that behind us."

Judy finally found her voice again. "Sandy, what are you going to do? It sounds like time is of the essence with the primaries going on right now."

Sandy nodded and turned his attention once again to Vito. "How the hell would this thing be financed?"

"I'll take care of that."

"How could you do that? There are campaign laws, and you said you'd have to maintain a low profile."

"Again, we use cut-outs. No one would know the money came from us. You'd be the best financed candidate in the race. We'd set up a Super-Pac as well, which would act as an arms-length campaign machine. All the campaign finance laws would be observed, without any possibility of being caught in a violation. We would make certain of that, and, trust me, we're good at this."

Sandy rubbed his chin, feeling overwhelmed by all that he'd heard.

Vito pressed. "You want revenge. This is the best way to get it. And you want to do the right thing for your country. You're a patriot, you know that. Stopping Lincoln Berwick will be a triumph that you'll always be able to look in the mirror and be proud of."

"I don't think it's enough, after all that I know now."

"What do you mean?"

Sandy rubbed his bloodshot eyes, and lowered his voice to a near whisper. Vito leaned in closer as he spoke. "The two people who engineered the terrorist attack that killed my family and hundreds of others, need to die. Meagan Whitfield and Bob Stone. I intended to kill them myself. That's been driving me. I haven't even shared that with my friends here, but I need that resolution. For Sarah, Liam and Whitney. And for myself."

Judy gasped.

"I'm sorry, Judy."

Vito reached over and put his hand on Sandy's shoulder. "My best advice to you is not to give it another thought, Sandy. Your ultimate revenge will be victory at the polls. Don't let this consume you. It's not healthy. Trust me. I know more of such things than you do."

Sandy felt a sudden surge of adrenaline through his veins. And a fire in his gut that he hadn't felt in what seemed like forever. "Forever" being before the slaughter of his wonderful family.

"I must be crazy. But, watching that lunatic get elected president would drive me even crazier. It's strange, but, I don't want Linc to die.

I don't know why. Maybe it's because we once had a history together, or maybe it's that stupid Honor Code that might still be drummed into me. I just want him stopped. He can't become our president."

All of a sudden, Sandy slammed his fist down on the coffee table, so hard that the cups rattled and the pot teetered. He was surprised at how persuasive Vito had been, which meant that maybe he was primed and ready anyway, and just needed a shove in the right direction.

"Okay, let's do it. I'm in. As Judy says, time is of the essence, and no one has ever accused me of being indecisive or a procrastinator. Put the wheels in motion, Vito. I trust you."

43

As if there'd been a flip of a switch, the room snapped out of its sombre mood and came alive with a cacophony of cheers. Sandy felt the excitement, and it felt darn good. Suddenly it was real. He'd made a decision, and he knew, at least in his own mind, there was no going back now.

Judy ran over to him and wrapped her arms around his neck, while Bill, Lloyd, and Vito fist-bumped. She whispered in his ear, "I'm so proud of you. It's going to be exciting. You were always meant for greatness."

Sandy pouted. "Hey, I was already kinda great, wasn't I?"

Judy gushed, giggling like a teenager, "Of course! But, now you're going to change the world!"

Sandy kissed her gently on the cheek. "Judy, I'm not really doing this to change the world. My motivation is probably the wrong one. I'm only doing this to stop one man."

"Sure you are. But, don't you think that will change everything if you can pull it off? Can you imagine what kind of a planet this would be with Linc as the leader of the free world?"

"Well, when you put it that way—"

"Yes, dear Sandy, I'd say your motivation is probably as good as it gets. So, stop thinking that way—right now. You're doing a great thing, and you should be proud." Judy giggled again. "And, can you imagine the look on Linc's face when you announce that you're running?"

Vito had resumed his seat in the corner armchair as he calmly watched the four friends celebrate. After a few minutes of banter and laughter, he quickly brought them back to reality.

"Okay, folks, there are a few things we have to do. First, I need to listen to that recording and you can fill in the blanks for me as to what happened that night in the van. As well, I'll take the recording off your hands, Judy, and keep it safe until such time as we decide to release it to the public."

"I'll be glad to get rid of it, Vito. It makes me nervous."

"I can imagine. Secondly, I'll make some phone calls and get your campaign organization started, Sandy. You'll need a campaign manager, first and foremost. There are some power brokers out there who will swing things into place quickly for you, including the tools needed to finance the campaign. As I said, the money will flow quite willingly once you've announced, but we'll make sure from our end that sufficient funds are always there regardless of fund-raising. Again, we'll use cut-outs to guarantee none of the money can be traced to the Cosa Nostra."

Sandy shuddered. "Okay, lots to do. Be careful on the money front. No violations."

"No worries. You need to pick a time and place to announce your candidacy. It may be too late now for you to get your name on the ballots in the remaining primaries, but that's not really a concern. The delegate count is so fragmented amongst all the Democrat candidates, that there will be no clear winner by the time the July convention rolls around. You'll be well known and favored by then, and, if all goes well, acclaimed at the convention over all of the others."

"Okay. I'll need some serious momentum between now and then."

"Yes, you will. I'm sure you'll be up to the task, Sandy. It will all go to plan."

"I like your confidence, Vito."

Vito nodded. "After you announce your candidacy, your house will be hounded by reporters, day and night. You'll be on the road doing speeches most of the next couple of months anyway, so it won't bother you too much—but it might drive your neighbors crazy. Before you make that announcement, though, there's something you have to get out of your house."

Sandy frowned. "What's that?"

"That PEP weapon. You've broken every law imaginable by having that top-secret prototype in your home. You know that. You've taken out classified secrets accumulated during your work with the Pentagon and cloned the damn thing in your basement. And now you've used it to kill two people. That can't be traced to you, as far as we know, but if that weapon is discovered, you'll be in a heap of trouble. Once the media start stalking your block, you'll have lost your chance to get it out to a safe place. Any movement in and out of the house will be captured on film. And, if you do succeed in landing the Democratic nomination, the Secret Service will be all over you, including every inch of your house."

Sandy massaged his forehead with his fingers, feeling a headache coming on.

"You're right, Vito. Got me thinking now."

"I'll take it off your hands for you. I'm your best bet. I'm sure your friends don't want to babysit it for you, and we wouldn't want to take the chance of them being caught with it."

Sandy stood and began pacing the room. "No offense, Vito, but handing over a top-secret weapon prototype to the Cosa Nostra doesn't exactly give me a comfy feeling."

"I understand. But, I have several safe places for it to be kept under lock and key. In fact, I have vaults. That's where it should be and probably remain forever. You can't take the chance of being caught with it, and, maybe because I'm the Cosa Nostra, I'm your most secure choice—ironic as that sounds."

Bill jumped in. "He's right, Sandy. You have to get it out of there."

Sandy continued pacing. "I don't know…"

The tone of Vito's voice changed—slightly lower, and firmer.

"Let me gently remind you, Sandy, that you never did fulfill your promise to me after I set up that fake identity for your visit to Triple-L. You pledged to give me a demonstration of that weapon. I'm true to my word—my word is my bond. You need to be true to yours. I still want that demonstration, just for my own amusement and curiosity, but now I'm offering to also bail you out of a jam. I'll keep it safe and sound to make sure you don't go to prison for the rest of your life."

Vito paused, fixing Sandy with a penetrating look.

"And, a few minutes ago, you did say that you trusted me. Were you being honest, or just patronizing me? I don't like being patronized, Sandy."

Sandy stared into Vito's dark eyes for several long seconds.

For the first time, he was starting to understand what it meant to be friends with the Mob. Vito had never pressured him before now. This was a first. It was gentle pressure, but there was no mistaking the tone or message in his words. This was how the Cosa Nostra did business. But, Vito did have a valid point that Sandy couldn't deny. He'd broken the law—probably several laws. Serious infractions. He would indeed go to prison if it was discovered that he'd used military secrets to build his own prototype.

He had very few options as to where to stash the damn thing, but it seemed at the moment that Vito's efficient enterprise was indeed his best one.

"Okay, Vito. I'm going to trust you on this as well."

*****

Bill joined Sandy on the trip back to Boston. Vito followed behind in his stretch limousine, driven by faithful chauffeur and jack of all trades, Nunzio.

Nunzio was a nice guy, kinda quiet, very big, menacing to look at, and probably a cold-blooded killer if truth be told.

They figured that the limousine provided more than enough space to haul away the PEP.

The car was as silent as a library for most of the drive. Sandy was thinking hard about what he had just committed to. His life would never be the same now. But, it had already changed drastically more than two years ago. With the loss of his family it was as if his very life itself had also lost its purpose.

Now, although the prospect of running for president, and *being* president, was scary, he finally felt as if some purpose had returned. He would get his revenge, but in a way that Sarah and his kids would have been proud of him for.

His purpose in life had now become a mission of stopping a

dangerous man from becoming president by stealing that crown right out from under his nose. Just like the competitions he and Linc used to have back at West Point, but this time the competition actually had real life consequences.

Bill broke the silence. "Are you excited?"

"Overwhelmed is probably the right word right now, Bill. But, I feel the fire in the belly, so I guess that's a good thing."

"It is. Lloyd and I want to join your campaign. We'll both take leaves of absence from our jobs and be there for you. We all share the same mission. To breathe easy again, and stop a lunatic.

"I think that once you announce, and Vito releases that recording, our safety will be guaranteed. And, if you can beat that prick, the justice will be sweet." Bill paused. "But then you'll be president. I hope that after inauguration you'll still talk to us."

"Well, for you," Sandy said, floating a sideways glance at his friend, "how does secretary of the treasury sound? You're one of the most successful investment bankers on the planet, so that would be right up your alley."

Bill laughed. "I'll consider it, although it would be one hell of a drop in salary. But, some things are just worth doing even when the money sucks."

Sandy chuckled. "Yeah, it will be a big drop in salary for both of us. Being president doesn't carry the paycheque that I'm used to either. As for Lloyd, well, I'm thinking that with his background at NASA, secretary of education would be perfect for him."

"I think he'd take it."

Sandy pulled into his driveway, and Vito's car slid in right behind him.

Once inside the house, they went straight into the basement. The most important task that awaited them was dealing with the item standing in the corner of death, alone and forlorn, its ominous red light flashing the silent message that it was eager and ready for new orders.

Sandy led them over to the PEP machine. Bill and Vito just stared at it in awe.

"This is it?" Vito asked. "This is the thing that vaporized those thugs?"

"Yep, this is it. Doesn't look all that impressive, does it?"

Sandy pulled a plastic garbage can up against one of the basement walls, and aimed the weapon at it.

"Watch this."

He described the operation of the machine, pushed the activation button, and worked the remote. Within seconds the garbage can disappeared silently into a tiny pile of dust.

Vito muttered under his breath, "Sweet Jesus."

"Okay, Vito, now that you've had your demonstration, let's get it bundled up and loaded into the limo. I've fulfilled my promise to you. Please, though, promise me that you'll keep it safe and secret."

Vito made the sign of the cross. "You have my word."

An hour later, after the machine had been packaged up and stashed away on the rear couch of the stretch, the three of them were back in the house drinking coffee.

Faithful soldier, Nunzio, stayed outside and kept watch over the precious cargo.

"So, that machine simply pummelled those two guys into a pile of dust?"

"Vito, that weapon is ground-breaking. It's scary to think of how it might be used on battlefields, or by terrorists if they managed to get their hands on it. There's no limit these days to what science can accomplish."

"Astonishing. And, you said you chased their car away afterwards?"

"Yeah. I went outside with one of their guns, and the driver panicked."

Bill glanced around the kitchen. "Where's the gun? Do you still have it?"

Sandy got up and walked over to his broom closet. "Believe it or not, I shoved it in here with all the cleaning stuff."

He handed the gun to Bill. "Here it is. I knocked it out of one of the guy's hands when they were stalking me in the kitchen."

Bill examined it, paying particular attention to the barrel. "Sandy, this is an AR-15, but this gun couldn't have given you even a scratch. It's equipped to fire blanks."

He pointed to the mouth of the barrel. "I'm kind of a gun hobbyist. See this red thing? This is a BFA or Blank Firing Adaptor. Military grade BFAs are red or orange, civilian are yellow. They use these for training new recruits so no one blows their balls off. This gun was firing blanks. Its barrel was adapted."

Sandy took the weapon from Bill and studied the barrel. "I never noticed this red thing."

He passed it over to Vito. "I'm guessing you know about this stuff. Is Bill right?"

Vito looked at it and nodded. "Yep, he's right. They couldn't have hurt you with this. And it's safe to assume the other guy's gun—that you vaporized—was equipped the same way."

Sandy sat down hard, and clasped his hands behind his head. "So, they were just trying to scare me."

"Looks that way."

"But...why? What was the point? If these guys were sent by Linc's campaign, why wouldn't they just kill me?"

Vito winced. "We'll never know now."

44

"...and, I'm certain that some of you are looking at me, standing at this podium, wondering to yourselves what makes this man think he is qualified to be president. Admittedly, ever since I decided to run, I look at that same man in the mirror every morning while shaving, and wonder the same thing.

"And every morning, I arrive at the only conclusion that makes any sense to me. Plain and simple, I know that I'll be a really good president, one who will respect the rights of all Americans; be they liberal or conservative, black or white, red or yellow, legacy citizens or new arrivals."

Sandy stopped speaking as the audience of several thousand rose to their feet and applauded. He was commanding the stage in the massive auditorium at the Boston Convention Center and had been speaking for about forty-five minutes.

He'd already unofficially announced his candidacy a couple of weeks ago on a cable news talk show. Tonight, was the official announcement.

His campaign manager, Rod Crenshaw, had planted all the right seeds. Strategic leaking of teasers here and there, coy interviews with the media, and of course booking the convention center with a hint that a major announcement was coming.

Sandford Beech wasn't a household name at the time all of the hoopla started, but he quickly became one. Media hype was Crenshaw's strength and he used print, television, and social media to his advantage. In fact, his efforts practically overwhelmed the news cycles in all three mediums. The man was a genius at strategic positioning, and Sandy was shocked at how quickly he'd become a celebrity.

Sandy's status as a hero, and medal winner, was blasted everywhere—more so than Sandy was comfortable with. But, he knew he had to back off and let the experts do their thing. If left to him, his profile would never be known. Because, Sandy wasn't prone to boast.

Rod Crenshaw had set him straight right from the beginning: "Sandy, if you intend to make a serious run of this, you have to back off. You don't have to blow the horn—we'll do it for you. But, that's what wins elections. Trumpeting a verifiable profile, or, if not verifiable, embellishing it to the point of euphoria. In other words, if we have to, we just make shit up. Luckily, with you, we have a lot to work with. It doesn't look like we'll have to make any shit up."

So, Rod went to work. The West Point connection was emphasized as well as detailing Sandy's acts of bravery at the Quincy Market attack. Of course, he focused on the deaths of the loves of Sandy's life, and Sandy's selfless act of killing the terrorists and saving countless lives before even checking to see if he could save his own family.

Sandy was uncomfortable with most of this, but he let Rod do his work. He'd reluctantly accepted the reality of what made voters vote, and what made them learn to love a candidate.

His hero status was now firmly implanted on the campaign, and in every news organization that covered it. And, true to form, every news outlet wanted a piece of him. Because he was new, fresh, and a shot in the arm to what had so far been a boring Democratic primary season with yawn-inducing candidates who engaged no one.

None of them had Sandy's pedigree, although all of his Democratic opponents were indeed bona fide politicians. The fact that Sandy wasn't a politician worked in his favor. He was a curiosity for that reason alone.

But the hero thing was working better than anything. He could tell just by the way people talked to him, looked at him, applauded him, wolf-whistled him. The adoration in their eyes was hard to ignore. Everyone loved a hero.

And Sandy was left with the depressing thought that voters were pathetically shallow. How easy it was to hypnotize them into worship.

Which probably explained why Linc had been equally successful at brain-washing a large portion of conservative voters.

A significant fringe portion of conservative voters were gaga over Linc because he was delivering to them a message of intolerance, fear, anger, and hate.

And liberal voters were gaga over Sandy because he was a genuine hero, and supportive of equality, fairness, love, and hope.

But both he and Linc were just spewing words. Voters had no assurances that either of them would actually be true to those words. Which merely reminded Sandy that words indeed meant everything in campaigns, but, that memories would fade after the excitement was over.

His keen intuition about himself told him that, in only the short time since he'd made the decision, his brain had made the distinctions, accepted the realities, and adapted accordingly. Sandy could feel that he was slowly and surely becoming a politician and that his brain had rationalized what needed to be done.

He raised his arms in the air, motioned with his hands for the crowd to stop their cheering and resume their seats. They complied immediately, and he was astonished at the power in his gesture.

He was in a world now that he never could have imagined, and he was surprised at how much he was enjoying it. In fact, he was a bit ashamed of himself for how much he was enjoying it.

He continued his speech, expertly using the microphone to his advantage. Allowing his voice to resonate its pitch up or down, depending on the emphasis needed. Sandy had always been a powerful public speaker, and this was the grandest stage he'd ever occupied.

He had their rapt attention and decided to hit them with the closer.

"Most of you would love to ask me why I'm running for president. Well, I have nothing to hide. I never had any ambitions to be a politician, but sometimes the average man has to step up to the plate."

Sandy composed his features in a look of humility. "I am just an average man, despite the way I'm being portrayed in the media. I decided to run for president because I'm disappointed by the message being delivered by the leading contender for the Republican nomination. I'll even mention his name, which seems to be a taboo in politics. I don't care about taboos—I'd rather tell it straight up."

The newly minted politician swept his gaze across the crowd and took in the looks of expectation, of encouragement.

"Senator Lincoln Berwick, from the great state of Texas, is running on a platform of hate, division, and fear. I became concerned, listening to his speeches, and became even more concerned realizing that his message was resonating with voters. No doubt he will be the successful Republican nominee, and I decided that I couldn't live with myself if I allowed him to go on from there to defeat the Democrat nominee. And, from what I've seen of the roster of Democrat candidates, none of them have a chance of defeating him.

"I, on the other hand, can and will, defeat him. I want to be your Democratic nominee. For, if I am not your nominee, I predict that Lincoln Berwick will be the next President of the United States, and I worry about that."

The crowd rose from their seats and cheered again. Sandy waited a respectful few minutes before motioning them to quiet. As before, his command had an instant reaction.

He was astonished at the magic of it all, and equally astonished that he was actually getting pretty good at this command and control stuff. Much easier than he thought it would be.

"So, my answer to the question of why I'm running for president is a simple one. I want to stop Lincoln Berwick from occupying the Oval Office. And, perhaps other politicians who preceded me over the last few decades had that same simple reason for running as well. Just to stop someone else.

"It may not be the best reason to enter politics, but, perhaps that's just an honest answer that most have been afraid to admit to. So, I'll admit to it, and I'm confident that the message I have for Americans is far better for the country than the message he's delivering, and for that matter a better message than all of the other candidates as well. Thank you, ladies and gentlemen, for coming out tonight to witness this historic moment. I am now officially in the race to become President of the United States!"

As he knew it would, the crowd erupted.

Sandy raised his arms in salute and gave the cheering throng time to vent its enthusiasm before once more signalling for quiet. He wasn't finished yet.

"I plan to break the mold as a candidate," he said. "Starting right now! So I'm prepared to take a few questions. Just give me a second to move down along the ramp to be closer to you."

45

Sandy made his way along the stage, while security cleared a path for him to walk down the ramp that was extended into the crowd. This had been Rod Crenshaw's idea. To bring sort of a town hall setting to the end of his speech. If it worked, Rod wanted him to do it at all of his rallies. Would set him apart from the other candidates, make the crowd comfortable with him, and help create the image of the "common man."

Sandy walked down onto the ramp, saying a silent prayer that he wouldn't trip and fall on his face. The ramp was about three feet off the ground, allowing him to be close to the people lining it, while at the same time being just far enough up from them to avoid being swamped. Following a discrete distance behind him were two burly security guards, paid for by the campaign. As this was all new to him, Sandy was comforted that they were there.

He stuck his microphone under his arm and signed a few autographs along the way. The ramp extended about fifty feet out into the auditorium, and people were crammed in along the edges trying to get a closer look at him.

One of his campaign organizers down in the crowd signalled for him to stop. The man's index finger pointed down at the top of the head of a well-dressed man. Sandy knew this was his cue to take a question. The campaign guy handed the man a microphone.

"Dr. Beech, thank you for taking my question. You mentioned in your speech that you were against foreign military interventions. Can you elaborate on that, please?"

Sandy smiled down at the man. "Yes, glad to. In simple terms, I don't think America should be involved in offensive positions in foreign lands. Our military should be defensive in nature, kept at the ready to defend our country and its interests, not to attack other countries in attempts to get more friendly governments in power. We interfere far too much, and it's no wonder we're despised in many countries. We've created chaos, deaths of innocents, and a refugee crisis that is out of control. We did that not because we were threatened, we did it because we felt it was our right to interfere."

"But, we have a large military budget, Doctor. Do you intend that to be maintained?"

"No, my plans involve reducing that budget substantially over a period of years. Presently the annual budget for the Pentagon is well over $700 billion, and a lot of Americans aren't aware of the fact that we have close to 800 military bases in 130 countries. Yet, no other country has a base on our soil.

"Why do we do this? In my opinion, it's to be ready and able to interfere. We have to back off. The tax load on citizens is unsustainable, and our relationships with other countries are in tatters from the chaos we've caused. It has to end. My plan over my first term in office is to close 100 bases, as a good start to reducing our presence to no more than 500 bases over my two terms in office."

A resounding applause from the audience accompanied Sandy on his stroll further down the ramp.

He was signalled again, and he stopped to take a question from a young man wearing a Harvard jacket.

"Sir, you mentioned your plans to revise the tax structure in the United States. I'm studying tax law, so I'd be interested in knowing what your thoughts are."

"Thank you for the question, young man. Yes, taxation will be one of my priorities. This great country presently has a crushing debt of $23 trillion. The amount of money that comes off the average person's paycheque just to pay the interest on that debt is staggering.

"We can't continue like this. We have to begin paying the debt down, and I know that's harsh medicine, but someone has to find the courage to begin the process. I will begin it, and hopefully my successors will continue it. Because, that level of debt won't be paid off in my lifetime, and at the rate we're going, maybe not even in your lifetime.

"So, taxes have to rise—my plan involves raising it primarily on the wealthy and upper middle class. The remaining tax brackets will be essentially unchanged. But, contrary to what my Republican opponent is promising, there will be no tax cuts under my administration.

"And, as I mentioned in my previous answer, the Pentagon budget will begin to come down, as will the number of military bases we have around the world.

"And, since other politicians won't talk about it, I will. The unjustified wars in Iraq, Aghanistan, Syria, Libya, and Yemen have cost the American people approximately $15 trillion, and that's a conservative estimate. Eliminating cruel interventions like those will alone begin to be felt in a positive way back home, and eventually bring taxes down.

"Just think, our national debt would be forty percent of what it is right now if we hadn't wasted money so recklessly in fighting useless wars, let alone the lives that would have been saved. And, let's look back even further—Viet Nam was another mess that we should have stayed out of. The financial cost of that war still hasn't been accurately determined, although the cost in lives is well documented."

There were cheers and whistles from the crowd as he walked further down the ramp. So far, despite how controversial his answers were, the people seemed to appreciate them.

He was stopped again by a question from a pretty lady in a striking red dress.

"Dr. Beech, thank you. I hope you don't mind my question, because it's a bit personal. Your family was slaughtered in the Quincy Market terror attack. Yet, you seem to sympathize with immigrants from Middle Eastern countries, and you are opposed to attacking those countries. Can you explain how you're able to feel that way considering your personal loss?"

Sandy hesitated for a few seconds. He hadn't anticipated a question like this, although he should have. He felt his eyes well up with tears, but he resisted wiping them because he was afraid that would appear dramatic and opportunistic.

"I'm okay with your question. Thanks for having the courage to ask it. My easy answer would be that if one day we're able to fix the daily carnage on our streets of Americans killing Americans, perhaps we could turn our attention to the comparatively minor rate of murders committed by immigrants and refugees.

"As for the Quincy Market attack, this fact hasn't received much media coverage, but, the killers that day were home-grown Americans, not Muslims immigrants. They left notes that indicated support for the terror group, ISIS, but those three men were not even of Middle Eastern descent, and ISIS did not claim any credit for the attack.

"Yet, despite that, politicians and the media have somehow convinced Americans that the attack was organized and planned by radical Islamic fundamentalists. This tells me one thing, and one thing only—the American people deserve to hear the truth, and not fed with propaganda to support an agenda of hate."

"Are you saying that the Quincy attack was politically motivated?"

Sandy paused. "All I'm saying is that the aftermath of the attack was propagandized by opportunism. And, the facts were twisted and not disclosed accurately. The American people deserve better."

"Are you accusing Senator Berwick of doing that in his speeches?"

Sandy swallowed hard. "I'm not accusing anyone. I'm just stating the facts."

He started to move on, but she wasn't finished.

"Doctor, excuse me, but one more question, please?"

Sandy nodded agreement.

"The recent attempted sarin gas attack on the Holy Cross Cathedral was reported to have been planned by a renovation firm that was run by Muslims. What are your thoughts on that?"

He shook his head. "I have no comments on that. It's still under investigation, and there may be more to that story than meets the eye. We have to wait."

She persisted. The way she asked her questions caused Sandy to suspect that the pretty lady in the striking red dress was a reporter, although she wasn't wearing credentials.

"Senator Berwick has condemned that thwarted attack as being just another example of terror by Islam. Do you support his assertion?"

"No, I don't. I believe in commenting only when I have the facts."

"Do you know more than you're admitting, Doctor? Once again, I'll ask if Senator Berwick is one of those opportunists you referred to earlier. And, were Americans involved in planning that attack? Was it to be a false flag, sir, a ruse?"

Sandy started moving further down the ramp. "When the facts become clearer, I'll have more to say. I'm not going to comment on fairy tales. Thanks for the questions, ma'am."

There were a few isolated claps in the audience, but, overall, the sudden silence was deafening.

A campaign organizer signalled another question. Sandy figured this was probably a good time to bring this to an end.

"Okay, just one more question. Yes, sir?"

An African American man, holding a pad of paper and pen in one hand and the microphone in the other, moved up to the edge of the ramp. His demeanour also screamed reporter.

"Doctor, my research has uncovered the fact that you and Senator Berwick were classmates together at West Point. Is that correct?"

Sandy didn't expect this. "Yes."

"Were you friends?"

"At one time, yes."

"My sources have told me that you were both members of an elite group called the Honor Guild. And that you were expelled from that Honor Guild for breaking some sort of code of honor. Is that right, Doctor?"

Gasps in the audience. Sandy realized that his back was against the wall. Lying would accomplish nothing.

"Yes, I finished off my education at West Point after I left that particular unit."

The man looked down at his notes.

"Sir, is it true there was some kind of scandal that you blew the whistle on? Was that why they considered that you broke the code of honor? Tattling on your classmate? And, was it something to do with the death of an underage girl that Lincoln Berwick had been involved with?"

More gasps from the audience.

Sandy's throat was as dry as sandpaper. His instinct told him to just shut up, but he knew he needed to say something and just get out of there fast.

Struggling for saliva, he said the only thing that popped into his head.

"Sir, this is a campaign event, and I don't intend to sully it by commenting on unsubstantiated rumors about another candidate. This is not what I came here for tonight, and I don't intend to play the game of dirty politics. That's not my style."

Sandy turned his attention away from the reporter and looked out over the audience.

"I look forward to a positive campaign where the views of both sides are respected, even though, at times, there will be disagreements. I strongly disagree with my opponent's message, and I'm sure he disagrees with mine also. That's democracy, and that's America. God bless America."

The crowd was on its feet again.

Sandy waved to each section of the room, to no one in particular, but, of course, this is what politicians were expected to do. Make each person think he was waving to just them.

Then he bowed in respect.

The crowd kept cheering, and a human wave took shape, swaying from one end of the room to the other. It was easy to tell that the several thousand in attendance were engaged, hooked, and effectively hypnotized. Even with the controversial and shocking questions that had been asked, the people seemed to be in the palm of his hand, as would future crowds, he hoped.

Sandy glanced upward for just a moment, thinking a silent prayer to Sarah, Liam and Whitney. Hoping they were watching. Hoping they were proud.

He kept a confident smile painted on his face, as he'd been coached to do, and braced himself to keep that smile lit up until he'd gracefully made his exit out through the back of the stage.

Then he'd be able to relax, breathe normally again. And, even frown if he wanted to.

And he had some reasons to frown.

Why were those two questioners not vetted by his campaign? Why were their questions allowed, when they were clearly reporters? This was supposed to have been a town hall session for voters, not a press conference. And both of those reporters seemed to have information that was sensitive and generally unknown.

He gazed out over the crowd while continuing to wave with both hands.

Suddenly he gasped, as his eyes stopped on a figure standing five rows from the front, swaying along with everyone else.

Goosebumps rippled down his spine as Sandy fixated his gaze straight into the eyes of a ghost.

46

Sandy jumped off the ramp and began pushing his way through the crowd. Ignoring the cries of protest from his two security men, he aimed blindly in the direction of where he'd seen the ghost.

Squeals of delight accompanied his unplanned safari into the masses. It was hard for him to move, with pads and pens being thrust into his face by eager autograph seekers. And trying to dodge phones now that he was down on the floor with everyone else, was impossible. He knew he'd be appearing in countless selfies that attendees would treasure for posterity.

He could hear the frantic panting of his security team as they tried to keep up with him. Finally, one of them succeeded in grabbing him by the shoulder and spinning him around.

Slightly muffled by the roar of the crowd from Sandy's unexpected star turn, he heard one of them—a guy Sandy thought was called Frank—grumble through clenched teeth, "What the hell are you doing, Dr. Beech? This is not secure."

Sandy put his mouth up to Frank's ear, and cupped his hands. "There's a man in the crowd, moving towards the exit. He's short, chubby, and balding, wearing a green jacket and a green Celtics ball cap. He's a threat. I'm not going to be able to reach him through this crowd, but maybe you can."

Frank glanced toward the exit. "Okay, let me try to grab him. But, you have to head backstage with Victor. Now!"

Frank used his bulk to push faster through the crowd than Sandy had been able to do, and the other security guy—who Sandy just learned was named Victor—grabbed hold of Sandy's arm and started leading him back to the ramp.

He whispered, "Dr. Beech, you'd better sign a few autographs and smile for a few photos while you're down here. This will be spun by the media as alarming if you don't attempt to make it appear as if this was your attempt at a crowd-pleaser."

Sandy stopped in his tracks. "You're right. Keep an eye on me while I wander a bit."

He shook a few hands, signed a few autographs and posed for some pictures. All the while, he had one eye on the exit doors. All six feet, seven inches of Frank was pushing his way out into the concourse, but Sandy saw no sign of the guy in the Celtics hat.

As Sandy signed his last autograph, he began to doubt himself, and who it was he thought he saw. It was crazy. Too crazy to comprehend.

*****

He was sitting backstage with his campaign and security staff, scanning through video footage of the crowd on a computer monitor.

Frank leaned over his shoulder. "Anything?"

Sandy shook his head. "Haven't seen the right angle yet. And he's a short guy, so wouldn't be easy to spot."

"I'm so sorry I couldn't grab him, Doctor. I checked out the lobby and outside of the convention hall. Didn't see anyone by the description you gave me."

Sandy shook his head. "No worries, Frank. The crowd was huge—like finding a needle in a haystack. Maybe my eyes were just playing tricks on me, anyway."

Sandy rubbed his eyes and turned them away from the monitor just as Rod Crenshaw entered the room through a side door.

He strode over to Sandy wearing an impatient grimace on his face. Rod was tall, blonde, movie-star handsome, and had an efficient air of authority about him that caused the room to become instantly silent.

"What's going on here? Been waiting outside in the van. We have a fund-raising dinner to attend, Sandy—$5,000 dollars a plate. If we don't move our asses we're going to be late, and these aren't the kind of people we want to keep waiting."

Frank held up his hand. "Calm down, Rod. Dr. Beech was

concerned about someone he saw in the crowd. We're scanning some footage to see if we can spot him."

Rod leaned up against the wall. "I missed the last part of your speech, but I heard it went well. Then, someone told me that you jumped down onto the floor. Is that what you were doing? Trying to confront this person?"

Sandy nodded. "Yes, I was. Stupid of me, but I just reacted."

"Well, don't do that again, Sandy. It's too risky. That's why you have Frank and Victor. Leave things like that to them."

"You're right, Rod. Was probably just imagining things anyway."

"Was it someone you know?"

"Someone I knew. But…he's supposed to be dead. So, I must have been hallucinating."

"What's his name?"

"Don't want to say."

"Okay, well, describe him to me."

"Short, fat, balding, puffy face, wearing a green jacket and green Celtics cap."

Rod put his arm around Sandy's shoulder, and turned him away from the computer. "You've just spent a couple of hours on your feet and delivered one hell of a rousing speech. Exhaustion and adrenaline can play tricks on all of us from time to time. I want you to head out to the van, lay your head back, and relax. Let me look through the rest of this footage for you. That's what campaign managers are for. To do the crap stuff, so you candidates can shine. Okay?"

Sandy nodded wearily. "Good idea. I was probably just dreaming, anyway. Finish up here and I'll see you out in the van."

Rod smiled. "Glad you agree. Our mutual friend would be very disappointed in me if he knew I was allowing you to get all stressed out."

Sandy frowned. "What mutual friend?"

Rod leaned in closer and whispered, "Well, Vito, of course."

"I wasn't aware that you knew Vito."

Rod shuffled his feet. "Not as well as you probably do, but I know him as being just someone on the fringe of the campaign."

Sandy folded his arms across his chest. "He's not supposed to be on the fringe of anything. Vito can't be associated with this campaign at all."

Rod shook his head. "No, you misunderstand. Of course, he can't be involved. He's completely in the background. He just pulled some strings to make certain things happen for you. That's all."

Sandy drummed his finger into Rod's chest. "Are you one of those strings he pulled? Did he choose you to be my manager?"

"No, not at all. Not directly at least."

"How indirectly, then?"

Rod's eyes blinked several times and flicked away from Sandy's for just a second. He seemed nervous.

He lowered his voice to a whisper again. "Sandy, don't be so naïve. Vito has been a big help to you, in more ways than you realize. This is how politics works. Sometimes we deal with people who hold cards we wouldn't want to play. Trust me, I've been at this a long time, and every campaign has a Vito or two in the background. Not to worry. We know how to insulate candidates from benefactors like that."

Sandy stared into his baby blue eyes, and this time Rod stared right back without blinking.

"You come highly regarded, Rod. Apparently, you're one of the best. I guess I'm going to have to trust you."

Rod squeezed his shoulder. "You can trust me. And, you'll be glad you did. So, for now, go on out to the van and leave this searching stuff to me. You've given me a good description of the guy. If I find him in any of the footage, I'll show it to you to see if it's who you thought it was. But, if he's indeed as dead as you say, then we're going to be looking at a pretty spooky video."

*****

Rod cleared everyone out of the room, and sent Frank and Victor out to the luxurious travel van to keep Sandy company. He sat down in front of the laptop where all the crowd videos had been downloaded and began his scan.

He was proud of his candidate. One of the brightest and most charismatic he'd ever managed. He could feel it in his bones that

Sandford Beech could go all the way, and with Rod's expert help, the man could easily be in the Oval office in less than a year's time.

A dream candidate, and one who had been groomed without him even realizing he'd been groomed. That was the best part, because every sincere bone in Sandy's body was committed to a cause out of pure unadulterated passion. An honest passion, something that was rare in politicians. Committed to a cause that was greater than any one man. Something that had existed in the politicians of long ago, but certainly not in modern times.

But, Sandy was naïve, as all decent people were. The good doctor was a genius and a genuine hero, but idealistic as hell. Which was both a good thing and a bad thing. Hopefully, over the course of the campaign he'd develop a thick skin and become more realistic about how things had to be done in the rough and tumble world of politics. Rod considered Sandy a project, almost like in the movie, My Fair Lady. He felt like he was Professor Henry Higgins, and Sandy was Eliza Doolittle. And the project was to transform the best presidential candidate in a generation into a hard-nosed leader who would inspire millions of people into an agenda of power and prosperity that would rival the heights of the Roman Empire.

Suddenly Rod clicked Pause on the monitor, and he stared hard at one of the crowd stills. Then he enlarged it.

"Shit!"

He pressed the Delete button, and continued to scan. The fat little man in the green Celtics cap popped up in four more scenes. Rod clicked Delete again.

Then he sighed and picked up his phone. Punched a speed dial number and waited for the familiar voice to answer.

"Hello?"

Rod spoke in hushed tones, just in case someone was still lurking outside the door.

"It's me. Our puppet is back in the country. Causing some mischief. Perhaps he thinks his payday wasn't big enough?"

The man sighed in exasperation. "Okay, leave it with me."

47

"You were supposed to use that Judy Nichols as leverage. Were supposed to do something to her and her precious daughter. You still have time. He might drop out of the race if you take drastic steps."

Meagan allowed a wry grin. "No, we're not going to do that. No need."

Linc banged his fist on the table. "What do you mean, no need? Sandy's ahead in the polls for the Dems. He's going to get their nomination next month—no doubt about it. We have to stop him."

Bob Stone reached out and put his hand on Linc's shoulder. "It's too late to do anything like that, Linc. He's too far along in the race. We can't take a chance on something backfiring on us. And there is that apparent issue with you and that young girl. You never told us about that. You should have."

"That's false. Nothing happened."

Meagan leaned forward in her chair. "The media has been having a field day with that rumor. All sorts of conspiracy theories. Luckily, nothing concrete, but your poll numbers have dropped a bit. Anything you want to tell us about it? Is there possibly any truth to it? Did you have sex with an underage girl? And…did she die?"

Linc shook his head, but Meagan noticed that his eyes betrayed him.

"Well, then, we'll just have to do our best to plant some distractions. Keep the media focused on other stories."

The Senator's voice elevated to a full octave higher. "This was supposed to have been a sure thing. We never counted on Sandy entering the race. How did that happen? I know I can beat him, but he wasn't the one I was supposed to have been competing against. If he wins the nomination for the Democrats, I'll be in for the fight of my life."

Bob shuffled some papers and stuffed them into his briefcase. "Well, then, you'll just have to fight for your life. You two are at opposite ends of the spectrum, but conservative voters love your message. You're still the odds-on favorite."

Linc shook his head in disgust. "But that's now; this is just the primaries. In the general election, I'll have to compete for all voters, not just conservatives."

Meagan stood. "Bob and I have a meeting to attend. Stop your whining; get out there and compete. I'll be honest with you—it feels like you've lied to us. God help us if you did. There had better be nothing to that story about the girl."

*****

It was the second meeting of the year for the Aufsteigen Group. A crucial one, as the presidential campaign was in the final lap. Senator Lincoln Berwick was the favorite to become the Republican nominee—and Sandford Beech, miraculously, seemed to have the Democratic nomination locked up in his favor, despite having entered the race in its latter stages.

There were twenty-six important people sitting in the conference room; the combined wealth of the group being almost beyond measure, particularly since a lot of their wealth was sitting comfortably in offshore bank accounts beyond the reach of the IRS and anyone else who had the nerve to challenge them.

A tall bespectacled man walked to the podium. In defiance of modern times, he had a file folder in his hand instead of an iPad. He opened the folder and began to speak.

"I will bring the formal stage of our meeting to order. As is customary, our given names will no longer be used during the solemn portion of this meeting. You all have German labels that identify you only to the people in this room, and I ask you that you all please follow our protocol and use only those labels. Thank you.

"We have a situation before us that is unprecedented. Our investment in Triple-L has paid dividends to us, perhaps beyond what any of us or our predecessors envisioned over the last few decades.

"But, the time is now, and we have the brass ring within our grasp. This is the first time any of our specimens have reached the point where they are of age to compete for the highest office in the land—indeed, in the entire world."

He looked up at the group and smiled.

"We don't just have one candidate in the running, we have two. Both major political parties have been hijacked unknowingly by our creations. Those two political parties have no idea of the quality of the candidates they have, or what their origins are. We in this room do know, however, and we are confident that America has never been in such a strong position as this before. Not in the entire history of the Republic.

"The name of our esteemed group, Aufsteigen, means Ascension. Our goal from the beginning was to have an Ascendant. Due to our unprecedented planning and manipulation, we are in the enviable position of having two Ascendants, not just one. We should all be very proud indeed, and I compliment the members of our group who were so active in engineering events to the state that we are at today.

"The papers I have in front of me are more than two decades old, yet due to our knowledge of genetics and our investment in the most revolutionary sperm bank in the world, the words in these papers carry relevance that is timeless.

"As all in the room are aware, both candidates are products of Triple-L and were students at West Point at the same time. Both were also chosen for the Honor Guild, although one was expelled due to certain…ah…violations. I won't go into those, but rest assured those violations of his were carried out with the best of intentions. Which only underlines, to us at least, his superior character traits.

"These papers in my hands are psychological evaluations of both candidates, conducted during the time they spent in the Honor Guild at West Point.

"I'll start with who I will refer to as Candidate A.

"As with previous votes we have taken pertaining to candidates for the Senate, we try to stay objective here. Although most members will easily guess who is Candidate A or Candidate B, we keep names out of it. You are to make your decisions based on the qualities that we want in the presidency.

"So, for Candidate A, I'll read a brief synopsis of the psychological profile.

"He is a man driven by ego, and ego alone. His personality is assessed as being at the highest degree of narcissism. Power is important to this person, as is the need to crush all opposition. His brain is superior, and it has the ability to quickly analyse complex situations.

"Selfishness is a trait exhibited by him in almost every human interaction. Not capable of affection, devoid of the ability to appreciate any semblance of love of others. A sociopath of the highest order. He has difficulty controlling his anger as well as his need to win at all costs. Sometimes can be a loose cannon and leans in the direction of bullying as a tactic to achieve his goals. A high achiever, one who can accomplish any goal he sets his mind to.

"Now, to Candidate B.

"He is brilliant in every sense of the word. Charismatic, and has the ability to garner affection and adulation from almost all sectors of society. A humble man, despite his obvious talents.

"Achieves victories without really having to try too hard. Wears his emotions on his sleeve at times, and effortlessly demonstrates empathy with others. Leads by example, and people follow him willingly.

"Idealistic and stubborn. Not easily swayed from his ideals and principles. Coercion may sometimes work, but his conscience is always working overtime in the background. Capable of deep emotion, and loyal to a fault.

"Falls in love easily, and returns love willingly. Capable of great accomplishments solely due to his ability to incite loyalty. Followers tend to be confident in his leadership due to his natural charisma and honesty.

"Motivated by the pursuit of good triumphing over evil. Obsessed with always doing the right thing, not only for others, but for the appeasement of his own conscience.

"So, there you have it. We will now call for a vote. And the motion we're voting on is a simple one. It is this: Do we want Candidate A or Candidate B to be our sole Ascendant and the next President of the United States?

"A simple majority will determine the answer, and, after the vote we will all speak as one voice.

"Needless to say, we have the opportunity of a lifetime here as we are fortunate for both political parties to have Triple-L specimens at the top of the polls. In essence, we of Aufsteigen will win no matter who wins.

"It comes down to who will be able to execute our agenda the best. Are there any comments in favor of one or the other before we hold the vote?"

A hand raised near the front of the conference table.

"Yes, Prinzessin, speak your mind."

Prinzessin rose from her seat. "Allgemeine, in my view, both candidates are strong, but the candidate most motivated by the essences of ego and power would serve our group the best. My vote will be for Candidate A."

"Thank you, Prinzessin. Are there any more comments?"

A man sitting beside Prinzessin stood.

"Yes, Soldat?"

"I second the comments from Prinzessin. Candidate A is my choice."

"Thank you, Soldat. The floor is still open. Further comments anyone?"

A large hand was raised in the back of the conference room.

"Yes, Drachen, please share your thoughts."

A tall man dressed in a black linen suit accentuated by a red silk tie, rose from his seat. All eyes turned in the direction of the imposing figure blessed with thick black hair and a dark Mediterranean complexion. Drachen always commanded attention—his presence usually sucked the oxygen out of any room.

"Allgemeine, with all due respect, I will disagree with Prinzessin and Soldat. The candidate with the qualities of character, honesty, and humility would make the most effective President of the United States.

"While he might be harder to control, he will be far more trustworthy in the long run for the Aufsteigen Group, and more likely to fulfill our agenda. Of course, he would require a certain amount of exertion and influence from us, but in the long run, the effort would be worth it. Candidate A is a loose cannon and reckless. My vote will be for Candidate B."

"Thank you, Drachen. Last call for comments. Anyone else?"

The tall bespectacled chairman of the Aufsteigen Group, known at these ceremonial meetings as Allgemeine, banged the gavel.

"Seeing no further hands raised, the floor is closed. We will now call for a vote.

"For Candidate A, a show of hands, please."

He counted the hands.

"For Candidate B, a show of hands, please."

He counted those hands, and jotted down the results on a pad. Raised his head to address the group.

"The vote count is thirteen to twelve, in favor of Candidate A. It has been recorded as to how each of you has voted. In my role as Chairman, I only vote in the event of a tie.

"And, of course, with the composition of our group, there could only be a tie in the case of unexpected absences of one or more members, or, sadly, in the situation of one or more deaths. In this case, we have a clear decision, and all voting members are present and accounted for.

"Candidate A is our Ascendant and choice for president. We will now speak as one voice and rally our resources behind that candidate. Which could mean drastic sanction against Candidate B if it becomes clear that he is winning against our choice, but no such sanctions will be permitted earlier than the two-month span of time prior to the election.

"We will all be committed to the cause we have voted on here today.

"A procedural reminder to all of you, however. If, prior to September tenth of this year, exactly two months from the date of the general election, any members of our group become deceased, the vote will be immediately recalculated. If the result changes in favor of Candidate B instead of Candidate A, we will follow protocol in support of Candidate B.

"In closing, good luck to us all, good luck to Candidate A, and God bless these United States of America."

48

The celebrations continued until dawn.

The new Hyatt Regency in Portland, Oregon, was christened in fine style.

Adjoining the Oregon Convention Center, it had been built to attract big events, big spenders, and big news.

Nothing bigger could have been anticipated than what had just happened on this hot July 21 evening.

Thousands of eager Democratic Party delegates, attendees, and power brokers, had just wrapped up their nomination convention.

This final night was the biggest celebration the party had ever seen in its history—because the result came out of nowhere.

A candidate who had been a dark horse only a few months ago, declaring his entry late into the primary contest, transformed, literally overnight, from a dark horse into a white charger.

And, despite the fact that he had won no primary contests whatsoever, he still won the nomination.

When the voting took place on the final day of the convention, none of the candidates achieved the required 2,382 delegates out of 4,763. They all fell far short, with some delegates even refusing to cast their votes the way the primaries had dictated, causing a crisis that had to be resolved by the party executive.

Urgent meetings were held, ideas were proposed, and rule changes were made.

The executive was surprised how many delegates had mutinied from party rules, and actually just exercised what they insisted was their entitlement to "write in" their choice for nominee.

Dr. Sandford Beech, the dark horse, had succeeded in attracting hundreds of votes from these mutineers on that crucial first ballot.

Other delegates started voicing their wish to "write in" as well, after seeing the dismal results from the first ballot for the three official candidates.

The Oregon Convention Hall became a noisy place indeed, with thousands of passionate delegates and party supporters insisting that caution be thrown to the wind, and to hell with the stupid rules.

Clearly, the three weak candidates were worse than weak—they were pathetic.

But, what was clear to virtually all of the attendees, the one candidate who no one considered "official" because he hadn't won, or even participated in, one single primary, was cresting as the favorite.

Without even participating, he'd attracted several hundred votes on the first ballot.

If the rules were relaxed, and true democracy was followed, allowing freedom to vote on conscience and instinct alone, then and only then, would the party be able to embrace its proper nominee.

In other words, attendees insisted, in loud and raucous terms, that the Democratic Party finally show that it was democratic. A novel thought indeed.

Fearing a complete breakdown of the Democratic Party, a possible riot, and a colossal embarrassment on nationally-broadcast television, the executive capitulated.

They made the announcement that rules and protocol would be ignored due to the unique situation, and that the convention would be thrown open to voting on an individual basis, with no consideration given to what had been committed to in the months-long primary season.

The die was cast.

The crowd, for the most part was ecstatic. This had never happened before in the history of the Party, and everyone felt they would be part of new history now.

Dr. Sandford Beech from the great state of Massachusetts, won overwhelmingly on the second ballot, garnering votes from 3,500 delegates, well above the majority that was needed.

And in his victory speech, which contained all the right words, and all the right magnetism, he announced his running mate.

The four-term senator from New York, Caitlin Atwood, would be the country's next vice president if the Beech/Atwood ticket won in November.

History was made once again, as Caitlin was only the second woman ever nominated for VP, and, if they won in November, she would be the very first elected vice president.

Dr. Sandford Beech promised his adoring crowd that the greatest country in the world would once again become that sparkling beacon of freedom and compassion.

He was rewarded with a thundering ovation that lasted for what seemed like forever.

Sandy was now the Democratic Party nominee for President of the United States of America.

Only a week earlier at the Republican Party convention in Dallas, Senator Lincoln Berwick had secured the Republican nomination.

The race was on.

A sprint over the next four months until the general election on November 10.

Americans would vote on that special day for their next president, their choice being between two former classmates who had raced against each other countless times back at West Point.

Americans didn't completely grasp, however, how special and unique this election really was. For the very first time in history, not just one, but both of the candidates, had been designer babies. Chosen for greatness before any quality time had even been spent in the womb. Lives created by sperm that had, remarkably, been several decades old before being resurrected from frozen slumber. Resulting in two lives destined to achieve the highest pinnacles of success solely on the basis of genetics.

*****

Sandy wasn't a partier, but he endured nonetheless. The convention hall planned to rock and roll until dawn, but he managed to sneak off to his suite in the Hyatt long before that.

No one would miss him. The partiers were probably too drunk to even remember why they were there. They were celebrating an historic event, sure, but just like at weddings, once the bride and groom left, no one usually seemed to care all that much.

His suite was spacious and sumptuous. More than he needed, but the campaign organizers insisted he have nothing but the best. He wasn't going to argue.

Lloyd, Bill, and Judy joined him for a drink in the wee hours of the morning. They were all relieved to escape the noise, and hanging out in Sandy's suite was the kind of celebration they enjoyed much more than mingling with hordes of strangers down in the convention hall.

Bill raised his glass. "A toast. To the next President of the United States!"

The four friends clinked glasses.

To Sandy, it all felt surreal. The four of them had endured so much over the last few months, and right now it seemed like a dream, a fantasy, that they were actually celebrating something he had never envisioned and never even wanted. But, now, he wanted it. He wanted to make a difference.

It was strange, he thought, how quickly priorities could turn on a dime.

Each of his friends had taken leaves of absence from their jobs to perform key roles in the campaign over the last couple of months.

They were full-time employees of the Beech for President campaign, and while their responsibilities were exhausting, they each still found time to get home to their friends and families every few days. Again, all paid for by the campaign.

Judy's daughter, Cynthia, had moved in with Judy's sister in New York, and would be there until the election. After that, who knew what the future held?

Sandy was determined to find roles for each of them in his administration if he won the presidency, so they'd all have to move to Washington to join him. Precocious Cynthia had already hinted to Judy that she expected them to move into one of those famous and trendy Georgetown brownstones that were frequently featured in political thrillers.

Lloyd walked across the room and gave Sandy a big bear hug. Then he stood back, resting his hands on Sandy's shoulders.

"This is kind of unbelievable. It's happened so fast. You raced to the top, and no surprise of course. You're about as presidential as any candidate could possibly be. You'll be great as president—it's an honor to say I was your classmate, Sandy."

Sandy chuckled. "I know. It's odd. I'm still trying to get my head around it all. There's still so much to think about, just the 'getting elected' part. But, beyond that, I have to be more concerned about how to actually be president, which of course, I know absolutely zero about."

Bill chimed in. "Hey, you're entitled to Secret Service protection now. The nominees of each party automatically get that perk 120 days before the general election."

Sandy shook his head. "I don't want them yet. Too constraining. I'll wait until I'm actually president. Until then, I still want some semblance of freedom."

Judy made a face. "Is that wise? Wouldn't it be far safer with those pros?"

"Maybe. But, I have four security guys that the campaign is paying for, so I'll just continue with them for now. They're ex-military, so probably just as good as the Secret Service, anyway. But, at least with these guys, I can tell them to piss off occasionally. Once I agree to take on the Secret Service, I lose that ability. So, for now, I think I'm fine."

Lloyd put down his glass and started for the door. "C'mon, Bill, let's go. We'll leave Sandy and Judy to reminisce about the good ole days on this special night—or, should I say, morning?"

Bill glanced at his watch, and followed Lloyd out the door. "Christ, it is indeed morning. Okay, goodnight, you two. Tomorrow is the first day of the rest of our lives, and I have a feeling that it's not gonna be dull."

*****

She was lying across his body, her sweet face resting on his chest. Her nakedness was warm and comforting, a feeling that Sandy hadn't experienced since he'd lost his wife. In fact, it was a feeling he thought he'd never experience again.

Her naked beauty wasn't much different than he remembered from back in their college days. Sure, they'd both aged a lot since then, but, remarkably, neither of them had changed too much.

A few extra pounds here and there in spots that would have caused them angst in their younger years, but still pretty minor in the grand scheme of things. And to be expected, with a couple of decades of distance from when they'd been lovers.

But they weren't lovers anymore. At least, not for now.

Sandy planted a gentle kiss on Judy's forehead.

"I'm sorry."

She slid her fingers across his lips and whispered, "Shush—nothing to be sorry about. It happens."

"It's never happened to me before. It's—humiliating."

Judy raised herself up on her elbows, and stared into his eyes. "No, it's not. It's just being human. We'll try again some other time."

"That would be nice. But, now that this has happened, I'll be thinking about it. I'll probably need to get good and drunk next time so I can forget."

"You can't forget. Your brain won't let you. But, you can relax and realize that you don't have to prove anything to me. We're not kids anymore, and we have a history between us that most couples don't have."

Sandy kissed her on the lips, then took a peek under the blanket. He chuckled. "Still nothing to report."

She cradled his face in her hands. "Sandy, dear, there are also a few other things you may not be able to forget all that easily. You know what I mean."

He sighed. "Yes, I do. I don't know if those things are a factor or not, but it's been over three years now since my life came to an end. That sounds kind of ominous, but it did indeed end. Pleasure hasn't been a priority for me ever since that happened.

"My work at MIT and the Lincoln Lab has consumed me—and I allowed it to. And, revenge has been foremost on my mind during my idle time. Wanting someone to pay, someone to hurt. It's been an obsession.

"And, now this—I soon may be President of the United States. I'm realistic enough to know that such a job will not have much pleasure attached to it. In an odd sort of way, I've been doomed ever since my family died."

"Did you ever seek counselling?"

Sandy shook his head. "No. The nuclear physicist in me told me that no insights would be more scientific than my own. Silly, I know, but probably really just more arrogant than silly. Counselling probably would have helped me."

"I can't imagine what it must have been like to lose your entire family all at once like that. It's impossible to get my head in that space."

Sandy sighed. "I still love her, Judy. I'm being perfectly honest with you. You deserve that. And I still adore my kids. That's not healthy at all. They're gone. I'm alone. And no one has yet paid the price for what was taken from me."

"Maybe the unhealthiest thing for you is to still think about revenge. If you harbor those feelings, even after you crush Linc in the election, you'll never be able to truly enjoy your life the way you deserve to."

Sandy squeezed her soft shoulders and gently kissed her on the nape of her neck.

"Sage advice, my dear. I'll try to take it. In the meantime, if you're patient with me for a while, I may be able to get my mojo back."

Judy slid higher up on his body until her breasts rubbed against his chin. "I like a challenge, Sandy. You'll be my project, how's that?"

He laughed. "Just don't squeal to the tabloids. I don't want my first term in office being labelled a flop before it even starts!"

49

The celebrations lasted for a week. Parties, fund-raising dinners, late night cocktails. Sandy was exhausted.

In between all the high-fives and drinks, there were endless strategy meetings.

Rod Crenshaw had laid out the itinerary for the next three months, which would basically take them right up to the eve of the election. And Sandy was well aware that Linc's campaign would be undergoing the same process.

Sandy was surrounded by people now whose names he couldn't remember even just minutes after being introduced. Rod was bringing on new handlers every day, and each of them seemed capable. From what Sandy could recall, their resumes were all strong.

But all of them seemed like hired guns, experienced with campaigns, but not much beyond that. They were basically professional campaign people, brought in for one purpose: victory. Their claims to fame were congressional races, gubernatorial campaigns, and even as lowly as mayoralty races. Most seemed thrilled to be part of a presidential campaign, which Sandy guessed would be the motherlode if you were a professional campaign whore.

He was finally back at his own house in Lexington—for the first time in weeks. Campaigning had taken him to several states, as well as non-stop appearances on the cable news networks. It was mind-numbing work, but he had to admit that it had helped to keep his brain sharp. The constant barrage of trick questions thrown his way tested his ability to dance on his feet. And he'd danced well, according to the media.

Recent polls, however, had shown Linc holding the lead in

national counts, by about ten points.

But that gap had been tightening with each poll taken.

A point here, a point there—slowly but surely, Sandy was closing the gap. He knew he was at a bit of a disadvantage, as Linc was a nationally-known figure, being a senator. Sandy, on the other hand, was still a comparatively unknown quantity.

But that was gradually changing, the more that people got to know him. He and Linc were like night and day, and the qualities Sandy was exhibiting on the campaign trail allowed the contrast to stand out. Linc's message was one of fear and anger—Sandy's was one of hope and respect. It all depended on what kind of government Americans wanted, and how they wanted to live their lives.

Linc had continued the message that he'd started his campaign with. He seemed to be a one-trick pony, hammering away at the terrorist attacks that had grabbed the public's attention in the last few years.

Even though 9/11 was a long time ago, he not so gently reminded the public of it whenever he had the chance. In his speeches, he pounded away at the Boston Marathon bombings and the Quincy Market slaughter. And, as if that weren't enough, he emphasized over and over again how the Holy Cross Cathedral had just been a heartbeat away from being the worst sarin gas attack in the history of the world.

Clearly, his campaign had every intention of making Massachusetts a swing state, one the Republicans could finally steal away from the Democrats. If they won that state and a handful of other traditional Democrat states, the presidency was going to be gift-wrapped for Senator Lincoln Berwick.

Sandy was determined to prevent that.

He strolled aimlessly around his house, savoring the comfort of being back in his own space—away from the crowds, reporters, and campaign schmoozers.

His permanent security team was now up to six, and they were with him all the time, everywhere he went. Tonight, they were posted at all corners of his property. Keeping the spying public and nosy reporters at bay. And, hopefully, anyone who wanted to take a shot at him.

They'd wanted to post two men inside the house as well, but Sandy refused. He didn't want the sanctity of his refuge disturbed by strangers, even strangers armed with M15s committed to ensuring his safety. He was only prepared to go so far with this security stuff. He needed his peace once in a while.

Absent-mindedly, he wandered down to his basement. For a moment, he was taken aback at not seeing his faithful PEP weapon with the flashing red light. It seemed so long ago now that he'd entrusted it in the care of Vito Romano. It felt strange knowing it was no longer standing sentry in that strategic corner of his basement; the corner that saw the disintegration into piles of dust of two intruders who, at the time, had seemed intent on killing him.

He was still puzzled at discovering that the two men had actually been shooting blanks. That they weren't there to kill him at all. It had only been theater, designed to scare him.

Or—designed for a different reason?

He hadn't had much time to think about it, but it was indeed strange. If they'd been attempting to scare him, it hadn't worked. Because, shortly after, Sandy had declared his candidacy for president.

But perhaps they'd merely intended to deter him from disclosing what he'd learned from that corrupt deputy mayor, Christopher Clark. By that time, Linc's campaign was well aware of Sandy's involvement with Clark; his impersonation of a client at the Triple-L sperm bank; and his interference in the attempted terrorist attack at Holy Cross Cathedral. So, he had become a pain in the ass to their agenda.

As well, Linc might have suspected that Sandy knew about the rape and death of Monica Hartwell decades ago. A skeleton that could not possibly be allowed resurrection if Linc had any hope of becoming president.

But, whatever the intent was of the commando action scenes in Sandy's house, the two men had paid with their lives. And nothing had happened since.

Sandy still had regrets that he'd allowed the Pulsed Energy

Weapon out of his sight, but he knew Vito was right. He couldn't take the chance on being caught with the most advanced prototype of the directed energy weapons he'd been working on at the Lincoln Laboratory. The damn things were classified, and he'd broken several laws by having a miniaturized version of one of them in his house without clearance. Vito was a wise man.

But, it bothered him that he trusted the man so much.

Vito was second in command of one of the nation's most successful and brutal crime families, and next in line to be Godfather. Now, here he was, in possession of one of the most secret weapons in existence, as well as being the phantom organizer and financier of Sandy's campaign.

Sandy wondered how his life could have spiralled so out of control that this was the kind of person he now trusted. How had this happened? And, so fast?

But Vito had been with him every step of the way. Saved his life, provided assistance whenever Sandy needed help to pursue his mission of vengeance. And then, wisely, had counseled Sandy to pursue vengeance in a different way, a more civilized way. To defeat Linc in a way that would hurt him the most. At the polls.

The kind of vengeance that would do the most good for the country, and provide Sandy with the best salvation possible.

It would give him closure.

Whereas, allowing the election of a man who personified evil would only give him a lifetime of sleepless nights.

Linc's campaign messages were disturbing, and Sandy knew the man would be dangerous if he ever won the White House. Particularly since Sandy knew that the Quincy attack that killed his family had been engineered by the man's campaign. And, they'd almost succeeded in doing it again at the cathedral.

Sandy knew deep down in his soul that sitting idly on the sidelines watching such a man become president would condemn him to years of regret and an even stronger need for revenge.

He thought back to the altercation at the cathedral, and shuddered when he considered what might have happened if he hadn't intervened.

An intervention only made possible by the information he and Vito had extracted from the terrified deputy mayor.

Sandy muttered a few curse words under his breath as he remembered back to that moment in the Cosa Nostra safe house. The moment Vito declared that the sleazy fat man was dead, despite his heroic efforts at trying to revive him.

The same sleazy fat man who still haunted Sandy. The dead man that he'd convinced himself he'd seen alive in the adoring crowd a few long weeks ago. Swaying along with the masses, five rows from the front.

50

Vito loved his bullet-proof Cadillac Escalade. Specially equipped to protect him in the manner that he deserved to be protected. As the next in line to assume the mantle of Godfather of one of the most powerful and sophisticated crime families in the United States, he was precious merchandise.

Crime had changed over the years, and Vito chuckled to himself as he thought back to the stories he'd heard of the old days. The executions in broad daylight, the heads of horses placed strategically in the beds of traitors, the broken kneecaps, the kisses on the cheeks of those chosen to die.

And Hollywood always glorified the violence, almost romanticized it, if that was at all possible.

Nowadays, the Cosa Nostra was just big business, like any other big business. They had their fingers into virtually everything, and they only used violence when there was no other way. It had been recognized by the young up-and-comers that power was no longer achieved through the barrel of a gun. In fact, just the mere threat of violence was usually enough in today's world, particularly when the targets knew who it was that was doing the threatening.

The industries that the Mob had their fingers into would shock the average American. Products that they shopped for every single day in supermarkets and big box stores, were providing dividends to the people the public knew only as the scum portrayed in movies like Goodfellas.

But the most important product that the Cosa Nostra invested in, in this brave new world, was politics. It was recognized that nothing could be accomplished by gangsters in respectable businesses if they didn't have power through politics.

Legislation that could favor their needs in tax laws, and the relaxation of regulations governing everything from transportation to construction, had to be influenced. The only way to influence that was to have the right people in all the right places.

From municipal politics all the way up to the senate and beyond.

And beyond was where the Cosa Nostra had their sights. Now it was finally possible. For real.

It was thought to be real back in the '60s, but that hadn't worked out the way they'd hoped. Not enough leverage, not enough control. The candidate simply took the Mob's help, took their money, and then turned on them.

Not this time. The Cosa Nostra was populated with smart business people now, not the thugs of the past. Although, at times, thuggishness was still needed. More importantly, though, clever manipulation was the tonic that paid the best dividends.

Vito declared out loud, to no one in particular, even though two of his associates were sitting in the passenger cabin of the SUV with him, "Tonight we salute our ancestors. Once in a while, they were right."

Polite and patronizing laughter filled the cabin, until Vito raised his authoritative hand in a signal that meant, simply, "Shut the hell up."

Vito sat in silence as the SUV moved its way through the evening traffic of Baltimore, Maryland, towards a destination on the outskirts of the city. Kind of out in the countryside as it deserved to be, because, it was after all, a golf course. Aptly named Scenic Acres Country Club. Beautiful scenery that Vito would have enjoyed at any other time. But, not this evening, because scenery wasn't on his mind tonight.

The election of a president was on his mind tonight.

He glanced out the window as he thought back over his history with the two people he had a rendezvous with at Scenic Acres. Well, they didn't know he had a rendezvous with them, but that didn't matter. It wasn't that kind of rendezvous.

He looked at his watch. Just a few minutes until they arrived at the lookout point that gazed down over the clubhouse. They'd be about three hundred yards away, but basically invisible. His SUV was black, the sun would have almost set behind him at the time of the rendezvous, creating visual blindness in his direction, and, hell, what he would be doing was invisible as well. So, a nice relaxing adventure tonight.

To be sure, though, just in case, his two bodyguards and the driver were armed to the teeth with firepower that local authorities would be helpless against. As well, there was that lovely bullet-proof feature that the Escalade brought to the party.

The SUV arrived at its destination. The driver backed up as close to the edge of the cliff as he could, and aimed the rear of the vehicle in the direction of the vast circular driveway that majestically adorned the front of the clubhouse down in the valley.

Vito glanced at his watch again, and pulled a phone out of his suit pocket. Laid the phone on his lap and adjusted the knot of his red silk tie. He almost always wore red ties. They made a statement that no other color could make, in his view. Red was his signature.

"Now we wait," again uttered to no one in particular.

They didn't have to wait long.

Vito answered on the first ring.

"Five minutes? They'll be leaving together? Okay. Is the valet bringing the car around? Make and color?" Vito hung up, opened the door, and signalled to the driver to pop the lift gate.

He walked around to the back of the Escalade and crawled into the cargo area, making sure not to bump the ominous, but understated, machine that was mounted innocently on its telescopic tripod.

He edged himself to the back of the Pulsed Energy Projectile and hit the power button. He was happy that Sandy had given him such a thorough demonstration down in his basement of how the machine functioned. Vito marvelled at how easy it was to operate such a high-tech weapon. Sandy had designed it so well that even a trained chimp could figure it out.

He picked up a pair of binoculars and focused them in on the front promenade of the Scenic Acres clubhouse.

There they were—laughing, clapping, high-fiving. Happy as pigs in shit.

A man and a woman—two people who thought they had the world by the tail. And, until tonight, they certainly did.

A white Lincoln Continental pulled up and the valet jumped out. Handed the keys to a driver, who then held the rear doors open for his two happy passengers.

Vito twisted the neck of the PEP and levelled it in the direction of the Lincoln. Looked through the scope, adjusted the focus, and locked in the image of the vehicle into the photo memory of the directed energy weapon.

The way Vito understood it, from what Sandy had explained to him, the energy of the PEP would now be sent only to that one object, the white Lincoln with its three occupants. Invisibly and silently. Nothing else in the general vicinity of the car would be touched.

Vito made the sign of the cross, raised the binoculars to his eyes for the last time, and pushed the activation button.

He watched in morbid fascination as the white luxury vehicle and its occupants transformed, instantly, into a large, but harmless, column of dust.

51

Vito was relaxing over a cup of coffee in the back room of a café. He used this private room once in a while, just for those special meetings that needed more of an intimate touch.

He pulled out his phone and checked for messages. There were several, but one in particular he'd been expecting.

Sandy had avoided contact with him since the campaign started, but Vito knew he wouldn't be able to resist getting in touch once the news hit about the two top campaign organizers for Senator Berwick.

Vito chuckled and shoved his phone back in his pocket.

Sandy was demanding a meeting and Vito knew why.

Well, it could wait a day or so—the best strategy was to leave Sandy dangling from a branch for a little while longer. Let the news prey on his mind a little. He was already putty in Vito's hands, but he'd be jelly after the next news was splashed.

News that Vito was intent on creating today, in this very café.

He reflected over the last couple of days.

The media had gone into a feeding frenzy, trying frantically to report on the strange disappearances of Meagan Whitfield and Bob Stone. It was the only story that was being covered, considering that they were the highest profile officials in Berwick's campaign.

Yet, no one had any answers. Both the local Baltimore police and the FBI were investigating, but, there was nothing to investigate.

A car with a driver and two passengers had disappeared into thin air, in front of the horrified eyes of a few dozen people lounging around in front of the country club.

The media outlets managed to force themselves onto the scene within mere minutes after the strange phenomena occurred, and interviewed countless witnesses.

All of them told basically the same story: "They got into the car, and then—they were just gone."

The usual experts were called in by the cable news networks—experts who scrambled to come up with some kind of explanation.

Spontaneous combustion was the most common theory, ridiculous as it sounded, because there had been no reports of flames, smoke, or heat.

Just a big pile of dust on the circular driveway where the car had once been.

The closest anyone got to the truth was a retired general, who surmised that it might have been some kind of laser weapon. The PEP wasn't technically a laser, of course, but his guess had been the closest.

Not one of the experts interviewed ventured that it was a directed energy weapon, a pulse emitter. The PEP did of course use an infrared laser, but the laser's involvement only served to start the reaction that forced rapidly expanding plasma towards the chosen target, faster than the speed of light. Enough plasma to totally disintegrate anything in its path.

Painless deaths, and not the least bit messy.

Vito surmised that his Cosa Nostra ancestors would have loved a weapon like this—no muss, no fuss. No bodies lying in the streets, no bullet-riddled cars, or blood-spattered suits.

Some media were so freaked out over the incident that they'd broached the outrageous subject of alien abduction.

Even if Whitfield and Stone hadn't been with the Berwick campaign, this incident would have been front page news. Because, it was just so sensational—and just so weird.

But, as it involved two top strategists for the leading presidential candidate, it made the story international in scope.

New conspiracy theories were being spun by the day, and the one that seemed to have the most legs was that it had been an assassination attempt on Berwick himself. That, the killers thought he was in the car.

Vito laughed to himself over that one. *There was no need to kill Berwick; he was going to be done in without a bullet being fired, or plasma being directed.*

No, Berwick was far more effective just being left in place, twisting and turning during the final leg of the campaign, giving voters a clear choice.

A bruised and battered Berwick, or a fresh, clean and honest Beech.

Voters didn't like uncertainty, and while Berwick was leading in the polls for now, that would change overnight. He would flounder in the final weeks, due in no small part to what Vito was going to do today in this café.

The café was in the Brooklyn area of New York, just a block away from a private Catholic school run by priests and nuns.

His guest for coffee today was Simon Coburn, the chief news director for the third largest cable news network in the country.

Vito had summoned him to meet at 3:30, being respectful enough to schedule the meeting location close to where Simon picked up his eight-year-old daughter, Wendy, every day from the Catholic school.

Simon was a single father, and had struggled over the last few years following the premature death of his wife and the illness of his daughter.

A sad story, and, to a point—but, only to a point—Vito did indeed feel sorry for him. Simon had become a business opportunity for Vito, just one of many media executives he controlled. And controlling the media and the messages being splashed out there for public consumption were the most powerful weapons of all.

Vito laughed out loud. Well, maybe the second most powerful weapon, now that he'd seen what the PEP could do.

The door to the private room opened and in walked Simon, escorted by one of Vito's burly guards. He rose from the table, and waved his hand in the air signalling the guard to leave the room.

Simon's steps were tentative as he walked up to Vito to shake his outstretched hand.

"I hope you can make this quick, Vito." He glanced at his watch.

"I have to pick up Wendy soon."

"Sit down. I won't keep you too long. I wouldn't want to keep Wendy waiting. You're a good father, Simon. You've had to do double-duty since Leslie's passing, and I admire you for that. Family is everything."

"Thanks, Vito. It's been hectic lately, too. What with the presidential campaign in its final weeks and the television debates about to start. Not to mention that strange incident in Baltimore. We're scrambling trying to cover that. But, how can we cover something so strange? There are no explanations for what happened, and it's put Berwick's campaign in kind of a negative spotlight right now. He's trying to spin it as an attempt by someone to stop his campaign, attempting to cast some suspicion on Beech's team. It's a puzzler, that's for sure."

Vito chuckled, and adjusted the knot of his red silk tie. "You news types love this kind of stuff. Great for ratings."

"Great for sleepless nights is more like it."

Vito poured Simon a cup of coffee from the thermos sitting on the table.

"Have a sip of java. It's strong, and should give you enough of a jolt to get you through the next few hours."

"Thanks. So, what did you want to see me about?"

Vito reached into his briefcase and pulled out a video cassette player.

Simon laughed. "There's a fossil if I've ever seen one!"

"The recording is on an old cassette. I didn't bother to convert it, because there's nothing better than an original."

"What's this all about?"

"In short, the end of Berwick's campaign."

Vito clicked Play.

After the five-minute recording was finished, Simon sat back in his chair and rubbed the temples of his forehead.

"You want me to release this?"

"Yes."

Simon sighed. "I can't do that, Vito. This is an uncorroborated recording."

"The names are cited on the tape—the girl's name and Berwick's name. And even though the tape is old, it's easy to tell that it's Berwick's voice. Simon, he raped and caused the death of a fourteen-year-old girl. You don't think the public deserves to learn what a monster he is?"

"Vito, no argument there. But, we have rules of engagement. I can't name you as the source, I can't say where this tape came from, and I can't verify that it's legitimate. Can you at least connect me with the man who made this recording? I can use him as a named or unnamed source."

"He's dead."

"Well, then, there's nothing I can do, Vito. I'm sorry."

"You could simply say that the tape was mailed to you from an anonymous source."

"It's still unverified. Irresponsible journalism. And nothing less than a smear job against a politician."

"Do you want that lunatic to be your next president?"

"That's not the point. I can't ignore ethics and jeopardize my network's reputation just because I don't like a candidate."

"Yes, you can."

Vito rested two massive hands on the table, clenched his fingers together and cracked his knuckles—the sound reverberating around the walls of the small room.

"Let's take a little walk down memory lane, Simon.

"When Leslie was dying of that heart disorder, your insurance ran out. In desperation, you went to a loan shark, paying 100% percent interest, eventually crippling you. You'll recall that the loan shark worked for us. I erased your debt, and paid for Leslie's heart surgery. Alas, it failed, and she died anyway."

Vito noticed that Simon's face had turned a bright shade of red, and his hands were starting to tremble.

"Then you discovered, through a very astute doctor's observation, that Wendy had the same heart disorder as Leslie. A genetic pass-through. You had no money left. I stepped up for you and paid the $500,000 for her heart transplant. Wendy now has a new heart and a long life ahead of her—because of me."

Simon lowered his eyes. "I've always been grateful to you for that, Vito."

"Being grateful isn't enough. I own you. I didn't do it because you're a nice guy—even though you are. I didn't do it because I like you—even though I do. You know these things, you're not a stupid man."

Simon looked up, tears clouding his eyes. "I'd get fired if I did this. What good would I be to you then?"

Vito shook his head.

"I wouldn't need you anymore. This would be the coup de grace, above and beyond all the other things you've done for me. So, let them fire you. But, I'll assure you of this—if you do what I'm asking of you, we'll take care of you. You'll never have to work again, I can assure you."

"How do I know that?"

Vito's face twisted into a grimace of feigned hurt.

"Now you insult me. I've always been true to my word, and I pulled out all the stops to make sure that Wendy didn't die. You'll just have to trust me. One thing about the Cosa Nostra, Simon—correction, two things—information is the first currency to us, and the second currency is our word. We are always true to our word. If we promise a favor, we deliver. If we promise someone they're going to die, they die. As well, you and I are both good Catholic boys. There's a certain honor with us Catholics."

Simon looked at his watch. "Oh, you've just reminded me. I have to run. Need to pick up Wendy. I'll consider your request."

Vito pushed the release button on the cassette player, and handed the tape to Simon.

"No, you won't consider it. You'll do it. I expect this recording to be splashed all over the news tomorrow."

Simon made a face and reluctantly took the tape, shoving it into his suit pocket.

"I said I'll consider it."

Vito rose from his chair and motioned Simon to follow him to the back of the meeting room. He pulled up the blinds, exposing a clear view to the street behind.

"Take a look, Simon."

Outside, standing on the street, was sweet little Wendy. She was holding an ice cream cone. Beside her, with an arm around her slender shoulders, was a priest.

Vito smiled at the sight. "Isn't she cute? You must be so proud. I knew you'd be pressed for time today, so I arranged for Father Angelo to pick her up from school for you."

Simon stared straight ahead, unblinking. "I've never met a Father Angelo at her school."

"Well, you wouldn't have. Angelo's not really a priest; he just likes to dress up in priestly costumes once in a while. Has some lovely robes, too. Funny thing about our religion, Simon—kids raised in Catholic families and who attend Catholic schools, tend to put priests up on a pedestal. That collar gives them saintly status, particularly in the eyes of an eight-year-old girl."

Vito's voice took on an ugly tone. "With all that we adults now know about the decades of child abuse by some of those perverts, kids really shouldn't trust priests at all, should they? But, Catholic parents are always torn between the desire to put lipstick on a pig, versus protecting their kids. It's a real conundrum for them. Inevitably, they still choose the lipstick."

52

The roar of the rotors was overpowering despite the earphones. Designed to be able to communicate with the pilot, but also to dull the sound. But they didn't work on the sound dulling thing, and Sandy had no desire to communicate with the pilot. So, he pulled them off because they were just darn annoying.

He looked out through the small side window of the helicopter and noticed that they were passing over Cape Cod, out to the open sea. A yacht was the apparent destination—a large one. He and Vito would be alone, except for the discreet staff of twenty that his host—and whoever else used this yacht—kept around to cater to any and every need. And, Sandy figured, just to steer the darn thing.

Sandy had ditched his security staff, and taken a cab to the small Lexington municipal airport. There, the chopper was waiting for him.

While he felt strange allowing himself to be flown out over the coast to a waiting yacht, he knew it was the best thing for security. Being seen with Vito, and, heaven forbid, photographed, would be the death knell of his campaign. He knew that, but, all the same, he felt uncomfortable being stranded on a yacht with one of the top kingpins of the Boston Cosa Nostra.

The helicopter turned on its side and began a slow gradual descent towards the water. Sandy saw the yacht as the chopper began its curved approach. A massive boat. He couldn't even begin to guess what it was worth, as he'd never even been on a yacht before. It was silver and adorned with searchlights beaming out and rotating from the sides of the hull.

He knew, from what he'd read of these super-yachts, that those lights were actually sensors that triggered an alarm inside the ship if someone approached within a predetermined range of the hull. A boat that had these security systems also apparently had escape hatches that led down to the bottom level, where a submarine waited to be dropped into the depths.

The chopper stopped its run and hovered above the ship, slowly lowering itself to a landing pad on the top promenade.

It was a beautiful night to be out on the water—warm, with the sunset pending within the next hour. Sandy wished he were here for different reasons and with a different someone. He would have at least had the benefit of enjoying himself.

He jumped down from the chopper and lowered his head. A tall man, dressed in a rain slicker for whatever reason, with an assault rifle strung over his shoulder, motioned for Sandy to follow. The man led him through a doorway to a gangway, which stretched down the entire length of the ship. They were on the top level, and from what Sandy had been able to tell from the air, the yacht had at least four levels, plus the lower hull—which presumably held the fabled submarine.

Halfway along the gangway, the guard turned left and Sandy followed him down a steep ladder to the next level. Another gangway, but this one was adorned with small chandeliers, and the floor had plush carpet instead of the industrial steel they'd clanged along on the upper level. They passed by several closed doors. Sandy guessed these were private quarters for guests or staff—probably guests, though, since this level seemed to be pretty plush.

The rain-slickered guard stopped at an open double doorway, then stood off to one side, motioning with his hand for Sandy to enter. To this point, after two gangways and one steep ladder, the guard hadn't yet said a word. Not that Sandy was in the mood for idle chatter, but it was disarming to be treated in that fashion—particularly since everyone on this boat presumably knew who he was.

He entered the room and resisted the urge to gasp. It was large. A dining room table sat in the middle, with a large crystal chandelier hanging from a ceiling that looked like it had been painted by Michelangelo. To the right of the table was a large sitting area. Leather sofas, carved mahogany coffee and end tables, and a fully equipped bar with a long counter that would rival *Coyote Ugly*.

To the left of the dining room was what looked like a more casual area—a large director's desk and several casual seating areas. There were no papers on the desk, just a large-monitor computer and an empty glass. Behind the desk, running along the upper wall, were ten TV screens, each tuned to different news and business channels.

To say the least, Sandy was overwhelmed—and a wee bit intimidated. He figured that must have been Vito's intention.

"Welcome, Mr. President!"

Sandy whirled around at the sound of the familiar voice, just in time to see a large Mediterranean head pop up from behind the bar.

"Forgive me for startling you. I was down on my hands and knees, looking in the wine cooler for some good Italian vintages."

Victorious, he held up two bottles.

"Found one I think you'll enjoy. Lucky for us, I had two bottles left. A beautiful Bruno, 1993. Was supposed to have been a good year, but with this wine, any year is good."

Sandy frowned. "Bruno?"

"Oh, sorry, that's short for Bruno Giacosa Barolo Collina Rionda."

Sandy chuckled. "Okay, I get now why you just call it Bruno."

Vito walked around to the front of the bar and placed the bottles down onto the smooth marble.

"About 800 bucks a bottle. I think the long name is just to justify the long price!"

He pressed a button along the side of the bar, and almost instantly a white-coated servant appeared. Vito pointed to the bottles, and within seconds they were opened and breathing in the salty Atlantic Ocean air. The servant retrieved two glasses from the cabinet and poured a small amount for Vito to taste.

He sniffed, breathed, sipped, snorted, and finally gave the thumbs up.

The servant then filled both glasses and disappeared through a side door. As he twisted his body through the narrow doorway, his jacket raised just slightly enough for Sandy to notice a holster and pistol on his hip.

Vito motioned to Sandy to take a seat at the bar. Then he sat down beside him and raised his glass in a toast. "Cheers to the next 'leader of the free world!'"

Sandy let the man's glass hang in the air. No toast, no friendly clink.

"I don't intend to toast you, Vito. That's far too civilized for a man who's deceived me. I'll consider it only after you've come clean."

"It's rude not to toast, Sandy."

"It's rude to lie to a friend, Vito."

Vito placed his glass back on the counter without taking a sip.

"Fine, then. Ask your questions."

Sandy took a deep breath before asking the question that he already knew the answer to. "You used my PEP weapon to kill Meagan Whitfield and Bob Stone, didn't you?"

"Yes, of course."

"I trusted that in your care, Vito. It was so that I wouldn't be discovered with it."

Vito chuckled. "This sounds kind of like a robber being indignant about being robbed."

"What?"

"You broke numerous laws just having that thing in your basement. So, don't get virtuous on me. I saved you from being caught."

"But I trusted you not to use it. As you know, I'm on leave of absence right now during the campaign, but I got a call from my boss at the Pentagon asking me for my opinion on what kind of weapon could have caused that kind of annihilation. I'm a physicist—I couldn't lie. And, they know I've been working on that weapon. I had to admit that in my opinion it was a directed energy weapon. He seemed to appreciate my honesty, and I don't think he was alarmed at all. We both agreed that some power, perhaps foreign, has such a weapon and might have decided to use it to sway the presidential race. Either in Linc's direction in an attempt to make him a martyr, or in my direction."

Vito rapped his knuckles on the counter. "So, no harm done."

"What the fuck are you talking about? Three people lost their lives!"

"I don't appreciate your language, Sandy. Keep it clean, please. Anyway, they had to die. I had to swing the vote—and even you wanted them dead."

Sandy raised his voice again. "There's no guarantee those murders will sway the vote in my direction."

"Not that vote. The vote at the Aufsteigen Group. You lost thirteen to twelve. I needed two deaths of members who'd voted for Linc. I figured his two top campaign officials were the best choices."

"How the hell do you know about those votes? It's a secret society; the proceedings of their meetings are never made public. And what kind of vote was that, anyway?"

Vito sighed. "I told you a bit about Aufsteigen during one of our last meetings. I told you they were supporting Berwick's campaign. Because, at that time, he was the only chosen one in the race. Then you entered the race, and voila, we had two chosen ones. A vote was needed to decide which one we'd support during the duration of the election cycle."

"What do you mean by 'we'?"

Vito rested his elbows on the bar and turned his head to face Sandy.

"I'm a member of the Aufsteigen Group, Sandy. Have been for fifteen years. In fact, I represent all of the Cosa Nostra families in the country. I'm fairly influential, representing about $3 trillion in assets from all of the families combined, but I wasn't influential enough to have the vote go in your favor at our last meeting." Vito shrugged.

"Linc won that vote, which meant that certain trouble would have been coming your way if I hadn't acted. Those people don't fool around—your life might have been in danger if they decided upon some drastic sanction to take you out of the race. It could have been as simple as an invented scandal to ruin your life and your career—or, they could have just assassinated you. But my elimination of Whitfield and Stone changed the vote—twelve to eleven in your favor. You're safe now, and pretty much guaranteed to win the White House. See, I saved your life again, and made you president, too. Are you ready to toast yet?"

Sandy just stared at him. He knew his mouth was hanging wide open in shock, but try as he might, he couldn't close it.

Vito raised his glass again, a sinister grin painted across his face. "Toast?"

53

Sandy had spent the last ten minutes in the gold-adorned bathroom adjoining the opulent dining room. Not fitting behavior at all for such a bathroom, but most of his time had been spent with his face in the toilet bowl, throwing up. Sandy splashed water on his face, rinsed out his mouth, and then just stared at himself in the mirror. Staring back was someone he no longer recognized.

He hissed, "You fool! How could you have been so stupid?"

Doing his best to compose himself, he ran his fingers through his blondish hair, pulled a bottle of eye refresher out of his suit pocket, and popped a couple of drops in each of his baby blue eyes.

He knew what he had to do.

Sandy opened the door and strode confidently back into the dining room.

Noticing that Vito was now sitting in the lounge area, he joined him. Sat down in a leather seat facing him. He knew he needed to somehow get some control back. Right now, he felt like he was in a straitjacket.

"So, this whole relationship between you and me has been nothing but a charade. You've played me all the way."

Vito nodded. "You asked me to be honest with you, and that's how I'm going to be. Some of it was a charade, but not all. We had no idea you and your family were going to be at the Quincy Market the day of the attacks."

Sandy leaned forward and interrupted. "You were in on the planning of that attack?"

"Of course. It was an Aufsteigen operation. Designed to give Berwick a platform that he could preach on. But your presence there was not anticipated. Neither was your hero moment. And when you were presented with that medal, and you threw it back at the general, that's when we decided you were to be the second Ascendant."

"Ascendant?"

Vito nodded. "The chosen ones for positions of power we refer to as Ascendants. After your rebellious act during the medal ceremony, you were the perfect choice to be the contrarian to Linc. Our most desired position was to have two Ascendants, one representing each political party. That way, we'd be guaranteed to have one of our people from the Triple-L sperm bank in the highest office in the land, indeed, the world. Both of you are offspring from the finest genetic stock on the planet."

"What the hell is my heritage? The least you can do is tell me who my father is. Surely, you have that information."

"All I'll tell you is that you're both from the same father. You and Linc are half-brothers. The Cain and Abel analogy. Isn't that special? The Triple-L stock consists of sperm from fifty elite donors, but you two happen to be from the same donor."

Sandy rubbed his forehead. "This is so fucking twisted, it feels like I'm in the middle of a nightmare. So, you were part of the planning of the Quincy slaughter. All those people killed, including kids, for God's sake. Whatever happened to your professed compassion for families? You were one of the assholes who killed my family—as well as a couple of hundred others, half of them children."

"Please, I'll ask again—watch your language. And, let's be clear—your family was collateral damage. Not intended."

"That time you saved my ass at Triple-L, was that staged too?"

Vito shook his head. "No. I helped you gain access to that lab so that you'd have an appreciation of the heritage you came from. Dr. Schmidt took it too far. We were watching you, and listening, as you know, and we were concerned that he was going to destroy our precious package. My men burst in and saved you, and those men they shot really did die."

Sandy stood up and started pacing the room.

"Now I can finally let myself believe my own eyes. That little prick, Christopher Clark, didn't really die, did he? You and he just acted things out, right? I was certain that I saw him at one of my speaking events. My eyes weren't playing tricks on me, were they? He's alive."

Vito shook his head. "He's not alive. He didn't die back then; we paid him off and whisked him out of the country. But he is dead now. He got greedy."

""I see. And, the cathedral? All fake?"

"You were meant to go there and stop it. We made sure that everything was on hold until you showed up. There was never any sarin gas in those canisters. It was just a ruse, and the sarin gas rumor was planted by us."

"Why?"

"We needed to give you a purpose, Sandy. We're well familiar with what motivates both you and Linc. He was used and played as well. Both of you had to endure some theater.

"With Linc, it's all about power and ego. With you, it's all about integrity, justice, rightful vengeance, and honesty. Again, like Cain and Abel. You're at opposite extremes of the pendulum.

"That was the beauty of our strategy, to manipulate both of you into candidacy. Because the stupid voters out there tend to mark their ballots on emotion—a good portion of them anyway. We needed two opposite extremes for them. Dr. Evil versus Dr. Good. And voters tend to vote *against* someone, as opposed to *for* someone. Simple, but true. In our view, we couldn't lose." Again, that shrug.

"But, what worried me, personally, was when I found out from you about that fourteen-year-old girl that Linc brutalized and killed back in your West Point days. We didn't know about that—or, at least I didn't know. And, I have no idea whether Whitfield and Stone knew about it and just covered it up. Didn't matter, I couldn't live with him being the winning candidate. Up until then, we were all perfectly content to have either of you in the Oval Office. But, that story about the girl did it for me. When I couldn't convince enough of my colleagues at Aufsteigen to vote in your favor, I had to take matters into my own hands against the Group."

Sandy pitched his voice almost at a whisper. "You released that tape recording. It's all over the news. The man's ruined. Not that I care, but that recording seems to have shifted the election totally in my favor now."

Vito nodded. "Yes. He is ruined. He'll never recover from this. The presidency is yours."

"When it is, what will you want from me?"

Vito laughed. "Oh, who knows? It will be nice to have a friend in the White House. Aufsteigen will have their little requests from time to time, pertaining mainly to banking issues, oil and gas, mining, trade, yada, yada, yada. As for the Cosa Nostra, we'll have a few requests of our own, on some of the same issues, but a few others as well—criminal justice, pardons, money-laundering, drug laws, prostitution, immigration. It's a long list, but we'll try not to overwhelm you."

Sandy shook his head and lowered his eyes. "I trusted you, Vito. Even though we came from different sides of the street, I considered you a friend."

Vito got up and walked over to the bar. He punched the same button that he'd punched before, and, again, the white-coated servant appeared within seconds.

"Tony, give us some music. Play that favorite song of mine—you know the one, the snake thing."

Vito walked back to the lounge area with two fresh glasses of Bruno. He handed one to Sandy, and sat down. "Let's sip our wine and listen to some music, shall we? I think you'll find this song enlightening."

The speakers in the ceiling crackled to life, and a song that Sandy remembered from the oldies stations began to play. *'The Snake'* had been a popular song back in its heyday, and what struck most who'd listened to it were the lyrics themselves. Those lyrics had real meaning back when Sandy had first heard the song, but more just out of amusement then. Now, there was no amusement. Because, clearly, the song was being used by Vito to tell Sandy in no uncertain terms who he really was, and how Sandy had been used. The song was now a weapon of shame rather than just an amusing little tune.

Sandy listened to the song intently, even though he knew the lyrics off by heart. He felt a sinking feeling in his stomach as the song came to an end. A feeling that turned into an acid burn once he looked up into Vito's eyes, and perhaps for the first time ever, into his soul. Vito's smile betrayed the evil that lurked within, a smile worn by a man who knew he no longer needed to pretend.

"Did you enjoy that song, Sandy? It does say a lot, doesn't it? Kind of a connection to reality. Your biggest strength, Sandy, is that you're one of the good guys. And, your biggest weakness is that—you're one of the good guys. You'll have to be aware of that advice once you're in office."

Vito raised his glass. "Well, since you won't toast me, I'll do a solo toast. To you, Mr. President."

Sandy stood.

"Get your fancy helicopter to take me back. I'm done listening to your bullshit. Sorry about the language—but, kindly, fuck off. As soon as I get back I'm announcing that I'll be withdrawing from the election. Find yourself another Ascendant."

Vito Romano, second in command of one of the most powerful crime families in America, laughed mockingly, and then just pulled his phone out of his pocket.

"No, dear sir. You won't be withdrawing."

Sandy watched as he slid his big fingers gently across the screen of his phone.

Sandy heard a recording of his own voice talking about how he wanted to kill Meagan Whitfield and Bob Stone as revenge for the deaths of his wife and children.

Then a new recording.

Just Sandy's voice again, describing the intricacies of the Pulsed Energy Projectile weapon. And his voice naively continuing, instructing how to operate the deadly machine and explaining what it was capable of.

Sandy stood frozen in the middle of the opulent lounge of a gangster's luxury yacht. Feeling like he was in the throes of one of those rare nightmares, one of those scary realistic storylines when you kept begging yourself to wake up. But you couldn't. And the story continued, and you usually ended up running for your life.

At that moment, staring up at a surreal crystal chandelier in a yacht probably purchased with laundered money, Dr. Sandford Beech, the next President of the United States, felt an invisible straitjacket squeezing the life out of him.

54

The old man muttered a curse and waved his wife away with one frail hand, while struggling with the other on the push rim of his wheelchair. Angela usually manoeuvered the stupid contraption around for him using the handles attached to the rear, but once in a while he just needed that feeling of independence again.

Angela sighed in exasperation. "You're still a stubborn old man, Herman."

He laughed and coughed at the same time. "Yes, and that's what you love about me."

They both enjoyed speaking English to each other around the cavernous home. Somehow, English seemed to fill the rooms with tones easier on the ears than German. Or, perhaps it was because English just sounded much friendlier than the harsh German that he'd spoken for a lifetime—a lifetime that had now reached 130 years.

Herman Braxmeier spoke excellent English, although only a handful of people knew that he could. He liked it that way. He was also fluent in Spanish, and that fact was also known to only a select few. When he was in town with his guards, he could listen in on side conversations without anyone knowing he could understand. That sneaky little tactic had allowed him to dispense with four disloyal soldiers already.

Herman had always believed in, and practised, the leadership style known in Germany as *Fuhrerprinzip*, the "leader principle." Such a style, when executed properly, demanded and succeeded in obtaining absolute obedience of all subordinates to their superiors.

He spun his chair to the side once he reached the door in his foyer; squeezed the handle and turned it. Then, before Angela had the chance to nag him once again, he spun both hands on the push rim and headed out into the courtyard.

He looked up at the sky. It was another warm November day in Salta, Argentina. Herman was glad to be here, rather than down in Buenos Aires. Salta was in the foothills of the Andes, 4,000 feet above sea level. The air was fresh, thin, and a lot cooler than the cities at lower altitudes. Even though the air was thin, he'd never had any breathing problems, despite his advanced age.

It was true, of course, that he was luckier than most. Good health and longevity was easy to achieve when you had gold, jewels, artwork, and raw hard cash to throw around. And Herman had been throwing it around for decades. He made sure that everyone he paid off knew that if he died, the riches would stop. Angela would get it all, and she was a lot younger than he was. As well, she had no need for secrecy the way Herman did. Angela was a native Argentinian; nothing to hide, no one to hide from.

He felt at home in Argentina. It had a modest population of forty-four million, but a full two million of its citizens were fluent in German. A few of his old friends had lived and died here over the years. Some were still around, and he saw them once in a while. They reminisced about the good old days, the days of power and glory, the days of wine and roses.

In fact, they'd all assembled here in this very courtyard for his birthday back in April. Even a few of his old friends who were living in Brazil made the trek to celebrate with him. They all paid homage, just the way they used to back in the Fatherland. They were all much younger than him, of course, so they were really more like subordinates than friends. But, Herman never really had any friends anyway, as he'd risen so fast in the power structures of Germany that everyone he met became an underling before they could blink.

Herman had rewarded all of the attendees at his party with autographed copies of *Mein Kampf*. The signature he used was the name they were all more familiar with. He would never truly be Herman to them.

He wheeled his chair around the gardens in the courtyard, and wondered why he'd never taken the time in his early life to appreciate such beautiful things as flowers. He could have given himself a break once in a while, but the obsession and drive within him never allowed him to relax. Not even to smell the roses.

He appreciated those things now, and had for the last few decades.

He enjoyed television, particularly American shows. And he loved playing chess in the Salta town square, with anyone who would dare. He couldn't remember the last time he'd lost at chess.

Everyone took him for granted because he looked so frail, but they underestimated the power and fire within him that mere competition always brought out. He still loved to win, and couldn't accept anything as common as failure.

Even back in the waning days of the war they'd underestimated him. Did they really believe that a man as superior as he, would just accept defeat? Take his own life? Capitulate? Did they really not think that a Plan B would have been set in motion long before the final collapse of Berlin?

Herman shook his head slowly from side to side as he thought back. Then he just laughed out loud at their stupidity.

His fleet of stealth submarines, laden with riches, had departed long before the fall of Berlin. Maybe they even knew that, but the arrogant Americans could never admit to the world that their inferiority had been overshadowed once again by the brilliance of a select few.

Submarines that had specific destinations—Brazil, Argentina, Venezuela, Peru, Chile. A few of his underlings eventually made their way to the United States and Canada, hoping to live out the rest of their lives in peace and tranquility. But, predictably, they were caught. Stupid fools.

Herman chuckled as he remembered all of the Hollywood war movies he'd watched over the last few decades. Some he'd even watched several times, just because they were so humorous. Angela never found them all that funny—she'd make strange faces at Herman as he doubled over in laughter. But he couldn't expect her to understand.

As far as the Americans were concerned, they'd won the war single-handedly.

And with the power of America, they also had the power over the history books.

But if the truth were properly told, the Russians won the war. Herman hated the Russians, but he had to give them credit. He'd underestimated their ability to fight in winter conditions, and, admittedly, had overstated his own. And the Brits and Canadians—they were relentless. Herman knew that the course of the war would have been a lot different if he hadn't dared to take on the Brits. And if he'd just left Russia alone.

But he couldn't stop himself. Winning created such a rush of adrenaline that it was impossible to bring a halt to it, even when the odds were clearly against him. He just needed that feeling, over and over again. Even though Herman wasn't a gambler, he suspected that the feeling was similar.

But the American version of history always made him laugh. The country that had waited three years to find the courage to get involved in the war, and only then after they'd been attacked by the stupid Japanese.

To this day, they still professed that they understood Nazi Germany more than any other country. Yet, they hadn't even been able to detect a large fleet of submarines crossing the Atlantic, escaping the collapse of a once powerful nation. Right under the noses of the self-obsessed nation that had bragged about total control of the vast Atlantic Ocean.

Herman smiled as he considered that the Americans still had no idea whatsoever of what his genius had accomplished down in Antarctica. Again, right under American noses. While the war was going on, with distractions everywhere, there'd been another front. A secret front. And, once again, an undetected front.

The wheels had been put in motion under the thick ice decades ago, ready for an awakening one victorious day. The country that had been bragging to the world about winning the war, patting themselves on the back about being a superpower, while at the same time fueling their never-ending paranoia about Russia—were entirely clueless about what had been going on under the ice.

One fine day, at the right time, during the right crisis, there'd be an awakening. The ice would rule, in ways that no one could have ever predicted.

Herman wouldn't live to see it. He knew that. But, he took comfort in knowing that he would be spitting in their arrogant faces one final time.

He looked up at the sound of a low flying helicopter. A hand extended out of the side window and waved. Herman struggled to raise his frail hand to wave back, just as he managed to do almost every day at this time.

This was his daily newspaper delivery. However, he'd been so nervous the last couple of weeks that he'd stopped his daily delivery. And refused to watch television or listen to the radio. Computers weren't a part of his life, so there was no temptation there.

Despite the prospects for success, Herman was still a suspicious man, as he'd always been. He'd had visions of some last-minute crisis, something being discovered that might scuttle the election result that he so longed for. A constitutional confrontation that might declare the election null and void.

Angela had arranged for the helicopter delivery to commence again today, because today was a very important day. She knew that her Herman had to know.

The newspaper package contained American newspapers, and only American newspapers. Herman was obsessed with America. And excited that maybe, today, he'd finally hit the motherlode. The ultimate revenge on an arrogant and dishonorable enemy.

Angela ran out the front door at the sound of the helicopter, and dashed to the spot in the courtyard where the package landed.

She picked it up and walked over to where Herman was sitting patiently in his wheelchair.

She knelt down and kissed him gently on his withered cheek.

"Are you ready, mein Fuhrer?"

Herman nodded, and smiled at hearing his old title being used by the woman he loved. Such respect, such devotion. That was what he missed the most from the glory days, back when every single person was prepared to kneel at his feet.

She tore apart the plastic covering and handed him the first paper on the top—*The Washington Sentinel.*

He unfolded it and spread out the front page on his lap.

Reading the headline, he broke out in a smile that was wider than any smile he'd ever allowed in his life: "Sandford Beech Elected President."

He gazed longingly at the photo of the blondish-haired, blue-eyed man, standing at a podium, both arms raised victoriously in the air.

Herman turned his head to the side as he felt a tear begin to drip down his cheek. Angela, in her usual gentle fashion, wiped it away with her pinky, reassuring him silently, with just the touch of a finger, that it was perfectly acceptable for the powerful to cry.

"That was a happy tear, mein Fuhrer."

Herman nodded. He pointed at the photo and gazed up into Angela's adoring eyes. He started to say something, but, stopped himself.

She cocked her head to the side, and smiled warmly at him. "Go ahead, say it."

Herman looked up, turning his attention to the sky, wondering if this day might be celebrated with a solar flare or some other celestial event.

But he couldn't ignore the actual real-life event that was sitting right there on his lap.

His weary war-torn eyes rolled back down to the front page of the *Sentinel.*

He pounded his index finger triumphantly into the center of the photo.

"My son."